Canceleer

From the corner of her eye Iseult saw the wild peregrine launch itself from its perch. Out of the light came a rushing core of matter, a dark comet cutting through the laws of space and motion. In the same split-second the crow hurled itself out of the tree. There was a 'crack' and it came apart, flopping out of a cloud of feathers. Bounding up from the impact, the Barbary shot a glance over her shoulder, rolled and fell, side-slipping in to the kill. Bracing herself against the crow's death spasms, she snapped its neck.

Case was jumping up and down, yelling 'Did you see that? Did you see that?' He gulped in an effort for calm.

'I saw it,' Iseult said, 'just a blur, an impression.' She looked at the sky, half expecting the falcon's course to be imprinted on the air. 'She did something funny, sort of spun round.'

'That's it,' Case said, getting excited again. 'Her signature. It's called a canceleer. I told you she was a belter.' He sank down and cupped his chin in his hands, grinning at the Barbary as if he had created her himself.

**Also by the same author,
and available from Coronet:**

RITES OF SACRIFICE

About the author

Windsor Chorlton was born in the north of England in 1948 and was a senior editor with an international publishing company before becoming a full-time author. A keen falconer and wildlife photographer, he has explored Morocco's Atlas Mountains to study rare birds of prey. He is the author of one previous novel, *Rites of Sacrifice*, set in the Himalayas against the background of the Tibetan guerrilla war.

WINDSOR CHORLTON
CANCELEER

CORONET BOOKS
Hodder and Stoughton

Copyright © Windsor Chorlton 1992

First published in Great Britain in 1992 by Hodder and Stoughton Ltd

Coronet edition 1993

British Library C.I.P.
Chorlton, Windsor
Canceleer.
I. Title
823[F]

ISBN 0 340 58023 2

The characters and situations in this book are entirely imaginary and bear no relation to any real person or actual happenings.

The right of Windsor Chorlton to be identified as the author of this work has been asserted by him in accordance with the Copyright, Designs and Patents Act 1988.

This book is sold subject to the condition that it shall not, by way of trade or otherwise, be lent, resold, hired out or otherwise circulated without the publisher's prior consent in any form of binding or cover other than that in which it is published and without a similar condition including this condition being imposed on the subsequent purchaser.

No part of this publication may be reproduced or transmitted in any form or by any means, electronic or mechanical, including photocopying, recording or any information storage or retrieval system, without either the prior permission in writing from the publisher or a licence, permitting restricted copying. In the United Kingdom such licences are issued by the Copyright Licensing Agency, 90 Tottenham Court Road, London W1P 9HE.

Printed and bound in Great Britain for Hodder and Stoughton Paperbacks, a division of Hodder and Stoughton Ltd, Mill Road, Dunton Green, Sevenoaks, Kent TN13 2YA (Editorial Office: 47 Bedford Square, London WC1B 3DP) by Clays Ltd, St Ives plc. Typeset by Hewer Text Composition Services, Edinburgh.

For Bill Massey

Canceleer, verb. 1 Of a hawk: To turn once or twice upon the wing, in order to recover herself before striking. 2 To turn aside, to swerve or digress.

Oxford English Dictionary

To make two or three sharp turns in the descent when stooping.

J.E. Harting, *Bibliotheca Accipitraria*

1

When the whore had finished her business with him, John Wesley Dearborn headed for the souk, intending to buy a present for his four-year-old daughter Lauren, who was homesick for America and missing the playmates she had made during their vacation in the Great Smokies.

His lapse – the first in sixteen years of marriage – had been so bizarre that in his mind he was condemned to play it over and over again.

That afternoon he had visited the Aguedal Gardens and rested with a book in the shade. Perhaps he dozed, because when he saw the three women, he thought at first that they were part of a dream. They were watching him in silence from the trees, their veils drawn across their faces. From that first moment, everything seemed to happen in slow motion. One of the women was walking away, but before the trees swallowed her, she turned and looked over her shoulder, her eyes gleaming like black olives. And Dearborn had found himself following, stumbling deeper into the garden, expecting the figure gliding ahead to disappear. But always she would stop and draw him on with her eyes until at last he emerged into a glade around the ruins of a pavilion beside a pool where insects danced on still water. And there, lying among shards of turquoise tiles, with lizards panting on the walls and the sweat running down his back, he had fucked the silent veiled woman, staring down into her sceptical black eyes.

Oh God, he thought, what have I done?

It was a measure of the strain he was under, he told himself. The vacation with Magda's aged mother had been testing enough, God knows, but the return to Morocco had constituted a trial of biblical proportions. During his absence, work on the dam had been hit by a strike called over the deaths of three labourers in circumstances which contravened even Moroccan codes of industrial safe practice. The project had also been plagued by minor acts of sabotage – apparently the work of local Berbers whose valley, *insh'allah*, would be 200 metres under fresh water by the turn of the year.

For three years drought had oppressed the south. The Dearborn household had returned to the villa to find the well parched and the garden a dust bowl, the gardener having run off to Casa with the maid and various items of furniture. On the second day back, the family dog, a feather-brained setter, had disappeared without trace. The next evening, Lauren had called her parents to admire the nest of scorpions she had found under her bed. Magda had met these emergencies with characteristic fortitude but had assumed an intimidating silence, charged with hostile currents.

He reached the Djemaa el-Fna and matched his pace to the flow of humanity moving across the square. He stood head and shoulders above the crowd – a lanky man in a three-button linen jacket and black slacks, the academic severity of his face relieved by a boyish lick of hair. By training he was a student of medieval Islam; his doctoral thesis had been on the *iq'ta* land grant system and its significance in the financing of Arab and Seljuk opposition to the First and Second Crusades. He had spent most of his professional life, however, in foreign service on behalf of the US government – first in Beirut, then in Tehran, and finally in Beirut again, leaving each posting to the roll of artillery fire. Now, at forty-three, he was employed to oil relations between the Moroccan Ministry of the Interior and a Franco-American consortium which had landed a contract to build a showpiece barrage in the High Atlas. Despite the handsome salary, Magda believed that his career had taken an irrevocable downward turn, and in moments of self-candour, Dearborn was inclined to agree. But the hell with it; he was through with hanging his ass on the line. No more civil wars; no more trying to square principles with political expediency.

From the centre of the square came the *tam-tam* of Saharan drummers warming up for the evening theatrics. It was a pristine September afternoon, the heat and dust of high summer abated, the air clear enough to trick the senses into believing that the mountains to the south were only a walk away. The Marrakechis scrutinized him with care, but nobody pestered him. One or two middle-aged men inclined their long Maghrebi faces in distant salutation. Most likely they knew him by sight. Marrakech was a small town; this part of the medina still retained the transient air of a desert encampment.

Hearing an American voice, Dearborn looked up to see a tourist couple tacking in his direction, under pressure from three street kids.

'I told you honey,' the man said, 'keep moving. Once they get a hold on you, you've had it.'

'Morton, I believe I'd rather go back to the hotel,' his wife said, pitting her bulk against his guiding hand. She appeared to be on the verge of hysteria.

'Hell no, this is exciting,' her husband declared, half raising his video camera in anticipation of a spectacle.

'I don't know, honey. It's not what I expected.'

'Wait until it gets dark. That's when the action begins – snake charmers, fire-eaters, acrobats. It should be really something.'

Suddenly the woman rounded on the youths. 'Can't you guys understand English? I don't want to visit any Berber market.'

'Okay fellows,' her husband announced, 'we're properly took care of and don't need your interference.'

'Morton,' his wife declared in a faint voice, 'I'm getting a headache.'

Her husband hesitated, sweaty with misgiving but determined not to concede. Dearborn stepped forward, begged the couple's pardon and then, addressing the kids in such Moroccan Arabic as he had learned, told them to get lost.

The woman flushed in gratitude. 'I told Morton we should have hired us an official guide, but oh no, he insisted we come down here on our own, even though they warned us at the hotel that these guys won't leave you alone until they have you all wore down. Lord knows what they would have done if you hadn't chanced by.'

'Nothing serious, ma'am,' Dearborn said, and pointed at a pair of gendarmes strolling by. His gaze lingered on the officers. It seemed to him that the police presence had been much enlarged since he left on vacation. There had been labour trouble in Casa, too, and violent bread riots in the Rif.

'Would that swing in your voice indicate you're from Georgia?' the woman inquired.

'Charlotte, North Carolina,' Dearborn told her. 'But I left home a long while ago. I work here,' he added, anticipating the next question.

Morton was resentful of his intervention. 'Nice town?' he demanded, eyeing Dearborn for gone-native signs or worse.

'Very nice.'

'It says here,' the woman said, tapping her guide-book, 'that the Djemaa el-Fna used to be an execution ground.' She looked about with mild distaste. 'That's what it was, I guess.'

'Yes ma'am, the Congregation of the Departed, right up into this century. They used to stick the heads on spikes on that wall right there.' Dearborn began to disengage. 'Have a real pleasant vacation now,' he said, backing off, holding up his hand.

He left the square by a side-street, his gaze wandering after a young girl who dipped her lashes when she noticed his attention. Forbidden fruit, he thought, picturing again the thrilling, awkward encounter with the whore.

Lust assailed him, and shame, and a dull resentment. It had been weeks since he and Magda had made love;

months had slipped by since they had enjoyed any degree of intimacy. Trying to define the moment when the relationship had altered, Dearborn could only conclude that the rift had been tacitly ignored, blurred by the routine pleasantries and concerns of family life until now the gap between them yawned like a chasm. His heart trembled in sudden apprehension, the fear of loss. If Magda went, Lauren went too.

At the end of the street he turned into a lane largely given over to the recycling of motor tyres and the reclamation of electrical goods. Taking a left, he followed a row of carpenters' shops and passed under an arch. On the other side was the deep shade of the souk, shot through with pencils of dusty light. In seconds his bearings were scattered. Allowing his instinct to guide him, he threaded the maze, pausing at stalls piled with synthetics, leather and copper, dawdling to breathe in the scents of cumin and coriander and mutton. In the end he bought a pair of embroidered *babouches*, but though he knew Lauren would like the slippers, the choice left him unsatisfied. On impulse, he asked for directions to the Mellah, the old Jewish quarter.

After a couple of false starts, he emerged from the souk into a street hung with the signs of tooth pullers and barbers. The lanes off it grew narrower. Above the canyons, swifts sliced the desert blue into crescents. The siren call to prayer sounded over the roof-tops and merged with all the other summonses. The houses pressed closer and between them veiled women in black hurried up passages barely wide enough to admit a person. It all contributed to a mournful air of desertion. There were few if any Jews left in the Mellah; nearly all of them had emigrated to Israel in the early 1960s.

Rounding a corner, Dearborn laughed in triumph, pleased that his sense of direction hadn't played him false. On the pink-washed walls hung the cages of the bird market. He had left it late, though, and only one dealer was still trading, his stock reduced to a few linnets and goldfinches. The linnets sang sweeter, but the gaudier finches would hold more appeal for Lauren. Dearborn bought a pair in their wicker cage.

As soon as the purchase was completed, he regretted it, anticipating Magda's disapproval. The garden was full of songbirds; it was wrong to cage a wild creature. Well it was too late now. He could always release them. Yes, that's what he would do. He would let Lauren keep them tomorrow and then she could liberate them in a family ceremony that would give pleasure and satisfaction to all.

He became aware of a commotion taking place around the next corner. The bird dealer had gone to investigate and Dearborn followed, but before he could see what was going on, the dealer turned and shooed him away. '*Allez, allez.* There is trouble here.'

There certainly was. A crowd had formed about a hundred metres down the street and in the middle, enmeshed in a circle of flailing arms, a man was lashing out.

Dearborn grinned – a lot of shouting and foot-stamping, sound and fury signifying nothing more than a neighbourly wrangle.

At that moment the circle drew back, shocked into silent clusters. Someone was on the ground, pitched over on hands and knees. From the women present rose a high-pitched ululation. A man in workman's clothes came half-walking, half-running towards Dearborn, trying to fend off the tentatively restraining hand of a plump, officious-looking fellow in a white *djellaba* and canary-coloured slippers.

At first Dearborn only noticed the blood marring the stout man's robes, but then he became conscious of something peculiar about the workman's face. 'Good God,' he murmured, realizing that the man's cheek was hanging open. The fat man shouted at him to get away.

'Go quick,' the bird dealer ordered, pushing him in the back. 'The police will be here soon.'

Everyone was running now, disappearing into doorways and alleys, the women flapping like hens. In a very short time the street was deserted except for the man on the ground.

Dogs were barking all over the neighbourhood. Slowly the casualty pushed himself to his feet and staggered in the opposite direction. 'Shit,' Dearborn said, torn between going to help and getting the hell out. Swearing softly, he set off in pursuit, still clutching the birdcage.

The man was lurching and seemed to be holding his stomach, occasionally feeling for support with one hand. Walking quite slowly, cursing at every second step, Dearborn passed a blood-stained knife and an even bloodier circle where the fight had taken place. Blood smeared the wall where the man had reached out. Committed now, Dearborn broke into a run, reaching the injured man just as he put out his hand, grabbed a doorpost and swung to the ground.

Dearborn put down the cage, his innards screwed tight. From chest to feet the man was painted a glistening scarlet. Blood was still welling out of his abdomen.

'Keep away!'

Swinging round, Dearborn saw that one bystander had stayed on the scene, standing off at a distance.

'Call an ambulance,' Dearborn shouted. 'Hurry!' He looked for something to staunch the flow. He stripped off his jacket but the sacrifice would have been useless. An artery must have been severed. The man was trying to speak; it sounded as if fish-bones were stuck in his throat. Dearborn put his face close. The man mumbled something about a house. He mumbled something that sounded like 'call him', gave an exhausted smile, and died.

Sirens had begun to bray. The goldfinches hopped from perch to perch. To his dismay, Dearborn found that his own clothes were stained with blood. No point in trying to leave the scene. He stepped back and forced himself to examine the dead man – handsome cosmopolitan face, flash suit of vaguely Italianate cut, gold watch or a convincing imitation of it, decent shoes – not the usual Moroccan rubbish. It must have been an attempted robbery, Dearborn decided, recalling the injured workman. But in that case, why had the crowd not gone to the aid of his victim? They had been in a frenzy. To Dearborn's eye, it had looked like a mob attack.

'His name is Ben-Yacoub.'

Dearborn whirled. A pair of squint eyes gazed at him from under the hood of a homespun *djellaba*. It was an old cripple hunched in the shade of a tank where the women of the neighbourhood drew their water.

'What happened?' Dearborn asked, his voice faint. His hands were trembling and a chill had settled on his flesh.

'His father was a silversmith,' the cripple said, speaking a version of French. 'I knew him well.' He pointed a scrawny finger. 'That was his house.'

The man had died in the doorway of number nine.

'Why didn't anyone help him?'

The cripple seemed not to hear. 'He told me he had been living in Casablanca, but that was a lie. His family went to Israel like all the other people in this street. I'm the only one left.'

Although Dearborn's brain was stalled, he began to sense the outline of something nasty. He peered at the dead man, estimating his age as mid-thirties. Flies had already clotted on his belly and on his eyes. 'When did you say he left Marrakech?'

'He was a child when they went to Israel, but as soon as I saw him I recognized him. He has his father's face in every particular.'

'Good Christ,' Dearborn whispered. 'Are you saying you haven't seen this man for thirty years?'

'That's what *he* said,' the old cripple announced in triumph. '"How can you remember what I looked like?" he said.' The cripple tapped his withered legs. 'What else have I got but my memories?'

The sirens were close now. Dearborn overcame a last-moment impulse to flee. 'What was he doing here?'

The cripple shrugged. 'It is for the police to decide, but in my opinion Ben-Yacoub is a Zionist spy. Why else would he change his name and pretend to have lived all of his life in Casa?'

'Oh shit,' Dearborn breathed.

The first gendarme came round the corner, stopped to take in the scene, scrabbled at his holster flap and advanced at a run, waving his pistol in an undisciplined manner that made Dearborn step smartly into the centre of the street and put both hands in the air.

They took him in the back of a Renault to a newish concrete building surrounded by ornamental pools close to the racecourse. A captain of police received his statement, made a furtive phone call and then transferred him to an unfurnished cell equipped with a one-way window. Dearborn was confident that eventually any misunderstanding would be cleared up, but he was familiar enough with Moroccan custom and procedure to realize that the authorities would sink their teeth deep before relaxing their grip. He had an awful premonition that the incident would prove too much for Magda, and then he thought, what am I saying? I'm an innocent man. She's my wife.

Some incalculable time later, he was taken out of the cell, escorted to an office and seated across a desk from a tall, aristocratic Moroccan wearing sunglasses metalled like a blowfly. He did not introduce himself, but Dearborn detected a Gallic poise, caught a faint whiff of the SDECE or *deuxième bureau*. But which? In terms of a suspect's welfare, it made all the difference.

From behind the reflective glasses, his interrogator made a leisurely examination, his elegant hands playing with a silver cigarette case. Noticing Dearborn's attention, he offered him the opportunity to smoke – English brand with gold rings. Dearborn declined. His interrogator selected one for himself, inserted it into a holder and posed with it. Behind him hung a recently updated portrait of King Hassan.

'You are a Zionist spy.'

'You know who I am. You have my statement. I'd be

grateful if you contacted my embassy and informed my wife.'

'You are a Zionist spy. No advantage can be obtained by denying it.'

'If I can't speak to my embassy, I would like the presence of a lawyer.'

'What were you and Ben-Yacoub doing in the Mellah?'

'I can't speak for Ben-Yacoub or whatever his name is. I was buying a present for my daughter.'

'You are a Zionist spy.'

'Look, I work for the Bowyer Corporation.'

'You are an engineer?'

'No, I work on the public relations side.'

His interrogator lit his cigarette and exhaled satisfaction. 'We know who you are, Doctor Dearborn,' he said, switching to English. 'The Zionists recruited you in Beirut.'

Dearborn sagged back, aware that he was in for a long haul. They had done their work well, he thought, but so they should. We trained them. 'There's a simple way to settle this,' he said. 'Ask the Israelis.'

His interrogator turned to the policemen with astonishment.

'I know damn well the Mossad has a semi-official presence in Morocco – an arrangement of mutual advantage. They'll tell you I have nothing to do with them.'

His interrogator consulted a sheet of paper. 'You worked in Beirut as an agent of the United States government?'

'I refuse to answer that.'

His interrogator scanned the sheet again. 'Your job was to co-ordinate with Israel's Phalangist allies,' he said, and raised his head.

Dearborn's blood ran cold. They had the whole fucking file. 'I refuse to answer any more questions.'

'Why did you visit Marrakech today?'

'To do some shopping. I've only just got back from vacation.'

'You were in the Djemaa el-Fna.'

'Yes – briefly. I met a couple of American tourists. They shouldn't be hard to trace.'

'And before that?'

'Shopping in Gueliz.'

'The shops are closed in the afternoon. You did your shopping in the morning and then had lunch. Where did you spend the time between three and five-thirty?'

'Taking a walk in Aguedal.'

'For more than two hours?'

'I had a doze.'

His interrogator took off his glasses. He had noble, probing eyes. 'Where were you between three and five?'

Sweat beaded Dearborn's forehead. 'With my mistress,' he mumbled.

'Her name?'

Dearborn swallowed hard.

'Name?' his interrogator demanded, pen poised.

'I forget.'

His interrogator looked at him with no expression.

'It was a casual encounter.'

His interrogator gave him time to stew. 'Where did this . . . this transaction take place?'

Dearborn looked at his shoes, staring at ruin. 'In a pavilion not far from the Bab Ahmar.'

His interrogator sent a small signal to the captain, who went to the door and murmured to an underling before taking his place again.

The questions continued, leading in circles, until Dearborn was incoherent and the room was filled with smoke. Finally, his interrogator rose and walked out, leaving him in the company of the captain and an officer who sat excavating his nostrils and eating the contents. Dearborn slumped. This was the outer circle of hell. This was what he had coming for betraying Magda.

His interrogator returned and ordered him to stand, then led the way down a corridor. All part of the disorientation process, Dearborn thought, and took deep breaths to face whatever ordeal was coming.

But his interrogator was standing with a telephone in his hand, holding it out to him. Trembling, he took it.

'You're in trouble, cowboy,' said the voice of Jerry Cody.

Dearborn closed his eyes.

'What were the fucking Israelis thinking of, recruiting an anti-Semite like you?'

'I'm in no mood, Cody.'

There was a small silence. 'Did they knock you about any?'

'Not as yet.'

'Well I'm damned if I'm coming down there to bail your smug ass out. Now you listen to me, John Wesley. You're a vital witness and if you know what's good for you, you'd better extend your total co-operation.'

'They've had all I've got to give.'

'We'll see. Make sure you're on the morning flight to Casa.'

'I'm going home, Cody.'

'No problem. Hold out on us and it's bye-bye, cowboy.'

'Believe me, I'm clean.'

'Ha ha,' Cody said, and banged down the phone.

Someone took the receiver out of Dearborn's hand and replaced it on the rest. He looked at it with dull eyes. 'Can I call my wife?'

Only then did he see that it was three in the morning. Somehow the connection was made and Magda came on. 'I'm sorry,' he said. 'I was a witness to a crime.'

'The embassy told me,' Magda said, sounding tired and not worried at all.

'I'll try to get home tonight, but I have to catch the morning flight to Casa.'

'It's not worth the trouble, then.'

'Magda, are you okay?'

She hesitated, gathering wrath. 'No I'm not. On top of this . . . this trouble you've got yourself into, a wild animal tried to attack me as I was putting out the garbage.'

'An animal? Christ, Magda, what kind of animal?'

'A wild boar – in the alley between the house and the gardener's hut. I smelt it. It was disgusting.' Magda let out a wail. 'What if it had been Lauren?'

Dear God, Dearborn marvelled, it's one damn thing after another. Next it will be boils and locusts. 'I'll be home tomorrow evening,' he said gently, 'and I won't leave until the house is sorted out from top to bottom.'

Magda's silence stretched. 'John,' she said eventually, in a voice that made his neck hairs stiffen, 'we have some serious talking to do.'

'Yes,' Dearborn said miserably. 'I guess we do.'

2

After the wettest summer in journalistic memory, the weather had turned with the leaves, bringing high polar skies scrawled with lines of geese. Case, driving a decrepit Toyota estate with two peregrines and a brace of pointers on board, came down off the moors at dusk and turned south on the coast road. Across a slack arm of the sea the Sutherland hills were printed black on the clear dying light.

Squinting up at a formation of geese, Case put one wheel on the verge, provoking a rattle of bells from the rear. He glanced in the mirror. Hunched and hooded, the falcons settled back into their stance, adjusting their balance like commuters on a lurching train. Their perch was the rim of a wicker dog basket with the pointers curled asleep inside. Case yawned. He had been up before dawn, tracking a falcon that had raked away in pummelling rain the previous day.

As drowsiness settled on him, he found himself playing over last night's row with Catty. He was aware of having behaved badly, but how could she expect him to take on a wife and kid? In a week he would be out of a job. Unless he came up with thirty thousand by Christmas, he would lose the house.

For days he had been wearing out ideas, but no matter how he turned it over in his mind, the scale of his predicament baffled him.

He felt the beginnings of helpless anger. Looking back into his life, it seemed to him that every time he'd got a stake in something good, it had been snatched away. Okay, a lot of kids get dumped at birth, but how many lose their foster mum too? Thinking about her gave Case a bad feeling. He was only three when she died, too young to understand what cancer was, and for years he'd been sure that the adoption had been called off because of something *he'd* done. In a way, he still did. 'That kind of thing can mess you up for life,' he said, his own voice taking him by surprise.

It certainly hadn't done him any favours, he concluded.

Watching the sky up ahead shading down into night, he recalled the years in the Home and thought of the supervisor – Fryer his name was, fat pooftah bastard. Case remembered Fryer telling him how the school reckoned he was bright enough to take GCEs, but all the time he was talking, his hand kept kneading away at his groin, not as if it sought pleasure, but as if it wanted to hurt. Case grunted, flashing a shot of Fryer toppling back over his desk, hands clutching his bloody face.

After that there had been three years of roads and building sites and Jim Skelton, who had looked after him like a brother when he found he was only fourteen. Thinking about Skelton made Case grin. For his sixteenth birthday, Jim had taken him to a pub where the women chalked their price on the soles of their shoes. Jim had lived on the sunny side of life. He was an aristocrat of the construction trade who ate steak for morning bait and drove a grader with four-wheel steering that came sidling out of the motorway mists like a giant cranefly. He was from a hundred-acre farm in Mayo – forty acres when the tide was in, he used to say. Case had learnt a lot about the countryside from Jim – how to dynamite salmon pools and smoke pheasants out of their roosts, how to set a snare and work a ferret. Poor sod. They were planning to work in the Gulf together, because the police were after Skelton for bigamy. He was mental where women were concerned – married women in particular, provided they weren't his. In the end it was the death of him. He fucked a ganger's bride on the carpet as her husband slumped snoring on the sofa after the wedding thrash, and either the wife confessed or else the bloke wasn't really asleep, because the next week he crushed Jim's head with the bucket of his JCB.

And then there had been the Paras.

Memories of foreign tours and balls-aching stints at the Depot froze on an image of Lieutenant Andrew Ridley, who had encouraged his interest in falconry and got his brains blown away in the barn of an Armagh farmhouse nearly five years ago this month, when they were both twenty-one.

Any road, Case vowed, dissolving the past, he wasn't going to let it go this time. He still had three months to turn the situation around. He was prepared to take drastic measures. That was one advantage of having no family, no ties of blood or kin. There was no one to answer to but himself.

And Catty.

The horn of an approaching car blasted his thoughts. He wrenched the wheel and nearly slewed into a wall. 'Wanker!' he shouted, then realized he'd forgotten to turn on his lights. He bared his teeth in a guilty smile. The other car had been an Inverness taxi, miles from base and heading north.

It was after nine when he reached town. A disconsolate huddle of youth was hanging out around the war memorial, sharing take-aways from Luigi's caff. Case halted under their stares and left the engine on lumpy idle.

An anaemic Viking wearing shredded denim detached himself from the group. Behind him came a black-eyed Goth in leather and fluorescent Lycra. Her mouth held a tremulous smile.

'Hello Pat,' she said. 'Did you catch anything?'

'Nowt to boast about,' Case said. He had screwed her once, up against a wall on the sea-front, his hand over her mouth to quiet her vocal paroxysms.

After many a glance to left and right, the Viking slipped a packet wrapped in clingfilm into Case's waiting palm. Case handed over twenty Scottish pound notes. He had acquired a taste for dope in Ulster, where it lightened the long hours standing to behind shutters and sandbags. He tossed the packet in his hand. It weighed next to nothing.

'What's the going rate wholesale?' he asked.

'Trade secret, man.'

Case smiled at him. 'Divn't get lippy, kidder.'

'Depends on the quality. This is good shit, man – Afghan. The guy I get it off pays twenty-five an ounce in Edinburgh.'

'I mean at source.'

'I don't know – maybe fifty, sixty a kilo.'

On the way to the Mill Inn, Case calculated that less than fifty kilos would solve his problems. For two long beats of his heart he really thought he might do it. Why not?

The Mill Inn was backed up against a desert of conifers facing the sea a mile outside town. Over time it had acquired a dance hall, a restaurant and a caravan park with shop-cum-video library. The forecourt was agleam with cars. A police car marked time at the entrance, waiting to pick up the weekly quota of drunks.

Case parked his heap next to Donald Thain's old Champ. It bristled with lights and was equipped with brutish crash bars. OFF-ROADERS DO IT ON ALL FOURS said a sticker on the back. Beside it stood a Zephyr in two-tone pearlescent with ultra-wide whitewalls, chromed side mufflers and a bonnet scoop. It belonged to Archie, Donald's son, who had been the man in Catty's life before Case came along.

Crofters and foresters, check-out girls and shepherdesses twitched in the strobes of the dance hall. High amplification shivered the Toyota's windows. At the doorway, a pair of bouncers with gelled hair stood locked in a clinch, big shiny faces rapt with concentration. They were adjusting each other's bow ties and didn't notice Case as he went by. He walked past the restaurant, where farmers in tight collars ate microwaved meals served under plastic musketry and Black Watch wallpaper.

Case went into the toilets. His reflection slid past in a mirror – spare sallow face, dreadlocks faded to the colour of cinnamon, slanting eyes as pale as a juvenile hawk's. Delinquent, he thought. Sometimes it bothered him, not knowing what kind of nature he'd inherited, not knowing which features belonged to which parent, not knowing who they were. Most likely both of them were still alive. He wondered if his mother ever thought of him.

Shit, what odds did it make?

In defiance of the trend, the public bar had survived in its original state. To gain admittance, Case had to go down three steps and stoop under the door-frame. The floor was stone-flagged, the seating area separated by wooden partitions worn as smooth as glass, the paintwork stained the colour of weak tea. An old labrador was camped in front of a coal fire. There were no women present; the customers were mainly older men with faces ravaged by outdoor labour and booze. Some had been there since opening time and wore work overalls. Over the bar the telly was tuned to a darts tournament. In the corner a real match was in progress.

At Case's entrance, conversation went stationary for a moment. Case was used to voices stalling when he appeared in public places. He was a gamekeeper of sorts, in a part of Scotland where poaching was a part of the local economy. Also, his origins and reputation aroused unease and a measure of disapproval that had grown stiffer since Catty's condition became apparent. When he visited the supermarket on his weekly shop, women in harsh wool overcoats nudged each other in the aisles. If he confronted them, they crooked their elbows around their handbags and lifted their chins in affront. Small town, he thought, small minds. Sod them.

Donald Thain was leaning against the bar, telling his Queen Mother story to Bill the postie, who was wiping glasses and casting glances at the telly.

'. . . so this English chauffeur asks Sandy to reverse. "Back up yourself," Sandy tells him. "Now listen, my man," the chauffeur says, pointing at his car, "I'll have you know I'm driving the Duchess of Buccleugh." "Oh aye?" says Sandy, pointing at his own passenger, "And fit do ye think that is – a heap of shite?"'

'She's a grand lady, right enough,' Bill said, staring at the box. 'Old as the century, God bless her.'

'So's the joke,' Case said, sliding on to a stool.

'Fit like?' Thain said, making space for him.

'Not so bad. How's it going at the Lodge?'

'Just fine. Mr Valentine says he's expecting you the morn. I'd say you'll have a grand day for the hawking, but the grouse are wild. Very wild.' Thain finished his drink and called on Bill to rectify the situation.

With his white mane, Old Testament eyebrows and regimental moustache, he looked the very picture of a staunch Highland keeper. Forbes Valentine, a wealthy English falconer who took the Lodge each summer, employed him to handle the dogs, and it was only fair to say that he had a canny way with them. But basically he was a garage owner who turned nasty in drink, and Case had no liking for the man. His wife Maggie minded the Lodge, and more than once Case had seen her face bruised, her eyes blacked.

Bill placed a pint of heavy in front of Case and served Thain with a double Bells and a Skol chaser. Thain watched with care as Bill prepared to add lemonade to the whisky. 'Easy man,' he ordered. 'Just titillate it.'

Ten seconds later the whisky was down the back of his throat. 'Aye well,' he said, 'we pass this way but once.'

'Why do yon buggers have to be so fat?' Bill inquired, looking at the telly. 'Look at the gut on that one.'

'Helps their balance,' Case suggested, 'lowers their centre of gravity.'

'Wheesht laddie,' Thain said. 'If that was the secret, my wifie would be champion of the world.'

Some connection in his brain led his eyes to the agricultural supplier's calendar tacked to the shelf of malts. September's girl sprawled naked over a straw baler.

'Now there's a rare pair of hurdies,' he observed. 'I like a lassie with a bit of beef on her.' He turned to Case, his face a caul of ruptured veins. 'That reminds me. I didn't see Catriona Bell at the shop. Away, is she?'

'Invergordon,' Case said. 'A friend's wedding.'

'No doubt you'll be thinking of regularizing your own relationship.'

Case let it pass.

Thain squinted at the array of bottles. 'I was talking to her father this very day. "Donald," he said, "I'll not stand idly by watching that man abuse my daughter's emotions." "William," I said, "it's a bit late to be fretting about her emotions."'

When Thain laughed, his chest sounded like shingle shifting on a beach. Case placed both hands on the bar.

Thain slapped him on the back. 'What's wrong, man? Can you no undercastumble my vocability?'

'You're an evil bastard,' Case told him.

Thain became thoughtful. 'Is that a fact?' he mused. 'Well, let me give you your character, Pat. You're like your damn hawks – aye getting above yourself. That's why you won't wed the ironmonger's lassie. You'd rather be chasing after Mr Valentine and his fancy friends, indulging in God knows what wickedness. Oh, I ken fine what goes on at the Lodge.' Thain fixed Case with a terrible biblical eye. 'Panty parties,' he said. 'Orgies. Drugs.'

'Wouldn't you like to know?'

'I ken one thing. Mr Forbes Valentine is nothing but a polished thug. Laugh away, but the polis have their eyes on that one.'

Case gave Thain a sideways look.

'Aye, they were up searching the Lodge after he left last year. They weren't local boys either. From London, Maggie says. They were rooting about for a whole day.' Thain closed one eye and nodded in slow time to underline the gravity of his accusation. 'Acting on information received.'

'And I bet I know who supplied it,' Case said. He was intrigued, though. 'What were they after?'

'That I cannae say.' Thain drained his glass and banged it down. 'It would take more than a day to work yon mannie out. He's got one of them A-rabs staying with him and the two of them were on the phone to Spain all day. Gey angry they were.'

Along the bar, a crofter who had been staring into his drink slowly slid to the floor. Strong hands hoisted him back into place. At closing time, the same men would assist the crofter to his pick-up, lift him behind the wheel, switch on the engine, select first gear and send him on his way unconscious.

Case was confounded by gloom. His problems were too vast. He would have to find a job in town, put himself down for a council house, marry, give up his hawks. He drained his glass. 'Well that's me,' he said. 'I'm away.'

'Bide a moment,' Thain commanded. 'Bill, same again, and ask Archie to step over.' He watched Bill going through his routine. 'You'll be looking for work,' he said.

'I'm open to suggestions,' Case said, trying to make his voice pleasant.

'And a place to live. There's a lot of interest in that ruin of yours. Doctor Thomson's putting in an offer.'

'He's going to be disappointed then,' Case said. 'I've got first refusal and I'm not refusing.'

'Good luck to you,' Thain said. 'Mind,' he added, 'it won't suit the new laird to have you staying on at Auchronie. No, not at all.' Thain took stock of Case's incomprehension. 'Man, have you not heard?' he declared in mock astonishment. 'Croll's taken a new keeper.'

'You're lying,' Case blurted, loud enough to turn heads.

'Bill,' Thain called in the silence. 'Tell Pat about the new keeper for Auchronie.'

'He's a boy from Moray,' Bill muttered, not meeting Case's eye. 'He's to start in the spring.'

'But Croll said he didn't need a keeper.'

'Ach, he wants a man whose face fits.'

Case concentrated on the whites of his knuckles. 'You're saying Croll gave me my cards because I'm half black.'

Thain laughed his viscous laugh. 'Half black be buggered. I've seen blacker on Orkney. What man ever saw a darkie with your colour of eyes? No, Pat, it's just the . . .' Thain shook his head in his effort to find the appropriate words. '. . . the all-over look of you.' He dropped his voice. 'What for do you wear yon fuzzy-wuzzy hairdo? Damn me, it looks like bloody pipe-cleaners. Now, now,' he said, jerking back, 'you know I don't hold with this racial prejudice. It's the colour of a man's soul that counts. We're all God's bairns, that's my philosophy.'

A lump worked its way up from Case's chest and lodged in his throat. Through his humiliation, he heard the darts players calling on a man called Geordie. The crofter who had passed out manoeuvred himself upright. Chin up, chest out, feet feeling for each step, he made his way to the mark. Darts were put in his hand. He took aim, blinking to dislodge the obscurity ahead, and released the missile. *Plunk*, it went, slotting into double top. After several failed attempts to raise his arm again he loosed the second dart. *Plunk*. Treble twenty.

Into Case's mind swam a vision of Croll – glad-handing, hard-as-nails, shit-faced Croll. *Plunk*. A hole opened up between his eyes.

'No doubt of it,' Thain observed over the cheers of the darts players, 'you've little cause to be fond of the new laird.'

He tugged Case's sleeve. At the door stood young Archie – a cultural throwback wearing a greased quiff, aubergine drapes, brothel creepers and a string tie clasped with a silver death's head.

'Pat,' Archie said.

'Archie,' Case said. There was no love lost between them.

Donald Thain wiped his moustache and levered himself off his stool.

With his mind tangled, Case followed them out. Fiddle music and war whoops came from the dance hall. In the shadows two girls were patting the shoulders of a distraught friend. A cap-sized moon floated low in the sky. The Thains led the way to a Range Rover parked in a far corner. The driver opened the front door for Case; the Thains climbed into the rear. Archie rested his mechanic's hands on the back of Case's seat.

'This is Mr McCrum,' Thain said.

'Delighted to meet you,' the driver said in the genteel tones of Edinburgh. He had a cherubic face, highly coloured, and wore country clothes. On the windscreen a sticker declared him to be a member of the British Field Sports Society.

Case's hopes took a tentative step up. 'Nice to meet *you*,' he said, extending his hand.

'Mr McCrum's up for the fishing,' Thain said. 'I was explaining your situation.'

McCrum nodded with every show of sympathy. 'Donald tells me you were an excellent keeper.'

'I still am, sir.'

McCrum sucked on his teeth. 'But I'm thinking you'll not find it easy getting another position.' He let the statement hang in the air. 'Not with a conviction for poaching.'

'Lord Orr gave me good references,' Case said in a stiff voice.

McCrum laughed. 'I wish to God I'd seen it – you creeping up on that deer and all the members watching from the clubhouse. Man, whatever possessed you to shoot a deer on the golf-course?'

'It was a bet,' Case muttered.

'He stalked it with a shotgun,' Thain pointed out. 'Shot it dead on the sixteenth green.'

'Aye, I heard you're a rare shot,' McCrum said. 'Paras, so I understand. Magnificent breed of men.' He gave Case's thigh a tentative slap.

Case began to discern the shape of something ugly. 'What is it you're after, Mr McCrum?'

'I'll not waste words,' McCrum said, sliding something into Case's hand. He switched on the courtesy light.

It was fifty quid, plus a business card. *Alexander McCrum, High Class Butchers. Licensed to Deal in Game.*

Sounds of breakage and female shrieks penetrated the car. Scuffles had broken out on the dance floor; figures swayed across the lighted windows. The music had stopped. Case glanced at McCrum's polished chops. He could hear Thain's wheezing and smell the rum-and-Coke on Archie's breath.

It all gave rise to a feeling of threat and not belonging.

In Northern Ireland he had been seconded to the Military Reconnaissance Force, a volunteer unit that worked with IRA informers. Waiting with a Fred outside some bar or club, he could never escape the fear that the informant was playing a double game, setting him up for ambush.

'Thanks,' he said, pushing back the money. 'I don't want to know.'

'Keep it,' McCrum insisted. 'Croll's a bloody fool to let you go without compensation.'

'Aye, yon staggies will have to look after themselves this winter,' Thain observed.

Case turned. 'Have a care what you say, Donald.'

'Damn me, the man's asking to be plundered.'

'Listen, I'm not daft enough to shit on my own doorstep.'

'We're not talking about one or two beasts,' Thain said. He surveyed all directions and spoke in a rapid hush. 'You ken the strath above Achnagarron. It holds all of Auchronie's deer at the back end. Last season there were nigh on eighty.'

'I know how many fucking deer Auchronie holds.'

McCrum intervened. 'I'll take every beast you can shoot. Fifty pounds each.'

'Split four ways,' Thain added. 'Man, you're looking at a thousand pounds for a night's work.'

Case wrenched himself round. 'You're drunk, Donald, fleeing. Nobody's going to shoot eighty deer in one night.'

McCrum squeezed Case's knee. 'Well now, I know where I can put my hand on a machine-gun. An ex-Para like you will have no problem using such a thing.'

'But you divn't understand,' Case said, looking at each man in turn. He gave an astonished laugh. 'I'm their keeper.'

Archie sniggered.

Case's anger collapsed in a wretched sense of his own stupidity. He had called McCrum 'sir' and greeted him with a deferential smile. After all the knocks he'd received, he still made the mistake of taking people at face value. Lord Orr had told him he'd got a job for life; Catty had insisted she was on the pill; Croll's voice had been sorrowful when he announced he would have to let him go.

'Fuck you,' he whispered. 'Fuck you all.'

'No need for a snap decision,' McCrum said.

Case threw the fifty quid in his meat-eater's face and climbed out, slamming the door behind.

Thain powered down a window. 'There'll be no work for you in these parts,' he shouted.

'Shove your work,' Case called. 'I'm off to Morocco.'

'Morocco, is it?' Thain shouted after him. 'Well, that's no kind of place for Christian folk.'

3

Iseult O'Dwyer reached the Lodge well after nightfall, having accomplished the eighty-mile journey from Inverness by taxi. The driver had lost the way when he turned off the highway, and they had spent two hours chasing their headlights over a moorland wilderness. By the time they found the Lodge, Iseult was frayed and ratty and on the edge of tears. She sat in the fug of too many cigarettes, waiting for the driver to finish calculating the mileage. Wiping her window, she peered at the mist-dimmed lights of the Lodge. It was a Victorian Gothic pile, huge and unlovely. In all other directions the world was circumscribed by darkness.

The fare was more than ninety pounds and Iseult was nearly fifty short. She offered a cheque.

'I have little use for the things,' the driver said with the meticulous diction of the region. He was pissed off because of her smoking and because she had made him miss his Friday night darts.

Someone had appeared at the porch. Her heart jumped as she recognized the tall figure of Forbes Valentine. She tried hard to clear her mind of fatigue.

'Wait,' she said, and ran over.

'Who have we here?' Valentine said, peering into the murk. His teeth were bared in apprehension or the semblance of welcome. 'My God, it's Cathal's sister. Iseult, what an unexpected pleasure. How clever of you to find us.'

'Can you lend me fifty pounds?'

'But of course,' Valentine said, after slight hesitation. He was staring at the taxi, as if he suspected that someone else might get out.

He paid the driver in person. There was an invitation to take a dram, a polite refusal, Valentine's hearty goodnights, and then the squirt of gravel as the taxi departed. They watched its lights dwindle.

'I do hope he finds his way back,' Valentine murmured. 'It's so easy to lose your direction on these moors.' He turned to Iseult. 'And now,' he declared, showing all his fine teeth, 'you must come in and reveal the purpose of your mission. This *is* a surprise.'

He led the way through a hall smelling of wet clothes into a well-lit foyer. The walls were wood-panelled and hung with antlers and photographs of grinning hunters squatting beside rows of game. Laughter chimed through an open doorway.

Iseult hung back. Her mouth was foul-tasting from one cigarette after another; her skin felt second-hand.

Valentine checked and turned. He was in his early forties, fair and evenly tanned, with the face of a weak king and the manner deceptively likewise. By profession he was an investment strategist.

'Dear Iseult,' he murmured, lifting a rope of her heavy hair. 'How beautiful, how so like your brother. I always think of you as twins, you know. How *is* my playboy of the western world?'

'Worried sick,' Iseult said, her voice already breaking.

Valentine took a backward step, concern shading his features. 'Oh dear, do I hear the sound of wolves howling at his door?'

'I've been searching for you high and low.'

'We are a little off the beaten track,' Valentine conceded. 'That's because I'm on my annual retreat.' He glanced at the dining-room door. 'I'm incommunicado,' he whispered.

'But you were supposed to phone Cathal.'

'Only when the deal was finalized.'

'Isn't it?'

27

Valentine spoke as though fearful of verbal ambush. 'Not as yet, no.'

'In that case, you'd better repay what you owe.'

'Owe?' Some colour wasted from Valentine's cheeks. 'How vexing,' he said. 'Not only was confidentiality an absolute condition, but I distinctly told Cathal that the money was non-returnable. You know, Iseult, your brother deserves to be chastised.' He frowned at his polished brogues. 'Did Cathal explain the nature of the operation?'

'Some kind of currency deal. I don't know. All I care about is that he gets his money back.'

Valentine laid a cool finger against her lips. 'Ssh,' he said. 'We'll decide what's to be done later. Yes, let's. Come and meet my guests.'

Sick with panic, Iseult let herself be steered into the dining-room. It was a mis-match of massive Victorian furniture and commercial-grade carpet dyed a sudden shade of orange. On the back of a carved chair, in a position of ceremony, sat a large, pale, hooded hawk. A dozen men and women were arranged around a long table covered with the shambles of dinner. Some of the women had a catwalk gloss and appraised her from top to toe with a killing glance. One or two of the male guests clambered to their feet.

'A traveller delivered from the storm,' Valentine announced. 'Let me introduce Iseult O'Dwyer. Iseult is the sister of Cathal, a dear friend from New York. She's a rather marvellous painter and she's come all the way from Inverness by mini-cab.'

Iseult registered smiles and a stiff murmur of welcome. The light made her queasy. Her period was due and it put everything out of phase. She found herself seated, a glass of wine placed before her. Valentine took his place at the head of the table. Iseult refused food. Conversation became general.

'Iseult's brother is a recent client,' Valentine said to the guest on his right. 'Iseult, this is Rafiq Saad.'

Saad rose and made a small bow. He was short and impeccably attired, with a matinée star's moustache and eyes like wet stones.

'I may have mentioned the account,' Valentine told him. 'A rather delicate exercise in international capital redeployment.' He sent a warning glance Iseult's way.

'Your brother's affairs are in excellent hands,' Saad pronounced.

'Apparently Cathal thinks not,' Valentine said, toying with a glass.

Saad elevated one eyebrow.

Valentine sighed. 'He's poured out his problems to his sister. I must say, it's very enterprising of Iseult to track us down.'

Saad examined her in a way that made her feel particularly uncomfortable.

'Please call him,' she said.

'Believe it or not,' Valentine told Saad, 'the terrible man has sent Iseult to ask for his stake back.'

Once again, Saad made his face express astonishment. 'This young lady's brother is a puzzle for me. Why does he not come to Britain himself?'

'My brother and I are very close,' Iseult snapped.

'Ah yes, there are no secrets within the family. I am Lebanese and I understand this very well.'

Anger clarified Iseult's confusion. 'Since you understand so much, perhaps you can tell me what's happened to Cathal's quarter million.'

'For God's sake, Iseult,' Valentine hissed.

Saad flapped a hand. 'No, no,' he said, 'the young lady's concern is understandable. Tell her please, Forbes.'

Valentine looked unhappy. 'Well,' he began, eyeing the tablecloth as if a script was printed thereon, 'speculative ventures, by definition, carry a degree of risk in proportion to . . .'

'Speculative?' Iseult cried. She jumped up under the swoop of fear. 'You've lost it, haven't you?'

Her outburst jarred the room into silence. Heads turned. Valentine ran his hands through his hair.

A trill of laughter escaped the girl sitting next to Saad.

'Money, money, money. That's all I've bleedin' heard since I got here.'

She was a puppy-fatted bimbo with candid blue eyes and Page Three breasts just about contained in a silk halter.

Saad insinuated one hand beneath the table and did something with it that made the girl squirm and her smile sicken. 'Money is what makes the world spin round,' he murmured, his eyes on Iseult.

'Love is,' the girl gasped, trying to push his hand away. 'Love is what makes the world go round.'

The other guests pretended that a more interesting spectacle had appeared at the opposite end of the table.

'Business and love,' Saad said, still working his hand, still staring at Iseult. 'For Chelsea they are the same.'

'Geroff,' Chelsea panted. 'You're embarrassing me.'

Iseult scraped back her chair. 'I'm going to call New York.'

Saad made a lazy signal and Valentine rose too, spots of colour burning in his cheeks and something like fear in his eyes.

In furious silence, Valentine marched the corridors, Iseult trailing in his rear. The institutional decor and fusty air were an oppressive breath from her grandparents' house. She felt as if she were being led to a place of punishment. Her room was at the top of a tower, reached by a winding staircase. Valentine flung open the door to reveal a frame bed and damp wallpaper. A stained wash-basin occupied one corner. Iseult shuddered in the cold.

Valentine pointed at an old black handset squatting on the dressing-table. 'Do remember that it's a public line. Oh, and calls are metered. You can pay for the call and the taxi before you leave. I imagine you'll want to get back to London tomorrow.' He went and stood at the window. Outside, the darkness was total.

Iseult took the phone and sat on the bed. Anxiety grew within her like a foetus. She lifted the receiver, hesitated, and dialled his number in a fumble of panic.

On the fourth buzz the connection went live.

'It's me Cathal. I've found him.'

'Hold on,' a light American voice said, 'Cath, it's for you.'

Iseult, clutching the phone, heard an exchange and then a door shut. Even in her distress, she couldn't help wondering about the soft-spoken man who was keeping her brother company. Verdi played in the background. She became aware of someone at the other end of the line.

'Cathal, I've found him. He's with me now.'

'Where?'

'Scotland, the middle of nowhere. I've been driving round in circles half the night.' Tears had mounted to her eyes.

'Ah, now rest yourself my darling girl. It's a marvellous job you've done. Put the bastard on, will you.'

His accent had mellowed into a smooth cocktail of Dublin and New York. She pictured him sprawled in a chair – white shirt, dark hair, a glass winking in his hand. Even on the phone, Cathal had a physical presence. A dart of tenderness pierced her.

Wordlessly, she offered up the phone.

'Cathal, dear heart,' Valentine said, smiling down at Iseult. 'How utterly delightful to hear you. But look, I do think it's naughty of you sending Iseult on your errands. The poor girl's quite distraught. No, no, I assure you, nothing *I've* done.' He turned his back on Iseult and walked away as far as the phone allowed. 'How irritating for you,' he said, 'but can't you exercise some of that irresistible charm?' He waited for the answer, his smile growing more determined. 'Now listen, Cathal. No, listen. Tell your friends that . . . Look, tell them there's been an unavoidable delay. I emphasize – a *delay*, not cancellation. If you can keep them at bay for six weeks, your patience will be rewarded manifold. Yes, I know I said the twentieth or thereabouts, but these things don't run on rails. Let me . . .'

A jabber of transatlantic protest cut him off. His smile grew weary. Shielding the mouthpiece, he rolled his eyes at Iseult. 'Quite deaf to reality,' he murmured. At last the static ceased and Valentine began speaking again. 'I do sympathize, but the rules were perfectly clear. No profit without risk and no . . .'

Whatever Cathal said, it erased Valentine's smile. His mouth compressed in a thin line. 'The bottom line is "no",' he said. He listened for the reaction. 'Frankly, I don't give a fuck. I've extricated you from one mess and that's the limit of . . .' He heaved a breath, fighting to keep his anger in bounds. 'Now look, Cathal, if you persist in behaving in such an unprofessional manner, you'll upset my colleagues. They may want a word with you. Do I make myself plain? Don't imagine I wouldn't. What?' His mouth grew tiny. 'Oh!' he exclaimed, his eyes blinking fast. 'Oh.' With trembling hands, he shoved the phone at Iseult.

She listened in a daze.

'. . . are tame rats compared to what I'll send after you, Forbes.'

He had reverted to a Belfast accent.

'It's me, Cathal.'

Behind her Valentine slammed the door.

'He's gone,' Iseult said.

The long interval ended with a tragic groan. 'You're going to hate me, Iseult.'

She tried to harden her will against whatever was coming.

'The deal,' Cathal said at last. 'I lied.'

Iseult laughed bitterly.

'I wanted to save you from worry.'

'Save me from worry?' She did feel hatred then. It soured her throat. She swore that never, never again would she let him use her. *Never*! 'I don't want to hear,' she cried.

'I've been a dope, Iseult. Do you understand – a dope?'

The word hung between them. The fear had been there all the time, at the back of her mind. 'You stupid bloody fool,' she cried.

Cathal sighed. 'It's worse than that,' he said. 'I borrowed the money from old friends.'

'More fool them. They can bloody well . . .' Iseult's voice stopped. Her mouth turned arid. 'What friends?'

'Old friends from Dublin,' Cathal said. 'Old comrades.' He allowed a silence to draw out. 'I was holding it on deposit for them.'

'You're lying,' Iseult said. 'You're lying again,' she shouted.

Cathal made a sound between a laugh and a groan.

Iseult crammed her knuckled hand between her teeth. 'You swore you had nothing more to do with them,' she whispered.

'Ah well,' he said, and breathed a musical sigh. 'It's not that easy.'

Her mind blanked. 'There's nothing I can do. You'll just have to tell them the truth.'

'The truth will kill me, Iseult. That money was for the cause.'

'Sweet Jesus,' she moaned.

'Hush now, and let me think.'

She heard him strike a light and suck in smoke. She groped for her own pack, lit the cigarette with shaking hands, took one puff and stubbed it out on the bed frame.

'There's only one way for it. Tell Forbes. Give him chapter and verse – Belfast, Dublin, old friends. Frighten the bastard.'

'I won't do it,' she shouted. 'I won't.'

'Time's running out,' Cathal said. 'In two weeks my friends will be calling for their money.'

Iseult swallowed. 'Whatever I say won't make any difference,' she said in a small voice. 'Valentine's only part of it. There's a Lebanese here called Saad. He's involved, too. He scares me.'

'Not as much as my friends scare me. You know them by reputation, I think – the Poet and the Landlord. No,' Cathal said in a lulling voice, 'I'd say the balance of terror is tilted our way.'

Iseult saw the Landlord's florid face, the Poet's stringy hair. Terror manifested itself with sickening clarity.

'It's not a question of Valentine or me,' Cathal said. 'It's both or neither. You'll be saving the two of us. Just the threat will be sufficient, and there's an end to it.'

'There'll never be an end to it.'

'There will, my darling girl, I promise. You don't know how miserable I've been. Every night I lie sleepless thinking . . .'

'Stop it!'

He seemed not to hear. 'After you left, I went to pieces, you see. I tried to forget with drink and gambling and business went to hell. And then up popped smooth-talking Forbes like an answer to a prayer, promising riches untold. Pure madness, but I was not myself at the time. You'd made me crazy, you see.'

She took the phone from her ear and smothered it against her breast. But Cathal's words continued to issue forth. An image of his long hands came into her mind. 'Leave me alone,' she whimpered.

'I'll leave New York. We'll go to California and start from scratch. We'll find a house by the sea where you can paint and I can . . . well, what happens to me doesn't matter. Please, Iseult, come back. Nothing's right without you. You're my only hope.' He paused. 'Iseult,' he said in a sharp voice, 'is it shame that's turned you cold?'

Dropping the phone, she dashed for the wash-basin and retched. She dashed water into her face and scrubbed until the flesh smarted. She flung back her hair. A hellhag confronted her. She clawed the image with her nails and dropped weeping on the bed. A minute passed, but the phone wouldn't stop squawking. The sound made her think of bald unfledged birds, beaks blindly groping. She saw her brother, dead. With a mew of pain she grabbed the phone.

'Cathal!'

'I thought you'd gone,' he said, his voice heavy. 'I thought you'd left me for good.'

Something tore in her chest. 'Oh, Cathal,' she whispered. A tear broke in her eye and slid down her cheek.

'Shut the door.'

Valentine was alone, pacing the room with the great hawk on his gloved fist. Under its saffron feet was the carcass of a grouse.

'This is Freya,' he said, 'an Iceland gyrfalcon, the gift of a Saudi prince. In medieval times they were worth a king's ransom.'

The gyrfalcon lifted its bloodied head and fastened its gaze on Iseult. It was a wonderful creature, the colour of birch bark and lichen. It bent again and closed its beak on the grouse with a visceral crunch.

Valentine stopped his pacing to examine a framed photograph on the wall. 'I've taken the Lodge every season for fifteen years,' he said. 'Look.'

Iseult recognized a younger Valentine, sparsely bearded and wearing a Tyrolean hat with feathers. He stood at attention among a group of Gulf State princelings with falcons on their fists. Behind them were a few girls with staunch, professional smiles who looked as if they were there to model rough-weather gear.

'Happy times,' Valentine said, his eyes softening in recollection. 'Some Foreign Office type hit on the idea of using the Lodge as a centre for informal diplomacy during the oil crisis. We used to travel up on a special train – civil servants, sheikhs and the finest whores money could buy. Shepherd Market used to be quite *denuded*. Once, we roasted a whole sheep on the forecourt while a bagpiper walked up and down playing the "Lament for the Viscount of Dundee". Tacky but rather wonderful – a cross between a Walter Scott pageant, a public school bun-fight and a production of the *Desert Song*.'

In the big room, Iseult seemed small to herself, remote from her surroundings. She crossed her arms and hugged her shoulders.

Valentine's mouth twisted in disdain. 'I only return out of

nostalgia. The moor's been sold to a Belgian consortium who rent it out for corporate hospitality weekends. Nowadays a stay at the Lodge is nothing more than a works outing for cost accountants.'

'Cathal told me,' Iseult said.

Valentine turned. 'Forgive me. I'm neglecting my duties. Can I offer you a drink?'

She let him pour a pale whisky. He took one for himself and they sat down at the huge table, selecting chairs some distance apart.

'Well,' Valentine said, with an off-centre smile, 'I do hope the moral dimension isn't going to be an issue.'

'Only the money,' Iseult said. Her voice sounded as if it came from someone else. Her coolness astonished her.

'You know, I share Rafiq's puzzlement. Cathal had no right to involve you. It's so ungallant.'

'He must have the money back.'

'He's not the only one out of pocket, you know.'

'Give it back,' Iseult intoned. She felt she had reserves of power.

'I don't have it.'

'Saad's got it, hasn't he?'

'Nonsense.'

'He's involved up to his nasty eyes.'

'Only as another dissatisfied customer.'

'I'll ask him myself,' Iseult said, rising.

'Don't,' Valentine pleaded, reaching out. 'I really wouldn't.'

'Then where is it?'

Her cry alarmed the falcon. It flared its great wings.

'If I tell you,' Valentine said, 'you must agree to leave Saad out of it.'

Iseult nodded.

Valentine stroked the falcon. 'Your brother,' he said, making a cautious start. 'Basically, he's a con man.' Valentine let this information sink in before continuing. 'Cathal formed an off-the-shelf company for investors wishing to speculate in the futures market.'

'I don't know anything about that kind of thing.'

'It's quite simple. The futures market involves speculating on the supply of commodities before they have been produced. It's a hit-and-miss business at the best, but in Cathal's case, there *were* no commodities, no trading operations of any kind. He simply pocketed the investors' money. When returns fell due, he would persuade his clients to invest their nominal profits in another imaginary deal. Usually they took his advice, but if they insisted on their money, he paid them out of new investment funds. It was a high-wire scam, Iseult, and he was bound to fall off in the end. Some of his clients threatened to file suits. Cheques started bouncing. When I met him he had less than $300,000 dollars to cover more than 10 million dollars in liabilities.'

'How did you meet him?' Iseult asked. Somehow the question held more significance than the unaffected explanation of Cathal's fraud.

'In a Greenwich Village nightery,' Valentine said. 'It was infatuation at first glimpse. Your brother is a monster of charm.' Valentine slipped the grouse from the falcon's clutches. 'There, my beauty, that's quite enough.'

'Were you lovers?' Iseult asked, and looked away at once. Her composure wilted. Does he know? she wondered. Had Cathal confided in him? The thought was sickening.

'Let's stick to business,' Valentine said in a gentle voice. He hesitated, as if he had lost the thread. 'To cut a long and woeful tale short, Cathal needed a million to get clear. On my advice, he bought into a cannabis deal with the last of his capital. He didn't have a thing to lose except his stake. It was deposited in a Gibraltar bank while the buyer went to inspect the goods and help organize shipment. Normally, he wouldn't have taken the risk, but this was a huge deal – thirty tons.'

'How much is that worth?' Iseult asked, in order to make sense of it.

'The media exaggerates these things grossly. At source, a million; on the street, as they say, thirty million. Of course, those are the extreme ends of the market. At the minimum,

Cathal stood to double his investment.' Valentine nuzzled his whisky. 'Anyway, the buyer visited the supplier as planned. Everything was in order. The next day he was supposed to return to Spain and transfer the money.' Angrily Valentine gulped his drink.

'Well?'

'He never arrived. He disappeared.'

'Where?'

Valentine was in two minds. He glanced at the door. 'Morocco – Marrakech.'

Iseult tried to order her thoughts. 'So the money's still in Gibraltar.'

'Locked in the buyer's numbered account. Untouchable, alas.'

'I thought you were the accountant.'

'Correct. Believe me, my involvement with your brother was exceptional – an act of friendship which I now regret. I don't make a habit of touting for custom. I'm a financial adviser.'

'You launder drug money.'

'We agreed to leave moral considerations aside, Iseult.'

'Why don't you raise another million and go ahead with the deal? What's one million set against thirty?'

Valentine looked tired. 'Fox might have been arrested. He could have been kidnapped. Until we find out what's happened to him, we can't risk making the shipment.'

'Fox?'

'Digby Fox. He's the buyer.' Valentine knocked back his drink. 'Look, once we've cleared up the mystery, we can start things moving again. Give it six weeks.'

Iseult smiled at her hands. 'Too late, Forbes. Cathal has only a fortnight left.'

'I'm awfully sorry, Iseult. I really don't know what to suggest. Cathal isn't the only one with disgruntled clients. In fact, I suspect that his friends will prove a jolly sight more accommodating than mine.' Valentine's features settled in a morose smile. 'Cathal wasn't exactly defrauding old-age pensioners out of their nest-eggs, you know. His clients were greedy people looking for a way to make big profits from money that should have gone to the tax man. Most of them will walk away from their losses rather than risk disclosing their financial affairs in court.'

'Aren't you bothered about where Cathal got the quarter million?'

Valentine shrugged. 'Cathal could charm money out of a rock.'

Iseult gave an exasperated laugh. She was exhausted beyond caution, but still she cringed back from the brink. She thought of the Poet and the Landlord and shuddered. The very threat would be enough, Cathal had said, but it seemed that such spectres, once conjured forth, would not so easily be put to rest.

'The quarter million belongs to the Green Cross.'

'A charitable organization? God, how very like Cathal.' Valentine tried to wipe the mirth from his face. 'Sorry, Iseult, but you must admit it has its droll side.'

'The Green Cross is based in Ireland.'

'Well, I don't expect the little sisters of mercy will be too hard on him.'

'Belfast, Forbes.'

Valentine's grin was replaced by a frown. He lifted his chin, as if searching for something just beyond the fringe of memory.

'Forbes,' Iseult said, with a tenderness derived from her murderous power, 'the Green Cross is a support organization for our friends across the water.'

Various reactions chased across Valentine's face in comical succession. He faked a laugh. 'Really, Iseult, that goes beyond acceptable limits.'

'The Provos, Forbes.'

Blood withdrew from his face. He stood tall, his nostrils pinched. 'I want you out of this house first thing in the morning.' He took a backward step and stumbled against his chair. The falcon bated in a jangle of bells, striking one wing against the table. Valentine struggled to bring it back to his fist. 'You crazy Irish bitch,' he panted. 'This is a rip-off. The IRA wouldn't have anything to do with an irresponsible faggot like Cathal.'

The demons Iseult had summoned made her remorseless. 'Next week, two IRA activists will fly from Dublin to New York.'

'Your brother put you up to this. I recognize his style. It's pure fantasy.'

'I know these people. I know what they are capable of.'

'I beg you, Iseult, stop this charade. The people we're dealing with don't take kindly to threats. Forget Cathal. He'll drag you down with him.'

'Why do you think he didn't come himself?' Iseult demanded.

'Because he's got you to do his dirty work.'

'Because the Brits have got an exclusion order on him.'

'Ridiculous,' Valentine said. His eyes roved the room as if he had misplaced something. The falcon stared at Iseult with its beak agape.

'Seven years ago Cathal was arrested in Amsterdam on an arms smuggling charge. He went to America after the Brits tried to extradite him. It was in the papers. Look it up if you don't believe me.'

'I don't,' Valentine said, but his skin had taken on the grey of putty.

'Return the money, Forbes. That's all you have to do. You can afford it.'

Valentine showed his teeth in the rictus of cornered prey. 'If your precious brother is mad enough to cheat on the fucking IRA, he deserves to take the consequences. My God, of all the crazy fucking . . .'

'They won't stop at him, Forbes. You know how they feel about drugs. When they find out where their money's gone, they'll come after you.'

He sat down in one movement. His stare clung to hers.

She went to him and stroked his hand. 'They'll kill Cathal,' she said. 'They'll kill Cathal, and then they'll kill you.'

4

A black Marine wearing trainers and an Oakland sweatshirt ferried Dearborn from the airport in an Oldsmobile with a small machine-gun clipped under the dash. Marvin was his name, and after establishing this, Dearborn sank into the back seat and muffled a yawn. He had slept for only forty minutes – closing his gritty eyes on the vertiginous take-off from Marrakech and opening them to find himself taxiing towards the Casa terminal. His jacket was a ruin and he had had to purchase an unsatisfactory replacement from the night manager of the Mamounia Hotel where, at his own request, the police had deposited him at 4.15 that morning. He had nicked his parched face shaving. Fastidious in matters of appearance, he felt in no condition to present himself to the world.

'The boss said you worked together in the Root.'

Dearborn jerked as if summoned by a voice from the past. He saw the driver's eyes on him in the rear-view mirror.

'That was some freak show, huh?'

Dearborn grunted. Unwilling to pursue the subject, he looked out of the window. They were cruising down Morocco's showpiece stretch of freeway, built to whisk plenipotentiaries between the airport and Rabat. Cables overhead carried portraits of the king decked out in the red and green national colours. The plain on each side was baked the shade of wheatmeal, the horizons smudgy with heat.

'Boy, we really loused up there,' the driver said.

Meaning, *you* loused up, Dearborn translated.

'I-ran, Lebanon, Libya. I'll say one thing for our Middle East policy: it's consistent.'

'We call it negative infallibility.'

The driver showed his teeth. 'Maybe you want to tell that to the Marines who got blown away in Hooterville.'

Dearborn locked eyes with him in the mirror. No, he was too young to have been in Beirut in '83.

'My big brother,' the Marine said, reading his thoughts.

'Did he get home?' Dearborn asked, forced to voice the awful thought.

'Most of him did,' the driver said, taking his right hand off the wheel and waggling his fingers.

A police jeep drew alongside, its occupants peering across, the passenger speaking into his radio. Marvin threw a casual salute and the Jeep fell back, staying with them until they reached the Rabat turn-off.

'Aren't we going into town?' Dearborn inquired.

'Saturdays, Mr Cody takes lunch at his country club,' the driver replied, and worked his tongue in his cheek.

Beyond the capital the road narrowed and ran through an avenue of eucalyptus with tattered foliage. It was local market day and the verges were crowded with villagers. Trees began to skirt the horizons and Dearborn glimpsed shuttered villas set amid olive groves. The pacific face of colonial Morocco, he thought – the legacy of General Lyautey, whose 'native politics' campaign, resurrected under such euphemisms as 'hearts and minds', had seen service in countries as far afield as Angola and Vietnam.

'I guess this place must seem like a resort spa after the places you've been,' the driver said.

'I guess.'

The driver curled his lip.

He kept a blessed silence as they headed on a minor road into the Forest of Mamora, through gladed stands of cork and wild pear posted with *Chasse interdit* signs. After about five kilometres, he turned off under an arch decorated with a steel frieze of horses. On one side of the well-paved track, a herd of pedigree Charolais grazed on pasture as green as Astroturf. On the other a young Moroccan woman in tight breeches was schooling an Arab mare, touching its haunches with a light whip.

'Will you look at the ass on her?' the driver breathed, slowing to a crawl.

Dearborn felt lust rear its sluggish head.

'Too rich for my taste,' the driver said, and speeded up.

At the end of the track, a trio of security men admitted them to a sweep of gravel behind an imposing villa draped in bougainvillaea. The driver parked in a tree-shaded bay among other expensive automobile imports and stayed in the car while a flunky in a red tarboosh attended to Dearborn. He was led round the front through a rose garden and arbour where there was a gardener for each hundred square metres. Sunlight created rainbows in the spray of lawn sprinklers.

With the appearance of sweeping the ground in his path, the servant ushered Dearborn on to a terrace set with wrought-iron tables occupied by beautifully barbered middle-aged Moroccan men. Several of them seemed to be in the company of their daughters.

Cody was seated at a table on his own, under a fig tree heavy with fruit. 'John Wesley,' he called, the extravagance of his greeting calculated to draw attention. 'Glad you could make it.' He bounded on to the terrace, meeting Dearborn halfway, shaking him by hand and elbow. 'Smile, cowboy,' he muttered through a gritted smile. 'I had to kiss a lot of ass to spring you from pokey.'

With many a hearty gesture, he led the way to their table.

'You could try using a bit more discretion with your help,' Dearborn said when they were seated.

'Marvin give you a hard time?'

'He as good as accused us of being a couple of burn-outs living in lotus land.'

'And who's to say he's wrong?' Cody said, lighting up one of his small cigars.

In his late fifties, he appeared to have a lot of fuse left. He was grizzled and stocky with a neck like a Prussian *Junker* and chalky blue eyes. He was from Texas, from a family of sod-busters as dirt-poor as Dearborn's own. Among their Ivy League colleagues, it had been a bond between them, even though Dearborn affected the manners of the officer corps.

'Business can wait a minute,' Cody said, snapping a finger at an instantly receptive steward. 'Let's catch up on life.' He puffed on his cigar and smiled. 'How's my little girl?'

'Lauren's terrific,' Dearborn replied. 'She's already started reading.'

'That's wonderful,' Cody said, but his smile grew remote. His own son had died in childhood. His wife had left him soon after. He had never remarried.

'Magda settling in?' he inquired, with a degree or two of coolness. He and Magda had never taken to each other.

'She's finding it a bit rough,' Dearborn said, keen to get that topic out of the way.

'I never could understand why you buried yourselves away in the mountains.'

'It's close to the dam. She said she wanted to experience the real Morocco.'

'*This* is the real Morocco,' Cody said, jerking his thumb at the other patrons. 'Feudalism dressed in an Armani suit. It reminds me of Lebanon in the old days. See that dude in the riding outfit. He's huge in bauxite. His grandfather was a Rif brigand – specialized in kidnapping European women. Everyone was happy. He got a ransom, the papers got a great story, and the ladies came out with a smile on their faces.'

Cody had the disconcerting habit of letting his eyes roam about while he talked. He had been a fighter-bomber pilot as far back as the Korean war, and he still looked as if he was forever scanning a console of instruments.

Without consulting Dearborn's opinion, he ordered mineral water and a bottle of estate-bottled *vin gris* – which he pronounced 'grease' even though his French was perfectly serviceable. He liked to play the role of the ugly American.

Behind the wine steward an under-manager hovered with a servitor's grace, holding a brace of freshly plucked partridges on a chased metal dish. Cody palped the birds' breasts, examined their beaks and claws, and expressed approval. 'New season's,' he said. 'The secret of game is kill it young and eat it fresh.' He stuffed a napkin into his collar. 'So how's progress on that dam?'

Dearborn explained about the labour troubles.

'You could have more. Some old cleric is stirring up the villagers. Personally, they get my sympathy.'

'They'll settle for the compensation.'

'Ever been up into that back country?'

'No,' Dearborn admitted, shamefaced. 'I plan to go.'

'Do it. It's fabulous territory – real wild. I was in those mountains last fall, hunting moufflon. I swear to God, John, I saw a leopard. Listen, why don't you come along on my next trip?'

'I'm not the hunting type.'

'What in hell do you do with your free time?'

'I started writing a book.'

'About Morocco? Forget it. That old guy in Tangiers has copyright on the place.'

'It's history, not fiction. Anyway, I like to spend time with my family.'

Cody nodded as if he was trying to convince himself of Dearborn's sincerity. 'I was thinking about you this morning,' he said. 'I was walking down a sunny street but I found myself looking into the shadows. And I thought, yes, that's the kind of country this is – light and dark, good and evil, with only one step separating them.'

Until moments like this, it was easy to forget that Cody was a devout Christian, a member of a fundamentalist sect headquartered in Austin that exacted a tithe of his salary.

Dearborn took a sip of water. He felt a little faint.

'Now some people are attracted to the shadow,' Cody said, letting his eye dwell on Dearborn. 'They turn their back on the light and they abandon themselves to sin of all kinds. They become weirdos or deviants.'

'What category have you got me filed under?'

' "A" for asshole, but that's only a provisional assessment. Colonel Douaz – the guy you spent last night with – gave me the full report.'

'How cosy.'

'Be grateful he was in town. Some of his co-workers don't think they're having a heart-to-heart until they hear the sound of bones popping.'

Dearborn ran his hand round his shirt collar.

Cody grabbed the edge of the table as if he meant to overturn it. 'Screwing a whore in a public park,' he hissed, hunching forward, 'I do not believe it. I'm fucking amazed.'

'So am I,' Dearborn said, plumbing a chasm of shame. His eyes slid away from the cold blue fury of Cody's gaze. In a cypress across the lawn, white egrets festooned the branches like candles. They made him think of his wedding day. 'Magda and I haven't been getting along too well,' he admitted.

'I'm not talking as a friend. I'm not talking as someone who reveres the sanctity of marriage. I'm talking as Security Co-ordinator to His Majesty's government.'

Dearborn tried to rally. 'I've been out of it for four years,' he pointed out. 'Lord knows, my personal life isn't much to brag about, but at least it's mine to call my own.'

Cody pointed a shaking finger at him. 'You'd better see a doctor before you force yourself on Magda, because by God, John, if I hear you've gone and polluted her, so help me, I'll cut your fucking balls off.'

'It won't happen again,' Dearborn muttered. He threw back his head and vented a sigh.

Cody subsided, glowering. 'I suppose I ought to give thanks that it wasn't the sin of Sodom.' He slapped the table in renewed rage. 'What the hell's the matter with you?'

'I'm not standing up to life too well, I guess.'

'Try kneeling then,' Cody said, jabbing a knife groundwards, his eyes afire.

Dearborn was spared Cody's evangelical counsel by the arrival of the first course – *croûtes aux écrevisses aux fines herbes*. Cody applied himself to the crayfish with gusto. Dearborn picked at his portion.

'So what were you and Ben-Yacoub up to?' Cody demanded between mouthfuls.

Dearborn threw down his napkin. 'Okay,' he said, 'that's just about it.'

'We still haven't got a make on him,' Cody said, unperturbed. 'But he's a wrongo and no mistake. He was carrying the papers of a Casa fruit exporter – first-class forgeries, real pro work.'

'What about the murderer?'

'Picked up at the bus station – a Berber peasant who got carried away by the excitement.' Cody paused over a forkful. 'Half an hour before he was murdered, the victim was drinking mint tea at the Café de Paris. He appeared to be waiting for someone. Next he showed up in the Mellah, walking down the street, checking out the houses. Some old guy saw him and recognized him as a Jew called Ben-Yacoub. A crowd gathered like it always does in this country and a local big shot suggested they call the police. That's when Ben-Yacoub panicked and pulled a knife. The peasant tried to grab him, got cut and pulled his own blade – stabbed him twice in the gut. Then you came along.' Cody popped food into his mouth.

Dearborn nodded, replaying the scene in his mind.

'You went to the victim's aid,' Cody said. 'Anyone else remain on the scene?'

'Only the cripple. Everyone else beat it.'

'Uh-uh. There were a lot of eyes on you, and they spied another man hanging back in an alley – moustache, fortyish, tough.'

'God, I forgot,' Dearborn said, sweating at his lapse of memory. 'I sent him for help.'

'What's significant, John, is that the same man was seen sitting close to the victim on the terrace of the Café de Paris half an hour before the murder.'

47

'Another Israeli?'

'Moroccan, they say.'

'That's what I assumed,' Dearborn said. 'What do the Israelis say?'

Cody dabbed his mouth and sighed. 'Ben-Yacoub is nothing to do with them – official. They're putting an outraged face on it, claiming it was an outburst of anti-Zionist hysteria. They say they'll run a check through the immigration records, but you know the Israelis: they'll keep the result to themselves.'

A waiter whisked away Cody's plate and removed Dearborn's barely touched portion.

'What do *you* think?'

'*I* think he *was* an Israeli. Run through the evidence. He was looking for a house in the Mellah. The old man I.D.'d him as an Israeli called Ben-Yacoub and he died outside a house owned by a family of that very name who emigrated to Israel in 1961. Here's something else. A waiter at the café noticed that he had a Marrakech accent, so he commented on the fact that he hadn't seen him in town before. No, says Ben-Yacoub, a bit flustered, I'm from Casa, but my mother came from Tahanaoute. Now Tahanaoute is a town south of Marrakech that used to have a big Jewish population, so Douaz sends a couple of men to investigate. Bingo! Half a dozen old folk remember a woman called Miriam who married a silversmith in Marrakech called Ben-Yacoub. The officers go back to the cripple. "What was Ben-Yacoub's wife called," they ask. "Miriam," he says.'

Cody spread his hands.

'A lot of Jews in Marrakech were silversmiths,' Dearborn pointed out, 'and I bet a good percentage were married to women called Miriam.'

'You were there when he died. Did he say anything?'

'Something about a house, and then something that sounded like "Call him."'

'Language?'

'He was inarticulate. He was dying.'

Cody sighed and sawed at his roast partridge. 'Dammit, they've left out the liver. That's the best bit. *Garçon!*'

'Oh, God,' Dearborn said. 'I just remembered something else.'

Cody's head snapped up.

'The birds. I bought some finches for Lauren. I must have left them in the street.'

Cody let his breath go slowly.

For a while they gave their attention to their food.

'Here's another coincidence,' Cody said at last. 'Remember Vanunu – the guy who tried to blow the whistle on Israel's nuclear programme? He was a Moroccan Jew, too, from Marrakech – a close neighbour of the late Mr Ben-Yacoub and about the same age.'

He gnawed the last scraps of meat from his partridge, wiped the grease from his face and lit another cigar.

Dearborn fanned the smoke away. 'How many of those things do you get through a day?'

'As many as I can. I've made it this far – I figure, what the hell.' Cody's eyes darted about. 'I retire in eight months, John, and I want to go out clean. I've promised Douaz our total support on this one.'

'You and him seem pretty close.'

'It's not every day that one of my former associates trips over a body.' Cody leaned close. 'I want you off my conscience.'

Dearborn nodded. 'But apart from worrying about me, you're sleeping well?'

'Like a baby. Why?'

'Oh, it crossed my mind that maybe something was brewing.'

'I forgot how paranoid you are,' Cody said. He drank his wine. 'Brewing?' he inquired.

'The strikes, the riots – even the dispute at the dam. Is it just my paranoia, or are there more police on the streets than usual?'

'Look around,' Cody said, waving his cigar at the tranquil

luncheon scene. 'These are the powers in the land, and the only thing they're agitating over is the size of their wives' and daughters' next Hermès bill.'

Dearborn fiddled with his *demi-tasse* of cardamon-flavoured coffee. He could feel Cody watching him very closely. 'But like you said, it's a veneer. When you look under the surface . . .' He raised his head. 'When you look into the shadows, you see things differently. This is still a tribal society. Half the population is under twenty and too well-educated for the available jobs. There's a lot of urban unemployment and the peasants want food prices raised. The official opposition is a bunch of stooges on the make; the unofficial party's in jail. The army's got more toys than it knows what to do with.' Dearborn laughed. 'Suddenly I have a nasty attack of *déjà vu*.'

'Listen,' Cody said, examining the stump of his cigar, 'those others – in Tehran and Lebanon – they were losers. What happened to them was ordained in heaven. But look at Hassan. He's incredible. He's survived – what is it? – six, seven assassination attempts. Two fighter pilots shoot up his unarmed airplane, so he grabs the radio and says, okay guys, His Majesty is dead, and talks his way out of it. A colonel and his staff plan an ambush. There's an ambush alright, but who gets wasted? The fucking colonel. Five hundred troops storm a royal garden party. Thirty-five dead, but the king walks away without a scratch. I tell you, John, that guy's got all the *baraka* in the world.'

'Don't you think you're setting too much store by God?'

'Now, John,' Cody said in a reproving tone, 'the good Lord can bear any burden.' He called for the waiter. 'But just in case,' he added, 'he's got us, the French and the Israelis as back-up.'

'Well, if there's any divine fortune left over,' Dearborn said, 'I could certainly use a slice.'

5

Case came out into the flow country and snapped down the sun visor against the glare smearing the screen. Pools of standing water shivered in a fierce wind. On the other side of Scotland the quartz masses of the Torridonians looked like glass dissolving into sky.

He checked the odometer. Six miles since leaving the road. Another five until he reached the Lodge. He was late. Snow depth markers went past at a constant rate. On the track, run-off braided into streams. Case pondered his Moroccan scheme. He would need at least two grand, but even if he got the necessary, he still hadn't cracked the problem of how to get the goods out of the country. When he considered the consequences of getting caught, all his stomach muscles cramped.

Suddenly his flash of nocturnal brilliance didn't look so clever. With every passing mile his will grew colder.

A junction presented itself. He took the left turn, following the march of telegraph poles. Soon he had to drop a gear to accommodate the tilt of the earth, and then another as the gradient steepened. The clutch was slipping. By the time he reached the top, the radiator was boiling. He killed the engine and sat there, both hands on the wheel. The wind droned in the wires and found the corners of the car.

From up here he could survey fifty square miles. Below him the moor widened into a shallow stadium planed out by the passage of time and ice. In all that space the Lodge was the only thing to stop the eye. It was about a mile distant, marooned at the far end of a loch, its turrets exposed to all directions, its windows blinded by the sun. Seeing it again, Case couldn't restrain a laugh. It had been the sporting retreat of a nineteenth-century jute magnate whose baronial pretensions couldn't overcome his shopkeeper mentality. It reminded Case of the Co-operative Wholesale Society's main branch in his home town.

He took a breath, let it go slowly and released the brake. As the Toyota coasted, it flushed a covey of grouse. Case's blood tingled as he watched them hurl away. There hadn't been a better day for hawking all season.

Valentine's guests had spent the morning shooting over dogs on the heights above the Lodge. Languid after exercise and lunch, they reclined on a circle of turf around the remains of a prehistoric fort. The company watched Case's arrival without stirring, glasses arrested in their hands. From the shabbily expensive patina of their clothing, he guessed that most of them were British. Through force of habit he gave the women a once-over. Valentine's guests usually included a few tasty items – easy prey after a day on the hills, a hot bath and a couple of cocktails. He marked down two possibles – an eye-catching blonde and a stunning black girl with cheekbones tinted violet to match her exquisite tweeds. Another woman, standing at a forlorn remove, just about caught his attention.

Thain wasn't in evidence, thank God. Valentine was with the Arab bloke, talking into a cordless phone. Freya the gyrfalcon occupied his other hand. Young Alastair Sinclair, an aspiring falconer from Brora, was looking after Valentine's three German pointers and a cadge holding two falcons. Case recognized Vector, a rangy peregrine-prairie cross.

Valentine raised his arm in salute and tapped his watch in reproach.

'And you,' Case muttered. Valentine's lordly manner got right up his nose.

He walked to the edge of the high ground and braced himself against the updraft, assessing the conditions. The wind scribbled patterns on the loch below. A brilliant ridge of cloud was building in the east, but there would be no rain before nightfall.

Zipping up his combat jacket, Case returned to the car and raised the tail-gate. The pointers poured out, sprung wire in loose velvet, and went off sparring and vacuuming up the scents. Drawing on a buckskin glove, Case held his hand behind the Dancer's legs. At his touch she commenced a rusty wailing and stepped back. She was dark and solid, her back slatey with a lavender bloom, her buff breast stamped with black chevrons. In flying condition she weighed thirty-four ounces. The Barbary was ten ounces lighter, with a back of powder blue and a leopard-coloured chest marked by arrowheads.

Skirting the shooting party, Case searched for a site to set the falcons down. They had bathed and weathered at home, and half an hour's recovery would see them composed and ready to fly. He selected a spot sheltered by a bank of heather and tied the falcon to her block.

When he returned with the Barbary, he found one of the guests examining the Dancer. It was the woman he had seen on the edge of the company. She was cocking her head from side to side as if viewing an object in a gallery.

She turned.

Black-red hair hung in waves down her back and her complexion was as white as cold cream. Her eyes were bruised by lack of sleep, her mouth small and sullen.

Her silence unsettled Case. 'I'm Pat Case,' he said. 'I'm a friend of Forbes'. I'm keeper on the Auchronie estate. That's down the road forty miles.' His voice seemed to run on too long.

'Iseult O'Dwyer,' was all she said.

She was about his age and nearly as tall – big and soft and alternative, not a woman who worshipped fitness. She wore an old anorak over a sloppy sweater of furry caterpillar mauve, with black leg-warmers and jazzy red-and-yellow socks tucked into borrowed boots. She looked like an art student roused from bed by a fire alarm. She bared one startling white shoulder and scratched it.

Case rubbed his hands. 'What about this weather then?'

She glanced about with mild vexation.

'You're not up for the shooting then?'

'I hate blood sports,' she said without emphasis.

Case frowned. Her accent was familiar. There passed through his mind a montage of broken streets, sodden hills, suspect number plates viewed through image-intensifiers.

'What?' Iseult demanded, returning his frown.

'Nothing. You're Irish.'

When she didn't respond, he looked at the sky. Geese were passing over in wavering lines. Their calls shivered down his spine. 'Makes you want to go with them,' he said.

She received this opening with another silence. The falcons shifted on their perches, tracking the baying of the geese. The Dancer plucked at her jesses and scratched her hood.

'Are they yours?' Iseult asked.

Case stopped smiling. 'Why aye,' he said, his voice sliding into the whining dialect of childhood. 'Whose else would they be?'

'I was only asking,' she said. She looked bored. 'What are they called?'

'The dark one's the Dancer,' he said, glad of the life-line, 'and that's the Barbary.' He was confident in the choice and was scornful of Forbes' whimsical selection. His peregrines bore the names of major credit cards. A couple of seasons back, he'd named his team after an assortment of low-alcohol lagers.

'It's cruel to keep them blindfolded,' Iseult said.

Her deadpan criticism sliced through Case's guard. 'It keeps them calm when they're travelling,' he told her, propelled by an urge to justify. 'They think it's night. That's where the expression "to hoodwink" comes from. In medieval times,' he went on, drawn out by her silence, 'falconers used to sew up their birds' eyelids. It was called seeling. Hoods were introduced by Emperor Frederick the Second. He got the idea from the Arabs.'

He moved his weight to his other foot and still felt off balance.

'I think it's a sin,' she said, and looked away as if the subject was closed.

He flushed. Silly bitch, he thought. He slid a look at her. Her eyes were smoky blue, laced with black. Her pallor was disconcerting – white like porcelain. You couldn't call her beautiful. Her face was too long and her mouth too tight and moody. Nah, Case decided with something like relief, definitely not your type. He couldn't stop looking at her.

'What are you staring at?'

'Er, I was wondering if you were a bit French.' He gave a delicate cough, as if he had made an impolite suggestion.

'My mother was half Spanish,' she said, and took out a pack of Marlboro.

She smoked in the way he associated with women, furtively palming the cigarette and making a big deal out of expelling the smoke. He couldn't get her measure.

The two pointers returned from their frolic and pushed themselves at her. Nervously, she fended them off.

'They won't bite,' Case assured her.

'I wouldn't blame them if they did.'

'What?'

'They're half-starved. There's nothing more to them than fur and gristle.'

'They're working dogs,' Case said, trying to keep his voice loose. 'I could feed them quarter of their body weight now, and they'd burn it off by evening. They'll cover thirty miles today.'

'Poor creatures.'

Enough was enough, he decided. 'Do you know owt about dogs or hawks?'

She shrugged one shoulder in a way that made him work his jaws.

'So why divn't you keep your half-baked opinions to yourself?'

She flipped back her heavy hair and gave him a pensive stare.

He swung round at the call of his name.

Valentine was hurrying towards him. 'I thought I said one o'clock,' he said.

Case realized why he rarely accepted Valentine's invitations: the man treated him like a bloody retainer.

Valentine glanced at Iseult. 'I've spoken to Cathal,' he said. 'Everything's arranged. He'll have the money by Tuesday. Rafiq mustn't know. This is entirely a personal gesture.' He gave Iseult a slow, burning stare, as if to brand his instruction on her consciousness, then turned to Case. 'Alright,' he snapped, 'let's not waste any more time. We'll work the Heights. I'll fly Vantage first and we'll take it in turns from there.'

'Suit yourself. It's your moor.'

'Oh for God's sake, stop being so bloody chippy,' Valentine snarled, already heading back to the company.

'Prat,' Case muttered, narked that not only Iseult had been at hand to hear Valentine's put-down, but also Alastair, who Case thought of as his apprentice. 'Take the Barbary,' he muttered, picking up the Dancer.

Iseult stayed put, cradling her knees. Case was angry and uncertain how to proceed. 'Coming?' he demanded.

She looked around as if searching for alternatives. With uncertain grace, she got to her feet. 'I suppose so,' she said.

They had the loch on their right as they moved off. Half a mile ahead, Case's dogs had found their stride, quartering the ground at a flowing gallop, weaving a criss-cross pattern. Occasionally they stopped and raised their heads, waiting for him to acknowledge them or signal a change of direction. He was matching his pace to Iseult's, and he was peeved that she hadn't commented on their grace and steadiness. She had her head down, as if walking was an exercise that required thought. So far, conversation had been a series of lurches.

'How do you know Forbes?' he asked, making a last feeble attempt.

'Through my brother,' she said, not looking up. 'He has some of my paintings in New York. Forbes wanted to buy one and got in touch.'

Case received this breakthrough in communication with the sense of relief he got when a wild hawk took its first mouthful on his fist. There was also a component of relief in his pleasure. It was daft, he knew, but an Ulster accent could still set his neck hairs on end. He had an intuition that Iseult was a Catholic. She had mentioned sin.

He considered his next question with care. Art was a field in which he had never set foot. 'What kind of paintings do you do?' he asked. Christ, he thought, that sounded awful.

Going by her startled stare, Iseult thought so too.

'Oil painting, I bet,' he said before he could stop himself.

'Mostly.'

'Abstract?'

'Whatever that means.' She sounded cross.

Shame of his ignorance made his palms damp. 'Like Picasso?' he said.

'Picasso? Jesus, what made you say that?'

Case concentrated on the horizon and wished he could transport himself there. 'Because he's the only fucking modern painter I've heard of.'

Her mirth ceased. 'Not like Picasso,' she said at last. 'Let's drop it. I don't know anything about hawks, and you don't know anything about painting.'

'I'm not thick,' he said, and wished he hadn't. Everything he said seemed to fly wide of the mark. He thought about his books. He had hundreds of them, on all sorts of subjects, and he read nearly every day. The trouble was, what he picked up never seemed to be the currency of conversation, or if it was, his bits and pieces of knowledge only lured him up the blind alley of his own ignorance.

'Tell me about Forbes,' she said.

Nothing much came to mind. He had never really examined the relationship. He paused, choosing his way with care. 'Falconry's what we have in common, and I'm not even sure about that. He doesn't say it, but I know he thinks falconry's for the upper-class, not proles like me. He'd prefer to be back in the Middle Ages, when hawks were assigned according to rank – an eagle for an emperor, a gyrfalcon for a king, all that rubbish.'

'Last night he brought his gyrfalcon to dinner.'

'Freya,' Case said. 'About as deadly as a fashion accessory.' He hesitated. It wasn't right to slag Valentine, he decided – even if he was a lah-di-dah pooftah with too much money. 'To be fair,' Case said, 'he's a pretty good falconer. We have a different approach, that's all. Forbes likes to make it a social affair; he loves the company. Me, though, I'd just as soon go out on my own. To me falconry's more of a . . . well, in one old book it's called a "mystery". That means a secret skill.' He found himself aground on his own embarrassment. 'You don't want to know about that,' he said hurriedly. 'Listen, if you don't approve of killing things, what are you doing with the green-wellie brigade?'

'Sorting out the family finances.'

'Everything sorted?'

'It looks that way.'

'Jolly good,' Case said in a fake pukka voice. Alright for some, he thought.

She eyed the falcon. 'Why do you call her the Dancer?'

'Because she's so dark. Spanish Dancer.' He paused. 'Like you.'

She gave him a steady look. 'And the Barbary?'

'Ah, she's special. She's from Morocco. In Arabic she's called a *shahin*. That means noble.'

She looked at him oddly, as if she disbelieved him. 'You got her in Morocco?'

Case resisted an impulse to lie. 'Nah, she came from a

pet shop in Wigan. An animal dealer imported her illegally, and when they caught him, they gave her to me to sort out. She was a mess – half her normal weight, every flight and tail feather smashed. And her beak was so overgrown, she looked like a parrot. He'd fed her on cat food.'

'She looks very noble now.'

'She's okay.'

'Which one's your favourite?'

'I stopped having favourites. You always lose them eventually.' Case hesitated, wary of making a fool of himself again. 'A writer who kept hawks said that it was like love – the first one leaves a hole in your heart that all the others pass through.'

He glanced across to see if she had any idea what he was talking about. Her eyes met his and he felt a little shock, a freezing of the moment.

'But you said the Barbary's special.'

'The Dancer's captive-bred. She's imprinted. She thinks I'm her mum. Her manners are atrocious and although she's notched up a pretty good score at grouse, she's not what you'd call an imaginative hunter. The Barbary's in a different league. She has all the techniques, all the tricks. She's a haggard – a wild-caught mature bird.'

'I expect part of the thrill is being in control of a wild creature.'

Case laughed. 'I'm not too sure about control. The Barbary's always pissing off. I lose her half a dozen times each season. One day she'll go for good. I have dreams about it. She's trapped by her jesses in the top of a tree and I can't reach her.'

A few seconds elapsed. 'Do you know Yeats?' she asked.

'Rings a bell.'

Iseult stopped. She didn't say anything for a while, then she began to recite in a far-off voice. ' "Turning and turning in the widening gyre, the falcon cannot hear the falconer. Things fall apart; the centre cannot hold; mere anarchy is loosed upon the world. The blood-dimmed tide is loosed, and everywhere the ceremony of innocence is drowned."'

Case shivered. The air about him seemed to have congealed. He tried to speak, but the words got caught in his throat.

Head flung back, Case tracked the falcon climbing into the blue. He took a sighting on the dogs. They were frozen on point, backing each other up. Valentine was behind them, right hand raised, commanding silence.

'I thought you just let them go and hoped for the best,' Iseult whispered. 'You haven't been paying attention,' Case said.

'What happens now?'

'The dogs will hold the point until the falcon reaches her pitch. She'll show she's ready by making a couple of tight turns. When she's in position the dogs will be sent in to flush the grouse – and down she comes.' Case shielded his eyes. 'At least, that's the theory,' he murmured. 'If anything can go wrong, it will.'

'Like what?'

'Like that,' Case said, pointing at another sector of the sky, where a black star had appeared. The falcon had broken out of her orbit and was climbing towards it. 'Wild peregrine,' he explained. 'They're a nuisance.'

The two shapes converged and went crabbing down the wind. Pretty soon the sky had been wiped clean.

A groan rose from the guests.

'Is she lost?' Iseult asked.

'Looks that way,' Case said, grinning at her anxiety.

Valentine stumbled towards them. 'It's going to be one of those bloody days,' he said and glared at Iseult. 'We'll give her five minutes,' he told Case. 'If the grouse are still sitting, you might as well put the Dancer up.'

The dogs had held their point. Little tremors ran up and down their flanks.

The guests subsided into the heather some way off. Case

lay on his back, supporting the Dancer on his chest. Iseult rested her chin on her knees. The light had thickened and the wind was moderating. Young Alastair joined them.

'Alright, kidder?'

'Oh yes,' Alastair said, blushing to his roots. He was in his last year at school and pathologically shy.

'Decent morning?' Case asked.

'Nine and a half brace. Mr Valentine's Lebanese guest got a very fine right and left.'

'Plenty of practice, I suppose. Hey look, I'm going away for a couple of months. I was wondering if you could take on the dogs and hawks. Fly the peregrines if you feel up to it, but you'll probably have your hands full with the gos.'

The boy's face lit up and then clouded. 'Oh, but what if I should lose her?'

'Makes no difference to me,' Case said, and laughed at the boy's confusion. 'She's yours to keep, kidder.'

Alastair's jaw nearly hit the ground. 'Oh Pat,' he stuttered, his face like a stop light, 'I can't. She must be worth at least a thousand pounds.'

Case glanced at Iseult. She was occupied with a cigarette. 'You've done a good job on that old red-tail I gave you. It's time you got yourself a decent hawk.'

'Do you really mean it? I'll treat her . . .'

'Gerraway,' Case said.

Watching the boy run off, Case shook his head, thinking of the thrill his first falcon had given him. He transferred his smile to Iseult. The exchange had been partly for her benefit.

'What a dreadful place,' she said, gazing out at the miles of nothing.

It was like a drenching in cold water. 'You divn't know what you're on about,' he blurted. 'It's bloody marvellous.'

His passion failed to move her. 'But you're not from round here.'

'Tyneside,' he said.

'How did you become a keeper?'

He sat up, thinking here we go. 'You've heard of setting a

thief to catch a thief? Well, that's me. I came up to Scotland to work on the rigs. Two weeks on, one week drunk. One night, some mates bet me a hundred quid I couldn't shoot a deer. I shot it alright, but I got caught, didn't I?' Case wondered if he should own up to the prison sentence and decided on discretion. 'It was in the local papers, and Lord Orr – that's my old boss – saw it. He knew the sheriff who sentenced me and thought he was a pillock. He offered me a job. He was eccentric.' Case half rose. 'Nice man. Died last year. The new laird's just given me the bullet.'

He checked the dogs. They were holding firm. It was time to ready the Dancer. He took off her hood. She adjusted to the light in a blink, her eyes taking fierce bites of her surroundings.

'She looks like a highwayman,' Iseult said.

The Dancer roused, puffing up her feathers and then relaxing them with an explosive shake. She began to preen, drawing each primary through her beak. Then she stretched out each wing in turn and fanned it over its respective leg. When she had finished, she scissored her wings over her back and stared off at something beyond the sight of man.

Valentine was walking in a slow circle, holding out an aerial like a diviner. He handed it to Alastair.

'Time's up,' Case said, pushing himself to his feet.

He began to walk towards the boy, then halted. 'Fancy flying the Dancer?' he asked, seized by an impulse he regretted immediately.

Iseult laughed. 'You're joking.'

'Alastair's away to search for Vantage and that means I have to carry the Barbary. I've only got one left hand.'

'I couldn't,' she said, dropping her eyes.

'Nowt to it,' Case said, wondering what had got into him. He slipped the hood on again, reached in his game bag and took out a spare glove. 'Don't panic,' he told her. 'She'll sit quiet while she's hooded.' He rotated his hand so that the Dancer stepped on to Iseult's fist, then demonstrated how to wrap the leash and take up the jesses. 'Hold your arm into your side,' he said, crooking it for her. 'Apprentice Japanese falconers used to practise by holding an egg between their elbow and their ribs – but then the Japs always like to make things difficult for themselves. There. Keep her facing into the wind.' He took a backward step. 'How does she feel?'

'Alive,' Iseult said, her facing lighting up. 'Oh! I can feel her feet gripping.'

Under the pretext of examining her stance, Case let his eyes roam all over her. The light filled her hair with amber. He felt a little swoop low down, as if he had gone fast over the edge of a hill. He cleared his throat.

'Hold still a second,' he ordered, steadying her arm. From his bag he took a fingernail-sized blue plastic chip trailing a foot of antenna. 'Transmitter,' he said. 'Only weighs a couple of grams, but it has a seven-mile range.' He clipped the transmitter to the base of the Dancer's central tail feather, switched on a receiver belted to his waist and unfolded an aerial. The receiver began to bleep, changing volume as he rotated through a full circle.

'What the hell are you two playing at?' Valentine shouted.

'Get stuffed,' Case muttered. Satisfied, he undid the Dancer's leash. 'Keep hold of her jesses,' he said, preparing to unhood.

Iseult gripped so hard that her hand shook.

Case straightened up. 'Unhood her yourself. Take the button end of this strap in your teeth and pull on this end with your free hand.'

She shook her head, too nervous to speak.

'It's dead simple.' He held the strap so that she could take the button in her mouth and guided her fingers to the other end. He could smell her perfume. 'Pull. Harder.'

Between them they fumbled the operation. The Dancer flicked the hood off. Iseult froze, her teeth sunk into her bottom lip. The falcon gave her a high-intensity stare, glanced at Case, looked away and twitched its tail. Then it tried to scratch its chin.

'She'll go in her own time. Keep her facing into the wind.'

Iseult edged round as if she was hemmed in by a crowd. The Dancer reviewed her surroundings and roused. She bobbed her head at the pointers. They were about seventy yards upwind. She fanned her wings very fast, holding tight to Iseult's glove, and her eyes burned hotter. She spread her wings to full span so that she became weightless and Iseult's hand lifted. The wind buzzed through her primaries and she was free, skimming over the heather.

Case wondered if Iseult experienced the separation with a twinge.

A hundred yards downwind, the Dancer skidded round and headed back, driving past in a tinkle of bells. She beat upwind, swung again and came clipping straight at their legs, swerving away at the last instant. Back she came, over the heads of the dogs, feinting at the place where the grouse were lying. She sailed downwind, limbering up her wings and did not turn again until she was small in the distance. This time her wing-beat was deeper. She began to mount, and when she came overhead her eyes were set straight ahead. Soon she was a dark winnowing. She began to play with the wind, letting it throw her round and then cutting straight into it. She made a long curving pass over the back of the nearest ridge and sank out of sight. Iseult flashed Case an apprehensive look. Half a minute later the Dancer reappeared, shooting straight up. She rose and sank a few times, then flew back in a straight line, eyes patrolling from side to side.

'Let's be having those grouse,' Case said.

The Dancer was still climbing – at least three hundred feet now and going higher.

Case escorted Iseult around the point until they were facing downwind. He swore. One of the dogs was squirming forward. Twenty yards in front a grouse showed its head. The next moment it dashed across a break in the heather. Another followed.

'Shit,' Case said. The lead dog made another hesitant move and looked to him for advice. He lifted his hand and she went solid again.

The Dancer had passed into a different sky – a place without constraints. She was tiny, drifting a little with the wind.

'Give her a sight of this,' Case said, holding out a lure.

Iseult declined with a rapid shake of her hand.

Case began to swing the lure. The Dancer halted her drift and beat back. She turned on stiff wings and Case felt a swell of power.

'The centre holds for now,' he said, stowing the lure.

Suspended directly above, the Dancer revolved and stalled, a tiny anchor hooked into the wind.

'Wait,' Case said.

'What for?'

'A last look.'

This was the moment he cherished most, when everything came together. The little tableau they had created had the immobility of a tapestry – the frieze of spectators on the skyline, the dogs drawn out to their nerve-ends, the bow-taut shape joined to earth by an invisible chord.

'Do you want to finish it?' Case asked.

'I don't know how.'

'Come on then,' Case said, taking her hand and running down the wind. 'Yell,' he shouted.

'Yell what?'

'Anything you like.'

She gave an incoherent shout and the forces holding things together collapsed. The dogs sprang forward. A long way in front the grouse burst from the heather. Sunlight spilled from the Dancer's wings as she turned over.

She drove herself down then drew in her wings, a heavy teardrop falling vertically. She fell fast enough to outstrip the eye, so that Case saw her progress as a series of broken lines. She began to flatten out, describing a parabola. Already she was on a level with the grouse and fifty yards behind. They were racing away like fat bees. Now she was below them and almost up to the tailmost bird. She went past it as if it were a tethered balloon. She overtook another and though there was no sense of contact it stumbled in the air. The Dancer flung up, looped over and stabbed down. The grouse was still flying. The Dancer bound to it in full flight, her impetus carrying her on. She sank from sight.

Iseult was rooted to the earth.

'Not bad,' Case said.

Iseult blinked. She put her hand to her face and staggered.

'Hey,' Case said, reaching her just as she keeled over.

6

'Oh, go away,' she complained, trying to ward off the faces crowding in on her. They had unnaturally sharp contours, and when she blinked they fragmented into a mosaic before slowly coming together again. She shut her eyes but their voices continued to pester her, making ridiculous suggestions, when all she wanted was to lie still.

The voices became muted and eventually faded away altogether. She opened her eyes to see the guests retreating in a pocket of silence, like figures vacating a dream. The young keeper and his hawks and dogs sat beside her in a kind of aura.

'Feeling better?' he said.

She nodded to stop him talking.

'You've got a touch of exposure,' he said. 'You townees are all the same. Let you out of your cage for a few hours – and wallop.'

'Oh, yes,' she said, sitting up all at once, 'typical fucking woman, swooning away.'

'Foul language is one of the symptoms,' Case said.

Her abrupt shift of attitude played havoc with her senses. She made her eyes as full as she could in an attempt to stop her field of vision closing up. The wind kept the heather in ceaseless motion, and with her heightened consciousness she was nauseatingly aware of each quivering stem. She covered her eyes and breathed in and out.

'Lie down,' he said gently. 'You're as white as paste.'

She felt him place his jacket across her. 'It's my period, if you must know.'

He digested this information in silence.

'And I haven't eaten a bloody thing since yesterday,' she added.

'Whose fault is that, luv?'

'Don't call me that,' she muttered, pulling his jacket up over her face. It smelt gamey.

He took it away and squeezed her shoulder until she opened her eyes. 'Emergency rations,' he said, holding out a pack of sandwiches and a flask. 'I keep them in case I have to stop out for a lost hawk.' He filled a mug. 'Get outside that.'

It contained sweet tea and it worked miracles. She swallowed a pill to take the edge off the impending migraine attack and realized she was indeed famished. She wolfed two of the sandwiches and most of a chocolate bar before the attention of Case and his drooling dogs killed her appetite.

'Shouldn't you be with the others?' she asked.

'They'll get by without me.'

'You don't have to stay.'

'Makes no odds to me.'

'I can find my own way back,' she insisted.

'Sure you could,' Case said without conviction.

The moor was flat and everlasting, holding up pockets of water in whatever direction she looked. She hadn't a clue where she was. Simultaneous with this realization came awareness of her chafed and pinched feet. 'I've got blisters,' she said in a helpless voice.

He helped her take her boots off. 'You great soft thing,' he said, shaking his head and looking pleased.

She leaned back on the points of her elbows, studying him while he cleaned the bruised flesh and applied plasters. Under the wild hair, he had rather delicate features and eyes of a peculiar jade green – arresting against the slight olive caste of his skin. The effect was exotic and feral. Some women, she guessed, would find him attractive.

He wasn't at all her idea of a gamekeeper. In her demonology, nurtured by her grandfather's tales, keepers were burly, broken-veined men with cudgels and mastiffs and an abiding hostility towards their fellow men.

He had an industrial-belt accent that swallowed consonants and lacked pretensions to education, but he was obviously bright – thin-skinned, too.

'Am I hurting you?'

'No,' she said, 'it feels nice.'

The touch of his hands made her drowsy. She lay back and pictured the geese flying south and she thought of her flat in London, the bedlam of crowds, the comfort of anonymity. It was a soothing vision. She wriggled her toes. 'What are you doing?' she murmured. 'Hey,' she cried, 'stop it.'

He was bent over, kissing her foot. It was a chaste gesture. He looked up with a serious expression.

Flustered, she wrenched her gaze away. 'You've got an Irish name.'

'A nurse from Cork gave it to me.'

She frowned.

'My mum dumped me outside a hospital when I was two days old.'

'Oh,' Iseult said.

'It's okay,' Case said. 'It doesn't bother me.'

'What about your dad?' Iseult asked after a moment.

Case hunched his shoulders. 'Never knew him. I grew up in an orphanage.'

'I can't believe no one wanted to adopt you,' she said.

'Someone did. It didn't work out. After that I was a bit of a problem kid – always fighting and nicking.'

'You seem pretty together now.'

'Most of the lumps have been knocked off,' he said, brushing his shoulder. 'Give or take the odd chip.'

His laugh seemed to indicate an unmuddied spirit. Sadness passed over her. 'In some ways, I envy you,' she said. 'At least you've been free to make your own way.'

'Oh sure,' Case said, 'the luckiest guy in the world.' He knelt at her feet. 'I'll tell you what it's like being brought up in an institution. It's like the army, like prison – you live by the rules. Follow the rules, they tell you, and then you'll be fit to take your place in society. And you try to do like they say because you feel guilty about not being like everyone else. It's not until you get out that you find that the rules are like the clothes you've been wearing – cast-offs no one else would be seen dead in.' He nodded hard, as if this idea had never come to him before and was worth keeping.

'I didn't mean it like that,' Iseult said. 'All I'm saying is that families can fuck you up, too.'

'I wouldn't know.'

She plucked a sprig of heather. 'All I got from mine was a set of saints to worship and a pack of devils to hate.' She shredded the flowers. 'Sacrifices to celebrate.'

He gave her a quizzical look. 'Sacrifices?'

'Oh, you know – Collins and Connolly, King Billy and Cromwell.'

'You're Catholic,' Case muttered.

'Is it so obvious?'

'Where from?'

'Belfast – not one of the ghettoes.' Iseult laced her hands behind her head. 'My parents were lecturers at Queen's University.'

Case pursed his lips and fiddled with the tassel on his gauntlet.'But they were Republicans,' he said.

'My great-grandfather was a hero of the Easter Uprising. He was sentenced to death and then reprieved at the last moment.'

'An IRA member?'

'It was called the Irish Republican Brotherhood in those days.'

'When was that?'

'You Brits are so ignorant. Nineteen-sixteen.' Iseult sat up. Case was watching her in a way that made her uncomfortable. 'You don't want to hear about Ireland's tribal squabbles,' she said. 'It's so bloody depressing. I couldn't wait to get away.'

'From your parents?'

'They died when I was twelve. No, they weren't blown up

70

or shot; they were killed in a car crash. After that, my brother and I went to live with my grandparents in Dublin.'

Case cleared his throat and looked away over the moor. 'So how did they screw you up?'

'Well, it's not very funny losing your mum and dad.' Iseult felt her lip quiver and bit it ever so slightly to keep from breaking into tears. These bloody periods. They always made her so bloody labile. She took a shaky breath. 'God, how did we get on to this?'

'Sorry,' Case said. 'About your parents, I mean.'

'Oh, I got over it,' Iseult said, dashing the tears from her eyes. 'It's amazing how you do.'

They were on their way back, the dogs somewhere out of sight. Case was withdrawn and Iseult regretted what she'd told him. No Englishman could understand.

Realizing how close she had come to confiding in him about Cathal, she shuddered. In all her life, she had confessed to only two people – a psychiatrist and an American sculptress with whom she had had a brief affair. Not even the priests had dragged it out of her. She stole a glance at Case, wondering how she would have told him, imagining his reaction.

My brother and I were lovers, she said to herself in the comic voice people put on when they read out letters from the Agony Aunt columns. He got me pregnant when I was fifteen and I had to take a day off school for the abortion.

Put like that it really did sound funny – stupid adolescent Mick behaviour. Crazy laughter bubbled up inside her.

You poor girl, the friendly problems' page editor said.

Yes, but that isn't the end, Iseult answered. Three months ago I stayed with Cathal in New York. One night we snorted coke and ended up in bed. It was great.

Within her, a tremendous sense of outrage swelled.

'Are you going to fly the Barbary?' she asked to lighten the mood.

'Forbes may be flying one of his birds. There's already a wild peregrine and one trained falcon loose on the moor. Put the Barbary up and we'd have a flock.' Case spoke without looking at her.

'I've ruined your day,' she said.

'Nah,' he said, pretending to search for his dogs.

'You said you'd lost your job,' she said.

'Yep.'

'I expect you'll find another easily enough.'

'Reckon not.'

'What will you do?'

Case shrugged. 'Something desperate.'

Iseult sought to jolly him. 'You ought to advertise in the paper,' she said with fatuous cheerfulness.'"Desperate. Will do Anything."'

'Anything *legal*,' Case said.

'No,' Iseult said, sobering, 'now they just say "Anything."'

Case looked at her, his pupils small in his faded eyes. His features had gone sharp and tough. 'I don't need to use the small ads. I've got it worked out.'

'Oh?'

'Yeah, I'm going to Morocco.'

Iseult nearly tripped. 'Forbes is sending you?'

Case looked startled. 'Nah, it's my own idea.'

Iseult's mind was in turmoil.

'A hawk-trapping trip,' Case explained. 'It's the autumn migration. I ought to be able to catch a dozen or so Barbary falcons, and maybe a Bonelli's eagle or two. The Germans will pay a bomb for them.'

'Really?' Iseult said, still bewildered.

'See these two?' Case said, indicating the falcons. 'How much do you reckon they're worth?'

'I don't know. Alastair said the hawk you gave him was worth a thousand.'

'Oh, you noticed then.'

'If you're that broke, why did you give it away?'

'Because it's against my principles to sell hawks to friends,' Case said in a stuffy voice which he dragged out from somewhere.

'But not to Germans.'

'That's different. Last year, a falconer from Munich offered me two thousand for the Barbary. He breeds birds of prey and sells them. I figure if some box-head wants to make a profit out of my birds, he can pay for the privilege.'

'Is it legal to export them from Morocco?'

' 'Course not. I'll have to smuggle them out.'

'How?'

'I'm still working on that side of it.'

'Well don't get caught,' Iseult said.

They continued in silence, Iseult wondering at the coincidence.

'Looks like they've marked another covey,' Case said.

Iseult spotted the pointers, stitched into the skyline.

'I'm going to fly the Barbary,' Case said, as if he had been working up to the decision. While he stripped the falcon for action, he prattled on about her merits. 'She weighs not much more than a cock grouse. But look at her feet and beak; they're as large as the Dancer's. Keep an eye out for her stoop. It's unique – a kind of signature.'

Iseult made a polite show of interest. She remarked on the Barbary's rufous colouring and thin, Asian prince's moustache. In fact, to her eye the Dancer was the more beautiful.

Case cast the Barbary off without ceremony and she went straight into the wind, jinking slightly to get the feel of it, her wing-beat shallower and faster than the Dancer's. Soon she was gone.

'She'll be back,' Case said.

But when they came up to the dogs, the sky was vacant. They had reached the rim above the Lodge. The mountains under the sun had set back into solid form and the cloud range to the east had swollen to threatening proportions. Case nibbled his lip, scanning the sky in short arcs. 'Never praise a hawk before she flies,' he said. 'She'll always make an idiot of you.'

'Isn't that her?' Iseult said, pointing a tentative hand at a small point drawing a line across the sky.

In fact the falcon had circled back behind them and was now driving upwind again, already at an immense height. She was ranging wide of the point, indifferent to the set-up.

Case reached into his bag and came up with a pair of binoculars. But he didn't need to use them. 'No,' he said, 'that's not her.'

The falcon came overhead and went on going. Seeing the danger pass, the grouse took their chance and racketed off.

Now the falcon veered aslant the wind and Iseult picked her up against the cloud, energetic as a gnat.

'Hang about,' Case said, 'she's after something.' He brought the binoculars to bear. 'A hoodie,' he said at last, 'on a suicide mission.'

He passed the glasses to Iseult. Eventually she located the crow, making a high passage across the loch. She ranged right and the faultless rhythm of the falcon came into sight. The crow was trudging across its line of flight, shambling downwind like a pirate craft wandering across the bows of a destroyer.

'Look out, you silly bird,' Iseult said.

And at that moment the crow woke up. It hung in her field of view, wings treading air – a Comic-Cuts character suddenly faced with a cartoon foe. Then it began to ring up.

'Old hoodie's going to take it on fair and square,' Case said. 'At that height they might end up in the next county. Just as well it isn't the Barbary.'

Round and round the birds went, sometimes following each other's path like weary climbers, sometimes taking diverging courses, the crow mounting in tighter spirals than the falcon. Iseult's neck muscles burned with the strain. She did not dare to blink in case she lost the black flecks.

'Go on, crow,' she whispered.

They emerged into the blue over the cloud pinnacles, at the very edge of vision, still weaving into greater height, dwindling from sight, gone, ghost-images playing on her smarting eyes.

'I think the hoodie made it,' Case said a few moments

later. He took the binoculars from Iseult and kept watch on the sky.

At least a minute passed.

'They're coming back,' he said. 'Your hoodie isn't out of it yet.'

At first Iseult saw nothing, then one after the other two atoms came falling out of the sky – no, three; there was another descending mote.

'Is it the Barbary?' she asked.

'It must be a wild pair. They're flying as a team.'

They were stooping turn and turn about as if they were driving a nail, but then one of the falcons missed a beat, flying a big arc away from the crow. No, she was turning, gaining speed, bunching up. Briefly the dots intersected and streaked apart, the crow evading the strike with deceptive clumsiness, flopping like a rag, recovering and labouring on.

'Stone me,' Case said in a quiet voice, 'it *is* the Barbary.'

The blows were falling quicker, the falcons making shorter passes and run-outs.

Iseult heard the crow cough as a stoop grazed it. It plummeted, falling directly towards them, one of the falcons powering after it, not relying on gravity alone.

'There,' Case shouted. 'That one.'

The Barbary was shortening the distance, zig-zagging to reduce the crow's options. It was committed, unable to swerve. Iseult put her hand to her mouth. The Barbary must take it. She was on its tail, one bunched foot extended, stretched to snatch.

With a ripping of air, hunted and hunters hurtled beneath the ridge. Iseult had forgotten where she was. For a time gravity had lost its hold and she had been up there, in the sky.

A black wedge zoomed up, ran out of momentum and corkscrewed down. A moment later Iseult heard screeching.

'Come on,' Case yelled. 'They're fighting over the kill.'

Iseult broke into a trot, trapped in slow motion. At the edge of the slope she stopped as if she'd run into a wall. The sky was calm. The crow was unharmed. It had found refuge in a solitary rowan growing out of a rock gulley. On a boulder above it, one of the peregrines screamed its frustration. The crow cursed back. The dogs added to the commotion, but not even their clamour was going to shift it.

Case was stumbling and slithering down. The falcon took off and flew back and forth over his head. 'Wild tiercel,' he yelled up.

'What are you doing?' Iseult shouted down.

'Going to flush the crow.'

'Leave it alone.'

Surprise hung a silly smile on his face. 'It's only a crow,' he said. 'They kill lambs. I shoot them by the score.'

'Just you leave it alone,' she cried, scrambling towards him.

Case waited for her. 'Now look,' he said. 'Falcons don't like missing their quarry. The Barbary won't come back to a lure after having live prey in her clutches. I'm not going to risk losing my best falcon for the sake of a bloody crow.'

'It's my bloody crow,' Iseult said, 'and it beat your hawk fair and square. You said so yourself.'

Case opened his mouth, but thought better of whatever it was he was going to say. He scratched his head and laughed as if he couldn't believe himself. 'You're mad,' he said.

'I don't care,' Iseult said.

'Any road,' he added lamely, 'there's no point. It would be nothing better than a rat hunt.'

He looked around as if searching for a more compelling excuse. The crow had gone quiet and was putting its plumage back in order. The wild tiercel had alighted on the ridge above, still complaining.

'Where's the Barbary?' Iseult asked.

'Search me,' Case said. 'Most likely she's put in on the ground to get her wind back.' He frowned and raised the binoculars to his eyes, sighting on the wild peregrine. 'You've got your eye on her, though, haven't you?' he murmured. For a few seconds more he studied the falcon, then he pointed towards the western end of the loch. 'Somewhere up there,' he said.

An immense hush had settled over the moor. Shielding her face with her hand, Iseult peered into the failing sun.

'Look out,' Case yelled.

From the corner of her eye Iseult saw the wild peregrine launch itself from its perch. Out of the light came a rushing core of matter, a dark comet cutting through the laws of space and motion. In the same split-second the crow hurled itself out of the tree. There was a 'crack' and it came apart, flopping out of a cloud of feathers. Bounding up from the impact, the Barbary shot a glance over her shoulder, rolled and fell, side-slipping in to the kill. Bracing herself against the crow's death spasms, she snapped its neck.

Case was jumping up and down, yelling 'Did you see that? Did you see that?' He gulped in an effort for calm.

'I saw it,' Iseult said, 'just a blur, an impression.' She looked at the sky, half expecting the falcon's course to be imprinted on the air. 'She did something funny, sort of spun round.'

'That's it,' Case said, getting excited again. 'Her signature. It's called a canceleer. I told you she was a belter.' He sank down and cupped his chin in his hands, grinning at the Barbary as if he had created her himself.

Chest heaving and beak hinged open, the falcon glared back, a wild creature now. A faint wail sounded on the wind and she cocked her head. The wild tiercel was being drawn up by the air, calling with a repeated, ascending note that faded out gently. Long after Iseult had lost sight of it, the Barbary kept her eyes on the sky, making a plaintive cheeping sound.

'She wants to go with him,' Iseult said.

Case was kneeling beside the Barbary, encouraging her to feed. 'So that's why you didn't see what was coming,' he said.

One of the crow's eyes was missing, the socket sealed up.

A shiver of bells found its way into her consciousness. The wind came in fits and the day was falling back on itself.

Shadows were already drawing over the far shore of the loch. From the water drifted an eerie cry. Rolling over, Iseult saw Case asleep, the pointers couched at his side, jaws grinning, the two falcons dozing near by, one leg drawn up under their breast feathers and their crops bulging.

Iseult smiled. In sleep, Case's sharpness smoothed out. With his long reddening hair, he reminded her of an illustration from one of her childhood books on Irish heroes – cunning Finn MacCool, slayer of giants. She remembered the way he had looked at her and the current that had passed between them.

The feeling was smothered by the doubt that had been gestating inside her. Perhaps Valentine was lying about his commitment to return the money. No agreement given under threat could be binding.

'How strange that you should be going to Morocco,' she said, impelled by an impulse from nowhere. 'My brother's got a friend there who he's lost touch with. He's been trying to contact him.'

Case opened one eye. 'What's his last-known address?'

'I can't remember,' Iseult said, unable to stop herself. 'Marrakech, I think.'

'Shouldn't be hard to find him. What's his name?'

With horror, Iseult saw what a pit she was digging. 'Actually, he's more a business partner than a friend. He's called Fox,' she said. 'Digby Fox.'

'I'll look him up.'

'No really,' Iseult said, desperately trying to climb out. 'It's a bit awkward, you see. Fox used to be in business with Forbes, and it ended in some disagreement over money which Forbes said was owing to him.' She uttered a laugh of pure panic.

'I won't tell Forbes,' Case said. 'Look, if you're not doing anything tomorrow, come down to my place and we can talk about it.'

'Thank you,' Iseult said. 'You're very kind.' She lay back as if lowering herself on to a bed of nails, her blood pounding in her ears. Gradually, her nerves straightened out.

'This Yeats bloke,' Case murmured sleepily. 'Irish is he?'

'Was,' Iseult said, seizing on the distraction. 'He was a friend of my great-grandfather.'

'Did he write any more poems about hawks?'

'Not that I remember.'

'Pity. Sounds as if he knew what he was on about.'

A vagrant breeze raised the feathers on the falcons' thighs and Iseult was struck by the birds' archaic symbolism – their plumed leather hoods with velvet panels, the armoured legs with their thongs and silver bells, the cruel weapons. They looked so self-contained – located right at the dead centre of their being.

'I know a ballad, though,' she said.

'The only ballads I know are about Sunderland football team.'

'It's English, in fact. It's called *The Three Ravens*.'

'Let's hear it then.'

Iseult composed her thoughts. 'There were three ravens sat on a tree. They were as black as they might be. The one of them said to his mate, "Where shall we our breakfast take?" "Down in yonder green field there lies a knight slain under his shield. His hounds they lie down at his feet, so well do they their master keep. His hawks they fly so eagerly, there's no fowl dare come him nigh . . ."'

She broke off with a laugh.

'Go on.'

'I can't remember.'

'Have a bash.'

'No, it's gone. The knight's lady finds him, kisses his wounds, buries him and then dies herself. Oh yes, the last line goes: "God send every gentleman such hounds, such hawks and such a leman."'

'What's a leman?'

'A lover,' she said, looking away.

She heard him come to her. 'Here,' he said. 'It's from the Barbary. Something to remind you of today.'

He cradled a hawk's bell in his outstretched hand. She took it, put it in her shirt pocket, and let her head sag against his shoulder.

'Iseult,' he whispered, 'I'm . . .'

'Don't say anything,' she whispered back.

A small bird in the rowan tree began a song and broke off, startled by its own presence. Silence crystallized around them.

7

Dearborn placed a kiss on his sleeping daughter's damp forehead and crept out of her bedroom, trying not to break the fragile mood of the evening. A storm was in the offing, deadening all but the most local sounds. Down in the valley the lights of the village prickled like the fires of a besieging army. Behind the house the limestone peaks stood out as white as paper against the night sky.

At an open window, Dearborn paused to watch frames of lightning collapsing soundlessly at the northern limits of the earth. For the first time since his return to Morocco, he experienced something approaching tranquillity.

He entered the kitchen so quietly that Magda remained unaware of his presence. She was at the table, writing. She had tied her dark blonde hair up and beads of moisture glistened in the down on her long neck. Softly he went to her and placed his hands on her shoulders.

'I love you, Magda.'

One of her hands found his. The other covered her writing – an airmail letter. Beside it lay the Bible his daddy had given him.

'Is Lauren asleep?'

'I hope she doesn't have nightmares. We were reading *Tom Thumb* and she insisted on two repeats of the bit where the farmer cuts open the wolf's belly.' Dearborn began to massage his wife's shoulders. 'Did you hear what I said?'

'I heard,' Magda said, and gave his hand a little pat.

'Always have, always will.' Dearborn's mouth skewed in sudden rancour. 'Don't I get something in return?'

Magda glanced over her shoulder with a luminous smile. 'Sometimes you sound like you're ten years old.'

Dearborn's hands stopped moving. A weight seemed to descend on him. 'Sometimes that's how I feel,' he said in a bright tone. 'A kid lost in a big bad world. I need a statement of confidence, a star to steer by.'

Magda turned and studied him as if she was seeing him anew. 'John, you know how fond of you I am.'

'Fond?' Dearborn exclaimed, recoiling. 'What's fond for God's sake?' The shock impelled him to the counter, where he poured himself an intemperate measure of vodka and added ice with shaky fingers. His shirt had gone clammy. 'Fond,' he marvelled, and took a quick gulp. 'Jesus,' he gasped.

But Magda had transferred her attention elsewhere. She was staring across the kitchen with an expression that chilled the alcohol in his veins.

'What is it?' he whispered.

She flashed him a peculiar smile. 'A snake. It followed me into the kitchen.' She pointed with care towards the door. 'I came in. The doorway was empty. I'd taken two or three steps when Ayesha began shouting and I turned to see it slithering around the corner.'

Dearborn blinked. It crossed his mind that Magda might have been taking some kind of medication. He opened his mouth, then thought better of the question. 'Was it a big snake?' he succeeded in saying.

Silently, Magda spread her arms to full width.

Dearborn swallowed surreptitiously. 'If it was that big, it wouldn't have been poisonous.'

'What do you know about it?' Magda shouted, jumping to her feet. 'You weren't here.'

'Honey, all I'm saying is that you don't get poisonous snakes of that size in Morocco. Was it black with a red mouth?'

Magda waved her hand as if she found the subject wearisome. 'It was dirty brown with zig-zag markings. Ayesha called some men but they were too frightened to go near it. I had to kill it myself.'

'What with?' Dearborn asked in a husky voice. A rock viper, he thought with horror. A fucking venomous snake right here in the house.

'A hoe. I took it off one of the men.'

Dearborn stared at the tiled floor, expecting to see dried snake blood and scales. He experienced a dizzy sense of unreality and countered it with a swift slug.

'The heat has stirred everything up,' he said, finding his voice. 'That's what's causing these damn happenings. But the weather's breaking. In a couple of weeks it will be cool and everything will settle down to normal. Just look at it as nature having . . .' He limped to a stop, alarmed by the set of Magda's features. 'Listen,' he said, 'we agreed to talk.'

'I think maybe the time for words is past,' Magda said, and went over to the stove. She still walked with a dancer's short gait, feet splayed, back erect. She lifted a lid and stirred. 'It's only *tagine* of lamb,' she said, wiping her brow with the back of her wrist. 'I don't know about you, but I'm not hungry.'

'I'm not blind, Magda,' Dearborn said. 'I can see the gap that's opened up between us. I know that if we took away the talk about Lauren and the domestic arrangements, we wouldn't be able to hear ourselves speak for the silence. But what I can't understand is when it started. It wasn't always like this. We used to have real empathy.'

'You want me to fetch my diary?'

Dearborn flushed. Magda did indeed keep a diary. Once, driven by curiosity, he had stolen a look – only once. He could no longer recall exactly what it was his eye had alighted on, but whatever it was, the memory was so scalding that he had to fortify himself against it with another drink.

'Give me an instance,' he muttered. 'Give me a starting point.'

Magda pushed out her bottom lip and shrugged. 'Beirut. You stopped telling me about your work. You lost weight and looked worried all the time.'

'It was a worrying time.'

'Then one afternoon you brought a Christian Lebanese to the apartment – Anthony I think his name was.'

Dearborn's heart hit. Tony was a very bad and dangerous man even by the generous latitudes Dearborn had worked by in his Lebanese days. 'I remember,' he said.

'You were in the study together and I could hear you arguing. He came out to use the loo and I saw him down the hall. He thought he was alone and he was wearing his thoughts right on his face. I could tell exactly what he was thinking.'

'What was that?' Dearborn mumbled, knocking back his drink.

'That if you cheated or disappointed him in any way, he would do you terrible harm. Then he saw me. He knew straightaway that I was looking right into him, but he didn't try to cover up. We stood there staring at each other for what seemed an age, and then he backed away, smiling and nodding in recognition of our perfect understanding.'

'For chrissake,' Dearborn said, 'the guy was on our side.' A spasm of guilt twisted his entrails.

'A week later a Phalangist bomb went off in West Beirut. There were rumours of American involvement.'

Dearborn opened his mouth to deny the allegation but found that no words would come.

'And you brought that . . . that beast into our home.' Magda walked up close to him, her jaw tensed. 'The same evening we went to a benefit concert for Beirut orphans. Afterwards you hugged me and said: "God, Magda, how lucky we are." I realized then what a coward you are, how easily you can wipe your conscience clean. So long as someone else does the dirty work, it doesn't affect you, does it?'

Dearborn had begun to tremble. 'Look, there's no purpose served by dragging up the events of years ago. You said it yourself: I'm a nobody now – a highly paid gofer.'

'Who happens to be involved in another murder,' Magda cried, thumping the table with the heel of her hand. 'Who spent last night in jail. Who had lunch with Jerry Cody.'

'Coincidence – like all the other crazy things that have been happening.'

'John, if you taught me anything, it was never to believe in coincidence.'

Dearborn tried to master his own anger. 'I'm your husband,' he said. 'I'm not in the business of lying to you.'

Magda rested both hands on the table and hung her head. 'John, I'm a half-Jewish Hungarian whose family were shot and thrown into the Danube. I know when to heed a warning.' Her gaze settled on the Bible. '"I have been a stranger in a strange land."' She looked at him and shrugged. 'I'm going home.'

'Give it a few more months. I can't leave now.'

'I understand that, John, but there's nothing stopping me and Lauren. She's hardly seen her country. My mother's nearly eighty and I don't intend to have her dying all alone.'

'I've told you before – she can live here with us.'

Magda laughed. 'My mother in Morocco? She'd perish inside the day.'

Dearborn gave in to his anger. 'Well that would be one problem solved.'

Not dignifying his response with a reply, Magda poured herself a small bourbon, crossed to the open doorway and stared out over the valley. Dearborn took the opportunity to replenish his own glass. Fortified by the booze, he looked on his wife with resentment.

'You've worked it out to your complete satisfaction, haven't you? You don't want to discuss the problem. The only debating you do is with that fucking diary.'

'You're right, John,' Magda said. 'I'm being selfish.' She looked across the room towards him, but her eyes were focused elsewhere. 'Since we got back, I feel like I'm living in a cloud. I wander from room to room, looking for myself.'

'What about Lauren?'

'She's not enough. Besides, she needs friends of her own age.'

'We'll move into Marrakech then. Hell, it was your idea to find a place in the mountains.'

Magda raised her glass as if she wanted to propose a toast. 'I'm leaving you, John. I need some time to find myself.' Her mouth assumed an ironic twist. 'Corny isn't it?'

Dearborn rushed to take her in his arms. 'It isn't,' he said in a fierce whisper. 'It isn't corny at all. Listen, we can work it out together. We can both benefit.'

'No, John,' Magda said, detaching herself. 'You complicate things too much.'

'You're having an affair, aren't you?' Dearborn shouted, his cool completely gone. 'It's that divorced lawyer we met at the Getsingers', isn't it.'

'Oh, John,' Magda said, smiling with mingled pity and disgust.

A fly fizzled into extinction on the electric insect trap and a moment later the sky lit up. Instinctively, Dearborn began to count the seconds, but he had only reached two when thunder detonated right above the house. A wind gusted through the door. He went to shut it.

'Leave it,' Magda said. She went out on to the patio, turned her face to the sky, and gave one of her cat-like stretches that made her breasts strain against the thin cotton of her shirt. A few warm splashes fell, pitting the dust, then stopped. Dearborn had an urge to seize her, to take her by force, to violate her right there in the dirt and the storm-filled air like he had the veiled woman in the gardens.

'Listen,' she said, stilling him with an upheld hand.

The air was filled with a strident rasping so universal, so encompassing that at first Dearborn failed to hear it. 'Frogs,' he said, and laughed bitterly.

'There's no one else, John. There never has been and I'm not looking for that kind of change right now. All I want is to go back to making my own arrangements.'

Rage flared on another roll of thunder. 'When I met you, you didn't even have a passport. You were dancing for fat cats in Beirut and blowing them for fifty bucks.'

Upstairs, Lauren cried out.

'Just because you took me away from that, you think you own me.'

'Bullshit. I've always regarded you as a partner.'

'Partnerships aren't always equal.'

Lauren called for her mummy.

'I have to go, John.'

With something akin to hatred, Dearborn watched his wife climb the stairs. 'You can forget about a divorce. There are no grounds.'

'We'll discuss the practical side when you're sober,' Magda said. She hesitated but didn't turn. 'I'm sorry.'

'I don't want your sympathy,' Dearborn shouted. He flung his glass and it shattered across the patio. 'I want your love.'

'I'm sorry,' Magda repeated, and went up.

For a while Dearborn couldn't move. His senses had deserted him, his wits failed. He lurched to the counter, poured another drink and rounded on the empty room. He could not believe how abruptly he had been reduced to such abject helplessness. Why had it happened? Where was the tragic flaw? His gaze alighted on the Bible. 'A stranger in a strange land.' He knew his Bible. That was Exodus.

He snatched up the book, fumbled it open and put on his reading glasses. 'Ha!' he exclaimed, finding the spot. '"And if thou refuse to let them go,"' he declaimed, '"behold, I will smite all thy borders with frogs: and the river shall bring forth frogs abundantly, which shall go up and come into thine house, and into thy bedchamber, and upon thy bed . . ."'

He broke off, senses swimming, unaccustomedly drunk. The thunder was almost continuous now, forked by bolts of excruciating violet. Rain drowned the roaring of the frogs. He turned the page and began to read again. '"And the Lord sent thunder and hail, and the fire ran along upon the ground; and the Lord rained hail upon the land of Egypt."'

He looked up. 'Where's the hail, Lord? You forgot the hail.'

A crack of lightning lit up the valley. Dearborn guffawed

and went back to the Book of Moses. After frogs came lice, and after thunder and hail the locusts descended. He had already encountered blood and flies. That left a grievous murrain and . . . flipping the page, Dearborn felt his skin creep. 'And the Lord said unto Moses, Yet will I bring one plague more upon Pharaoh . . . About midnight will I go out into the midst of Egypt: and all the firstborn in the land of Egypt shall die . . .'

Dearborn cast a glance towards Lauren's bedroom and threw aside the Bible as if fearful of contamination. Going to the cupboard under the stairs, he unlocked a steel case, took out a Beretta and crammed a magazine home. Then he staggered out into the deluge. At the next thunder-clap he fired back. Circling unsteadily, blinded by the rain, he emptied the pistol at the heavens, while all around the earth trembled and flashed under the assault of celestial artillery.

When the clip was finished, he lowered himself on to a garden seat and hung his head, the gun loose at his fingertips, letting the rain pummel away his thoughts. He was in a near-insensible state when Magda found him.

'It's Jerry Cody,' she said, putting a hand on his shoulder. 'He says it's urgent.'

Dearborn stood up and made his way stiffly into the house. He hadn't heard the telephone. He picked it up without thought.

'We got an I.D.,' Cody said in triumph. 'The old man was right. The victim's name was Hazan; his family changed it from Ben-Yacoub when they got to Israel.'

'I'm glad you cracked it,' Dearborn said, wiping wet hair from his forehead.

'You can forget about him, John. He was a nobody.'

'Right now, he's the last thing on my mind.'

'Our sources say he never adjusted to life in the Promised Land, took to crime.'

'Well, he's paying now.'

'What's wrong, John? You sound strange.'

'You've caught me in the middle of a crisis.'

'Magda?'

She was watching from the bottom of the stairs, arms crossed, rubbing her shoulders as if she was cold.

'She just left me,' Dearborn said.

Cody exhaled a sigh from the bitter well of experience. 'It's a fucking war,' he said.

8

'And then there was this German falconer,' Valentine said, 'Lothar his name was – manufactured bathroom furniture.' His glazed eyes sought Case. 'Typical Kraut, wasn't he, Pat? – demanded industrial levels of productivity from his hawks and wore a toupee like a dead spaniel.' Valentine choked into his drink. 'Lothar insisted on flying his falcons to the fist instead of using a lure.' Valentine assumed a War Picture Library accent. '"Ze falke zat only returns to ze lure has not been properly disciplined, ja?" So there we are at seven in the evening, rain chucking down, ze falke refusing to come back and Lothar going insane. "Stuff this," Pat says, and strolls up behind him, whips off his rug and tosses it up to the falcon. Now she won't come back to anything else.'

The company laughed with varying degrees of comprehension. Valentine's face lapsed in a vacant grin. Case couldn't remember seeing him hit the bottle before. From upstairs came the knocking of antique plumbing. The other guests had already bathed and changed. Saad the Lebanese was with Chelsea, the eye-watering blonde. Valentine had parked the gyrfalcon on the back of a great oak chair carved with a coat of arms featuring a mailed fist and seashells. There was a burst of applause as a handsome youth emerged from the kitchen in a striped apron, displaying a shining salmon on a white dish.

Case checked the doorway again, his heart beating high in his chest at the prospect of Iseult's entrance. As if he hadn't got enough to worry about, he was in love – or as close as made no difference. Mixed with his excitement was terror of the consequences. He would have to tell Iseult about being in the army. There was the problem of Catty, not to mention work, the house, Morocco . . . Bloody hell, he thought, awed at the amount of punishment he was lining up for himself.

'What a pity we did not have an opportunity to see your *shahin* from Morocco.'

Looking down, Case saw that Saad had materialized at his elbow. He mustered a polite smile. 'You are interested in falconry, Mr Saad?'

'On my family's estate lived a man who hunted birds with a small . . . I do not know the word in English. In Arabic it is called *bashiq*. It has eyes like bright stars.'

'A sparrow-hawk.'

Saad arched his brows in surprise. 'You speak Arabic.'

'Nah – only a couple of words.'

'In the summer, when I was a child, this man would sometimes take me into the orchards before the day got hot to hunt the . . . a bird like a small *perdreau*.'

'Quail.'

'Yes, the hunter would whistle like a father quail and soon this bird's wife would answer – "peep, peep, peep" – coming closer and closer until – poof – the *bashiq* flew into the corn like an arrow. Afterwards, the hunter would take me back to his house and tell me stories while I ate coffee and bread.' Saad gave an infinitesimal shrug. 'All finished now.'

'Where was that, Mr Saad?'

'My father's estate was near Baalbek, in the Bekaa Valley. Since then I have only seen hunting with hawks in Morocco.' Saad made the most of his inconsiderable height. 'Some years ago, I was honoured to spend several days with His Majesty and his guests on a royal hunt.'

Case would have liked to hear more, but Valentine was hovering behind the Lebanese. 'Spare a minute?' he inquired, grimacing apology at Saad. 'Vector's grouse gave her rather a rough and tumble,' he explained, 'and I'm sorry to say she broke a primary. I wonder if you'd mind taking a look.'

Saad gave way with grace. Case's spirits took a plunge.

Tomorrow, Iseult would take the train south and he would never see her again. On Monday, Catriona would return from her friend's wedding. His fantasies collapsed. The future loomed.

'Just popping out to inspect an injured hawk,' Valentine called.

Outside, the stars over the loch were beginning to plot the course of the night, but the eastern sky was opaque with impending rain.

'Any joy with the Barbary?' Valentine asked.

'A hoodie,' Case said, the thrill of the hunt gone.

'Never mind,' Valentine said, and staggered into Case. The slip seemed to trigger anger. 'I must say, Pat, it was bloody inconsiderate of you sloping off with that Irish bitch.'

Case's neck prickled. 'She fainted. I didn't notice anyone else offering to take her back.'

'Serves her right. Gatecrashes my party, embarrasses me in front of clients, and then steals my falconer away.'

'I'm not your falconer, Forbes,' Case said, his voice dulled in warning.

Valentine appeared not to hear. 'Did she tell you what brought her here?' he asked. He peered at Case, his eyes glinting.

'Money.'

'Quite,' Valentine said, after thinking about it.

'I wanted to ask you about her paintings. She told me you'd bought one.'

'Only as a favour to Cathal. Grotesque thing – all red and black, like a heavy menstrual flow.' Valentine stopped dead. 'Good God, Pat, don't tell me you find her *attractive*.'

Case knotted his fists.

'Really, Pat, if you insist on playing an away game, you'd be better off making friends with Chelsea.'

'The one with the big tits, right?'

'Much more your type. Besides, I thought your troth was plighted to that shop assistant.'

Case's jaws ached.

Some distance behind the house was an old stable block that served as the falcons' mews. Case held open the door for Valentine. The room was lit by a neon tube, but the falcons made the cold light sacred. They were ranged on perches above a wide shelf set at shoulder level. As they shuffled to face the disturbance, their bells scraped – a dry, churchy noise. The air had a warm ammoniac smell. Valentine expelled a long sigh.

Case examined Vector. He turned, frowning. Valentine's face wore an inane grin.

'Sorry about the deception, but I wanted a chance to talk without being disturbed. Alas, it's the end of the season for me. I have to shoot off on business early tomorrow and I may be away six weeks or so. Could I billet my hawks on you?'

'Sorry, I'm going away myself.'

'Yes, Thain told me you'd got yourself into a bit of a situation.'

'If you mean skint, jobless and about to be evicted – yes, I have a bit.'

'Of course I'll pay,' Valentine said, unearthing a wallet from his hacking jacket. With care he peeled off notes and offered them with a flourish. 'There. A hundred should more than cover the hawks' keep.'

Staring at the money, Case felt resentment curdle. 'You feed your hawks and dogs on garbage,' he said, 'and when you hold a shoot you lord it with your pals, stuffing yourselves on smoked salmon and champagne while the beaters make do with a can of Long Life and a pork pie way past its sell-by date. If my hawks make a kill, you insist that the grouse is handed over to you. Forbes, you're the meanest man I ever met.'

Valentine had grown immensely tall and thin.

'If that's your attitude,' he said, blinking rapidly to convey the anger he was holding back, 'I don't believe I'll be seeking your company next season.'

'Fair enough,' Case said.

The door opened and a burly, tanned man in Sunday pub

clothes strolled in, closely followed by another man who filled the entire frame.

'Hello Shirley,' the tanned man said in a quiet Cockney voice.

Valentine's face was flayed white. His Adam's apple bobbed.

'Forbes?' Case said.

The tanned man glanced at him. He wore a sweater patterned with red and black diamonds, dark slacks and crocodile-skin loafers with silver bars. His face was pitted with acne scars and good looking, though starting to blur at the edges. He had a fighter's nose.

The bloke at the door was built like a privy and had a personal stereo clamped to his skull, which was shaven except for a short tartan plot on top. He had tattoos on his hands, a curtain ring in one ear, and wore jeans and a bomber jacket with PRIDE OF THE NORTH stencilled on it. Someone had once come close to biting his nose off.

'Who are you?' Case demanded.

'Denis Low,' the tanned man said with a convivial smile. 'Secretary of the Waltham Forest Fishing Club. Me and my friends were in the area and thought we'd look up our old pal Shirley. Right Shirl?' He put a comradely arm round Valentine's shoulders. 'A word in private,' he suggested.

Slowly Valentine straightened his jacket. With the stiff gait of a trance-walker he went out. The tanned man gave Case a cheery nod.

For some time Case remained stock still, his mind racing, settling on nothing. He gave a startled laugh. What could two paid-up members of the hands-on school of villainy want with Valentine? He went to the door and put his hand on the light switch. The falcons' eyes followed him. They had flown a hundred miles, killed at a touch and now they were as still as cast metal. Stay out of it, Case told himself, plunging the room into darkness.

A rain was settling with deceptive slowness and the dogs were barking. A shouted order shut them up for a few seconds, then the racket started again. The kennels were beyond the lights of the Lodge and he had to grope his way forward. His pointers made white blurs. He put his hand through the bars of their run. Their hair was ridged on their spines and their jowls were rucked back from their jaws. They licked his hands and whimpered. 'Hush now,' he whispered. 'I see you.'

Wiping the rain from his eyes, he turned his head. The night listened back. Someone moved across a window. As Case walked towards the house, he made a point of not looking directly at the lights.

On the forecourt was a car that hadn't been there before. It was a top-of-the-range Mercedes with metallic paint and all the trimmings. An anti-theft eye winked on the dash. By the glow from an outside lamp, Case read the number plate – LOW 1.

Wincing at the crunch of gravel underfoot, he crossed to the window of the drawing-room. A television flickered unwatched in the corner. The guests had their backs to him, their attention directed at the floor behind the table. Valentine was among them, a whiter shade of pale, together with the two neds who had taken him away and at least one other stranger. Case realized that the gyrfalcon wasn't on her perch and he felt fingers walking in his guts. On the television, a building exploded in a slow cloud of dust.

Case went to the Toyota and swung up the tail-gate. He reached for his gun-case, withdrew the twelve-bore, checked the safety and entered the house.

The drawing-room had the hushed air of a sick-room. Valentine bore his shock with an astounded smile.

'Who's the woolly?' the tanned man called Low said, eyeing the shotgun.

'A keeper,' Valentine said.

'Oh, it's raining,' a voice said.

A phlegmy growling came from below the table. Case moved people aside. Stooping, he found the gyrfalcon dead, lying spreadeagled in a swathe of feathers. A brindled pit bull in harness and studded collar had its jaws fixed in her chest.

'No need for the shooter, mate,' a voice said. 'It was an accident. Max only wanted to play.'

Case straightened. The voice belonged to a young fat man with a hog bristle haircut and a lime-green tracksuit.

'This your dog?' Case said.

'What's it to you?'

'Get him off.'

Fatso looked at Case, his tongue working in his cheek. 'Easier said, mate. He's got a death grip.' Fatso grinned and nodded at the company as if he'd made an utter fool of Case.

'He will have if you don't shift him,' Case said, levelling the shotgun in one hand.

Fatso's smirk vanished. 'Alright mate, no need to get aerated.' Squatting on his hams he made cootchy-coo noises. Max's threats rose to another pitch of intensity and his eyes popped out on stalks and turned up so only the whites showed. Fatso stood and wiped his hands on his tracksuit. 'No fucking fear,' he said.

Case took a look around. There were four of them. Next to the tartan-haired heavy stood a tall thin man with blond hair brushed forward like a Roman senator and sprayed in place. He wore metal-rim tinted glasses, a pastel-blue suit with a Saint Laurent belt and white Gucci loafers. A gold cigarette lighter was poised for use and he had a gold Rolex on his wrist and more gold on his fingers. He looked as though he could have used a week at the seaside.

Turning his back on them, Case leaned the gun against the table, knelt down and took hold of Max's collar. The dog went solid – a high tensile spring. Its tail wagged and its eyes looked like they would burst.

'You're taking a bit of a risk there, son,' Low said.

'There's going to be blood on the ceiling,' Fatso warned. 'Old Max can bite through a ship's side.'

Case delivered a mighty uppercut to Max's prominent balls.

The dog whipped round even faster than Case imagined it would, jaws snapping shut half an inch from his forearm. He hoisted it away from the remains of Freya. It was like holding on to an engine. The huge hands of the body-builder came crushing down on his. Case glimpsed a dashed blue line on his helper's neck with a pair of scissors tattooed underneath and the instruction 'Cut Here'. Together they dragged Max off and held him until his owner clipped the leash on. Delivered into his care, the dog collapsed on its haunches and started licking its injured tackle.

Case collected the remains of Freya. He picked up the shotgun.

Fatso handed Max's lead to the heavy and blocked his exit. 'Oi, that was my dog you assaulted.'

'Be reasonable, Barry,' Low said.

'He's done Max an injury,' Fatso said.

'Leave it out. You could hit Max with an RSJ and he'd roll on his back and wag his tail.'

'Look at the fucking state of him,' Fatso shouted. 'How's he supposed to breed with his bollocks bashed in?'

'Hey,' Low said, 'hear the one about the chihuahua and the Rottweiler?' He draped a hand across Fatso's shoulders. 'This fellow goes into a pub and asks if anyone owns the Rottweiler outside. "Yeah," this big geezer at the bar says. "What about it?" "My chihuahua just killed him," the little bloke says. "Do me a favour," the big bloke says. "That Rott eats chihuahuas whole." "Yeah," the little guy says, "he choked to death."'

Nobody except Low laughed.

'I'm serious,' Fatso said, his voice going shrill.

'Alright,' Low said merrily, tightening his grip on Fatso, 'what's the difference between a Rottweiler and a social worker?' He looked to see if anyone had the answer. 'Easy – you stand a better chance of getting your kid back from a Rott.'

A guest giggled. Low's face brightened. 'Hello, Chel girl – and bless me, if it isn't Mr Saad. Gor, no wonder my Wednesday soirées have been so thin of late.'

Chelsea gave Low a tiny wave and cast a demure look at her fellow guests. One corner of Saad's mouth twitched in an affectless smile.

Fatso took a step towards Case. Low pulled him back. 'I ... said ... give ... him ... the benefit,' he intoned, shaking Fatso to the rhythm. He jerked his head at Case. 'You,' he said in a different voice, 'walkies.'

After dumping the gyrfalcon in a bin with the kitchen peelings and household dust, Case observed a moment's vengeful silence. Then he went down to the lochside. His hands shook. He had wrenched his shoulder and his guts felt as if they were crammed with rocks. 'A gyrfalcon for a king,' he said, and threw back his head and gave a bitter laugh. Rain splashed over the guttering of the Lodge and found its way down his chest.

It's nothing to do with you, he told himself. Back off. But he wasn't listening; he was trying to pin the facts together in a shape that made sense. Money had to be involved – criminal money. Case peered at the house and a slow shiver gathered at the top of his spine. In one of the corner turrets a solitary light burned. Within that light, Iseult lay asleep. She, too, had come on business, and like the four heavies she'd turned up unannounced. That's why Valentine was so poisonous when he spoke about her; that's why he was pissing off first thing tomorrow. Some kind of deal had gone wrong and he was scarpering.

Case's impulse was to dash to her room and ratify a few things, but his hunter's caution told him to hold off until he'd established a few co-ordinates.

Back in the house, he found the drawing-room deserted, a heavy application of salt marking the spot where the dog had killed Freya.

Valentine and his visitors were not in the dining-room. At Case's entrance, eyes slid away. The guests had had enough rude shocks for one evening. 'You were telling us about Jonty,' someone said, breaking the strained pause.

'God, it was so funny,' a girl said, and everyone laughed in grateful anticipation.

'Well, you know he's always wanted to be a jockey.'

'But he's far too tall.'

'I know. But he's on a diet and he's started cycling everywhere in a suit made out of bin-liners. He has this mad idea that it'll help him lose weight. Anyway, last Friday night he was cycling back from Bridget's when the liner got caught in his front wheel and he went over the handlebars – right on to the bonnet of a Jag.'

'Typical Jonty. Was he hurt?'

'No, it was parked. He was perfectly alright except – ' The girl gulped on premature laughter. 'God, it could only happen to Jonty. When he climbed off, he saw a man and woman inside, staring at him with absolute horror – and,' she declared, eyes swivelling gaily, 'they were absolutely starkers.'

'How gruesome.'

'The man was covering his naughty bits with an *A-to-Z*.'

Case's guts churned. He saw the guests as if through smoked glass.

'Where's Valentine?' he demanded.

Cutlery chinked. Eyes lowered. '*Mr* Valentine and his friends are in the billiards room,' one of the guests said. 'I rather think they don't want to be disturbed.'

Case had reached the door when a voice said: 'Young man.'

It was Saad, shaking his head as if he had divined what was going on in Case's head and considered it folly. Another piece of the picture, Case thought, not prepared to puzzle it out now. All the way to the door he could feel Saad's eyes following him like muzzle bores.

The billiards room was down a corridor at the back of the Lodge, next to the gun room. Case stopped outside. Chalk squeaked on the tip of a cue.

'Valentine?'

'Everything's cool, Pat.'

Case tried to adjust his breathing. Billiard balls clicked behind the door. It swung open and Fatso presented himself. 'Fuck off,' he said, hefting a cue.

In Portsmouth once, Case had seen some pub graffiti signed by a Para en route to the Falklands. 'Yea though I walk through the valley of the shadow of death, I shall fear no evil, for I am the evillest bastard in the valley.'

'You deaf?' Fatso demanded, taking a forward step.

The first time Case had been arrested, after an affray outside a pub in Stoke-on-Trent, he'd been thrown into a cell with no bed. When he'd shouted and banged for half an hour, the duty sergeant and two constables had shown up, smiling. The sarge had asked him if he could read, and then asked him to prove it by reading the notice above the door. In the split- second it had taken Case to discover no notice, the sarge had buried his fist in his stomach up to his backbone.

Fatso stiff-fingered him in the chest and he back-pedalled, putting up no resistance, letting the adrenalin rise like spring water.

In the army he'd been taught unarmed combat by a psychopath who was a disciple of the Zen masters and a follower of the way of the samurai. If the enemy is like the mountain, he would say, attack like the sea. And if he is like the sea, attack like the mountain. Case had never got the hang of it.

He pulled up his left sleeve, baring his tattooed wings. 'Tell us what that says.'

'I don't give a toss what it says.'

But Fatso couldn't prevent his eyes flicking aside, and that gave Case time to pull him forward and plant his forehead sweetly between the eyes. He kicked him in the groin and nutted him again as he folded over. He leaned over the groaning heap. 'It says *Utrinque Paratus*, kidder – and that means Ready For Anything.'

Through the door he saw the big bloke advancing, taking up a considerable amount of space, no particular expression on his face. Case winced, thinking of the hiding he had coming, when a billiard cue swung down in front of the big man's chest and he halted.

'That wasn't very nice,' Low's voice said.

Stepping over Fatso, Case went in, passing the big man, who shook his head at him in commiseration for what was yet to come.

All the light in the room was concentrated on the green baize where a snooker frame had been set up. Low, back turned, scalp showing on the crown of his head, was lining up a shot. Valentine was sitting on a window seat, his hands tangled in his lap and his eyes like sockets. The thin bloke with the chalky face and windproof hairdo was pulling on a fag. The pit bull was at his feet, some feathers caught in the angles of its jaw. It whimpered when it saw Case.

Low stroked the cue. 'Go on, my old son,' he said, following the ball with his nose. Obediently, it dropped.

He turned and subjected Case to long, intense scrutiny. 'You, my friend, are out of order.'

'Are these the punters you were telling me about?' Case asked Valentine.

'Punters?' Low said. 'Telling?' He turned to Valentine with an expression of resigned disenchantment. 'Telling?'

'He's lying,' Valentine cried, coming up off his seat. 'Why would I tell him anything? He's only a local keeper.'

Low poked him in the chest with his cue. 'Outstanding,' he said, 'I drive six hundred miles, stuck for three hours in the world's biggest contraflow system, and when I get here I find Shirley's been mouthing off about me to the local peasantry. Out-fucking-standing.' He stared at Valentine, awed by this embodiment of human frailty.

The sight of Fatso entering under assistance distracted him. Fatso was cupping his balls with one hand and holding his nose with the other. 'Bleedin' hell, Barry, your face don't look too clever.'

The big man eased Fatso into a chair and left him doubled up, then took up station behind Case.

Low breathed a sigh. He strolled up to Case. 'What's your name, son?'

'Pat Case.'

'You're a hard case, aren't you, Pat?'

'I can take care of myself.'

'You little rascal,' Low said, taking hold of his chin and rocking it. He had hairy knuckles and wore a big onyx ring with his initials picked out in diamonds. He nodded at the big man and Case was suddenly overwhelmed in his grip. 'You're a funny-looking gamekeeper,' Low said, palping Case's cheeks.

'How many gamekeepers do you know?' Case mumbled. His arms were wrenched behind; his shoulders burned.

'Point taken,' Low said. 'It just goes to show.' He let go of Case's face. 'Got any kids, Pat?'

'Not yet.'

'Nature's little miracles,' Low said, still dangerously cheerful. 'Don't let no one tell you different. You want to take good care of the family jewels. Know what I mean?' He glanced over his shoulder. 'Max!'

Max squirmed on his belly and stayed put.

'Come here, you daft pooch. Come to Denis. That's it. *Good* boy. Good *boy*!'

Case twisted. The big man held him with ease. He took hold of his dreadlocks and yanked back his head. Case could hear the hiss of his stereo and smell his aftershave. He felt Max snuffling at his legs. Low stooped and a moment later Max's muzzle was pushed into his groin.

'Cop hold of them particulars, Max. Go on, get your teeth into them. Lovely little cluster.'

Case braced himself, everything inside shrinking. Common sense told him that the dog wouldn't maul him, but the primitive brain core wasn't convinced. He grunted as the dog's muzzle pressed into his groin.

'Go on, you stupid fucking mutt,' Low shouted.

The pressure on Case's groin suddenly eased. He heard Max drop to the floor and scuttle off. His head was pushed forward.

'It's your lucky day,' Low panted. 'It turns out that Max is a pacifist. Me, though, I'm . . .' Low's face congested as he lifted the cue and swung it in a short arc. It whacked into the side of Case's left knee-cap and black nausea hit at almost the same instant. He went cold from the face down, all the vital fluids withdrawing through his spine. When the big man let go, he dropped as if he'd been severed at the hips. He writhed and mewed, his left leg dead except for the pain, his right leg bending and straightening in spastic, insect reflex. He managed to drag himself against the wall and get his back to it. Cold sweat greased his face.

The big man had hoisted himself on to the scorer's stool in the corner and was reading a magazine, his stereophonic ear-muffs still in place. Low was back at the table, pouring a glass of brandy. He selected another cue, weighed it and loosed a shot. 'Now, Pat, what's your nause?' he asked, watching the balls cannon off the cushions.

'. . . who you are,' Case whimpered.

Low held him under steady regard for a moment. 'Men of business,' he said. 'Haulage and leisure is my field.' He walked around the table. 'Pink,' he said. The pink leapt into the bottom pocket. 'That's Roy Besant,' he said, gesturing at the pallid man. 'Cash and carry.'

'Denis,' the man called Besant said in warning.

'Pat asked me a reasonable question and he's entitled to a reasonable answer. We're all reasonable men, Pat. Barry there is my sister's boy – wholesale fruit and veg. Max you've already been introduced to. And that,' Low concluded, pointing at the hulking figure in the corner as one might show off a particularly impressive zoo specimen, 'that is McGrory. Big Mac's a debt collector. Debts collected with discretion, that's him.'

Case feared his knee was broken. He did not dare put his fear to the test. 'Collecting from Valentine,' he croaked.

Low grounded his cue. 'Shirley's in deep shtook,' he conceded, after a moment's introspection. He squinted at the table, bisecting angles. 'Ever been to Spain, Pat? 'Course you have. Everyone has. Me and the missus go every year. With the kid gone, we thought we'd buy a villa, maybe retire there. So Shirley tells us about this mate of his who's starting a new development – lovely bit of property, own golf-course, near Marbella but not too near, if you know what I mean. None of your lager louts throwing up over the garden wall. One hundred and eighty thousand sovs for five beds and private pool.'

Valentine raised his head. His eyes were bloodshot.

'Now the catch is,' Low said, 'this geezer wants money upfront. But that's alright because he promises to make the deposit work for us – his very words.' Low held up an admonitory finger. 'I know what you're thinking, Pat. You're thinking what a mug. But this geezer isn't some moody foreigner; he's fucking English. Digby Fox he's called.' Low slammed the cue ball. 'He's only a fucking bishop's son, isn't he? I mean, with that kind of pedigree, you'd think my wedge would have been safer than with the Legal and General.'

'Go easy, Den,' Besant said.

Case rolled his head. He was woozy with pain. The light had turned swampy and he feared he might throw up. 'How was this Fox supposed to make your money work?' he managed to say.

On the scorer's stool, Big Mac looked up from his magazine. Low's coarse-grained face assumed the inertness of an Aztec mask.

'What's your game, Hard Case?'

'I'm just making sure that Valentine doesn't walk out of here a paraplegic.'

Besant snorted. 'He's trying to pull a stroke,' he declared. He had a London accent, too – more North Circular than Bow Bells.

'No worries,' Low said, him and Case still staring at one another. 'Me and Hard Case have got an understanding.'

He strode back to the table. 'Where was I? Oh yeah, that slag Fox. A couple of days back, an old friend gives me a bell.

Fox has closed shop, hasn't he? Trousered every penny and done a runner.'

'Fox hasn't stolen a thing,' Valentine said, his tone weary with repetition.

Low tendered a mournful smile. 'Oh yes, I forgot to say. Fox hasn't had it on his toes with my money. He's only put it in a bank and put the stop on it. I can't touch it without his say-so, and I can't get his say-so because no one knows where he is. The grief is, Shirley, I can't wait. The interest rates are killing me.'

'Forbes,' Case croaked, 'if you know where Fox is, you'd better tell them.'

'I can't,' Valentine said in a dead voice.

'What an entertainer,' Low said, and went crazy. At a speed to baffle the eye, he was in front of Valentine, lifting him by the hair until he was up on tiptoes. 'You fucking toe-rag. Give me El Fox or I'll give you stumps.'

'Forbes, it's no contest,' Case shouted.

'Hear that?' Low panted, banging Valentine's head on the wall for emphasis. 'Hear that, eh?'

'Stop!'

Low dropped Valentine as if he'd been burnt. 'I do believe Shirley wishes to assist us in our inquiries,' he murmured.

Valentine's eyes and nose were streaming. 'Please believe me,' he begged, 'I don't know what happened. He phoned to say that everything was ready for shipment and that he was going to meet someone in Marrakech.'

'You'll have to do better than that,' Low said, feinting with his right.

'A new business partner,' Valentine blurted, parrying the anticipated blow, 'an Israeli.'

Low nodded eagerly.

'That's all,' Valentine said, his eyes imploring each man in turn. 'Fox never even told me his name. He kept that side of the business to himself.'

Low looked to the thin man for counsel.

'Adds up,' Besant said, smoking furiously. 'Fox's record

is one hundred per cent. He had no reason to rip us off.'

'Add it up some more,' Low said, bending over Valentine and enunciating slowly. 'Put some meat on the bones.'

'I swear to God it's all I know,' Valentine whimpered. 'I think something went wrong in Marrakech and he's gone into hiding. Please,' he said, 'wait six weeks.'

Low stood breathing heavily, at a loss. He made a circuit of the table, growling under his breath. He stopped in his tracks opposite Besant. 'You know what this means,' he said. 'Someone's going to have to get down to Morocco a bit lively. Ever been there, Roy? Fancy a trip?'

'Not much.'

'I went once – two-week package to Agadir. Thought it would make a change from Spain. I should say so. The food was fucking diabolical. I thought a dog must have crawled inside me and died.'

Fatso dabbed his nose. 'Why don't I go? I could take Nicky and Mac and Stretch.'

'No chance,' Low said emphatically.

'Go on, Den. I could find Fox standing on my dick.'

'You couldn't find your dick in the bath. Besides, you don't speak Moroccan.'

'They speak French,' Fatso grumbled. 'French and Arabic.'

'Yeah, well that's more than you do.'

'How about Mac?' Besant said.

'Leave off. Mac has trouble speaking *English*.'

'Send Winston with him. Winston speaks French.'

'Winston's from Trinidad, you daft pillock. He'd stand out in Morocco like a fucking tax disc in Dalston. Send Big Mac and Winston? The Arabs would think it was the Third World War.' Low seemed quite shaken by the suggestion.

Besant brightened. 'Mellor owes us one.'

'Nah, nah, keep Old Bill out of it,' Low said. He was agitated. 'That's another thing,' he added, 'the place is crawling with filth – wollies everywhere you look, passport checks at every corner. It's your genuine police state. No, it's going to have to be someone legit.'

As he began another circuit of the table, Case started the task of regaining his feet, using his right leg and the leverage of his hands against the wall. Nobody paid him attention. When he was upright, he made a cautious trial of his left leg. Gasping pain, hot wires – but at least the knee had mobility.

'Private investigator?' Besant was suggesting. 'Hey, we could use a French outfit.'

'This isn't a bleedin' EEC joint initiative,' Low shouted.

Head pressed against the wall, eyes closed, Case remembered his first jump from a plane – standing in an open bay hypnotized by the ground unrolling a thousand feet below. No matter how well-trained you were, no matter how confident in the effectiveness of your gear, nothing prepared you for the act of stepping into space.

'I could find Fox for you,' he said.

For two long beats of his heart there was free-falling silence.

'There's always Olly,' Besant said. 'I know he costs, but. . .'

Low cut Besant off with an upheld hand.

'Let the kid have his say.'

'I know Morocco. I was there with the army.'

Besant snorted. 'Getting pissed with a bunch of hairy-arsed squaddies.'

'I've been back on my own.'

'He means he spent two weeks on a Sunseeker winter break,' Besant said.

'Fair play, Roy. Give him a chance.'

'My last trip, I was there two months.'

'Parlay vooz Fransays?'

'I get by. I know the Marrakech area. If Fox is there, it shouldn't be hard to find him. In fact I was planning my own trip to Morocco.'

'Denis, he's shitting us,' Besant protested.

Low ignored him, his eyes on Case. 'What's your interest in Morocco?'

'I was going to trap some birds of prey and smuggle them over to Germany.'

Valentine sent Case a dull look. Low's brow puckered. 'Is there money in that?'

'Yes.'

'Well I never,' Low marvelled. 'You live and learn.' He took a look at Case from a different angle. ''Ere, you're not a wooftah, are you?'

'Not so far as I know. Why?'

'Because the only bloke I know who has any time for Moroccans is as queer as a Cuban sixpence.' Low pondered, clocking up options. 'Ever been in bother with the law?'

'No.'

'Careful. I can pick up the mobile and have the form on you before bedtime.'

'I did six months for poaching a deer.'

'Any previous?'

'Breach of the peace, resisting arrest – nothing serious.'

'And they gave you six months? Gor, that's a bit heavy.'

'I shot it on the municipal golf-course. In Scotland, that's next best thing to a hanging offence.'

Low shook Case by the chin again. 'I knew you were a scallywag,' he said.

'You can't be serious,' Besant told Low.

'Got a better idea? So far you've suggested sending my sister's pride and joy, going in mob-handed, dialling nine-nine-nine and calling in the gendarmes. Next you'll suggest I get the Foreign Office on the team.'

'Yeah, but look at him.'

'Give him a haircut, get him some decent threads – he'd look alright. And he's got bottle. Look how he handled Max; look what he did to Barry.'

'He's shitting us,' Besant insisted.

'Shut it,' Low commanded. He thought a while. 'You poodle down to Morocco,' he said to Case, fingers keeping rhythm on his palm, 'you sniff around until you find Fox . . .' His fingers marked time. 'Then what?'

'Then I call you.'

Low made a fist and punched his palm.

'If it's so fucking easy,' Besant said, 'why don't we go ourselves – pack our buckets and spades, take the wife and kiddies?'

Low laid an arm around Besant and led him to a corner. They conferred.

'What regiment, pal?' McGrory asked in a throaty Glasgow bass, his intervention startling Case.

'Three Para.'

McGrory digested this, then inclined his head and spat. He hiked up his sleeve and tapped a particular area of tattooed forearm. 'Scots Guards,' he said, and returned to his mag. Case saw that it was called *The Puzzler*.

Valentine was avoiding all eyes, his jaw under tension.

Case leaned in his direction. 'Any objections?' he whispered.

Valentine closed his eyes.

'How much has Fox got in this moody bank of his?' Low demanded, returning from his conference.

Valentine made a helpless gesture. 'I'm not sure – a couple of million.'

Low rolled his tongue inside his cheek and exchanged a glance with Besant. 'So here's the form,' he announced. 'We're all going to Morocco. We're all Morocco-bound, to coin a phrase – and that includes you, Shirley.'

'Me?' Valentine exclaimed, sitting bolt upright.

Low spread his hands. 'Shirley, put your head on *my* shoulders. I took your professional advice.'

'You don't understand. It's not that simple.'

'Oh it is, Shirley, it is. I'm a great simplifier. If we don't come up with Foxy inside a month, the money is down to you – every fucking penny, plus a hundred for all the aggravation.'

Valentine uttered a wild laugh. 'Good God, man. What about my other clients?'

'What about them?'

'I've got the future to consider.'

'Worry about that when it comes. For now, I'm all the future you need to know. First thing tomorrow, you and me are going to motor back to London and have a look at your assets.' Low faced Case. 'You're on, Hard Case.'

Besant scowled through a lungful of smoke.

'If I find him,' Case said, 'I want thirty thousand. That's my bare minimum.'

'Fancy something to eat?' Low said to his companions. He began the move doorward. 'Not my problem, old son,' he called. 'Sort it out with Shirley. Get the full S.P. on El Fox.'

Fatso paused as he shambled past. 'You and me, pal,' he said, dabbing his nose. 'You and me.'

'One thing,' Case said. 'Why bother with Fox?'

Low halted at the door. 'If my friends heard I'd got taken off by a bishop's son, they'd laugh their bollocks off. Listen, I've got a sign on my trucks: OUR NAME IS LOW BUT OUR REPUTATION IS HIGH. Says it all.'

'What will you do to him?'

Low brooded. 'No illusions, Pat. You find him, you bell me and you go home.' He stabbed with his finger. 'Understand? Take any fucking liberties and I'll pull the world down over your ears.'

9

Iseult stopped and looked down the track the way she had come, across islands of gorse and ragged pines to the sea. On each side, trees stood tall in the silence. Over the woods some kind of hawk with broad wings climbed in unsteady circles. The light rose out of the ground in a thin haze, blurring the line between the earth and the sky and making the sea an extension of the land. It was a benign light, like the remembrance of things past.

With a small sigh, Iseult set herself to the slope again. Drugged with Migraleve, she had slept through the night, wandering downstairs in a swampy mid-morning stupor to find Valentine gone, his guests disgruntled and hungover, not caring to meet each other's eyes. Apparently there had been some kind of a party after she went to bed. She looked for Saad, but he was gone too. Nobody could say what the visitors had wanted. A falcon had been killed by a dog and the keeper had been involved in violence. Her first reaction had been to pretend that nothing had happened. She accepted a lift to Inverness from a couple driving south, and it wasn't until she spotted a sign to Auchronie that the implications hit home. She had demanded to be let out.

Now she tried to face the possibility that Valentine had told Case about Cathal. Unlikely, she decided. No, the fear that coiled inside her came from the growing conviction that Valentine would go back on his pledge to settle up with Cathal.

She looked up, exasperated by the long climb, to find the way guarded by a large unclassifiable hound that lay in the middle of the track, its head placed flat between its paws. She froze. She had a town-dweller's fear of dogs, and this one looked dangerous – rough-haired and wild, with citrine eyes shining out of a black mask. It rose, stalked forward and dropped again, tail sweeping from side to side.

'Case?' she called timidly.

The dog stood up and backed off, making her ears ring with its cavernous barks. Case appeared, hobbling fast. He secured the dog and surveyed her from a wary distance. He was wearing a battered pair of trousers and a khaki singlet that exposed his rangy, tattooed arms and made him look like a hooligan.

She saw from his expression that he knew about Fox. Thinking about the ridiculous tale she had spun him yesterday, she almost turned and fled. 'I decided to take you up on that invitation,' she said, working up a smile.

'I reckoned you might,' he said, his disposition ungracious.

Did he know about Cathal? She looked about, frightened to meet his eye. 'Your domain,' she said, taking in the panorama with a sweep of her hand.

Case nodded.

'The light's marvellous,' she said, under the weight of his silence. 'I saw a deer on the way up.'

'Roe,' he said. 'They're a pest.'

On this unpromising note, he turned and led the way up the track. Through a stand of birches she glimpsed part of the fabric of a building. She didn't know what to expect – a hovel of wattle and hides, a breeze-block cabin. It came into clear sight and she stopped with a laugh, her worries crowded out by surprise.

'Jesus,' she said. She looked from the house to Case and back again. 'How much of it is yours?'

'All of it,' he said, pride of ownership breaking through.

'Jesus,' she said again.

The buildings formed three sides of a square enclosing a grassed courtyard on which Case's hawks were weathering. The central section was a house, more or less intact; the right wing was a dilapidated stable block and the left wing a ruinous barn. In style it owed a lot to the Arts and Crafts movement. Above the front door was a pagan sun which Iseult had seen before, decorating the hoods of Case's falcons.

'The third laird built it as model housing for his estate workers,' Case explained. 'After the First World War the laird's youngest son took it over. He was an artist who was killed at Anzio and for forty years the house was left empty.' Case opened the door to a tacked-on porch. 'There were two dead sheep in here when I found it.' He pushed open the inner door. 'My bed-sit,' he said.

Iseult entered a stone-flagged, whitewashed room of baronial proportions, with two tiers of windows and a flight of steps leading to a gallery which must once have been part of an upper floor. A fireplace big enough to accommodate a small tree took up half of one wall. The opposite wall was monopolized by books on brick-supported shelves. Under the gallery stood an ancient black kitchen range and a bath and sink. The only other furnishings were a bulging sofa, a table used as a desk, a dining-table planed from a slab of pine and a couple of chairs.

Iseult spun round in the centre of the room, face raised to the light angling down from the windows. 'What a wonderful studio it would make. God, it's fantastic.'

Case grunted. 'It needs a bit doing.'

He was embarrassed; that was it. In her relief she took his face in her hands and kissed his cheek. 'It's a lovely house.'

'You'll stay the night,' he muttered.

'I'm booked on the eleven o'clock sleeper. I was going to ask you out for a meal. I passed a hotel a few miles back.'

'They cook all the food in the winter,' Case said, 'and bung it in the microwave for the tourists.'

'Is there anywhere in town?'

'Only Luigi's. He's an Italian POW who stayed on. The speciality of the house is deep-fried spaghetti sandwiches and they change the oil once a year – whether it needs it or not.' Case coughed. 'Have supper here.'

Iseult looked at her feet. 'That's kind of you.'

To her dismay, Case picked up his hawking glove. 'First we have to catch it.'

'I'm not up to it,' she said. 'My feet are sore and I ache all over.'

'Me too,' Case said.

They walked through a slant of golden light, the hound questing ahead. The trees were widely scattered – russet pines and birches printed black and silver. Spiders' webs sparkled with points of dew. The land was untended, falling back into wilderness.

Iseult darted glances at Case, trying to muster enough courage to raise the subject of the visitors. A goshawk balanced on his wrist, sulphurous eyes burning out of a hollow face. She swelled up, raising her crest, then subsided with a twitch of her tail and the sour rasp of a bell. As they passed through sunlight, her pupils dwindled to pencil points.

'She's in yarak,' Case said. 'That means she's got the blood lust on her. She's mental – a real terrorist.'

Iseult's head jerked.

'They have a different style of hunting to peregrines,' Case explained. 'Falcons take most of their prey in the air, by fair flight. Goshawks are birds of the forest. They kill at short range, by stealth and ambush. That's why they're always so keyed up.' Case sucked air in imitation of a rabbit's squeal. The goshawk's feet convulsed. 'She's bloody effective,' Case said. 'She'll take half a dozen head of prey in a day. She kills for the sheer love of it.'

Iseult gave the hawk a sideways look of loathing.

'You missed all the fun last night,' Case said in a conversational tone.

Iseult steadied her expression as best she could. 'It didn't sound very funny to me.' She let her eye dwell on his injured leg. 'Did they do that?'

'I asked for it.'

'Who were they?'

'Villains,' Case said. He squashed down his nose with his palm. 'Yer actual London gangsters.'

'I suppose they were after Valentine for money,' Iseult said, as if it wasn't of much consequence.

Case gave a grim smile. 'They're coming at him from all sides.'

Iseult shoved her hands in her pockets and scuffed the dead leaves. 'I expect he told you about my brother,' she said, her heart pounding.

'Mentioned him – said he'd invested a few bob in a deal that had gone down the tube.'

'A quarter of a million dollars,' Iseult said, stung by Case's offhand manner.

'Buying holiday villas in Spain?'

Iseult dropped her eyes. 'The drugs have got nothing to do with me,' she said. 'I hope you believe that.'

Case didn't respond immediately. 'I could never work out how Valentine got to be so rich,' he said. 'I asked him once. You have to be committed, was all he said.' Case smiled into the distance. 'It was quite a night for revelations. I always thought Valentine was a slack-jawed toff, but it turns out he was brought up in a council house at the end of Heathrow. Every time a Jumbo took off, it drizzled kerosene. His parents were airport maintenance staff. They still live there. We were up talking till gone midnight. I got his entire life story. The poor sod's almost human.' Case glanced at Iseult. 'By the way, he was very keen that I didn't speak to you.'

Iseult's heart seized. 'Why not?'

Case spoke as if he was feeling his way. 'You told me you came up to sort out the family finances. I heard Valentine tell you he'd get the money to your brother next week.'

'So?'

'So what's the secret? The heavy mob had to threaten to hammer nails through Valentine's joints.'

'Cathal's an old friend,' Iseult said, her palms clammy.

'That's not the impression Valentine gave.'

115

Iseult gave a fluttery laugh. 'He's scared for his reputation. He does a lot of business in the States. If this comes out, he's finished.'

'Yeah? Well, right now he's got more than his reputation to worry about.'

Panic brewed. 'You think he'll go back on his word?'

'You should know. Why else did you feed me that shit about Fox being an old friend of your brother's?'

Iseult stifled a sob. 'I wasn't thinking straight. I'm sorry. No,' she cried, fending off Case's hand, 'I'm alright.' She sniffed and tossed back her hair. 'How much is Low after?'

'Half a million quid. When he's finished with Valentine there'll be nothing left but small change.'

Iseult took the news in the pit of her stomach, square with her expectations. She uttered a short laugh. 'From the start, I knew it wouldn't be as simple as Cathal said.'

Case frowned. 'Does he do this kind of thing often?'

'He had a bad run on the money market.'

'And now he expects you to clean up.'

Iseult swallowed and tried to smile. 'He's my brother.'

Case pursed his lips. 'He sounds a right chancer. If it wasn't for you, I'd let him take his lumps.'

'What's that supposed to mean?'

'You asked me to look for Fox, didn't you?' Case said. He seemed distracted.

'But . . .'

Case had his finger to his lips. He pointed towards the edge of the wood and waved her on. The hawk's head was snaked forward, its plumage tight.

'Over on the far side,' Case whispered. 'See the burrows?'

Iseult stared into a sunlit meadow overgrown with banks of gorse.

A rabbit extended itself, lolloped a few steps and hunched again. Suddenly they all popped into focus. The nearest was about eighty yards away, twenty yards from sanctuary.

'Stop here,' Case whispered.

He limped from tree to tree, not making a sound. The hound shivered at Iseult's feet.

It was impossible to say which moved first. The hawk was in the air, a grey shadow rowing between the trees, and the turf was scrambling with rabbits, white scuts jinking. One rabbit had made a false start and the hawk veered in its direction. The rabbit saw it, stopped, jumped aside and the hawk shot past, turning wider than her quarry, which dashed off in another direction. Iseult's heart was in her throat. The gos grabbed the rabbit just as it seemed it must reach sanctuary.

Case stepped out into the sunlight and Iseult followed warily, as if she expected some new form of disturbance to erupt around her. The hawk was mantling over its prey, bloodied tufts of fur on its beak.

'Are you serious about going after Fox?'

'I'm a gamekeeper, aren't I? Gamekeepers catch foxes.'

'What's in it for you?'

'Thirty thousand quid. That's what Valentine has to fork out if I run Foxy to earth. Low and his neds are coming too. That should be a laugh. 'Ere we go, 'Ere we go, 'Ere we go,' Case sang.

Iseult felt a childish wrench of disappointment. 'I thought you said you could help me.'

'That's right. If I find Fox, I'll give you first shot at him.'

'What about Low and his friends?'

'Who says they have to know?'

'Why, Pat? I don't have any money.'

Case smiled like a child. 'Well if it isn't money, it must be love.'

A bluish dusk was gathering. The sun was netted in the branches. Wood-pigeons swerved overhead, reflecting rosy light from their breasts. A blackbird gave an alarm. The goshawk had taken stand in the crown of a pine after missing a pheasant. It turned its head, mad and thwarted.

'I'd say we have enough,' Case said, crawling over to

drop another double palmful of chanterelles on to Iseult's sweater.

'We can't let them go to waste,' she said. 'Jesus, Case, do you know how much these cost in London?' She dashed off in search of more of the golden trumpets.

Case followed slowly, keeping an eye on the hawk. Iseult sank to her knees among another patch of chanterelles, then recoiled with a grunt of disgust. From the base of a birch rose a giant fly agaric. The blatant symbolism of the white shaft and crimson spotted dome made her wince. 'Charming,' she said, pushing herself to her feet.

'What a beauty,' Case said.

'Careful,' Iseult said, as he stretched out a hand. 'They're poisonous.'

'Not necessarily. Siberian shamans use them as hallucinogens. The rest of the tribe drink their piss and get high.'

'Disgusting.'

'Only the shamans can eat the mushrooms raw.'

'That's what I said. They're poisonous.'

'Not to shamans.'

'How do you know if you're a shaman?'

'Trial and error.'

'I bet the Siberians aren't exactly queueing up for the job.'

'It's a highly coveted position.'

She burst out laughing. 'Case, where do you get all this useless information.'

'It's not useless,' he complained, ready to sulk, but then he too started to laugh.

They stopped at the same moment, their eyes meshing. His expression put a strain on her smile and made her swallow, knowing what his next move would be.

Gently, he pulled her towards him. 'Case,' she murmured. His lips smothered hers, softly at first, and she felt a shivery thrill and weakness. She took hold of him and moaned, but it was the wrong signal. His kiss grew harsh and suddenly she was no longer responding. She laughed in alarm. His tongue forced its way into her mouth and she felt frightened, under attack. 'Stop it,' she hissed, trying to prise herself free. His cold hand worked its way under her shirt and cupped her bare breast. She pulled his dreadlocks and drummed on his back. Loosing his hold, he grabbed her wrists, panting now. They struggled chest to chest. The hound growled. The goshawk lowered one great foot and sidled along the perch, lifting its feet like a sumo wrestler. Pain clouded Iseult's eyes as Case bent her arm back. He wrenched her wrist down, and bore her to the ground, straddling her. He changed his grip, sliding one hand beneath her shoulders and moving the other down her belly, fumbling at the zip of her jeans. She felt the force of his desire and with all her strength she levered her arm free and jabbed her elbow into his mouth.

He reared back, his face a study in pain and anger and astonishment. 'Why did you go and do that?' he whined. He smeared his mouth with the back of his hand and stared with disbelief at the blood.

In a few seconds the afternoon had turned ugly. The dog was whining and growling, ready to bite. Every aspect of Case seemed hateful. Already his lip was swelling up and it gave his face a lopsided, vicious look.

'You bastard,' Iseult hissed. 'You bloody English bastard.'

'I thought you wanted to,' he said, his voice going up.

'Wanted to what – let you fuck me?'

'Make love,' Case mumbled.

'You call that making love?' Iseult taunted, sitting up. 'It was like being mauled by a wild animal.'

Case blanched. 'You didn't give me a chance.'

'No man touches me unless I say so. Understand?'

'Well put it in writing next time,' Case shouted. 'You were giving out signals all over.'

Iseult hung her head and massaged her wrist. 'You hurt me.' Her anger came back at full strength. 'Bastard,' she shouted, taking a swipe at him.

Case caught her hand and held it, his eyes glittering. To her disgust, Iseult became aware that she was excited as well as scared and angry.

'Bastard,' she whispered.

For a moment she thought he would hit her. Then he flung her hand away and rolled on to his back, staring into the branches. His hound came and licked his face. He fondled its ears.

Iseult stood up, feeling a bit foolish. 'I'm going back,' she said, waiting for him to make a move.

Case sighed and pushed himself to his feet. He pointed up at the deserted pine. 'The gos has buggered off. I have to get her back before dark. If she stays out a couple of nights, she'll be completely wild.'

Iseult tracked Case at a distance as he went calling and whistling through the wood, following the electronic bleep of his telemetry receiver. Occasionally he stopped and turned, his eyes panning across Iseult as if she didn't exist.

It was like when she was a child and she had offended Cathal and he made her stew in her misery, even though it was all his fault. He could nurse a grudge for days, for weeks, and he always got his own back.

He had been a dark and secretive boy, clever and manipulative — his mother's firstborn and her favourite. After the funeral, they had gone to live in their grandparents' mansion outside Dublin. Grandpa was a bruising yahoo, the son of the hero of the Easter Rising and an IRA activist during the War. Molly his wife, ten years older, was a mouse who kept going on neat gin and bridge and the Church. The children had made few friends. Iseult had discovered art; Cathal had found consolation in a campaign of petty theft.

Grandpa had caught him in possession of a silver creamer belonging to a neighbour and knocked the bejasus out of him. That night she had gone to his room and held him and stroked him until he stopped sobbing and began to direct the movement of her hands. After that he often came to her room and in the rank darkness under the high ceiling they had taken their small illicit consolations.

It became a habit, a solace, a pact. One night, Cathal had told her that when he was a small child, their mother had sometimes soothed him by sucking his cock. It was common practice, he claimed, among the women of Spain. By now, Iseult knew her brother was a fantasist, but she bent to his demand, disguising her own excitement with a pretence of maternal resignation.

And so it had gone on until she was fifteen and Cathal was seventeen and the inevitable happened. Cathal, who had an instinctive familiarity with the ways of the world, found her a doctor who whipped out the foetus during school hours and sent her home in time for tea. In the months that followed, she had nightmares in which images of her smashed parents conflated with images of the tiny foetus. Cathal left home for Trinity, and a year later he organized her escape to London, where she worked as a waitress until she was old enough to go to art college.

They hadn't made love again until three months ago when, blighted by an affair with an alcoholic art correspondent twice her age, she had fled to New York. Cathal knew how to comfort her; Cathal knew all the secret places of her heart.

Until then she had been able to pretend that what they had done had had a kind of innocence – that she had been ministering to a casualty. But that morning when, for the first time, she woke in his bed by daylight and felt him beside her, she knew that her need had been the greater. She had been in love with him. She still was. It was his face she saw in the dark which she insisted on during love-making with others, and if she banished him, her mind stayed empty, a blank screen.

'She's shadowing the dog,' Case said.

Far ahead, the hound had started an outcry.

When they caught up, the dog was working a bramble thicket, tunnelling into one side and then dashing round to the other. Up in a dead pine, the hawk's eyes blazed like coals. Case waded into the thorns, beating with a stick. The hawk hunched forward, wired to every move.

Out bolted a rabbit, eyes rolled back in its skull. Down dropped the goshawk, levelling off near the ground. Three beats of her wings, and she had her prey footed. Iseult heard a thump, a squeal and a brief drumming.

Case made in to the hawk and extended his gloved hand. The rabbit gave a kick and screamed.

'Mother of God, it's still alive,' Iseult cried, her hand flying to her mouth.

Case took out a knife and cut the rabbit's spine.

Iseult peered through her fingers. Between wheezing, gasping pulls on fur and sinew, the goshawk fixed its paralysing glare on her.

'It's only nature,' Case said. 'Life goes on.'

Iseult cast a fearful look around her. The woods had been shocked into stillness. The dark was thickening up from the ground.

'Can we go back now?' she pleaded.

But instead he led her down a steep slope to a beach at the mouth of a shallow sea loch. The tide was low and waders fringed the sand-bars. The sun was at the edge of the forest and on the wounded sky ducks were flighting. At the head of the loch, above terraced lawns, stood a castle with flaring windows surrounded by great and carefully sited trees.

'My boss's country seat,' Case said, sitting down. 'He owns a chain of quick-fit exhaust and tyre centres.'

Iseult lit a cigarette and rubbed her arms to show she was cold. Case reached into his jacket and pulled out a couple of snapshots. Iseult noticed him hesitate before he handed them over. 'Don't be fooled by appearances,' he said.

Digby Fox had a pudgy face and thinning hair tied back in a short ponytail. Outfitted in a pair of Bermuda shorts that did his physique no favours, he was lounging by a pool in a garden that fell away from a brilliant white villa.

'His house in Majorca,' Case said. 'Chopin stayed there.'

He cleared his throat – a gesture which Iseult had come to recognize as a sign of awkwardness.

In the next photo, Fox was dressed in baggy cotton trousers, work shirt and espadrilles, and he was seated at a table on the terrace of a taverna, opposite a peasant in identical clothes, frowning over a chess move. Studying the two snaps, Iseult was unable to reach a judgement. Fox was a nondescript.

'Valentine reckons he's dead clever,' Case said. 'They met at Oxford. That's where Fox started dealing.' Case took back the pictures and twisted his mouth. 'Bloody waster,' he said, apparently provoked by this portrait of effortless intelligence casually squandered.

'Do you think he stole the money?' Iseult asked.

'Valentine swears he has no financial worries. He's loaded – like, he's a multi-millionaire and he lives on about fifty quid a week. No family, no expensive tastes.'

Iseult took a quick drag on her cigarette. 'What do you think happened to him?'

Case hesitated. 'I reckon it's got something to do with the Israeli he was supposed to meet.'

Iseult tried to avert her eyes from the sight of the goshawk excavating the rabbit's skull. 'Valentine said he might be dead.'

'You don't die in Morocco without attracting attention. It's not easy to do *anything* in Morocco without it being public property.' Case turned the rabbit's head so the gos could get better purchase. 'If he's there, I'll find him.'

Case's baseless confidence irritated Iseult. 'You don't even know where to start,' she said, grinding out her cigarette.

Case turned over one of the snaps. Iseult recognized Valentine's writing on the back. *Le Sanglier Blessé*, she read.

'It means the "Wounded Boar",' Case said, and coughed.

'I know what it means,' Iseult said. 'I lived in Paris for a year. Is it a hotel?'

'A hunting lodge in the Rif mountains,' Case said, 'but you won't find it in the tourist guides. It's a clearing house for the local hashish crop, run by the man who Fox visited – a French bloke called Lemonnier. According to Valentine, he's a count whose family goes back to the Crusades, but if Lemonnier is anything to go by, it must have gone badly downhill since then. His dad was shot for collaborating with the Nazis. Lemonnier himself was a member of the OAS. A fun character.'

'He sounds like a monster,' Iseult said, her interest withdrawing with her hopes.

'I fly out on Wednesday,' Case said with studied nonchalance. He paused. 'Fancy coming along?'

Iseult's mouth opened in disbelief.

'My French isn't too hot,' Case admitted. 'You'd be a great help.' His smile buckled under Iseult's appalled stare. 'Just a thought,' he said, scratching his ear.

Iseult gave a dismal shake of her head. Even if he did find Fox, it would be too late.

'Well,' Case said with a forced laugh, 'it's only money.'

For a while they sat with their own thoughts.

From the forest halfway up the loch, a file of deer had emerged – three adults and a calf. They stepped into the sea and began to plunge across, trailing blood-coloured wakes. They came up on the other side, shook spray from themselves, and cantered into the woods.

'They do that every day,' Case said, in a gruff voice.

It was his way of trying to make amends, Iseult realized, touched nevertheless. She studied him, no longer sure of her feelings. He was staring over the water, his thoughts a long way off. 'Don't go to Morocco,' she whispered.

Case looked at her from an angle. 'That's not what you said yesterday.'

'If Fox is dead, he must have been murdered; if he's alive, someone doesn't want him found.' Iseult held Case's eyes and he hunched his shoulders, as if the cold had got to him.

'Who would have guessed you were so well house-trained?' Iseult murmured, watching Case stack the dishes in the sink.

She was drowsy and a little drunk. The huge room with its glowing fire and dancing shadows was a pleasant place. Case had cooked rabbit with chanterelles and made her laugh with stories about the locals. For a moment she had a heady sensation of normality. She looked out of the window into the blackness.

'It must be lonely living here,' she said.

'Winters can drag,' Case admitted. 'But I've always got my books.'

Iseult wandered over to the makeshift library. The basis of the collection seemed to be out-of-date school textbooks. She smiled, imagining Case working through them in alphabetical order. 'You've got *The Taming of the Shrew*,' she said.

'Load of rubbish.'

'Even the hawking imagery?'

'I thought it was sexist,' Case said in the pompous tone he affected when he was unsure of his ground.

Iseult hid her mirth. She noticed a set of photograph albums in the bottom shelf and pulled them out.

'You don't want to bother with those,' Case said.

Ignoring him, Iseult carried the albums over to the desk. She opened the first one and skimmed the pages. Her interest sharpened when she noticed the same pretty, red-haired girl cropping up.

'Why are all your dogs and hawks female?' she asked.

'Bitches are more biddable and falcons are bigger and more powerful.'

Iseult digested this, looking at another photo of the girl, and was pierced by a little barb of envy. 'And redheads are sexier.'

Case turned. 'I meant what I said.'

Iseult looked up, smiling in incomprehension. 'What?' she asked before she could stop herself.

'I'm crazy about you.'

Iseult turned away with a wan smile, cursing herself for walking into it. A lot of men found her attractive, mistaking her looks and colouring and artistic interests for evidence of

125

sensuality. 'You'll be disappointed,' she said, trying to make a jest of it. Her face went hot in realization of the implicit proposition and she pretended to give her attention to the photos. Hearing Case come up behind her, she held her breath, not sure how she would react if he touched her.

Gently, he took the album away. 'If you're going to call your brother, you'd better do it now. There's a mist settling and we ought to allow an hour to get you to the station.'

The prospect of explaining to Cathal made Iseult hollow. 'I'll ring Valentine first. He should be back in London now.'

'No harm in trying,' Case said. He shrugged on his jacket and the hound stumbled to its feet. 'I'll be outside. Give us a shout if you get him. There's something I want to ask him.'

He was at the door when the phone rang. For a moment Iseult locked eyes with Case, seized by a delusion that it was Cathal and cringing under the feeling that he had caught her out in infidelity.

Case picked up the receiver. 'How did it happen?' he said eventually.

The answer made him click his tongue. 'What a plonker.' He listened, nodding from time to time, and then he said: 'Same deal? Okay, but make sure Fatso behaves himself and nobody gets under my feet.' He turned in Iseult's direction, his face hard-edged. 'Nah, I'll fly to Tangiers and meet up with you later. You'll have to front me a few quid. Yeah. And you.'

He put down the receiver slowly, feeling for the rest, and wandered over to the fire. 'That was Denis Low,' he said, holding out his hands to the flames. 'No point ringing Valentine. He's not at home.'

'Dead?' Iseult whispered.

'Legged it. Did a U-turn on the M1 near Watford, went through the central reservation and was last seen hotfooting it towards Dunstable.'

Iseult felt like she'd been kicked in the gut.

'Makes no odds to me,' Case said. 'Low's promised to pay the bounty if I get a result.'

Fury scalded up out of Iseult's confusion. 'That's all you're worried about, isn't it?'

Case's features turned inwards. 'Yeah well,' he said, 'we don't all have your advantages.' He went out, the hound padding after.

When he had gone, Iseult advanced on the phone and dialled in one angry swoop. Cathal came on almost immediately, brimming with gratitude and sounding drunk.

'What a girl,' he declared. 'The fellow was back to me inside the hour, swearing to return every last penny. If the Landlord himself had spoken to him, he couldn't have done a better job.'

'He's not frightened now.' She wanted to hurt; she wanted to twist the knife.

Cathal laughed. 'What's that you're saying?'

'He's out of your clutches,' Iseult cried. 'You'll not see a penny piece.'

'God save us,' Cathal murmured.

His tone quenched her anger. 'There's only one hope now,' she said, and against her own reason began trying to explain about Fox and Case and Low, getting hopelessly tangled. She stumbled to a halt and waited for Cathal's explosion of scorn. 'Even if Fox is in Morocco,' she added, 'it might take weeks to find him.'

'Hush,' Cathal said. 'I'm thinking.' He mused for a while longer. 'Stay there,' he ordered.

He was gone for several minutes. Iseult found herself leafing through one of the photo albums. She frowned as her eye fell on a picture of Case and another man standing in countryside with pistols dangling in their hands. She read the caption and felt as if she'd been dipped in icewater. *MRF, Armagh, 1983*.

Feeling sick, she flicked over the next page and identified a skinheaded Corporal Case in the front row of the shooting team of 3rd Battalion, the Parachute Regiment, inter-service cup winners at Bisley. She began leafing backwards and forwards, skimming images of Case in jump gear, made up with camouflage black, at ease in shorts on Cyprus . . .

Cathal's voice made her gasp. 'I can put them off for a month,' he said.

She tried to peer through the window. Case could be on the other side, watching her. Her flesh crawled. She slammed the album shut.

'Iseult, are you there? Did you hear me?'

'Cathal,' she said, finding her voice.

'This fellow Case.'

'He was in the Paras,' she said, her gullet burning. She was thinking of the way she had responded to his touch, wanting it.

'I don't care if he was a B-Special. Now listen, tell him you've changed your mind.'

'Changed my mind?' Iseult said, her mind no longer hers to command.

Cathal sighed in exasperation. 'About going to Morocco.'

'I'm not going.'

'I'll join you there. Let me know where you're staying.'

'I won't go.'

'For the love of God, Iseult, you're sentencing me to death.'

'There'll be death if we go to Morocco.' In the dizzy silence she seemed to hear an echo of her prophecy – a thin sound, like the squeak of a thumb on glass.

'Even if we can't find Fox, I have to get out of the States. Morocco's as good as anywhere.'

Iseult was too wretched to argue. 'I'm going to bed, Cathal,' she said. 'Call me tomorrow.'

'With him? With a Para?' His voice was sly.

The squalor of the situation admitted no denial, and suddenly she saw an opening for revenge. 'Yes,' she shouted. 'With a fucking Brit Para.'

'Mmm,' he said. 'Stimulating.'

10

She was cutting it fine for the train, Case thought, taking another look over his shoulder. Part of him wanted her to miss it; part of him wanted her out of his life and gone. It was hard to believe that little more than a day had passed since first he set eyes on her. It seemed that he had been engaged in a contest with her for as long as he could remember, always wrong-footing himself just when he thought he had got on equal terms. His fists tightened in shameful recollection of his behaviour in the woods. 'No fucking breeding, that's us,' he said to the hound.

Moonlight chilled his back. A fish lorry went south on the coast road, climbing through the gears, its headlights making prisms in the mist. Watching it, Case found his own thoughts turning south. Saad made him uneasy. So did the Israeli. The Israelis didn't mess about. Saad and the Israeli together? Perhaps Fox's disappearance was political.

He would need help, he decided, remembering Laschen, the mountain Berber who had guided him on his last two trips to Morocco. Laschen's French was as bad as his own and he had difficulty communicating with anyone outside his own region, but he had a hunter's quickness of mind and he was as tough as hide. Also, the village where he lived was hidden away in the Atlas, fifty klicks from a metalled road. If things went wrong, it would make a good place to lie up.

When Case next looked, the window was empty and the lights were dimmed. He checked his watch and saw that it was nearly half-ten. Iseult must have decided to stay. He stood up, his mind tugging both ways, and decided that on balance he was glad. As he kennelled the hound, he resolved on good behaviour. There wouldn't be another chance.

On the threshold he paused. Firelight glowed on the walls.

'I couldn't face the train tonight,' Iseult said, rising from the couch. 'I took a quick bath. I hope you don't mind.'

She was wrapped in a towel, her hair gathered up, one tendril hanging loose. The light from the fire bathed her skin in an opal sheen.

Case let his breath go slowly. 'I'll sleep on the couch,' he said, affecting indifference.

'Don't be silly.'

There was an awkward stand-off. Case stirred the embers, trying to work out an appropriate move. He heard the slither of material and risked a look. His heart gave one mighty lunge, and then all his blood coagulated.

'I've always wanted to do that,' she said, standing naked on the hearth.

She looked very tall and formidably white, with a heaviness of limb that Case found worshipful. Her breasts were no more and no less than what he'd expected – or what he'd imagined as he watched their mammalian quivers under her sweater. Her nipples jutted pink in the cold. Under his scrutiny she grew uncertain and crossed her hands over them.

By degrees he found his voice. 'Let down your hair,' he ordered, the words clotting.

Holding her head to one side, she shook her hair loose to the waist.

Case advanced through the flimsy guard and took hold of her. She went limp. Her skin was cold and soft. For a long suspension of time they kissed, then he slid to his knees down the white length of her. A small sigh flew from her lips.

She had an oaky taste that made him think of sherry. She gave a gasping laugh and tugged his head back. She held out her hands and led him up the stairs.

In bed it began to fall apart. To his disappointment, she insisted that the lights be turned out. She matched him move for move, but there was no melting, no rhythm and somehow, Case sensed, no passion on her part. In the darkness and concentrated silence he kissed her face and tasted salt tears and in an angry spasm she urged him on, going through the motions with phoney vigour.

'Don't stop,' she gasped.

'I don't know what you want me to do.'

'Anything. Anything you like.'

But Case had lost heart. Suspended in the dark over her still-straining body, he said her name.

Abandoning pretence, she fell back. 'I told you I was no good,' she sobbed.

'Why?' he whispered.

'I don't know. It's always the same.'

'I mean why go to bed with me if you didn't want to?'

'I did want to, and then . . .' she took a shaky breath.

'Never mind,' Case said, feeling useless.

'The truth is,' she said in a harsh voice, 'I'm in love with someone.'

'It can't be helped,' was the best that Case could offer.

'Remember what you said about your first love making a hole in your heart that all the others pass through?'

'Who is he? I assume it's a he?'

'It doesn't matter. It's hopeless.' She turned on her side and vented a long sigh. 'It's not very fair on you.'

His emotions buzzed like flies trapped in a jar. Absently, he stroked her hair.

'Case,' she murmured, 'will you take me to Morocco?'

'I'm not sure if that's such a good idea any more.'

She turned and gripped him. 'But you asked.'

Case intuited all manner of problems without being able to pinpoint one in particular. 'It's up to you,' he said.

'Would you mind if Cathal came along?' she said in a tiny voice.

Case groaned.

'For me,' she begged.

'For you,' he sighed.

She gave a vast, uninhibited yawn and snuggled down.

'I envy Cathal,' he said.

She tensed.

'I hope he appreciates all that you're doing for him.'

She didn't answer.

'I wish I'd had a sister like you,' he said.

She squeezed his arm and wriggled close, the tension going out of her. 'We can pretend,' she murmured.

Gradually her breathing slowed and deepened. Case tried to compose himself, but he felt he was balanced on a sword edge. 'If you prefer,' he said, 'I'll sleep downstairs.'

Her hand stole out, her fingers stroking in a way that put renewed strain on his nerves. 'Stay,' she murmured, her voice slurred with sleep.

He lay wide-eyed, his jaw locked, a degree of bitterness in his heart. What a fiasco. All it would take to round off the day, he decided, would be for Catty to walk through the door. That took the edge off his lust nicely, and in a short while he was asleep.

He awoke to the premonition of dawn, the windows silvered. Beside him Iseult gulped and sighed, finding another level of sleep. Raising himself on one arm, he looked down on her. Her white face was dissipated in the dark, her hair luminous with blackness. Swinging himself out of bed, he soft-footed down the stairs and dressed in the monastic light.

In the night it had frozen. The woods behind the house lay rigid and soundless, laced by fantasies in white crystal. Everything below was lost in mist stained by a blood-red sun. A pair of crows flapped from the top of a pine and flew into the trees with barbaric cries. Case's feet left black hollows in the grass.

He released the hound, checked the hawks and then returned to the house. After getting the fire going, he made coffee. Iseult was still fast asleep. He roamed along the unsorted rows of books until he located an anthology of ballads, sandwiched between Vol.II of Richard Francis

Burton's *Personal Narrative of a Pilgrimage to El-Medinah and Meccah*, and *Great True Life Adventure Stories*. There was nothing under 'Three' or 'Ravens' in the list of contents nor in the index of first lines, and it was only by chance that he spotted the title *The Twa Corbies*.

Mug and book in hand, he went outside and sat on a stump. *The Twa Corbies* was the Scottish version of the ballad. He worked his way through the dialect. The first two verses were similar, but when he reached the third, the tone grew dark. In this version, the hounds and hawks abandoned the knight to go hunting, and his lady deserted him for another mate, leaving him as carrion for the crows.

Case read the last verse aloud, finger moving along the lines.

> *Mony a one for him makes mane,*
> *But nane sall ken whar he is gane;*
> *O'er his white banes, when they are bare,*
> *The wind sall blaw for evermair.*

Frowning, he looked at the house, the last line keening in his mind.

11

Magda was as good as her word, requiring only four days to organize her leave-taking. She had always been an assertive personality; Dearborn had a weakness for the type.

At Casa International they played out a charade of happy families, receiving and dispensing advice and good wishes as if this was an ordinary day in an everyday world, and then Magda put her arm around Lauren and shepherded her through the security barrier.

'Safe journey!'

You can't do this to me!

But of course she could. The last Dearborn saw of them was little Lauren's face craned back over her mother's arm, wearing a dazed expression between incomprehension and pitiful realization that her world had shifted on its axis. He had seen it on orphans in Beirut.

The image clung as he paced the arrivals hall, for it was his fate that day to play escort to Ed Mozart, a Bowyer Corporation lawyer who was flying in from Paris to make an on-site inquiry into the disputes at the dam.

Any other time, the sight of Mozart would have lit alarms, but Dearborn was too mired in self-pity to take heed of the bantam strut, the hank of hair glued across the bald pate, the eyes like hard currency.

'I thought we might have lunch before going on to the office,' he suggested when they were in the car.

'I'm here to shoot trouble, Dearborn. I want to see the dam.'

'You mean right now?'

'Damn straight I do.'

It had been Dearborn's intention to spend two or three days in Casa to get on terms with his new status before returning to the ghosts in the villa.

'I'd better let them know to expect us,' he said, reaching for the car-phone.

'Make it a pre-emptive strike,' Mozart said, commandeering the phone for himself. He punched keys. 'Minnie,' he said, when contact was established, 'I've hit the beach. Here's where you can reach me. Any developments on the Saudi front and you prioritize me, you hear.'

Their route out of the city took them past a *bidonville* constructed of flattened oil cans and fertilizer sacks. Mozart stared at the shanties as if he expected to recognize a client. He opened his briefcase and withdrew a file and note-pad.

'Slide the political situation past me.'

'Oh, it's about the same as usual.'

Mozart stared holes into him.

'I'm sorry,' Dearborn said. 'My mind was on other things.' He drew a deep breath as if he was about to embark on a disquisition. 'Calm,' he said. 'Perfectly calm. I have it from an impeccable source.'

'And the dam.'

'We had some storms that brought down landslides and closed access for a day. The road's clear now.'

'Goddammit, John, I'm talking personnel.'

'They're still not happy about safety.'

Mozart made a note on his pad. 'It says here the accidentees had more than forty dependents. I do not, repeat *not*, believe that all of them are bona-fide beneficiaries.'

'Moroccans have big families.'

Mozart glared at Dearborn. 'What about the mad mullah?'

'She's not a mullah.'

'She?'

'That's right. She's hereditary keeper of a *kouba*. That's a shrine to a local saint.'

135

'I don't care if she's second cousin to the Virgin Mary; I want to know why she isn't in the slammer.'

'Because it wouldn't be good strategy. It would be bad strategy.'

'Is that *your* opinion?'

'Yes.'

'Is that what you told the Moroccans?'

'I concurred with their judgement, yes.'

'Dammit, Dearborn,' Mozart said, scribbling another note on the pad, 'that broad is eating at our schedule.' He grabbed the phone. 'Minnie, see if our ambassador can fit me in tomorrow – a.m., a.s.a.p.' He fell back, exhausted from the tough decisions Dearborn was forcing upon him. His palm circled wearily. 'What else?'

My wife left me, Dearborn wanted to say. 'Nothing,' he replied. 'It's been pretty quiet.'

Conversation flagged as they followed the tawdry plain south. The landscape matched Dearborn's mood. From now on, just the act of getting through the day would have to suffice, and he wasn't even sure if he could manage that. His family had been all the purpose in his life, and now that was gone – a scary thought for a man eyeing the plateau of middle age.

Mozart was about as sympathetic as a dispensing machine, but Dearborn had a need to unburden his heart. 'Two hours before you flew in, I saw my family off.'

Mozart drummed his fingers on his briefcase and looked down the long straight road, resentful of quality executive time a-passing.

'My wife and I agreed to separate.'

'You spoken to a lawyer?'

'We haven't reached that stage yet.'

'Here,' Mozart said, fishing for a card. 'Beat her to the punch.' He slapped the card on the dash and showed his teeth. 'Klein handled all three of my divorces.'

The phone bleeped. Mozart snatched it up.

'I know he's corrupt,' he said. 'Show me one of those

sonofabitches who isn't. The issue is, is his corruption within the budget parameters?' He was leafing through his diary. 'Okay,' he said, 'the seventh. Route me through Hong Kong. Let B.B. know. Oh, and be sure to give him my warm personal bests.' He replaced the phone. 'Got problems with one of our Chinese joint ventures.'

'What kind of man is Bill Bowyer?' Dearborn asked. 'I only know him from that *Fortune* profile.'

Mozart's face mottled with anger. 'That was the most partial, biased piece of reportage I ever saw. I tell you, John, B.B. is just about the completest man I know – hard-assed businessman, yes, but also a visionary – way ahead of the rest of us.'

'Mmm.'

'Terrific sense of humour, too,' Mozart said, and chuckled fatly. 'You hear about the time he had an audience with the Pope?'

'I don't think so.'

'Ed,' he told me afterwards, 'I never thought the proudest day of my life would be the day I kissed another man's ring. There you have the essence of the man, Dearborn.'

That about exhausted the small change of conversation. At Benguirir, Dearborn diverted to a minor road that took them south-east to the Marrakech-Fez highway. The mountains came in sight, hazy and insubstantial under the vertical midday sun. They skirted east for fifty kilometres before pointing south again into the ranges. In mid-afternoon, Dearborn passed the turn-off to the villa. 'I live up there,' he said, seeing empty rooms, the swing in the garden, the detritus of a marriage. He kept going. The metalled road ran out and they zig-zagged up a *piste*, crawling round a dizzy succession of hairpins in expectation of meeting one of the *camions* that trundled down at five-minute intervals. Gangs were making good the surface washed away by the rains. The mountains above were undifferentiated and dead-looking, but the valley below fell away into a green-black haze of irrigated terraces and orchards and villages.

Dearborn rounded the last corner and the dam smacked him in the eye – a marvellous monstrosity shouldering two mountains apart, with tiny figures dangling on threads over the central spillway and metal beetles crawling along its base. Dearborn slipped on sunglasses to ward off the glare of raw concrete. Mozart grunted.

The army post had been reinforced since his last visit. Two managers emerged from the site office and exchanged glances of dismay. Mozart leapt from the car, smile bolted in place, and bounded up the steps to greet the hastily convened welcoming committee. A bearded Frenchman and a laconic Okie were in charge of operations. There followed a confused round of introductions and the obligatory drinking of Fanta and mint tea.

'Okay,' Mozart said, jumping up after the first glass, 'I want to see where the incident occurred.'

Hard hats were produced and everyone crowded into a jeep. They drove up the mountain and stopped outside a tunnel. A gang of dust-caked men issued from the dark, pushing a wagon loaded with spoil. A young Moroccan engineer from the Anti-Atlas led them through din and hot vapours. At the end was a scene from Hades created by a rock-boring machine like a small tank or B-movie robot. Four men drenched in sweat were operating it; one directed the gouging drills, one fed it power, and the other two seemed to be there to stop it leaping out of control.

'This the culprit?' Mozart shouted.

The engineer signalled for the power to be killed.

'So what went wrong?' Mozart demanded, looking around with a forensic eye.

'Carelessness,' the Okie said. 'Lack of attention.'

Exhaustion, Dearborn wanted to say. What do you expect when men work twelve-hour shifts six days a week in conditions that would fell a horse? Day after day he saw them coming down the *piste*, sprawled in trucks like corpses.

'Who was in charge of the shift?'

Eyes turned towards the Moroccan engineer.

'Tell him he's terminated,' Mozart ordered Dearborn.

Dearborn blushed with shock. 'Ed, that's not my responsibility.'

Mozart barely glanced at him. 'You,' he said to the engineer, 'I want you off the site in twenty minutes. You,' he said, crooking a finger at Dearborn, 'show me this shrine.'

Sweating with anger, Dearborn stumbled in his wake. Back at the office, Mozart dismissed everyone except the driver. Dearborn made to climb in the jeep but Mozart ordered him to follow in his own car.

When the dam was completed, it would create a reservoir six kilometres long and one wide, drowning three Berber villages. Dearborn reached the turnaround above the last of these as the sun touched the mountain wall behind him. He climbed out, his shoulders stiff and his back cramped from all the driving. They were five thousand feet up and the air had a bite.

'Deep country,' Mozart said, staring off at a restless sea of forested hills that lapped against the wall of a high plateau.

Dearborn pointed down at the white dome of the *kouba*. 'Berbers come here on pilgrimage from all over the Atlas.'

'How about if we rebuilt it a hundred feet higher? Hell, it would look a real poem by the water's edge.'

It occurred to Dearborn that if his countrymen had a weakness, it was a failure to appreciate the symbolic value of things. 'It wouldn't be the same,' he said.

'So what's the big attraction?'

'There's a powerful curse on it.'

'Curse?'

'Before the French protectorate, shrines like that were the people's court. Say a man was accused of stealing a sheep. He and his family had to swear his innocence on the tomb of the saint.'

'Suppose he was lying?'

'Then the curse would fall on him.'

'I'd take my chances.'

'It wasn't as simple as that. When I say his family had to

swear to his innocence, I mean his entire kin, right down to the remotest cousins. If a single one of them refused, the accused man was presumed guilty. If he persuaded his family to perjure themselves, the plaintiff watched out until one of them went blind or lost his flock in a blizzard and then he could say that justice had been done. It worked pretty well.'

Mozart cracked an uneven smile. 'As a lawyer, I have to say it stinks.'

'No point hanging a shingle out up here. Nowadays, if a local has a complaint against a neighbour, he takes it to the district *caid* and the man with the biggest bribe wins. Same principle if it's a criminal offence. The police drive up, grab the first dozen men that come to hand and throw them in jail. Their families have to buy them out. The guilty party is the one left behind.'

Mozart gave Dearborn a narrow look. 'I would expect you to sound more judgemental.'

'Let your own values get in the way and you won't understand much about this country.'

'What values *do* you stand for, Dearborn?'

'Right now I'm in the process of making a re-examination.'

'I'll tell you what they don't stand for. They don't stand for the Bowyer Corporation.' Mozart began striding away with his rooster energy. 'You're out, Dearborn. Take a month's salary in lieu of notice.'

'Can I ask why?'

'It's all in here,' Mozart said, swinging his briefcase against his knee. 'We've been collecting the goodies on you for quite some time.'

'Bullshit,' Dearborn said. 'This is a political decision you jackass flunky lawyer.'

Mozart pointed at him, backing away. 'I'm glad I caught up with you, Dearborn. People like you are a virus in the corporate body.'

'Doesn't this line of work get on your conscience?' Dearborn called.

Mozart reddened up. 'I don't need lessons in conscience

from a shit-ass pervert like you. I know about you and your fornicating in public. Soon as B.B. heard, you were doomed. You hear me, Dearborn? *Doomed.*'

Dearborn sauntered across and leaned on the jeep. 'Doesn't anybody try to bust you in the nose once in a while? Because believe me, in a long life dealing with unpleasant little shits, you are about the most odious I've stepped in.'

A look of intense pleasure transformed Mozart's face. 'One time I had to lay off an entire workforce – four thousand men – in Brazil. Now this was the Mato Grosso, Wild Westville, and there was no plane out till next morning. So all day I was out and about in the company of those men, and believe me, they were tough. They were men. They were armed.' He signalled the driver to advance. 'You know what happened?'

'Nothing.'

Mozart's smile blossomed. 'Damn straight, nothing,' he shouted over the clatter of the engine. 'It was like their balls had been cut off.'

The jeep shot forward, leaving Dearborn leaning on air. 'I understand,' he said.

He didn't watch as Mozart was chauffeured away to his next showdown in Guangdong or Jedda or wherever. That was all finished. The irony was that if he had been fired a week ago, it might – just might – have brought him and Magda together. She had always hated his role as company stooge. Basically, she wanted him to be a teacher.

He took stock. Wife left him, no job, a widening reputation for sexual delinquency. Events were certainly moving on an inexorable downward track.

He sighed and the stream below sighed back. Water was life, renewal, hope. He found himself drawn down to it.

The descent was deceptively difficult, through terraced fields hedged with thorn and connected by a network of paths as tortuous as the ties of clan and marriage that had produced them. By the time he reached the trees the sun was nearly gone. Women were coming up from pasture, bent under loads of grass, driving thin cows with swinging udders.

They wore tribal colours of black and silver and cut-down rubber boots. They muttered blessings and touched their hearts but avoided his eye. They appeared to be either very young or old, although all ages must have been represented. Most of the older women carried huge keys on their girdles, signifying that they were holders of the house.

Men were re-arranging the irrigation system for the night, loosening a stone here, blocking a breach there – an insect-like operation. They worked fast, as if fearful of being caught in the dark.

And the light was failing fast, withdrawing to the highest peaks. Dearborn sat in the shadows by a pool, lobbing pebbles into the current. A bulbul delivered its fluting song from the thicket. Frogs belched. All kinds of thoughts kept rising to the surface and sinking under, dragged down by the undertow of memory.

One nasty piece of flotsam kept bobbing back, trapped in an eddy. When he had accused Magda of selling herself for money in Beirut, she had neither denied it nor expressed the anger that was her due – implying it was true or she couldn't care less what he thought. Either way, it was an unmanning thought.

He had met her in a club on the Corniche, belly-dancing. For three nights he returned to watch her slow, sumptuous gyrations, tormented by the fact that after each performance she left on the arm of some paunchy Lebanese – a different man each night. On the fourth night he had slipped the floor manager fifty bucks and asked for an introduction.

She was a political science graduate from Chicago and she had been working on a kibbutz in Upper Galilee. Disillusioned by orange-picking, she had travelled north and had her passport stolen. She came back to his apartment that first night and the magic she worked with her pelvis had left him wrecked. Dearborn made sure that the question of payment didn't arise by volunteering to donate the price of her air fare home.

She never went. She moved in with him and three months later they were married. He couldn't believe his luck.

The Company was less enchanted, making its disapproval known without specifying grounds. Dearborn told himself it was because Magda had strong Zionist *and* Palestinian sympathies, which she expressed passionately and not very logically on the Beirut diplomatic circuit. The thing was, no matter what Magda had cost him career-wise, he had never regretted it. Not even now. He was proud of his wife, her strength, her inability to compromise. Come back, Magda. I need you.

Something stirred in the trees behind him. He turned and was amazed to be confronted by black night. Floodlights had been switched on at the dam, transforming it into an artefact from a socialist realist film set.

He fancied he heard another stealthy rustle and his breath snagged. Cody had said there were leopards up here, but that wasn't true. Dearborn distinctly remembered reading that the last big cats had been killed decades ago.

That Cody and his redneck enthusiasms, Dearborn thought with sudden affection. What had he said? If you can't stand up to life, try kneeling.

'Oh God,' Dearborn began, 'I'm sorry I got pissed at you the other night.'

A mighty force took hold of him and hurled him through the air. He opened his mouth and choked on water. He was in the pool, held by both arms, something around his neck. It tightened and his vision filled with blood. Two men had him tight and his flailing legs couldn't find purchase. His mind was in split screen, one window in turmoil, the other quite lucid. I'm being killed, he thought. In a very short time I'll be dead. His foot made contact with the bottom and he pushed up, locking his knee, lifting his attackers bodily. Whoever had hold of him wasn't dislodged but must have been thrown off balance, for the ligature relaxed enough for Dearborn to gulp one breath of air before he was forced back under and the stranglehold tightened again.

There was nothing he could do. A rushing filled his ears and everything inside was congested. He no longer felt pain. It was like the last moments before succumbing to anaesthesia.

He was choking on water again, clawing at his throat and finding nothing there. His attackers had let him go. They were thrashing downstream. He was in the shallows, on hands and knees, retching. Now he could feel pain. It encircled his throat. He raised his head, half-blind, a wounded animal, and made out two figures on the bank – an old man, robed and bearded for the Day of Judgement, and a tiny girl, crying with fright.

In the village, his saviour's son provided him with an undersize *djellaba* and took away his wet clothes. They had put him in the guest-room, a place of hectic colours – swimming-pool-blue walls, red and gold cushions, two riotous tapestries, one depicting the *q'aba* at Mecca, the other a lyrical study of deer at a waterhole. Children's faces peeped around the door frame. The pain had moved into Dearborn's head, threatening to lift the top of his skull. His lungs felt as if they had been shaved.

The faces at the door scattered and a delegation filed in – his rescuer, who introduced himself as the village chief; a school-teacher wearing horn-rims taped with sticking plaster; and a tough-looking individual with wall eyes who had made the pilgrimage to Mecca.

They took their places opposite and opened proceedings with inquiries about his health and observations on God's mercy and wisdom. Civilities over, his hosts began to argue among themselves in their Berber dialect.

'Have you called the police?' Dearborn wheezed.

They looked at each other.

'The men who attacked you were not from this village,' the hadji said.

The *chef du village* nodded. 'They were not from this valley.'

'It was night,' Dearborn pointed out.

'They did not belong to this valley.'

Dearborn juggled with the problem confronting him. It was his duty to warn his employers – ex-employers – but if he summoned the gendarmes, they would bust the entire male population. The prospect of more time in police care swung the decision.

'Would you swear on the tomb of Sidi Brahim that my assailants are not from this village?'

His saviour regarded him with motionless eyes, then began to stand up, indicating that Dearborn should rise too.

Dearborn made a loose gesture of acceptance. 'I believe you,' he said. 'I won't involve the police provided you get word to this man.' He wrote down Cody's number and handed it over, together with his car keys. 'Do you know how to operate a phone? I don't care what you tell my friend so long as you make it clear he must come as quickly as possible.'

After conferring, the *chef* despatched his son.

Tea was brought on an electro-plated tray as big as a wheel. When it had been dealt with, Dearborn's hosts retired, telling him to rest before the evening meal. He lay on the divan, his thoughts pelting, until shock took hold and he fell into a doze.

He woke from unhealthy dreams to the barking of dogs and the *chef*'s dispassionate face. He followed him out on to the flat roof and saw headlights moving up the valley and blue lights spinning. On all the roofs, villagers watched as the convoy grouped at the turnaround. Faint shouts could be heard above the yelping of the dogs. Nobody offered Dearborn recriminations. His rescuers probably thought him a fool not to have insisted on calling the law in the first place.

The force made a noisy entrance to the village, meeting some shrill resistance from the womenfolk. The *chef* disappeared, leaving Dearborn alone on the roof.

First up was Cody, wearing a hunting jacket and an expression undecided between philosophical resignation and murderous intent. Behind him came Douaz.

'You were quick,' Dearborn croaked.

'Helicopter,' Cody said, indicating Douaz. He inspected

Dearborn's neck and whistled. 'Looks like someone put a *fatwah* on you, cowboy.' He turned his back and stared at the ridge-line. 'What in hell were you doing wandering around up here on your own? You know what these people think about the dam.'

'As of this afternoon, I don't work for the dam.'

Cody seemed helpless in the face of this twist. 'Oh boy,' he said. 'Oh boy oh boy oh boy. When you decide to screw up, you certainly go at it heart and soul.'

Douaz interrupted to put a few questions concerning the identity of the attackers. The suave colonel invited Dearborn to present himself at police headquarters the next morning, then left to organize the house-to-house.

'That's it,' Cody said. 'You're outbound.'

'Me?' Dearborn squeaked through his damaged throat, 'I'm the goddam victim.'

The *chef* and his son emerged, bearing an earthenware *tagine* and a butane lamp. When the dish was placed before him, Cody brightened somewhat.

'This is what I call the genuine article,' he said, dipping bread into the pungent grease. 'Start with mutton – mutton mind, not lamb. Add a quart of oil, a quart of water and let it simmer until the water's all gone. In Rabat it's fucking *nouvelle cuisine* time. Go on, eat.'

'I can't swallow.'

On the mountain a jackal howled. Desert stars had flowered. In the lanes the police were herding away the men. The women were tearing their hair and wailing.

'Cody, it wasn't anyone from this village.'

'They'll nail him.'

'I think they were professionals.'

Cody looked at him, a hunk of dripping mutton between his teeth. 'You're nuts,' he said, and worried the meat like a dog.

'That doesn't mean they weren't out to get me.'

'What makes you think they weren't local boys?'

'They didn't speak. They didn't make a sound.'

'If they'd been pros, they would have cut your fucking throat.' Cody pointed a shank-bone at Dearborn. 'No one knew you would be here today.'

'I might have been followed.'

Cody paused in mid-chew. He looked his age. 'Alright,' he muttered. 'Anyone coming past the dam would have been logged. I'll check with Douaz.'

'Cody, did you tell my employers about that . . . woman?'

Cody wiped grease from his lips. 'No, John, I wouldn't do that.'

'Because that slime-ball Mozart had been primed. He was sent here to do a number on me.'

'I would have thought the fact that you've been doing a lousy job was all the motive he needed.'

'If it wasn't you, it must have been Colonel Douaz. Why?'

'Why?'

'Oh come on, Cody, people are acting peculiar. It's like they're walking on eggs.'

Cody studied him, trying to dislodge a shred of gristle from his teeth. 'In three months' time the dam comes on line, right?'

'More like five the way things are going.'

'Late or not, the opening ceremony goes ahead as scheduled.'

'With his majesty cutting the ribbon or unveiling the plaque or whatever it is you do to inaugurate a dam.'

'That's an unwarranted assumption,' Cody snapped, 'and classified as well.'

'Come on, Cody. Everyone knows the King can't resist a grand opening ceremony.'

Cody fixed Dearborn with his eyes. 'This is a very sensitive locale, John, and you're spoiling the atmosphere.'

The assault had shaken up Dearborn's mind and half-thoughts were flickering like fish glimpsed in a pool.

'Suppose you're right about those killers,' Cody mused, wiping the bowl. 'Why would they want to whack you?'

'It has to be connected to Ben-Yacoub,' he said.

Cody belched. 'You never set eyes on him until he was dead.'

The harder Dearborn tried to pin it down, the more elusive it became. No, he couldn't get hold of it. He shook off his trance. 'Who have you got on the case?'

'Douaz has all the resources he needs.'

'I'm talking about people from our side.'

'It's the same side.'

'Yeah, but liaison.'

Cody was so angry he could hardly get his cigar lighted. 'I'm fucking liaison. Is that good enough for you?'

'Sure, Cody, don't blow up. So what's Douaz come up with?'

Cody mastered his anger. 'Ben-Yacoub, aka Lova Hazan, was a petty thief and doper. He had no political connections, no links with any intelligence outfit. He was probably here on a drugs thing, had a sentimental urge to take a trip down memory lane, and just happened to run into bad luck.'

'An Israeli misfit,' Dearborn murmured. 'Doesn't that alarm you?'

Cody relaxed. 'They're not as rare as all that.' He laughed, pointing at Dearborn's sorry attire. 'You should see yourself, John. You look like the Old Man of the Mountains.'

'How come I didn't see a report of Ben-Yacoub's death in the papers?'

'Christ, John, where's your sense of perspective? It's the start of the tourist season.'

Dearborn sensed that he was being played false. 'So the case is closed.'

'It's not top of my concerns.'

'With respect, Cody, I think you're wrong. I've got a feeling about this one.'

'Also with respect, John, fuck your feelings.'

'How about running a fresh pair of eyes over it? How about putting me on a short-term contract? I can make a few informal inquiries in Israel.'

Cody went very still. A moth incinerated itself on the gas

mantle. 'You're an analyst. You have no field experience. You'd fuck up.'

'That's partly why I want to get on this case. Listen, Magda despises me because for all those years I sat back and let other people take the risks.'

'Consider yourself privileged.'

'Please, Cody. I have no wife, no job, nowhere to go. I'm at a loose end.'

'Loose end?' Cody shouted, pointing a tremulous finger. 'You're a loose cannon and I want you off my deck.'

12

Cathal flew into Tangiers on a day of throbbing sunlight, the plane skidding down the runway like a blob of mercury. Case, watching from the observation roof, took a covert look at Iseult, trying to read her mood. What he could see of her face was tight and nervous; the rest was blacked out behind sunglasses. She had painted her lips shocking vermilion and secured her hair in an extravagant plait. With the straw hat and shorts she was wearing, the effect was strikingly unco-ordinated.

Two Moroccan airport staff were gawping at her – her whiteness, her bigness, her thighs. It irritated Case that she had made a spectacle of herself. Only dumb tourists wore shorts.

He could see the vulnerable tracery of veins under her sheer white skin and he found himself thinking that in years to come those veins would turn blue and varicose, the unexercised frame would spread and sag.

'Aren't you overdoing it with the ciggies?' he asked, watching her tap another from the pack. She smoked too much and she never showed up on time and watching her unpack was enough to give him a seizure.

'Leave me alone, can't you?' she said, looping a stray piece of hair back over her ear.

They had been together in Morocco for two days and already they were at odds. For a start, they had different metabolisms. Case liked to wake early and grab the day by the throat; he was fretting under the unscheduled delay imposed by Cathal's late arrival. Iseult was a creature of night, reaching her peak of vitality in the small hours. At two that morning, he had been condemned to watch from his separate bed while she smoked and read, smiling absently at certain passages and licking her finger before turning each page.

And now he had her brother to deal with.

He puffed out his cheeks and watched storks revolving on thermals, gaining height before sliding away south. That's where he should be headed, he thought, not hanging about in this crummy seaside town.

'There he is,' Iseult said quietly.

Cathal was wearing pastel tones and appeared tall, but Case could only infer his features through the waves of heat boiling off the tarmac.

They went down and waited in the tiled hall. It was a charter flight from Madrid.

'He's the dead spit,' Case murmured when Cathal emerged. It was unsettling – like seeing a positive and negative of the same image.

'Oh, he's better looking,' Iseult said.

Spotting Iseult, Cathal spread his arms and advanced, taking each of her hands in his. They stood like that for quite some time, wordless, before Cathal leaned forward and slowly, delicately, touched lips. Iseult burst into tears.

Case stirred the ground with his feet and pretended to admire a travel poster. When he dared look again, Cathal was smiling at him over his sister's shoulder – a wry smile that seemed to suggest a long and not entirely painless working knowledge of women's emotional ups and downs. He murmured something to Iseult and she turned, making a stilted gesture of introduction.

They were from the same mould – same luminous complexion, same deep amber hair – but Cathal was a couple of inches taller, his features better finished, his irises bluer and out-lined with black – very Irish eyes. His hair was straighter, swept back and parted roughly in the middle, which gave him a romantic poetic appearance without making him look too limp-wristed. But what made the vital difference was his animation. He sparkled. For a man who was only one skip ahead of his creditors, he seemed on remarkably good terms with himself.

'We were expecting you yesterday,' Case said.

'Rearguard action,' Cathal said. 'Withdrawing under cover of smoke.' He seized Case's hand in both his own. 'Pat, what can I say to a man who offers to rescue me from a grave of my own digging?' He shook his head. 'A good deed in a naughty world. You can't imagine how refreshing that is.'

'Er, that's okay.'

'I know,' Cathal said, taking his sister's arm so that all three of them stood linked in friendship, 'it was for Iseult's sake.' A fleck of her lipstick had transferred itself to Cathal's mouth. It looked like blood. 'A token,' he said, pressing a gift-wrapped package into Case's hand.

Case undid the wrapping to find a glazed Persian tile of a long-haired youth on horseback, holding a hawk aloft.

Cathal's eyes widened. 'Will you take a look,' he exclaimed. 'If Pat isn't the living image of that fellow.'

Iseult cast a glance over the gift and looked away, in a huff.

'It's sixteenth-century,' Cathal said. 'From Isfahan.'

'It's a fake,' Iseult said curtly. 'A forger called Flaherty turns them out by the score.'

Cathal laughed merrily, not abashed in the slightest. 'He's calling himself Somerville now. The last I heard he had disguised himself in doublet and hose and cod-piece, guiding tourists around the *Golden Hind*.'

'I don't care,' Case said, running his fingertips over the delicate crazing. The extraordinary thing was that the young Persian nobleman *did* resemble him. It gave him a sweet, sad feeling.

'You like it?'

'It's beautiful,' Case said. He stole a shy glance at Iseult, but she was blowing a sulky stream of smoke at the ceiling.

Fingers feathered his hand. Cathal was smiling into his eyes.

> *'But such as you and I do not seem old*
> *Like men who live by habit. Every day*
> *I ride with falcon to the river's edge*
> *Or carry the ringed mail upon my back,*
> *Or court a woman; neither enemy,*
> *Game-bird, nor woman does the same thing twice.'*

'Would that be Yeats?' Case said, embarrassed.

'Would that be Yeats?' Cathal cried, doing a stylized back-step of astonishment. 'By God, Iseult, why didn't you tell me that Pat was a fan of the great W.B.?'

'It was Iseult introduced me to him,' Case explained.

'Did she now?' Cathal said, smile diminishing. 'Good for her.'

Iseult flung her hair off her shoulders, forgetting that it was tied up.

On the taxi ride into town, Case sat in front, mulling over the next move.

'I'll be leaving for Marrakech in the morning,' he announced, striving for a casual tone. He swivelled round, then looked smartly to the front again, jolted by the sight of Cathal and Iseult nestled up as close as doves, their eyes closed, Iseult's lips slightly parted, Cathal stroking her hair.

'And where does that leave us?' Cathal murmured.

'Wherever you like,' Case said, rattled by their intimacy. 'Take a few days' holiday.' He sneaked another peep. Cathal was sprawled in the corner, Iseult's head at rest on his chest. 'Look,' Case blurted, 'it could take some time.'

'But you're on the scent,' Cathal said, massaging Iseult's shoulder. 'You have the sniff of Fox in your nostrils.'

'Give us a break. I only just got here.'

Cathal gave Iseult's head a playful push. 'Tchh, and here's you telling me it was cut and dried.'

Cat-like, Iseult rubbed her cheek on her brother's shoulder.

'I thought you were going to start at *Le Sanglier Blessé*,' she said drowsily.

'I changed my mind,' Case snapped, annoyed by her dopey attitude. At the same time he was imagining himself in Cathal's place. He shifted uncomfortably, crossing his legs on an erection.

'The Wounded Boar,' Cathal said. 'That's Lemonnier's place, is it?'

'We won't go into that now,' Case said, nudging a glance in the direction of the driver.

'But why can't we come to Marrakech? Honest to God, we won't get in your way.'

'It's not my way you have to worry about. It's Low's path you don't want to cross.'

'A very forthright gentleman,' Cathal murmured, and ran a fingertip down Iseult's arm, from the tender flesh on the inside of her elbow to the pulsing vein on her wrist. She gave a little jerk as he brushed a nerve.

'Stop!' he shouted.

A procession was crossing the road, led by a group of musicians playing hand-drums and pipes. Cathal scrambled out and Case joined him. The women punctuated the droning of the men with blood-tingling ululations. The party left the road and entered a disused brickfield. Rubbery smoke from a tyre dump behind an Agip service station drifted across their path. Long after they were just a twitch in the heat, Case could hear their chant.

'Africa,' Cathal said, turning to Case with dancing eyes. 'Where else would you find a party in the middle of nowhere?'

'It was a funeral,' Case told him.

But Cathal wasn't bothered by details. He raised his face to the yellow sky, the invisible burning sun. 'Ah,' he breathed, 'you can smell it – the passion, the cruelty.'

Against instinct, Case found himself grinning. 'I'd have thought you'd get enough of that in New York.'

Cathal's face twisted. 'It's a carcass, Pat – a maggot farm. The maggots turn into flies and then down come the spiders and gobble them up.' He shuddered. 'I tell you, I'm glad to be out.'

Case studied him, not sure if he was dealing with a fool or a rogue. 'And what are you, Cathal – spider or fly? Iseult didn't tell me exactly what it was you did for a living.'

'Financial services, Pat. Dull stuff.'

'What – like an accountant?'

'That's it, the very thing. A cruncher of numbers, not at all the healthy action-man character such as yourself.'

They were sparring, Case realized, enemies from the start. 'I hear you had some difficulty balancing the books,' he said, putting the needle in.

'Ah yes,' Cathal said, 'things got a little out of hand.' He slid a smile Case's way. 'But it was time to move on in any case. I was getting bored with myself.'

Although Cathal took unaffected pleasure in Tangiers, his enthusiasm was no match for the hotel where Case and Iseult were lodged. It was a cheap seafront establishment set behind palms like broken umbrellas. Above the entrance a rusting Coca-Cola sign creaked in the hot wind.

'Ah no,' Cathal said, 'I can't be doing without my little amenities.' He picked his way across Iseult's debris, parked himself on a bed, filled a tooth-glass with duty-free Bushmills and consulted the hotel guide. 'Les Almohades, I think.'

'I thought you were skint,' Case said.

'But *they* don't know that.'

'I'll come with you,' Iseult muttered, hurriedly scooping her belongings together, too craven to make eye contact with Case.

When they had gone, Case walked up and down, unable to settle, then did fifty push-ups very fast and stood in a tepid shower, wondering if he had made a big mistake.

The restaurant selected by Cathal for their evening rendezvous had been the palace of a Rif warlord. Case, dressed in clean army surplus, experienced some difficulty gaining admission. Finally, he was led through an iron-bound door, across a courtyard loud with fountains, and into an interior designer's vision of the Moorish good life. The waiters wore starched white *djellabas* and moved among the brass-topped tables and fibreglass arches as if they were on castors. The multi-lingual menu came without prices.

The ambience was somewhat blighted by a party of American tourists from a passing cruise liner. Banished to the darkest alcove, Case sipped a beer and watched a 200-pound lady in a crushed velvet Babygro swaying to the rhythms of a Rifian folk ensemble.

Cathal and Iseult made their entrance attended by flunkies fore and aft. At the sight of them, Case stood to attention, knocking over his glass. Iseult was wearing a dark dress and she had let down her hair and her face shone like an icon. She looked gorgeous. They both did. The tourists were impressed into silence.

In good loud French, Cathal demanded adjustments to the seating arrangements.

'You look smashing,' Case said humbly, reduced to cloddish reverence by Iseult's transformation. 'I never saw you in a dress before.' It was yew green, her mouth a bow of scarlet.

'Cathal gave it to me,' she said, and let her hand caress the material.

'I wouldn't know how to go about buying women's clothes,' Case admitted. 'Clothes for a woman,' he added hastily. He had the sudden feeling that the evening was about to go wrong. 'I feel a right scruff beside you two.'

Cathal's eyes flickered over him. 'Never mind,' he said, 'you can choose the food. Iseult tells me you're quite a gourmet.'

Case weighed the words for sarcastic content. 'I don't know,' he said uncomfortably. 'It must be pretty pricey.'

'Tonight, money's no object.'

Case's experience of Moroccan food was limited to peasant dishes. He suggested that they keep it simple.

They drank a bottle of champagne while they decided on the menu. Cathal talked non-stop of life at the leading edge of the enterprise culture. Bogus or not, he made entertaining company. Iseult was content to listen quietly, her eyes dipped. Any doubts Case had harboured were gone; he wanted her desperately. Every time he glanced her way, it brought a lump to his throat which he had to wash down with another swig.

He was mildly sloshed before their order had been taken. The waiter was young and beautiful, with lustrous black skin stretched over delicate bones. 'Now then,' Cathal said, watching him walk away. 'The unvarnished truth. What are our chances?'

'Pretty good. Can you remember how long Valentine said you'd have to wait for the money?'

'Too long.'

'Six weeks is what he told me,' Iseult said.

Case nodded. 'And Low. Not a few weeks or a couple of months, like you'd expect from someone pulling a figure from the air. But six weeks exactly. Now listen. Before Low turned up, Valentine asked me to look after his hawks – for six weeks. He said he had to shoot off on business. To me, that suggests he was planning to disappear until Fox showed up again. I think Fox got a message to Valentine, telling him he'd run into trouble.'

'Then Valentine must know why.'

'Nah, I was there when Low put the frighteners on him. He wasn't holding anything back.'

'The Israeli?' Cathal said.

Case knocked back his next drink. 'That's why I have to go to Marrakech.'

'Iseult mentioned a Lebanese – Rafiq Saad.'

Case glanced at Iseult, not pleased with Cathal's free and easy use of names. 'Another one of Fox's punters,' he said.

'From Iseult's description, he sounds more like someone who operates on the supply side.'

Case thought so too, but he didn't care for the way Cathal was making the running.

'The logical person to ask is Count Lemonnier,' Cathal said. He swirled his wine. 'Why don't Iseult and I take a dander up to *Le Sanglier Blessé*? It's only a day's drive.'

'Not a chance.'

'Don't overlook the fact that Lemonnier has quarter of a million dollars' worth of my hash.'

'I said forget it.'

Cathal pretended to breathe the bouquet of his wine. 'What do you think, Iseult?'

'Hey, we're not putting it to a vote,' Case said.

'Iseult?'

'I can't see what harm it would do,' she muttered, staring at her plate.

'Get the idea out of your head,' Case cried, glaring at each of them in turn.

'But why?' Cathal demanded.

Case wasn't entirely sure of his motives; all he knew was that he didn't want to advertise his presence until he'd picked up all available clues from the ground. 'Fox disappeared in Marrakech. That's the place to start. Lemonnier won't be too chuffed to know we're trampling around looking for one of his customers. We'll save him till last.'

Cathal's smile degraded. 'As you like,' he said. 'But suppose you tell me how you propose to get round the problem of Mr Low. When it comes to his attention that he's not the only one in the hunt – well, I don't want to sound churlish, but you can take chivalry too far.'

Faced by Iseult's ambivalent support, Case was beginning to think along similar lines.

'If I were in your position,' Cathal said slowly, 'and if I came up with Fox, I'd be tempted to go for the whole pot.'

'You've lost me,' Case said, floundering in Cathal's train of thought.

Cathal balanced his chin on the tip of his index finger. 'Finders keepers,' he suggested.

'Your brother's barmy,' Case told Iseult.

'Just floating the idea,' Cathal said.

Case's laugh jarred in his own hearing. 'The last person who tried to poach from Low ended up with his hand in a food processor.'

Iseult's eyes made circles.

'A telling point,' Cathal conceded. He studied Case over the rim of his glass. 'You know, Iseult, Pat's right. While he's tracking down Fox, we should do a little sightseeing. I have a shameful yearning to do Casablanca, even though I'm reliably told that it's a dreary old industrial slum.'

It seemed to Case's fuddled mind that Cathal was enjoying a joke at his expense. He leaned close, the better to focus. 'Just remember who's sticking his neck out.'

Cathal raised his hands. 'Count on it, Pat.'

Iseult stood abruptly and headed for the cloakroom. Case made to follow but Cathal stopped him with a shake of the head.

'Let's take the chance to get better acquainted,' Cathal said. He eyed Iseult's retreating back. 'Tell me now, would you call my sister beautiful?'

'Sort of,' Case mumbled. It wasn't the kind of question he was used to.

Cathal absorbed this with his drink. 'Someone said that beauty is the promise of happiness.' He frowned. 'Or was it goodness? Well, whatever. Beauty's the thing. Consider that serving boy who keeps fluttering his lashes our way. No doubt he has the morals of an alley cat, but with looks like that, who cares?' Cathal tossed back his drink. 'Whoever said love is blind wasn't using his eyes.'

Case lost some of this in a suddenly descending haze of alcohol.

'As paterfamilias,' Cathal said in a bored voice, still admiring the waiter, 'I suppose I ought to ask you if your intentions toward my sister are honourable.'

Case blinked dully.

Cathal waved his hand in dismissal. 'You're right. Who gives a shit about honour? What about love, though?'

'I've only known her a week,' Case mumbled.

'It's never too early. The delicate balance is struck in the first instance.'

'Balance?'

Cathal leaned close. 'Between fear and fascination.'

Case sat straighter. 'What the fuck's that got to do with love?'

Cathal pondered a moment. 'You're right again. I must be confusing it with sex.' His eyes darkened; his hand slid towards Case's. 'You're a fascinating fellow yourself, Pat, and I imagine you could be rather frightening if provoked.'

Case pulled his hand out of range. 'For a bloke who grew up in Belfast, you have a bloody funny way of talking.'

'Unless you're a weather forecaster, the Ulster accent isn't one of the most useful commodities for a boy who wants to make his way in the world.'

Drink had made Case aggressive. 'When were you last there?' he demanded.

'Five, six years ago.'

Case placed his tattooed arm on the table like a challenge. 'Me too.'

Cathal's eyes flicked down. 'Ah yes,' he murmured.

'I thought I'd have to free-fall through the ceiling in my red beret before you'd notice.'

'Well now, it's like meeting a man with a deformity. You act blind out of charity.'

Case was drunk enough to find the remark objectionable. 'You saying being a Para is a deformity?'

'Figuratively speaking, Pat.'

'It pisses you off, doesn't it?'

Only the unnatural glitter in Cathal's eyes showed that he'd been drinking. 'I'm like most Irishmen, Pat; I find it hard to forgive, but I always forget.' He shifted in his seat. 'Still, I'm glad it's out in the open.'

Case was suddenly demoralized. 'So the fact that me and Iseult . . . well, you know, me and Iseult.'

'On the contrary. Love the bridge and that.' Cathal's eyes ranged about until they found the beautiful young waiter.

'Anyway,' Case said, laid low by gloom, 'you don't have to worry on that score. Iseult's in love with someone else, so that's me sunk.'

Cathal's attention swung back.

'Some bloke in Ireland.'

Cathal lowered his head in deference to the news.

'I was wondering if you knew him,' Case said, his voice stiff.

A muscle in Cathal's cheek twitched. He pressed fingers to his brow. 'I do.'

'Iseult says it gets in the way of everything.'

Cathal glanced around as if he was anxious for the bill.

'Does he still love her?'

Cathal looked sombre. 'Oh yes, it's a life sentence. A tragic, impossible passion, Pat.'

'Why?'

Cathal winced. 'Look, Pat. It's rather painful, so if you don't mind . . .'

'Just tell me what he's like?'

Cathal laughed and frowned at the same time. 'Do you know – I can't work him out. But not a good man, not the man for my sister.'

'It's that forger, isn't it?' Case said.

Cathal seemed delighted by his intuition. 'That's the very fellow. Ah, he's a wild, mad bugger, Pat, with a string of broken hearts to his credit and the peelers of three countries on his tail.'

'So there's hope for me,' Case said in dogged, no-hope tones.

Spotting Iseult on her way back, Cathal winked at Case. 'There's always hope, Pat. Faint heart and all that.'

Iseult slowed as she reached the table. 'Have you decided?' she demanded, looking from one to the other.

'Total agreement,' Cathal declared, patting Case's hand to prove it. He caught sight of his watch. 'Would youse look at the time,' he exclaimed. 'I have to call New York. No need to break up the party. Everything's taken care of.' He paused and smiled down at Case, shook his head and moved off. On the way out, he stopped for a word with the young waiter.

When he had gone it was like being in a vacuum. Iseult made to get up, but Case caught her hand.

'Tell me what I've done wrong,' he demanded.

'All that violent talk makes me nervous.'

'I was worried Cathal was getting ideas of his own. Anyway, it's sorted now.' Case coughed. 'You and him seem very close. I expect it's because he's gay. I mean,' Case explained, blundering further into the swamp, 'it's a well-known fact that women feel more relaxed with gay men.'

Iseult wrenched her hand away.

Mired up to his neck, Case lashed out in panic. 'Look, I'm not trying to be rude.'

'Aren't you?'

'What's the big deal? I thought down your way it was compulsory.'

'You crass macho fool,' Iseult hissed.

In her contemptuous stare, Case saw his fears confirmed. 'I get it. It's because I was in the Paras.'

Her stare slipped away.

'I was going to tell you,' he muttered.

Her head jerked up, her mouth ugly. 'Tell me you served in a shoot-to-kill squad?' she cried, loud enough to hush the other diners.

He collapsed back in his chair and stared at the ceiling.

'I saw your sick little gallery,' she said in a vehement whisper. 'You and that public school psychopath, posing with your pathetic bloody guns.'

'Lieutenant Andrew Ridley,' Case said. His hands were

shaking and he was faint from adrenalin. He was nodding and smiling. 'You want to hear about him, hmm?'

Iseult was rounding up her bag and cigarettes. 'No I bloody don't.'

'Last time I saw him was three years ago,' Case said. 'I couldn't face it again. He was watching kid's telly, smiling and smiling, stinking of piss, brain-dead.' Case thumped the table. 'Your lot did that to him.'

He and Iseult had their eyes locked, mesmerized by each other's hatred.

'I'm going back,' she whispered, not making any attempt to move.

He grabbed her hand. 'Not yet.'

The *maître d'* glided over, concern masking his unction. 'Is anything the matter?'

'Fuck off,' Case told him, looking straight at Iseult.

'Let go,' she mouthed, beginning to struggle.

'Not until you tell me why you slept with me.'

Fear drove out the fury in her eyes. Her hand went as limp as a bird. The fear, he thought, the fascination. He could see the smooth white cleft of her breasts. His grip tightened. 'Give you a thrill, did it? Or were you fitting me up so I would help your darling brother?'

Slowly she sank into her seat. Slowly she disentangled her hand. He watched it drag across the linen.

'I didn't mean that,' he said. He passed his hand over his eyes, appalled by the amount of wreckage he had brought down on himself.

'It's true,' Iseult said in a wooden voice. 'I did it for Cathal.'

After a moment, Case uttered a harsh laugh. 'Well it worked a treat,' he said, scraping back his chair. 'You've got me right where you want.' He couldn't bring himself to look at her. He couldn't walk away. The restaurant manager was whispering to the doorman, plotting a discreet eviction. As the snatch-squad began to move in, Case scribbled on the back of the menu, hardly able to see. 'My hotel in Marrakech,' he said, throwing it at her. 'You'd better let me know where I can reach you. Be ready to shift yourselves. There won't be a second chance.'

She read the card, then looked up, her unspoken question plain to read.

Case shook off the doorman's heavy hand. 'Because I love you, stupid.'

13

'That was a shitty thing you did last night,' Iseult said, watching the road reeling in.

Cathal sat in the passenger seat, silent and distempered, his face soft at the jawline. 'Alright,' he said at last. 'How much was I light on the bill?'

'More than sixty pounds.'

'Holy mother! Whatever happened to Third World prices?'

'I had to borrow the money from Pat. God, it was awful.'

'I miscalculated the exchange rate, that's all. It was a genuine mistake.'

'Like all the others which someone else ends up paying for.'

Cathal massaged his eyes. 'Oh, stop harping on. Can't you see I have no pounce in me this morning?'

'And that's another thing,' Iseult blurted. 'Where the hell did you get to? I waited up till four.'

'Soaking up the atmosphere.'

'You went off with that waiter, didn't you?'

'For God's sake, stop acting the dismal housewife. I didn't throw a tantrum when you boasted about letting Pat fuck you.'

'That was different,' she shouted.

'Whatever turns you on.'

'It was for you, you bastard!'

'Watch it!' Cathal cried, as the hired Fiat veered into the path of an oncoming truck.

Iseult got the car back under control. 'You hate him, don't you?'

'I admit that as I lay in bed that night, imagining you gasping and writhing under some beery, sixteen-stone slob, I felt a certain anger – mixed with a degree of arousal, I have to confess.'

'Sorry the reality's so disappointing.'

'Oh, I wouldn't say that. I could almost fancy Pat myself. Such an unusual hybrid. Those cold eyes – like a March wind, to borrow from the immortal William Butler.'

'I'll scream if I hear one more line by that sentimental old fascist.'

'In that case,' Cathal said nastily, 'you shouldn't have turned him loose on an impressionable soul like Case.'

Iseult had no answer. The road made gentle curves.

'He's got to you, hasn't he?'

'Don't be silly,' Iseult said, so quickly that she must have been anticipating the question.

'Pleasing in bed, though?' Cathal said, laying his hand at the top of her thigh.

'Stop it.'

Cathal put his head close to hers. 'Tell me what it was like,' he murmured, working his hand towards the warmth.

'Cut it out,' she whispered, instantly wet.

'How big he is, how hard.' He ran the point of his thumb up the seam of her crotch. 'Every little detail.'

The sun seemed to have gone into eclipse. Vaguely Iseult heard the wail of a horn. 'You'll make me crash,' she whimpered.

Cathal laughed and withdrew his hand. 'Do you know what I'd like?' he said. 'Before this ends, I'd like it very much if all three of us could get together.'

Two or three kilometre stones went past.

'He thinks he's in love with me,' Iseult said tiredly.

'All to the good.'

A sign came up saying Casablanca was another eighty kilometres. Iseult swallowed.

'Cathal, Pat knows I found out about him serving in Northern Ireland.'

Cathal's eyes went small. 'I thought I told you to stay off that.'

'I couldn't go on pretending forever.'

'I suppose not. Actually, we touched on it ourselves. He tried to be provocative but I wouldn't be drawn. I hope you were diplomatic.' Cathal looked across. 'Iseult?'

'I lost my temper. We had an awful row.'

'You what?'

'Cathal, I accused him of being a murderer.'

'Stop the car.'

Iseult let the car coast to a halt.

'Say that again.'

'He upset me.'

'Get out, Iseult. Just fucking get out.'

Under the force of his anger she found herself standing on the verge. He scrambled behind the wheel and wrenched the car through a complete turn, slammed on the brakes and flung open the passenger door.

'No, honest,' Iseult pleaded. 'We went to a bar and talked. I made a mistake. I got it wrong.'

But Cathal wasn't listening. His eyes were deranged, darting about as if he saw enemies everywhere.

He scared Iseult. 'Where are we going?' she whispered, holding tight to the cheap padded dash.

Hours of jangling silence later, when they were deep in the Rif, Cathal began to laugh. 'Look at us. Anyone would think we were married.' He leaned across and kissed her cheek. 'I forgive you.'

She shut her eyes. Reprieve brought exhaustion. Her calf muscles ached from pressing an imaginary brake. Her arms were sore from hugging herself protectively. Cathal drove like a maniac.

He drew off the road and parked at the edge of a green ravine that zig-zagged through a gap in the mountains. 'Kif,' he said, pointing into the valley. 'Prime Moroccan shit – and 250K's worth belongs to me.' He smiled at

Iseult, all traces of anger and last night's excess gone. 'Lunch?'

They found a grassy spot among oleanders. The air was warm and soft and smelt of herbs. High ground encircled them, nearly naked now, but once forested with cedars. The sky was petrol blue and Iseult had a feeling that the sea wasn't far away. There was no one else in sight.

Cathal had brought a lavish picnic prepared by the hotel. Eyeing the champagne and *foie gras* and monogrammed linen napkins, Iseult felt familiar unease.

'I hope this lot's paid for,' she said.

'Plastic,' he said, patting his wallet. 'The resources of civilization are not yet exhausted.'

'It's got to stop, Cathal.'

He paused in the act of tearing a *baguette* and smiled at her, clear-eyed and innocent.

'You're a con-artist,' Iseult said, prepared to risk his temper.

'At least you recognize it's an art.'

'It's a sickness.'

Cathal nodded, as if she had made an intriguing point. 'By definition, the true artist is always a deviant.'

Iseult snorted. 'You always try to run rings round common sense.'

'No, listen; it's an interesting concept. In nature there's no such thing as a confidence trickster because, according to biologists, the strategy evolved by a species cannot be bettered by any dodge dreamt up by the individual. Therefore there can be no cheating. The hawk must always act like a hawk; the dove must always be dovish. Dull, eh?' Cathal produced a bottle of Dom Perignon. 'Fortunately, we're in a position to improve on dame nature.'

'Don't you ever feel guilty about the people you've defrauded?'

Cathal pointed a knife – property of Les Almohades. 'What would you say if I offered to double your money within the month – performance guaranteed.'

'I'd say you were a liar.'

'My clients don't. They swallow it whole. They gobble it up. Yum-yum.'

'They don't know you.'

'There's always a relationship,' Cathal said, prising out the cork. 'Look, a confidence trick is like sex. It requires collusion, an element of co-operation, the pleasure heightened by a whiff of guilt.' The cork popped into the air and champagne spurted out. *'Voilà!'*

'So your clients love to be screwed by you,' Iseult jeered, holding out her glass. 'All you're doing is relieving them of their guilt.'

'No pleasure without pain.'

'The Provos will be delighted to hear it.' A wild suspicion side-tracked her. 'Or maybe those bastards are another figment of your imagination.'

'They're real,' Cathal said, wincing. 'Oh yes,' he murmured, 'they're for real.'

The champagne lost its sparkle.

'How long have we got?' Iseult muttered.

'A month,' Cathal said, trowelling goose liver on to his bread. He cocked a mischievous eye. 'Convinced them I could double their money if they hung on until a foreign deal came off.'

Despite herself, Iseult laughed. She soon stopped. She shook her head in helpless reproof – as a mother remonstrates with a child who knows her love will always overcome her anger. 'You can't talk your way out of trouble forever.'

'Who gives a damn about forever?' With a sigh, Cathal stretched out on the grass, a glass of champagne balanced on his chest. Idly, he twined a rope of Iseult's hair around his fingers. 'Talking of sex and deception, I suppose Case must suspect ulterior motives.'

The champagne turned to vinegar in Iseult's mouth. Knowing that Cathal would snap into viciousness if she dropped her guard, she put on her brightest, hardest aspect. 'It was awful. I thought he was going to cry.'

'Delicious,' Cathal said, his chest bobbing with laughter. He sipped his champagne. 'Delicious,' he repeated, and then frowned, as if the drink held an unusual aftertaste. 'Odd, though, why he should continue this quest. But then again, perhaps not so odd when you examine his background. An orphan, no family, a confusing ethnic background. It all adds up to a desperate desire for approval.' He smiled admiringly. 'You've got a slave for life there, sister mine.'

'Don't,' Iseult said. She had just noticed how high and wide the sky was – how receptive.

He took another turn of her hair and pulled her down, began kissing her neck.

'Let's forget Lemonnier,' she whispered, her skin prickling. 'Let's go away.'

'Iseult,' he murmured, his hand unbuttoning her shirt. 'I've been granted a stay of execution, not a vacation. Let's make the most of the moment.'

Iseult watched his long hands enfold her bare breast and imagined cold eyes feasting on her nakedness. 'This isn't right,' she said.

'That's what makes it so perfect.'

She jerked loose. 'I'm talking about Lemonnier. We promised Pat.'

'Divided loyalties,' Cathal murmured. 'Now I really am jealous.' Gently he bit her.

She eyed him with puzzlement. 'You really do hate him, don't you?'

'Personal feelings don't come into it. Quite apart from my vested interest in Lemonnier, the logical place to start looking for Fox is with the last person to see him.'

'Pat's no mug.'

Cathal smiled. 'He's a fool in love.'

The phrase 'love is not mocked' popped into Iseult's mind. Although the sky was clear and fresh, she couldn't rid herself of the impression that the atmosphere had grown heavy, gravid with disapproval. 'You didn't answer my question,' she said, quickly buttoning up her shirt.

'About Case?' Cathal smiled as only he could – a smile that could soften wrath, untie purse-strings, twist heart-strings. 'I hate the bastard from the bottom of my heart.'

His candour humbled Iseult. 'But what if he should find Fox while we're with Lemonnier?'

Cathal sighed and popped an olive into his mouth. 'You're so otherwise, Iseult. You swore blind he didn't stand a chance.'

'But if he does?' Iseult said. Foreboding made her want to wring her hands.

'I dropped off our address in Casablanca. They can pass on any message.'

'And if there is no message? No Fox?'

'All the more reason to cultivate Lemonnier. We're sitting on hash mountain. Who knows? I may be viewing the uplands of a dazzling new career.'

'You don't know what you're letting us in for,' Iseult said, nervously eyeing the gap in the mountains.

'True,' Cathal said. 'But sometimes the pay-off is better if you don't think the situation through.'

They reached Aïn Arba, the town closest to *Le Sanglier Blessé*, just before sundown. The single street was wide and empty, divided by a strip of dust planted with dead shrubs, pre-cast concrete lamp-posts and a few broken gum trees strung with fairy lights. Frayed bunting and stars and crescents dangling on wire contributed to the jaded festive air. It was as if the inhabitants had forgotten to take down the decorations for a celebration in the distant past. Or perhaps they were still waiting for the party to happen.

A one-legged boy turned a cartwheel in front of the car.

'This is a very weird town,' Cathal said.

'It's not in the guide-book,' Iseult said, her gaze moving cautiously from side to side. She squealed. The one-legged urchin had popped up at her window.

'Where's the hotel?' Cathal inquired, keeping going.

Hopping alongside, the boy pointed up the street, and

followed with strenuous bounds as Cathal accelerated away. Defective eyes glinted from doorways and kiosks. They passed some kind of market square, with a café on one side and animal pens on the other, but there was no sign of the hotel. With a steadily failing heart, Iseult scanned the buildings. A line of trucks stood nose to tail in front of a row of lock-ups. They passed the police station. After a few more houses, the town petered out.

They turned and went back. Night had come down. Most of the street-lights remained unlit.

'I'm not staying here,' Iseult said.

'Think of it as the rough before the smooth.'

Cathal stopped near the café. A police jeep was parked outside, a hand poking out of the driver's window, languidly indicating that they should present themselves for inspection.

'Good evening, captain,' Cathal called. 'We're looking for the hotel.'

'No hotel,' the officer said. He was fat and sloppy, his eyes lacquered with suspicion. 'What are you doing in Ain Arba?'

'My sister and I are touring your beautiful country,' Cathal told him.

'Passports,' the policeman demanded, snapping his fingers.

He pored over the documents as if he was trying to crack a code. Iseult waited dry-mouthed.

'Relax,' Cathal whispered. 'Lemonnier's got the place in his pocket.'

Grudgingly, the policeman handed back their passports, then pointed out of town. 'There is a hotel twenty kilometres south.' He cranked up a smile that looked like it had been learned on a course. 'Very nice hotel, very pretty.' The smile stalled. 'But you must be careful of the road. Stop for no one.'

'That settles it,' Cathal said when they were out of earshot. 'I'm not budging.'

Business had picked up at the café. They sat at a table

outside the glass front. All the other customers were inside, clustered under a black-and-white television, listening with open mouths to a sermon delivered by a Muslim cleric.

A boy came out and flicked several comatose flies off the plastic cloth, then plonked down two bowls of thick barley soup. Cathal asked him about the hotel and he pointed to the blind side of the square. At the same moment, the jeep revved up and swung into the street.

'*Yalla*, I take you,' the boy said, the instant their bowls were empty.

He led them to a medium-sized tenement built on a plot of hard-packed earth. One wall had an ominous bulge and was clad with wooden scaffolding. Iseult felt moisture underfoot and made out a large stain, a slow seepage that spread out from the foundations. In the open doorway a desiccated man cowled like a monk stood waiting to receive them. Iseult had the feeling that if he opened his mouth in a smile, dust would trickle out. He deprived them of their passports before showing them upstairs. The light shed by the few bald bulbs had a diseased quality. Several times the proprietor stopped to warn them of missing steps. They had to press back against the wall to let three men pass. One of them looked at Iseult with addled eyes and said something which made the hotelier shriek with anger and shoo him downstairs.

'Smell the kif?' Cathal said, as they turned down a corridor marked off by flimsy blue-painted doors. 'Christ, you could cut it.'

Number 28 was their room – a cell two metres square with grey mattresses and smeared walls.

'No, Cathal,' Iseult said, shrinking back. 'I'd rather sleep in the car.'

'Courage,' Cathal murmured, taking her elbow.

'Is there a bathroom?' Iseult demanded.

'There is a bath-house near the mosque,' their host said. Something akin to a smile ghosted across his face. 'It is for men only.'

'Must be a truck-stop,' Cathal said.

But when Iseult went in search of a lavatory, she glimpsed through a half-open door a woman lying on a bed, and in the short moment that their eyes met, a surprising amount was communicated.

She found the lavatory at the end of the corridor. It was a hole in the floor, blocked and foetid. Gorge heaving, she stumbled back to the room and threw wide the door. 'So it pays not to think things through?' she shouted. 'Well, congratulations. Your incredible lack of foresight has landed me in a brothel.'

Cathal mustered a sickly smile. '*Le patron* wants to know if we'll be taking dinner.'

Iseult snatched his stock of Irish whiskey and drank straight from the bottle.

'We'll eat out and make an early start,' Cathal said.

Back in the café, the TV was showing a dubbed English cops-and-robbers series of the seventies, the men wearing flares and driving Ford Granadas and smoking hell for leather. The audience accorded the action the same respectful attention they had given to the *imam*. A card game had started in one corner.

'Global village,' Cathal said.

'Sheer hell,' Iseult said.

Cathal risked a cautious smile. 'I'm quite enjoying it. It has an endearingly lawless feel.'

Two boys were juggling kebabs on a charcoal grill. The same lad who had served them soup presented them with half a dozen skewers. They were delicious. Iseult saw that the police jeep had reappeared. When she looked again, it had gone, but a short time later it was back. Its behaviour made her edgy; it made her think that trouble was breaking out all over town.

'Do you know *Le Sanglier Blessé*?' Cathal asked the waiter.

The boy backed away, shaking his head to indicate that such matters were not for him to deal with, and disappeared into a back room. Moments later, a burly man in a bad suit came and stood in the doorway. After he had taken their measure, he strolled over and offered his hand with perfunctory civility. 'My name is Mohamed,' he said, touching his heart. 'Welcome.' He straddled a chair at the next table and studied them again, waiting for Cathal to make the first move.

'We wish to visit *Le Sanglier Blessé*.'

'It has been closed many years.'

'But the Count still lives there.'

'The Count?'

'Count Lemonnier.'

'Ah, the Count. He is in Tangiers. I do not know when he will return.'

'But how desolating. We were given an introduction by a friend.'

'A *chasseur*?'

'A business colleague – a man who has often done business with Count Lemonnier.'

Mohamed evaluated the claim from every angle. 'Who is this friend?'

'*Un Anglais*. Digby Fox.'

'Fox?' Mohamed repeated several times in laboured incomprehension. 'I shall ask my friend.' He rose and went away. A skinny man in natty clothes was waiting for him in the doorway, and they both turned and looked before going into the back room together.

'You'll get us arrested,' Iseult whispered.

'It's the only way,' Cathal whispered back.

Several minutes passed. Iseult's heart skipped a beat when the policeman came in, but after giving them a frustrated glare, he moved on to arrest a member of the card school.

Mohamed's natty friend swaggered to their table. He wore a suit like an oil slick and two-tone shoes of blue and grey. His eyes swarmed all over Iseult, his lechery so blatant it felt like physical molestation. 'I love English,' he said. 'English are my friends. English like lof.'

'We're Irish,' Iseult said in a stiff voice.

The natty man frowned. 'You not like lof?'

'No.'

The natty man's frown intensified. 'Beautiful lady, why you not like lof?'

'Lof?'

'Is very good. I like very much. Ha, ha, ha.'

'Oh "laugh",' Iseult said with huge relief. 'Yes, the Irish are great jokers.'

'I also,' the natty man intoned, hand on his heart. He threw back his head. 'Ha, ha, ha,' he howled.

Save us, Iseult prayed.

Tea was brought and the natty man assumed a weird pall of dignity, wielding the pot with the unction of a Chevalier de Tastevin. 'Moroccan whisky,' he said, insisting on clinking greasy glasses with his guests. He drank in silence, his pinkie cocked, his eyes probing Iseult, dwelling on the points of interest. 'Now my friends,' he said after the first glass. 'What do you want?'

Cathal repeated his request.

'Give me one hundred dirhams,' the natty man ordered, making a leisurely review of Iseult's breasts. 'I will phone the hotel.' He reached under the table to receive the money, his hand brushing Iseult's thigh.

'Urgh,' Iseult said when he had gone.

The television was broadcasting the international news. There was more trouble on the West Bank. On a visit to Tunis, the Moroccan King had called for a fresh initiative on the Palestinian problem.

The natty man returned. He elevated his shoulders and let them drop. 'The Count cannot receive you. He is not well.' Once more his eyes infested Iseult, roaming where they had left off.

'How disappointing,' Cathal said. 'I had hoped to discuss a matter of mutual benefit.'

The natty man waved as if dismissing a fly. 'Soon he will be well again – *insh'allah*. Stay in our beautiful town two days, three days and maybe the Count will see you. He is my good friend.'

'Alas, time presses. I have business in Casablanca.'

The natty man leaned right over to view the parts of Iseult hidden by the table. She squirmed and crossed her legs. 'Men are always worrying about business,' he confided. 'They ignore their women and this makes them sad. There is no hurry. This is a very interesting town – very much to see.'

'I'm sure,' she said, revulsion masquerading as polite interest.

The natty man clapped his hands. 'Tomorrow you go to Casa,' he told Cathal. 'I shall look after your beautiful lady until you return.' He bestowed a simper on Iseult. 'Tomorrow I will show you some of our *curiosités naturelles*.'

'Tomorrow we both leave,' Iseult said, finding her voice. 'First thing.'

'It is no problem for me. It will be an honour. You will come to my house and I shall give you a feast.'

'The beautiful lady says no,' Cathal said.

The natty man turned on him, smile thinning. 'Why do you speak like that? Am I not your friend? Do you think I'm a thief?'

'Of course not. But we've already made other arrangements.'

'What arrangements?'

'Mind your own business.'

'Go then,' the natty man said loftily. He stood and walked away muttering. Stopped by an afterthought, he jabbed his finger in warning. 'Do not take the wrong turning, my friends. The road to the Wounded Boar is closed.' His eyes gave Iseult a final contemptuous grope. 'It is not safe.' He walked away, and then noticing the curiosity of the other customers, he threw back his head. 'Ha, ha, ha,' he bayed.

'Get me out of here,' Iseult wailed.

'Shit,' Cathal said. 'I should have called Lemonnier from Tangiers.' He slapped the table. 'Stupid,' he said. 'Amateur.' He fell back against his chair, his eyes glazed with frustration. 'Now what do we do?'

'I don't know about you,' Iseult said, rising. 'But I'm going to drink enough to wipe out all recollection of today.'

In their absence, the hotel had filled up. Kif fumes fogged the corridors, sweetening the smell of sewage. Behind the cardboard-thin walls, men were shouting. Querulous music added to the din. Doors kept slamming. Iseult kept her eyes pointed straight in front. Inside their room, there was no abatement. It was like being inside the entrails of a poisoned beast.

She reached for the whiskey.

'Here,' Cathal said, producing a dirty cloth bag. 'Kinder to the system.' He took out a handful of unprocessed kif.

They shared a giant spliff, sitting opposite each other, knees touching. Gradually Iseult's mind stopped jumping. The dope took the edge off the noise. The room began to seem lighter and bigger and her fears not so overbearing. She thought that sleep might not be beyond her. She lay down fully clothed, trying to shut her mind to the vermin that infested the mattress.

Cathal stood at the small grilled window, smoking another joint. She heard him come and stand over her and she feigned sleep. Next thing, she heard the door handle turn.

'Where the hell do you think you're going?' she demanded, jumping up on to the points of her elbows.

'I forgot to call the hotel in Casa. Also, we're low on gas. There's a filling station down the road.'

'At this time?'

Cathal's expression was evasive. 'I want to get an early start. It's a long drive to Casa.'

'Like hell,' Iseult said. 'You're planning to drive up to the Wounded Boar. It's written all over you.'

'It's worth a try.'

'You heard that man,' Iseult cried.

'There may be another route. It's worth asking.'

'He wasn't talking about driving conditions. He was threatening us.'

'We've come too far.'

'You're damn right we have.'

Cathal slumped on the bed beside her and hung his head. 'Look, Iseult, for me there's no going back. I really went for this one. My credit's all gone.' He straightened up and put on a martyr's smile. 'With you too, I guess.'

'You make it so hard,' she said, her voice tapping a well of sadness. 'Every concession you treat as a surrender.'

He gave her shoulder a quick squeeze and stood up, ready to face the worst alone. 'I'll drop you off at the airport.'

Somehow, Iseult thought, he always left a question mark hanging. 'You're not going up there by yourself,' she said wearily.

He sighed and shrugged.

It would be easy to walk out on him, she thought. Easier than at any time in the past. She had seen his act too many times. He had changed, the charm faded. Or perhaps it was she who had changed. After all, people did, didn't they? 'I'll stick with you this time,' she said. 'After that you can . . .' She met his eyes and resisted the fear she saw gathering there. 'No more, Cathal. No more.'

Humbly he took her face in both hands and kissed her brow. 'Aren't you the brave girl, though?' he murmured, and stood rocking her head against his chest.

'Stupid,' she said, smiling through her tears. 'Stupid and scared.'

'Try and get some sleep,' he told her, stealing out.

But that was out of the question. Her mild high had broken down into agitation. She lay racked on her nerves, trying not to construct a picture from the whimpers and groans that penetrated the walls. For minutes on end she watched the door, tensed for the first slow movement of the handle. Drawing herself into a ball, she wrapped her arms over her head.

Midnight came and Cathal hadn't returned. A sudden, astounding silence prevailed. Iseult needed a pee. Locking the door behind her, she crept along the deserted passage. Unable to face the privy on her floor, she descended to the next landing. In the murky light she saw a girl in white flit into a room.

On her way back upstairs, she heard voices behind her and fled, dashing down the empty corridor, fumbling with the key as the voices came nearer, staring over her shoulder and almost falling into the room when the lock suddenly gave.

Under the trembling filament of the single bulb, three figures gaped at her. A woman lay on the bed, a man humped between her spread thighs, grinning foolishly. Beside the bed stood another man naked from the waist down, his tumescent sex shockingly, almost untenably long. It was the man she had encountered on the stairs when they arrived, now stoned out of his head. He held up his arms and came towards her, his cock stiffening in jerks, his face wearing the pained but rapt smile of a believer who has been vouchsafed a preview of Paradise.

Iseult tore her eyes away and looked at the door. Number 25. She dashed for her own room, ignoring a plaintive cry from behind. The door was unlocked. She flung herself through, slammed it shut and spreadeagled herself against it.

Cathal jumped up from his bed. A curly haired youth was sitting beside him, a copy of *Gentleman's Quarterly* open on his lap.

'There's a man after me,' she sobbed.

The youth acted first, going to the door and peering both ways. Cathal joined him. 'There's nobody there,' he said.

'We're getting out,' Iseult panted, cramming the few things she'd unpacked into her bag.

'This is Hassan,' Cathal said, indicating the youth, who offered an eager-to-please smile and held out his hand.

'Right now,' she shouted, throwing Cathal's bag at him.

14

Any hope of getting clear by daylight was frustrated by the state of the *piste* – the minor of two dirt roads to the Wounded Boar. It was laid on bedrock, and where the ballast had been washed away, the surface was as broken as a dry river bottom. Between potholes, Iseult kept an eye on the dark rear screen, expecting headlights.

With the coming of daylight, her dread of pursuit began to recede. They had reached a relatively flat section between the hills above the town and the ranges that were beginning to take on definition to the north. The land here was littered with black nodular rocks, like crashed meteors, but up ahead the terrain changed character, becoming complex, with white mountain spines standing up above wooded valleys.

Iseult became aware that Cathal was cursing to himself.

'Something wrong with the car,' he muttered. 'It isn't pulling.'

She took a two-handed grip on her seat and prayed. Behind them, the sun pushed over the horizon, blooding a flock of ducks that skimmed a lake to their right. The engine sounded strangled. 'Maybe you ought to change down,' Iseult suggested.

Cathal paid no attention. 'Come on,' he breathed.

'You haven't got the hand-brake on, have you?' Iseult said, suppressing her urge to scream.

Cathal brought the car to a stop, but left the engine running. 'Okay, genius, you have a go.'

They changed places in the dawn. Iseult's fingers were stiff and unfeeling. She revved the engine in neutral. It sounded fine. She selected first and the motor stalled. It churned and churned before coughing into life again. With the lightest touch possible, Iseult fed in the clutch. The engine expired.

For a while they sat there, neither of them daring to put their apprehension into words, then Cathal released the bonnet catch and got out. Iseult followed, shrivelled in the cold. Both peered cluelessly at the engine, Cathal giving this or that component a tentative prod.

'Beats me,' he said. 'It was fine yesterday. Maybe it's got something to do with the altitude.'

'Maybe you filled up with the wrong grade.'

'The bastards must have sold me watered petrol.'

The implications sank in.

'Give it another go.'

While Cathal pumped the throttle, Iseult peered down the road, arms crossed. The starter began to turn less energetically. A reek of petrol filled the air. 'Flooded,' Cathal said. 'We'll have breakfast and try again.'

The ground was ash-black and powdery. No vegetation grew at the water's edge, but there were fish in the lake. Iseult saw rings dimpling the surface.

'You should have let me bring Hassan,' Cathal said, sorting out the remains of yesterday's picnic. 'He'd know what to do.'

'So would Pat,' Iseult snapped back. 'But who needs a mug like him? Not Cathal O'Dwyer. Oh no! He'd rather troll round bath-houses picking up pretty boys.'

'I had to check out the road,' Cathal muttered. 'You never could give me credit for anything.'

'The account's deep in the red, remember.'

Cathal banged down a bottle of mineral water. 'You don't change, do you? All the time we were kids, you always had to be in the right.'

The accusation was so absurd that it robbed Iseult of breath.

'Grandpa, too. Nothing I ever did pleased him. Always comparing his glory days to my pathetic childhood. "When

I was your age," he'd tell me, "I was already a member of an active service unit." On and on he'd go.'

His intensity shook Iseult. 'Is that why you joined Sinn Fein?'

'It was practically forced on me.'

'I told Case he was lucky not to have a family. He couldn't understand.'

'You told him a lot, didn't you?'

They locked eyes. Cathal was the first to break contact. 'He asked me about the great love of your life,' he muttered.

Iseult matched his weary laugh.

'I didn't tell him,' Cathal said, sounding scared. 'I'd never do that.'

She scooped up a handful of the black dust.

Her silence made him falter. 'Would *you*?' he asked timidly.

'Tell Pat about the baby?' Smiling, she let the dust trickle through her fingers.

'I didn't mean that,' he said quickly. He hesitated. 'It's years since you mentioned it.'

'I never think of it,' she said, standing up in one movement and wiping her hands on her jeans. The sky had turned luminous. 'I'm going to wash,' she said.

Silver shapes were breaking the surface, often jumping clear. To Iseult, it seemed as if the fish were trying to escape from something. In a few minutes, the commotion stopped and if any stranger had chanced by he would have sworn there was no life in the depths. Iseult gave her face and hands the quickest of licks.

Cathal was trying to start the car again, draining the battery. The starter motor clicked and whined, clicked and whined. Cathal pounded the steering-wheel and rested his head on his arms.

Iseult looked along the track in both directions. The land was empty. The scale of it filled her with lethargy. 'How far have we come?'

Cathal rubbed his eyes. 'We started at five. It's quarter

past seven now. Say we've covered twenty kilometres. That leaves about fifteen.' He let the calculation float in the air, waiting for Iseult to pick it up.

She shrugged. 'One way or the other, we have to walk, and I'd rather die than spend another night in Ain Arba.'

They took what they considered necessary: the stale and soggy picnic scraps, one and a half litres of Sidi Harazem mineral water in plastic bottles, and a change of clothes which in Iseult's case included the green dress Cathal had given her. Both of them were wearing jeans and cotton jackets. Iseult's flat, thin-soled shoes weren't up to the job, but she had no choice. Cathal carried the provisions in a sporty tote bag.

At the end of the lake they came to an old metal sign warning trespassers not to go further. It was peppered with buckshot. They pretended it was invisible. Now that she had made up her mind, Iseult was determined to see it through.

Once she had found a rhythm, the exercise was quite pleasant. Away from the lake, the way wound up through scattered oaks where birds sang. They weren't the only travellers on the road. Walnutty little men joggled downhill, perched crossways on the rumps of their donkeys. '*Le Sanglier Blessé?*' Cathal called. But the men just wagged their fingers as if deploring a breach of decorum and bobbed out of sight.

Traffic dried up. Walking wasn't so effortless now. Sweat slicked Iseult's back. At this height and in this season the sun wasn't at full strength, but it was relentless, and they walked in the full light of it. They rubbed oil on their exposed skin, took a drink of the now-tepid water and set off again.

On all sides the trees climbed to the crests. Iseult watched an eagle soaring, one wing black, the other gold as it wheeled into the sun and was burned up. The glare was hurtful. Iseult stopped looking at the sky and watched her feet moving beneath her. Already they were blistered. She wouldn't let herself give in.

Hours passed. The sun reached its meridian. The birdsong

had stopped, leaving only the brittle sound of insects. Cathal swung the bag to the ground.

'You said fifteen kilometres,' Iseult complained.

'Can't be far now,' Cathal said, avoiding her eye. 'No need to rush at it. We'll take a break.'

When they had eaten, neither of them was in any hurry to move off. Iseult stretched out between the roots of an ilex. She found herself scratching the backs of her hands and wrists and saw that the skin was inflamed. Her lips were parched. She made herself examine her feet. Both heels were an angry red. She remembered Pat kissing her feet. That had only been a week ago. How extraordinary it all was.

A large lizard waddled from under a nearby rock and raised itself on squat legs. Cathal tossed a piece of cheese in its direction, but it took no notice. It opened a bright red mouth. Iseult watched its lime-green flanks heaving in and out and fell asleep.

A scurrying woke her. She saw the lizard's tail flick into a bush. The cheese had gone. She sat up, feeling faintly sick. Her sunburnt skin itched. Cathal looked at her, and she looked at him, and then they pushed themselves to their feet.

The sun was still high – a magisterial presence under which Iseult quailed. Her hair weighed a ton, the small of her back ached and her feet tortured her. She persuaded herself that the Wounded Boar must be around the next corner. Alright then, the one after that. She rounded the bend and saw, miles away, the road wandering along a hillside, with no end in sight.

Progress became automaton-like. At some point she found herself stationary, unconscious of where she was, and when she looked up she felt as if she was swooning into the sky. It was not a pleasant sensation. Cathal led her to shade and sat her down. 'We'll wait until it gets cooler,' he said.

Iseult asked for the water. She should have drunk more. With a lame smile, Cathal produced the remaining bottle. It was nearly empty. She drank what there was. 'I'd hate to be in a lifeboat with you,' she said without force.

They waited until the sun was well down. But the long stop was a mistake. Iseult's head thumped and cramp had taken hold of her legs. Her skin felt too small for her body. Her mind strayed.

It wasn't true that she never thought about the unborn baby. Hardly a day passed without her recalling those awful weeks – the heart-stopping moment when doubt turned to certainty, the agony of waiting, the day of release, walking back into the house, knowing she had got away with it. Even now, her escape made her dizzy with relief, and yet, and yet . . . She perceived what a burden she still carried. Her psychiatrist hadn't been able to lift it, only rationalize it; her American lover hadn't been able to share it, merely try to push it on to Cathal. A priest then, she thought, almost giggling at the idea.

Cathal was shouting, a wavering silhouette. She hobbled up to him.

Le Sanglier Blessé was grand in its solitude – a long stone house set on a faraway craggy hillside above a forest broken by primitive rock domes. A white track meandered up behind the house. Through a notch in the ridge, Iseult registered the harder blue of the sea.

'The Barbary coast,' Cathal said, and gazed about with satisfaction. 'What a set-up. Miles from anywhere, the Med on your doorstep, Spain a fast boat ride away.'

'And no unwanted callers,' Iseult said, trudging on.

'Hey,' Cathal called after her, 'he's not going to turn us away.'

The road dipped into the forest, and for the first time since leaving the car they walked in shadow. The domed outcrops glowed crimson. Iseult's face, hands and throat were on fire. She felt light-headed and her heart beat with unnatural speed. Cathal had reckoned the last leg would take no more than an hour, but Iseult had to rest every few minutes and the hour stretched to two. By the time they came in sight of the house again, it was only a light in the dark, an outcast star.

Iseult stumbled on something soft and animate that dragged itself away as if it was broken.

'It's alright,' Cathal said. 'It's only a toad.'

'I don't like toads,' she quavered.

Holding on to Cathal's arm, she tried to pick her way. She stopped caring. 'What was that?' she asked dully.

'Only a dog barking,' Cathal said. 'Come on, keep moving.'

He increased pace and it dawned on Iseult that he was scared.

The next bark stopped them in their tracks – a deep-chested baying sounding from on high. They whirled as another dog took up the cry, and swung again as another answered, and another, until it was impossible to separate the howling from the echoes. The stars burned as bright as flares and the crags stood out in hard silhouette, but Iseult couldn't see anything moving. She clutched Cathal. 'They're coming this way,' she whispered.

Cathal's face was blueish, his lips drawn back.

'Cathal, I think it's us they're after,' she whispered. 'That's what the man was warning us about.'

She heard Cathal swallow.

'What are we going to do?' she pleaded.

'We have to find a place to hide,' Cathal said, pulling her off the road.

The hue and cry was much closer. 'Christ, what are we going to do?'

The tumult stopped. She pictured the dogs running through the night.

'Get some stones,' he said, scrabbling on the ground. 'Hurry.'

A snarl sent them blundering into each other. Another spun them. 'They're all around us,' Iseult whispered. Her teeth were chattering.

Cathal fumbled in the bag and pushed something into her hand – a knife.

'I can see one of them,' she said, her voice calm.

It seemed abnormally large and misshapen. The stars struck sparks from its eyes. It padded towards them, then stopped. Other shapes ghosted out of the dark. She could hear them panting.

'They'll tear us to pieces.'

Cathal lunged forward, shouting. The dogs stood their ground. The pack leader showed the whites of its jaws and snarled. Its followers whimpered excitedly, jostling for position. The leader moved forward without haste.

Iseult closed her eyes and began to babble childhood spells.

'Shut up!' Cathal said. 'Listen!'

The dogs were more distinct. They had their heads turned away and they were growling. Iseult heard a busy humming.

Around a bend headlights appeared, turning the dogs' eyes to yellow glass. The pack shifted and snapped. The hum became a roar. The vehicle was approaching fast, taking the humps and potholes in its stride. The dogs were drifting away. The vehicle braked on gravel and doors slammed open. Iseult heard urgent shouts, feet running and then a burst of automatic fire. Bullets flailed through the branches. She was flat on the ground, Cathal half on top of her.

The vehicle was moving forward again, its lights on full beam, blinding her. She crawled backwards, shielding her eyes from the glare. The vehicle crunched to a stop and shapes passed across the lights. In front of her, legs arranged themselves in a wide-apart stance. Under their owner's unseen, unreserved scrutiny, she became aware that she had wet herself. A hand reached down and plucked the knife from her hand. Someone spoke in soft gutturals and another man laughed, tickled by the thought of her trying to hold off a pack of dogs with a piece of five-star cutlery.

The hand reached down again and gently raised her to her feet. Leaning aside, she vomited.

15

On the road up to Belvoir Castle, Dearborn had to slam on the brakes to avoid colliding with a troupe of small gazelles that suddenly appeared, airborne, a few yards in front of the windshield. They exploded past like tumblers, clearing the lane in a single leap. Dearborn swung himself out of the car and scrambled up the cutting, expecting to find that they had vanished as emphatically as they had appeared. But there they were, spring-heeling across a field of thorns, slowing to a dainty trot, bowing their necks to graze. And Dearborn gave an astonished laugh, because these gazelles, the creatures of Solomon, were feeding in a mine-field.

'Israel,' he said, imagining retailing the piquant piece of symbolism to Magda. And then he remembered that his wife and daughter were gone, fled, lost. He squeezed the bridge of his nose, the gazelles forgotten. A week hadn't been long enough to dull the pain.

He also had a medium-intensity hangover from drinking alone. He could have stayed with Jon and Eliana, old friends in Tel Aviv, but he was unable to face another analysis of the marital crack-up – especially since he suspected that the weight of judgement wouldn't come down on his side. Instead, he had driven to Jerusalem, checked into the King David and eaten in a Ukrainian restaurant, getting into a nasty row with the manageress when she insisted on payment in dollars at two-thirds the official exchange rate. What price the children of the dream, Dearborn wondered.

Before getting back into the hired Subaru, he checked the road curving back down the escarpment. It wasn't realistic to believe that the Israelis hadn't marked his arrival, but he had taken pains to leave Jerusalem discreetly, hoping to lose any tail for a few hours. Unfortunately, he had reached Nablus to find it popping with small-arms fire, and an IDF patrol had diverted him on to a back-road. Crossing empty steppe, he had halted by a burnt-out Merkava tank to consult the map, and as he wrestled with the folds, a motorcyclist distorted by heat shimmer came up half a mile behind, stopped for a few seconds, then circled and disappeared back into the haze.

Dearborn drove on. Despite losing time on the detour, it was only ten-thirty when he reached the castle ridge. A breeze sang chords in the wires and dishes of a listening post. Two soldiers guarded the entrance of the facility; if they were expecting him, they took care not to show it. He turned into the castle carpark. The ticket booth was unoccupied, the felafel concession untended, but the site was open. Dearborn crossed the dry moat and entered the ruins.

So far as he could tell, there were two other visitors – a young couple holding hands, with eyes only for each other. He put on his glasses and let his shoulders hang in a professorial droop.

Crusader castles had always fascinated him. He had visited Belvoir before and had no need of a guide-book. He put in fifteen minutes' browsing, then slipped through a breach in the eastern curtain wall.

Zwy Gur, dressed in short-sleeved white shirt and baggy tan slacks, was sitting on the edge of the glacis, his back to the castle, looking across the Rift to the heights of Jordan.

'I appreciate you meeting me like this,' Dearborn said.

Zwy Gur shrugged off the civility but indicated that Dearborn was free to share the view.

Dearborn settled beside him. More than a thousand feet below, water winked liked glasshouses among sub-tropical green. Pelicans were drifting towards the mineral blue of Lake Galilee.

'The Arabs called it the Star of the Winds,' Dearborn said.

' "Built like a falcon's nest among the stars," is how Abu Shama described it.'

Receiving no response, Dearborn edged a glance towards the Israeli. The years hadn't changed him one way or the other. Maybe he was a little fatter, softer under the eyes, but he was still a formidable proposition – squat, bald, a pelt of black fur on his arms, ugly as sin. He was of Iraqi extraction, his family having been airlifted to Israel in Operation Babylon.

Dearborn couldn't claim the bond of friendship. They had met on a formal basis in Beirut, through their shared interest in the Christian militias. Zwy Gur was a senior Shin Bet officer charged with the eradication of PLO fighters who had stayed behind after the main force had been evacuated – unsavoury work.

'I think I was followed from Jerusalem,' Dearborn confessed. 'Your people, I think.'

'We've been following you since you stepped off the plane,' Zwy Gur said, his voice sunk in the lower registers. 'Why did you visit the Arab market in Tel Aviv?'

Dearborn was flustered. 'I lost my way from the airport.'

'You went there to meet someone.'

'Not true. All I saw were rats.'

'Rats?'

'Hundreds of them, thousands. The square was carpeted.'

'Rats breed where there's filth.'

Dearborn gave a short laugh. Nothing changed. 'Do you know the history of Belvoir?'

Zwy Gur did another of his non-committal shrugs.

'You might find it interesting – instructive even.' Dearborn eyed the derelict walls. 'It was built for the Knights Hospitallers, a closed order of warrior-monks pledged to defend the pilgrim roads. It's one of the earliest concentric castles. The inner stronghold was occupied by the Hospitallers; the outer defences were guarded by mercenaries. They only held it for twenty years. It had a fatal weakness, you see. If the perimeter was breached, or if the mercenaries changed sides, the enemy could use the outer walls to hold off a relieving force. The stronghold became a prison. In 1189, the garrison surrendered to Saladin after an eighteen-month siege. It's been empty ever since.'

'Spare me the metaphors,' Zwy Gur said. He turned with intimidating slowness. 'Why is Lova Hazan so important to you?'

Dearborn breathed a covert sigh of relief. So there was a way in. 'He practically died in my arms. A few days later someone tried to murder me. I'm worried it could turn into a habit.'

'Maybe it was us.'

'I considered it, but where's the motive?' Dearborn gave a fatuous laugh. 'Besides, here I am, alive and kicking.'

Zwy Gur's slabby face moved in a sour smile. 'We're not infallible.' He went back to contemplating the view. 'So you've convinced yourself that Hazan's death and the attempt on your life are connected.'

More and more, Dearborn found himself doubting his own feelings. 'That's correct,' he said in a staunch voice.

'So where is it – this connection?'

'It eludes me. Another man was seen in the alley. Maybe he's it.'

'More. Describe him.'

'Moroccan. Tough face. I wasn't paying attention.'

'Perhaps Lova Hazan told you something he shouldn't have?'

This was more encouraging, but Dearborn had nothing to pad it out. 'I beat my brains out on that question for the Moroccans. Hazan said "nine" – the number of his family's house – then something like "Call him".'

'Call who?'

'It was just a sound; he was drowning in his blood.'

'Sure?'

'Sure.'

Zwy Gur slapped his thighs, making up his mind. 'Then I can't help you.'

'If I could only hear Lova Hazan's story, maybe I'd see . . .' Dearborn's voice faltered. Cody was right. This was nothing more than a deluded whim, an attempt to avoid facing up to his real problems. He ought to go home and set about finding a job. Maybe he had enough money to finish the book. The thought took hold. He looked down the Rift, his mind wandering over the march and countermarch of history. Yes, go home and finish his book.

Zwy Gur's slow voice caught him miles away. 'Lova Hazan was a no-good – a parasite. His family, they were decent people, but they found it hard in Israel. They never even learnt to speak Hebrew. His father couldn't find a silversmith's job so he settled on a Moroccan moshav near Beersheba. Hazan was no farmer. He dropped out of school and took a job as a mechanic in Ashqelon, but after a couple of months he was fired for stealing spare parts. He drifted, became a bum, hanging around the beaches in Elat, Netanya – wherever there were foreign tourists to impress. That's how he got into drugs. When he was seventeen he was arrested for raping a German girl at Elat's Club Mediterranean. She refused to give evidence and the charge was dropped.'

A flock of birds sprayed past, migrating to Africa. Zwy Gur's eyes followed them. Dearborn's stomach had tightened.

'Next year he was mobilized into the army. After six months he deserted.' Zwy Gur fanned his palms. 'Now he's dead and you know his story.'

'Hold on,' Dearborn said, waving his arms. 'When? Where? Why?'

'He disappeared in Lebanon in March 'eighty-three. He hasn't been back to Israel since. As for why . . .' Zwy Gur smiled, after a fashion. 'Members of his unit returning on leave were stopped at the border. They were carrying more than a hundred kilos of hashish supplied by Lova Hazan.'

'The Bekaa Valley, right?' Dearborn said, trying to subdue his excitement. 'That's where he must have been stationed.'

'If you say so.'

'So what happened to him? What about all the years since?'

'My responsibility is internal affairs,' Zwy Gur said. 'Lova Hazan hasn't been an internal affair for a long time.'

'But someone must have kept tabs on him.'

'No more questions.'

'The bare bones – that's all I'm asking for. How did he end up in Morocco?'

'That sounded like a question.'

Dearborn tried to get his mind back on the level. 'You could have refused me entry. You could have refused to see me. Instead you show me a glimpse of thigh, then slap my face. I don't get it.'

'I didn't come here to satisfy your curiosity. I came here for answers. You don't have any, so . . .' Zwy Gur rose. 'Your seat is reserved on the seventeen-thirty Paris flight. *Shalom*. Have a good journey.' He squeezed Dearborn's hand briefly and painfully, then began to stride away.

'No,' Dearborn called after him. 'Everything I told Cody and the Moroccans would have been on your desk inside twenty-four hours. There's another reason for putting me through this routine.'

Zwy Gur took a step closer and settled his dark eyes on Dearborn's face. 'You're not a friend of Israel, but you once did me a favour, and I want to give you something back – a warning. Go round interfering like this and it will be only a matter of time before you receive the answer between your shoulder-blades.'

Dearborn's eyes shifted under the Israeli's steady gaze. 'At least it proves Lova Hazan wasn't any common or garden trafficker,' he muttered.

Zwy Gur's face was a fortress. He turned to go.

'If I was sure it was in good hands,' Dearborn said, speaking with care, 'I'd be more than happy to drop it.'

Zwy Gur stopped in the breach. 'You don't have confidence in Cody?'

Dearborn flushed at his betrayal. 'His tour's nearly up. He's keeping his head down until the bell goes. He's leaving it all in Moroccan hands.'

'Colonel Douaz is very capable.'

'You know him?'

Zwy Gur's smile left something to be desired. 'I helped train him. From what I hear, that man will go far.'

'And Cody. Do you hear good things about him?'

'I'll walk you to your car, Doctor.'

Conceding defeat with a sigh, Dearborn climbed up to join him. They set off through the ruins. The young couple he had seen when he arrived were still present. He sensed them fall in behind.

'My sympathies about your wife,' Zwy Gur said.

Dearborn blinked away his surprise. 'Yeah, well, thank you.' He fell into step again. 'You married?'

To his even greater astonishment, Zwy Gur halted, brought out a wallet and showed Case a photo of a conventionally pretty blonde woman and two lovely teenage daughters seated at table in a modest dining-room. 'We married a week after the Six Day War – in Jerusalem.'

'Congratulations. What's the secret?'

'Of what?'

'Keeping the marriage going so long.'

'Keeping love alive,' Zwy Gur said in a chiding tone. 'Love.'

'Okay, love. What's the formula?'

'No formula. You have to water it. It's like a plant in the Negev.'

Dearborn smiled. Zwy Gur's family, he now recalled, had owned a date-palmery on the shores of the Euphrates.

'You find it funny?' Zwy Gur inquired.

'You make it sound like an irrigation project.'

The Israeli obviously didn't find the comparison misplaced. 'My father knew every tree in his palmery,' he said, his gaze fixed on the memory. 'He used to talk to them.' Zwy Gur's eyes rejoined the present. He shrugged. 'Every day I tell Hannah I love her. I surprise her. I show her I'm interested. I never take her for granted. Taking women for granted is fatal.'

'Sounds simple.'

'Simple? Sometimes the effort kills me. But it works and I'm the living proof. Why else would a beautiful woman like Hannah spend her life with a man who looks like a Streicher cartoon?'

'I'll bear it in mind.'

'Also, my other advice.'

'That too,' Dearborn said, meaning it. They had reached the carpark. He held out his hand. 'Don't worry, you've persuaded me to drop it.'

'I didn't say that.'

'Huh?'

'All I did was warn you of the risk.'

'That's good enough for me.'

'In Beirut you had a reputation for playing hunches. Sometimes they paid off.'

'Not the ones that mattered,' Dearborn said, seeing in his mind's eye the Beirut embassy blown apart, the corpses of his friends and colleagues limed with concrete dust, their hair burnt to the skull, their entrails everywhere. He straightened his shoulders. 'I was always a processor of information, never a gatherer. Besides, you were my only lead. I wouldn't know where to go next.'

'It's simple. Follow the money chain.'

'Huh?'

'Lova Hazan had no politics, no allegiances. All his life, greed was his only motive. Greed led to his death.' Zwy Gur opened his palms. 'So – follow the money chain.'

Dearborn frowned, his thoughts scattered. 'It sounds like you already know where it ends?'

'We both do – in a Moroccan alley. But some of the links are missing.'

'If you can't locate them, what chance do I have?'

Zwy Gur paused, weighing his words. 'Perhaps your former colleagues can help.'

As the silence lengthened, Dearborn had the feeling that the horizons were receding all around. He put his hand to his brow and turned on the spot, trying to recover his bearings. He peered at Zwy Gur through spread fingers. 'Are you telling me Lova Hazan was an American agent?' he whispered.

'An asset,' Zwy Gur said. 'Of short duration and limited worth, but an asset.'

Dearborn laughed without humour. 'I should have seen it coming,' he said. He shuddered to think of his narrow escape. 'No thanks,' he said, backing away. 'No thank *you*.'

'First he asks me for help,' Zwy Gur said, addressing the sky, 'then he says forget it.'

'You've got your own people.'

'I told you, Doctor: internal security is where my responsibility lies.'

'I'm talking about the Mossad.'

Zwy Gur didn't answer, but from the way he cocked his head in an expectant expression, Dearborn realized he had stumbled over one root of this affair. The Israeli must be after someone in his own security forces.

Zwy Gur gave a tiny nod. 'Natti,' he called.

The young man left his companion and came forward. They were both slim and dark, with girlish lashes. Dearborn suspected a Yemeni provenance. At a gesture from Zwy Gur, Natti handed over a buff envelope containing a single black and white photograph of a middle-aged, heavily bearded man on the deck of a small cabin cruiser. The subject had been photographed unawares.

'An Israeli?' Dearborn said.

'An American agent,' Zwy Gur said. 'Lova Hazan's case officer, you could say. His name's David Canova. He left the agency about the same time as you.'

'Never heard of him.'

'That's because he worked in Central America. He was an advisor to the El Salvador government and then he went to Panama. He left the service after he was linked to an arms-for-drugs deal arranged on behalf of the Contras.' Zwy Gur opened his hands. 'There, the first link.'

Very dimly, Dearborn saw the direction the chain was

heading and did not like it one bit. 'He left?' he asked. 'Or was pushed?'

'He was allowed to retire with dignity,' Zwy Gur said. 'He set himself up as an arms dealer in Madrid, but business hasn't been good. Call on him. He knows a lot about Lova Hazan.'

'But you've already spoken to him.'

'Not yet. He's very bitter and he drinks too much. When he drinks, he likes to rake over the past. He's like a dog returning to its own dirt. I think you'll have a lot in common.'

'I can't go against my own people,' Dearborn said.

'Believe me, you'll be working *for* them,' Zwy Gur said. 'Believe me.' Gently, he extracted the photo from Dearborn's hand. 'Natti and Esther will look after you until your plane leaves, and they'll be going back to Europe with you. They'll keep you from harm.' He led Dearborn to the Subaru and helped him inside. 'See how it goes,' he said, stooping to peer through the window. 'I'll be in touch from time to time. Trust me.'

Dearborn gave a short laugh. 'My daddy used to tell me: never draw to an inside straight, stay out of land wars in Asia, and if a man asks you to trust him, scoot like a coon.'

Zwy Gur stepped back, hand raised. His massive forearms made Dearborn think of Popeye. 'Try not to draw attention to yourself. No more scenes in restaurants.' He frowned. 'What is it about Israel that makes you act like that.'

'I guess it brings out the worst in human nature,' Dearborn said. He turned the ignition. 'Ironic, really, when you consider that the whole place is a monument to the universal idea of One God.'

'The simplest ideas are the hardest to agree on,' Zwy Gur said. He cast a glance over his shoulder. 'You didn't tell me what happened to the Crusaders here.'

'Saladin let them go. With full military honours.'

Zwy Gur looked back at the ruins, his nose twitching, as if the weathered stones still retained a trace of a human presence. 'Saladin was a Kurd,' he said. 'The Arabs would have cut their throats.'

16

Case made his way south by degrees, lugging a whopping hangover. From Tangiers he took a country bus to Casa, then transferred to a train that took all night to trundle its way to Marrakech. He travelled Economy and slept in fits, immobilized in a wooden compartment with sixteen guest-workers returning home with booty earned at the Renault plant outside Paris. At four he woke feeling hungry. He removed somebody's head from his lap, retrieved his kit, picked his way through the tangle of bodies and consumer durables, and went into the corridor. The buffet was an old man with a tea kettle heated by a tray of coals soldered underneath.

Breakfast done, Case dumped his kit under a window which was only a wooden shutter and settled down. It was like going back to Depot after leave. He took out the copy of Yeats he had bought in London and leafed through the pages, stopping at a line here, a phrase there. The wheels clacked and the wagon creaked and his head began to droop.

Suddenly he was wide awake. He read what was before him on the page.

> *What if I look upon a man*
> *As though on my beloved,*
> *And my blood be cold the while*
> *And my heart unmoved?*
> *Why should he think me cruel*
> *Or that he is betrayed?*
> *I'd have him love the thing that was*
> *Before the world was made.*

It was Iseult's voice he heard. He opened the shutter and stood with his face to the wind. It was still dark, the world unmade.

At break of day he stepped off the train. A white owl wafted down the platform ahead of him and he wondered if it was an omen. Roosters crowed. The air was like milk, the barren hills to the north black velvet trimmed with pink. A mosque's pre-recorded call to prayer was swallowed in its own feedback. In the station yard he bought a paper-cone of French fries, served with hot peppers and a glass of spiced coffee. The street smelt of red dust, oranges and shit. He'd arrived.

Ignoring the offers of a taxi, he set off walking through the French Town. The jacarandas were in blossom on the wide pavements, the blue flowers giving out their own luminescence. The avenues were already filling with traffic. His eyelids itched. Fatigue sharpened his senses; he felt that nothing could escape his vision.

By the time he reached the medina, the sky was whited out with heat. Out of sentiment, he checked in at the hotel which he'd used on his first solo visit to Marrakech; it was a fleapit with a Third Republic façade overlooking a denatured plot of open ground off the Djemaa el-Fna. A boss-eyed porter showed him to a room overlooking a lorry park. From experience, Case knew the trucks started running their engines at about three in the morning. The alternative was a room above an alley where kids were playing soccer. The air-conditioning unit was coated in a fur fabric of dirt, but it sounded as if it worked, and the cockroach in the wash-basin was nothing out of the ordinary. It would do for his purposes. He booked in for three nights, unpacked and within fifteen minutes was back on the street, carrying a bulky parcel.

'You want a guide, mister?' a kid demanded as he crossed the Djemaa el-Fna.

'I've already got one,' Case replied.

He wasn't sure if he had. At this time of year Laschen was probably back in his village.

'You are strange here,' the kid warned as Case plunged into the souk. 'You will be lost.'

He tagged along, his spiel faltering as Case threaded a course through the covered alleys. '*Attention, m'sieur*, this man will cheat you,' he said when Case stopped outside a leather emporium guarded by a black man with venality written all over his pudgy face.

'Laschen,' the fat man shouted, clapping his hands, 'your English *ami* waits for you.'

Crestfallen, the kid watched his prey vanish into the fat man's clutches. 'Give me some money,' he called. 'I am poor, you are rich.'

A small, wizened Berber dressed in yesterday's Western fashions came out from behind a curtain, shook Case's hand and put his own to his lips. 'Hello, gentle,' he said in lacklustre fashion.

His eyes were cloudy, webbed in creases, as if he toiled long hours in poor light, but in fact his eyes were fogged from staring into the sun. Not much more than five-foot tall, with legs like a wishbone, he was as hard as tacks. Case had met him on his first trip into the Atlas. That time, he had arrived during the last fortnight of Ramadan, but though they walked for eight or nine hours each day, in fierce heat and on switchback trails that climbed to more than 3,000 metres, Laschen never allowed anything into his mouth except a pebble to take the edge off his thirst. After the fast ended, Case discovered the Berber habitually got through two packs of Casa Sport a day.

He noticed Laschen sizing up the package in his hand and hefted it apologetically. 'I couldn't manage a television,' he said.

Laschen pursed his lips.

'It's a pressure cooker,' Case explained. 'Anyway,' he added, 'you can't get pictures where you live.'

Laschen took the gift with tepid thanks. Case wondered if he'd done something to offend him.

'I remembered the shoes for your children,' he said.

Behind Laschen's back, fat Moulay sucked in his breath and rolled his eyes.

'I hope your family are well and happy,' Case said, wondering why fat Moulay was grimacing. 'Is something wrong?' he demanded.

Moulay grabbed his elbow and led him away, his face settling in sombre folds. Laschen went and stood at the shop entrance.

'His family is *mort*,' Moulay murmured. 'All *mort*.'

'Dead? Oh no!'

'Ssh, it is better if he does not think of it. It makes him mad.' Moulay moved closer. 'His house fell down.'

'Christ, how?'

The fat man sneaked a moist glance at Laschen. 'There is a curse.'

'What curse?'

Moulay put his mouth to Case's ear. He was enjoying himself immensely. 'Many years ago, Laschen did a bad thing in his village. Now the *djinns* have taken his family to punish him. It is sad. This is why he is mad.' He stepped back, finger to his lips.

'Bollocks,' Case said. Ignoring Moulay's mouthings, he went over to Laschen, took his elbow and hauled him outside. 'Come on kidder, let's go get a kebab.'

Walking through the lanes, Case fell into thoughtful silence. What Moulay said had to be cobblers, but there was definitely something a bit iffy about Laschen. Case remembered how the men in his village stared at him without speaking, the women muttering with their hands in front of their mouths. Another thing: in most of the Berber houses Case had stayed in, his arrival attracted an influx of curious locals, but he couldn't remember anyone visiting Laschen's home.

They went to a working-man's café on the edge of the medina and ordered salad and *quaah* – kebabs with alternating pieces of meat and fat.

'Did the eagles we found breed this year?' Case asked.

'A shepherd ate the babies,' Laschen said.

202

Case wasn't shocked. Birds of prey had a hard time in Morocco.

'Have you been hunting?'

'Hunting is forbidden since they started building the *barrage*.'

Clearly, a lot had happened since Case's last visit. '*Barrage* – that's a dam, isn't it? Where?'

'At the bottom of the valley. Next spring all the villages south of Talate will disappear.'

The news saddened Case. He felt proprietorial about that valley. 'I'd like to take a last look,' he said.

'Tomorrow I take you.'

'First I have to look for a person – an Englishman who came to Morocco about two weeks ago. We arranged to meet in Marrakech, but he didn't tell me where he was staying. He was going to call me, but he hasn't. I'm worried something may have happened to him.'

'The police will tell you.'

'I've forgotten his name,' Case said. '*Je suis* stupid.'

Laschen didn't contradict him.

'It's very important that I find him,' Case said.

Laschen hunched one shoulder. 'Ask the police.'

'I'd rather not. You know what they're like.'

The salads arrived. Case scored the table-cloth with his thumbnail. 'Did you hear of any trouble involving a foreigner – an accident, *peut-être*?'

Slowly Laschen shook his head, his expression one of guarded puzzlement.

Case picked at his salad. It was diced very small in the Moroccan fashion. 'I was hoping you could help,' he said.

'I am not from this city,' Laschen said, eyes down, chewing fast.

'All I want is for you to ask around in the hotels, cafés, car-hire offices. Someone must have seen him.'

'I am very busy,' Laschen said, his eyes eluding Case's.

'I'll pay you.'

'I am very busy,' Laschen repeated. He was gobbling the last mouthfuls of his meal as if he couldn't wait to get away. 'I must go. Moulay will be angry.' He stood up. 'Goodbye, gentle.'

'Hang about,' Case said, also rising. 'What's the big hurry? A few minutes ago you were offering to take me into the mountains.'

'That is not what you're asking.'

'Okay, just tell me what's wrong.'

Laschen paused. He glanced at the other diners, then came back to the table. 'The man you want to meet. Is he a Zionist?'

Case stopped chewing. He, too, made a covert inspection of the other customers. 'No,' he said, 'the man I am looking for is a Christian – a Nazarene. Who's the Zionist?'

'I do not know.'

'Then why mention him?'

Laschen's eyes shifted doorward.

'Here,' Case said, taking out Fox's photo. 'This is the man I'm interested in.'

'Excuse me, I do not know him,' Laschen said, ignoring the picture. He walked out.

The Berber was all the plan Case had. He ran after him, catching up on the other side of the street. 'Wait,' he called.

Laschen kept going. Case fell into step. 'You always wanted to go to Amsterdam. How much money do you need to arrange a passport?'

'*Beaucoup*.'

'Well,' Case said, holding out the photo, 'you find Fox and *beaucoup* is what I'll give you.'

Laschen wavered. He looked up and down the street, then took the photo. He frowned. 'This is not the Zionist?'

'I already told you. Perhaps if you told me about this Zionist, I'd understand what's bothering you.'

Laschen pointed into an alley. 'He was murdered two weeks ago, in the Mellah.'

After parting from Laschen, Case visited a local barber who sang Bob Marley songs in tribute to his dreadlocks as he sheared them off. 'Now people will think you have been to Mecca,' the barber told him, holding up a tarnished mirror so that Case could see the incarnation of his old self – highly trained skinhead and government-licensed bovver boy.

He killed the afternoon watching a pair of lanner falcons that had taken up winter residence on the Koutoubia tower. When shadows began to slant, he strolled up the Avenue Mohamed V to call on the Waltham Forest Fishing Club in their four-star concrete blockhouse.

Low and team were at the poolside, and Case came up on them unobserved.

There was something defiantly, almost nobly Brit about the little gang – Low in split-new jeans and no shirt, a scrub of hair across his peeling shoulders, poring over the sports section of an imported tabloid; Fatso with a bulge of blubber over his Union Jack swimming trunks, chatting up a pair of dolly birds on a break from the typing pool; the man-mountain McGrory basting his pecs, his tattoos telling an epic tale of love and war and fabulous beasts, his dick curled like a snail in the briefest of cozzies; Besant lying flat out on a lounger like a blanched stalk of asparagus.

'Nobody likes us,' Case murmured to himself. 'We don't care.'

'Oi-oi, here comes low-life,' Fatso said. 'Who let you through the door?'

Low looked up, no give or take in his expression. 'Where the fuck have you been? We've been dwelling here two days.'

'Tangiers. I had a couple of things to sort.'

'Got anything?' Besant asked worriedly.

'Not a whisper,' Case said. Until that moment he had had every intention of sharing the news about the Israeli.

'Well you'd better get busy, hadn't you?'

'I'll need to tap you for some more money.'

'Don't tell me you've done the last lot.'

'I told you he was at it,' Besant said with morose satisfaction.

'It's for a Berber who's helping me.'

Reluctantly, Low peeled off some notes from a wad. 'Here's a ton. Tell your nark not to spend it all in the same shop. There's no more when that's gone.'

'I promised him a thousand if he came up with Fox.'

Low's head jerked. 'That was a bit previous,' he said, his tone dangerously quiet.

'He's following up a lead on an Israeli who was in town at about the right time.'

Alerted by Case's hurried delivery, Low let his stare dwell, probing for flaws in the claim. Eventually, he grunted acceptance. 'So long as you remember it's coming out of your bunce.'

Case nodded and made to withdraw.

'Where are you skiving off to?' Low demanded.

'Catch up on my sleep.'

'Not on my time, you're not.'

Case abandoned his retreat and perched himself on the edge of a lounger.

'You disappoint me, son,' Low said after a reflective interval. 'All that patter about knowing your way around Morocco, and when it comes to producing a result – zilch. Fortunately,' he continued primly, 'some of us have not been idle.'

Case's baffled stare came to rest on Fatso's smirk.

'While you were poncing about in Tangiers,' he said, 'we were putting Fox's mugshot about. Last night, we had a nibble. This geezer shows up, says he might be able to point us in the right direction.'

Case's eyes switched left to Low, who poured a bottle of lager, drank and wiped the rim of froth from his mouth. 'A plod,' he said.

'A policeman?'

'Start at the bottom and work your way down, Pat.'

Case blew a vexed sigh. Twelve hours into the hunt and they were in the public eye.

'What's your nause, Pat?'

'He's pissed off that we're first out of the trap,' Fatso said.

'First into it, more like.'

'Give me some respect,' Low said, his tone edged in warning.

Case took a few breaths to get back on even keel. The harm was done now. All he could hope for was to stay clear long enough to follow his own line. 'How can this bloke help?' he asked.

'Says he'll run Fox through the computer.'

'He won't be using his own name. He's got a dozen passports.'

'We know roughly when he docked in Morocco, and Shirley said he probably went through Casablanca. That shortens the list of runners.'

'Two days in Marrakech and the police toss Fox at you. I don't believe it.'

'Stand on me,' Low assured him. 'This geezer's kosher – just another pig hoping to stick his nose in the trough.'

'On what terms?'

'Negotiable – strictly according to results.'

Case shook his head. 'He can't be for real.'

'See for yourself,' Low said. 'You've got a meet with him this evening in – gracious me, looks like you'll have to miss the cocktail hour.' He clicked his fingers. 'Roy, where's that map?' Low prodded the *carte du ville*. 'Here we are – nice quiet crossroads in the palm grove.'

'No one knows I'm after Fox,' Case said. 'I'd prefer to keep it that way.'

'Diddums,' Fatso jeered.

Case rounded on him. 'If you believe a policeman is going to risk his job without demanding a bunch of readies up front, you're softer than I thought.'

'The boy's got a point,' Besant intoned, breaking the lengthy pause.

Low stropped his thumbnail on his chin. 'Alright, Mac. You'd better take yourself along, make your presence felt.'

'What's the collective name for stockings, socks and tights?' McGrory asked.

'Search me,' Case said, watching the crossroads.

He and the big man had established an OP in an abandoned construction project outside the old city walls. The crossroads looked as wide as an airstrip, pale between the walls of darkening palms. No traffic turned their way, for the road ran out, unfinished, a couple of hundred yards to their left, but the occasional home-goer turned in the opposite direction, where there was a distant swarm of traffic at the next intersection. The contrast made Case feel as if they had stepped across a divide.

'Hosiery,' McGrory said. 'Okay, try this one. A stupid, clumsy person? Three letters.'

'Don't tempt me,' Case said. Behind the building the medieval wall was rose-pink in the declining light.

'Oaf,' McGrory said. 'Right, which Verdi opera was composed for the opening of the Suez Canal?'

'The Magic Flute?'

'Aida,' McGrory said, pronouncing it 'Ada'. 'The Flute was Mozart, you dull git.'

Case blinked, then did a slow pan over the trees. The symmetry of the plantation was hard work on the eye, making it impossible to anticipate which direction trouble might come from. A moped buzzed round the corner – two up, young women, their robes ballooning. Case watched until they slipped into the grain of distance. The sky was a navy curve. In half an hour it would be dark.

Keeping one eye on the approaches, Case turned to McGrory. He nodded at the magazine. 'What's the addiction?'

'Big prizes to be won.'

'Yeah?'

'Last month I scooped the pot – a hundred and fifty nicker.'

'Get away.'

McGrory inflated alarmingly.

'I mean,' Case said with haste, 'I'm impressed.'

The big man was mollified. 'What do you think my IQ is? Go on, guess.'

'Haven't a clue.'

'Go on,' McGrory said, growing truculent.

'More than a hundred?' Case ventured, ready to amend his estimate at the first warning sign.

'A hundred and forty-five. Good enough to join Mensa.'

'You're kidding.'

'You calling me a liar, pal?'

'No way,' Case declared.

'No one calls me a liar,' McGrory said.

'Hey, what's that?' Case said, pointing at the far side of the crossroads.

The light had fallen to the level where shadows walked, but there was someone there – more than one, drifting out of the secretive trees. Three women, veiled from top to toe. They stood by the roadside, waiting in a surreal limbo. A car approached with menacing slowness, and stopped. A man got out and followed one of the women back into the trees. The other two stayed by the crossroads.

'Tarts,' Case said.

'I don't think much of your one,' McGrory said. He went back to his quiz book. Doves settled into the trees. A few stars prickled high up. The prostitutes had withdrawn.

'What is the official verbatim report of the proceedings in Parliament?' McGrory asked.

'Give it a rest.'

'Nervous?'

In fact Case's nerves were quiet, his mind empty. 'It reminds me of waiting for a contact in Armagh.'

'There was no hanging about in the Falklands. The Argies gave you as much contact as you could handle.'

Case temporarily abandoned his watch. 'You were there?' he asked.

McGrory pulled up the sleeve of his T-shirt and invited Case to admire the scene – an ink study of soldiers storming a hill. 'Tumbledown,' he said. He tapped a detail showing a hulking warrior rending an enemy limb from limb.

'You?'

'No rules of engagement on Tumbledown,' McGrory said. 'No fucking yellow cards.' He twisted his arm so that he could bring it under his tender regard. 'You ever kill a man?'

'Car coming,' Case said.

A mustard-coloured taxi drew up by the crossroads, dropped its passenger and drove away under sidelights. The women glided forth.

'Another punter,' McGrory said. 'Hey, how about giving them one when this is over? Go halvies.'

'A full dose for half-price isn't much of a bargain,' Case said. He tensed. 'Here, he's heading this way.'

Without a glance either side, the man walked over and halted twenty yards off.

'That's him,' McGrory said.

Case stepped from the doorway. The man tried out a couple of smiles before deciding on one that fitted. He wore an imitation tweed jacket and the uppers of his shoes were parting company from the soles, but the moustached, bully's face was a dead giveaway. A policeman, sure enough.

'Who are you?' he demanded of Case, dismissing McGrory with an awed glance.

'Friend of Mr Low.'

'Your name.'

'Arthur Scargill.'

'Passport, please.'

'Left it at the hotel.'

'What hotel, please?'

'The Mamounia.'

The man showed his teeth in derision.

'If you've got nothing to give us, we'll be off,' Case said.

'I have found your friend Monsieur Fox.'

Case hadn't expected anything else. 'What name is he using?'

The man seemed to have difficulty understanding the question. 'He is staying in a house by the sea. Here he is,' he said, unfolding a section of map covering the Atlantic coast. 'Take it. I have marked the house. From Marrakech it is three hours.'

'Let me give you some money,' Case said, offering his latest instalment from Low.

'No, no,' the man said, backing off as if Case had turned the evil eye on him. 'Tomorrow, after you have found your friend, I shall come to see you.'

'Go on,' Case said, holding out the notes as if he was luring a recalcitrant hawk.

The man flicked his tongue over his lips. He looked all around, then took Case's arm and escorted him into the building, where he took the money with humility. 'A little *cadeau*, you understand,' he murmured, making it clear that this wasn't the pay-off. 'I shall visit you tomorrow evening.'

'That'll be nice.'

'*À demain.*'

'Ta-ra.'

It was dark, the road silver between the black palms. The taxi had circled back and was waiting to pick up the man. Case watched its tail-lights dwindle until they merged with all the other lights criss-crossing the faraway intersection. The policeman was clearly running along with someone else's programme, but until Laschen came up with another line, it was worth joining the pack. Case had the feeling that a course had been plotted, and that whatever twists he made, he would end up at the same place in the long run.

17

Back in town, Case and McGrory went to deliver the news to Low. He was alone, taking a shower. Over the back of a chair hung a white tuxedo, frilled shirt and bow tie. He emerged in a shortie silk Paisley dressing-gown, smelling like a cottage garden. He stooped in front of the dressing-table and combed his hair – the robber baron holding audience over his toilet.

'Did he show?'

'On the nail,' McGrory said.

'And?' Low said, establishing eye contact via the mirror.

'Piece of piss. He even gave us an address.'

Low swivelled. 'Stroll on,' he marvelled. 'His actual last-known.' In his delight he broke into a sparring routine with McGrory, performing a quick run on the spot, a few fast jabs, a duck to the left and a dive to the right, finishing with a short hook pulled an inch from the big man's jaw. He broke away, panting, and nodded in Case's direction. 'So what's giving *him* the hump?'

'It's a set-up,' Case said. 'Has to be.'

Low put his playful manner away. 'I'll be the judge,' he said. 'Just give me the location.'

Case produced the map and pointed. 'Miles from anywhere,' he said. 'I know the area. It's dead lonely.'

'Good place to hide up,' Low observed.

'For whoever will be sat there waiting for us.'

Low breathed through his nose. 'I'm getting a bit weary of your style,' he said. 'Barry's right. You've got no bottle for this kind of work.'

'I'm an expert in this line of work,' Case said.

'Ask yourself something,' Low told him, reining in his temper. 'Why would the man waste our time? Deliver Fox and he's on a nice little earner, but no body, no dosh.'

Case maintained his sceptical silence.

Low nudged his chin doorward. 'Go get yourself a drink,' he muttered to McGrory. 'You done well.'

When the big man had left, Low sat at the dressing-table and examined his reflection. 'I must be going soft,' he said. 'Five years ago, if a casual had argued the toss like you, I'd have given him a smacking he'd never forget.' He shook his head in wonderment at the new image. 'Pat, you are causing me serious rickets.'

Case decided he'd better get it over with. 'Fox's Israeli partner was murdered here a fortnight ago.'

Low rose up, stumbling against his chair.

'I was going to tell you this afternoon, but I didn't want to scare Roy off.'

'That is fucking marvellous,' Low said.

As he advanced, Case held his ground and braced himself. Even so, the feint left him for cold. He parried the jab into the solar plexus but missed the left that caught him smack in the mouth. Low hit him again as he bounced off the wall, and he went down. Low stood over him, his dressing-gown adrift, reached down, hauled him upright with one hand and swung him against the wall. 'Tell me now,' he whispered, fist raised.

'It's only rumours,' Case mumbled through split lips, 'but the locals are saying he was an Israeli spy. He got into a brawl and a Berber knifed him.'

Low let go of Case. He went over to a cabinet and poured a glass of brandy. He drank it in one and closed his eyes, swaying slightly, breathing like a horse. 'Is Fox in the frame?'

'No. The word in the caffs is that an American was picked up on the scene. There's been nothing in the papers, but Laschen says he's an engineer working on a dam in the Atlas. The funny thing is, a few days ago someone tried to kill him, too.' Case broke off and dabbed his mouth with the back of his hand. 'Don't ask me what it means.'

Low shook his head, trying to settle the news into some semblance of order. 'You mention this to the policeman?' he said at last.

'No need to tell him what he already knows.'

Low began to stalk round the room.

'I handed over the hundred you gave me,' Case told him. 'At first he wouldn't take it, but greed got the better. It shows he's not working on his own initiative.'

Low stopped off to replenish his drink. He looked punchy and out of shape, no longer threatening. In an access of rage he kicked his bedside chair over. 'What the fuck is occurring?' he demanded.

'You could try asking Saad.'

'Rafiq? He's a fucking playboy.'

'Who works with Valentine.'

'Shirley does his accounts. Come on, Pat, you're winding me up.'

Case sat down on the bed, his legs rubbery. 'What's his background?'

'Pure gold. He legged it out of Beirut with the family fortune. Shirley brought him along to my club about a year ago. He's been a regular ever since. He's a sex maniac, changes girls like I change shirts. Remember Chelsea? That's his flavour of the month.'

'Fox's dope deal cost a couple of million. You put up a quarter, a friend of Valentine's chipped in a couple of hundred grand. That leaves more than a million unaccounted for.'

'No, no,' Low said, 'I saw Rafiq in Scotland, remember. If he'd just watched a million go down the tube, he'd have shown his displeasure. But not a murmur. Sweet as light.'

'Before you rolled up, Saad and Valentine spent two days phoning Spain. He wasn't so happy then.'

Low started to disagree before puzzlement, then anger got the upper hand. His face took on the primitive set that meant trouble. He made his way to the phone, dialled reception and demanded a London number. Then he righted the capsized chair and slumped on it. He looked up, eyes haggard. 'You kill me, Hard Case, you really do.' He massaged his nose with the heel of his hand. 'If Rafiq's crossed me,' he said slowly, 'he's history.' He smashed his fist into the wall. 'I earned that money,' he shouted. 'That was my pension scheme.'

Case caressed the swelling on his cheek where Low's second punch had made contact. 'What was it – a bank robbery?'

Low's glare faded out in a tired smile. 'Security blag in Harrow,' he said. He stretched and yawned. 'There's me, Roy, a couple of faces from Edmonton and three drivers. It goes like clockwork. We catch the men with the bags coming out of this factory and steam in. Bang! Only this guard doesn't know when to take a count, does he? I mean, ask yourself, Pat: here's this geezer on a take-home of less than a grand, plus luncheon vouchers, and he's up against three men with shooters. So what does he do? He keeps coming. We leg it over this footbridge, but he's still with us on the other side.' Low stared with vacant eyes and spread his hands. 'Roy gets carried away.'

'He killed him?'

'Hero, the papers call him. Fucking lunatic more like.' Heavily, Low poured himself another brandy. 'We're looking at life, and with my form I mean twenty, twenty-five.' Low banged the bottle down. 'And after all that, some fucking nonce whose old man used to be a bishop walks away with our hard-earned.'

'We don't know that,' Case pointed out.

The phone shattered Low's outrage. He snatched it. 'June?' he said. 'Put Derek on, will you. Yeah, we're having a super time. Wish you were here.' He waited for Derek to be summoned. 'Derek? No I'm fucking not. You wouldn't believe the rickets we've encountered. Now look. Rafiq Saad – yeah, golden-bollocks, lives up on the Bishop's Avenue with all the other millionaire towel-heads. I want him sussed, and sussed proper. Start with his girls; that should keep you busy. No, you berk, I'm not interested in his disgusting habits. I'm not putting the black on him; it's his business connections that interest me. Yeah, I know he's a valuable client.' Low's knuckles whitened. 'Do it, Derek.'

Low nodded at whatever emollient noises Derek made in response. 'Get a pair of eyes on him for the next two weeks. I want to know where he goes, who he meets.'

'Make that four,' Case said.

Low pulled a face, but didn't argue. 'Better make that a month, but take it easy – no climbing over his gaff. Bishop's Avenue is crawling with diplomatic protection.' Low's tone dropped. 'The next part might be delicate,' he said. 'Remember Mellor, the DI who was so helpful when we had that trouble with the club in Archway. Yeah, that's the one. Ask him to pull Rafiq's sheet, would you.'

Derek said something.

'A monkey might not be enough,' Low told him. 'It'll probably mean a visit to Special Branch, so use your commo.' Low waited. 'No, I do not know what nasties to expect. And no, I do not want you putting any questions to Rafiq personally. I'm saving the pleasure.'

Derek said a few more things. Low began to wind down. 'Oh, and Derek,' he said in conclusion, 'get hold of George. Ask him to organize new passports and shoot down here in his motorhome. And see if Olly's available, will you? That's right, things are as bad as that. See you.'

'What next?' Case asked when Low replaced the phone.

With no pretence of modesty, Low peeled off his dressing-gown. 'Rent a decent set of wheels,' he said, pulling on his pants. 'Big enough for five, but nothing flash. Then get yourself back here and we'll firm up our plans.'

'I'm skint again,' Case reminded him.

Low gave a long-suffering sigh. 'This trip is knocking lumps out of my cash flow,' he said, unbelting another hundred. 'If Fox isn't in that beach hut, it's going to be spam for Christmas.'

'You want me to take a look?'

'Appreciate it,' Low said, 'but this is a team effort.'

'They'll be waiting for us.'

Low paused. 'You could be right.' He buttoned up his shirt. 'In fact, bet on it. But there are times in life when you just have to go in on front.' He sniffed his armpits, didn't like the outcome, and sprayed deodorant. He shrugged himself into his tux. 'Here,' he said, looping the bow tie round his neck, 'give me an assist.'

'What's the big occasion?'

'Thought we'd do the Casino.'

'Rob it?'

Low laughed as if it was the finest jest in the world. 'It may come to that.' His laughter stopped. He lowered his eyes. 'Sorry I had to get physical, Pat. No hard feelings?'

'No,' Case said, grappling with the tie.

Low touched him under the eye. 'You'll have a right shiner.'

'I've had worse,' Case muttered.

Low admired his fist and sucked the knuckles. 'Used to be a bit useful,' he said. 'Even got an offer to turn pro.' He stepped back, shot his cuffs, and inspected himself in the mirror. 'What do you think?'

'Very smart.'

Low turned his attention on Case and found him wanting. 'You'd better clean up before showing yourself on the street.'

Case went into the bathroom and washed his face. Low hovered in the doorway.

'I had a kid who'd be about your age,' he said. 'Silly sod wrapped himself round a Nissan Cherry two days after his eighteenth birthday. His mother's never been the same since – in and out of Friern Barnet.'

Case judged it unwise to comment.

'You did right not to tell Roy,' Low said. 'His nerves haven't been too clever since . . . well, Pat, my mouth ran away with me there. You never heard nothing. One of these days I'll tell you my biography. What a story. I should be a writer.'

217

Case gargled and spat blood. One of his teeth was loose.

'You go your own way,' Low told him. 'I like that. I was the same at your age. Never could get on with the law.' He adjusted the angle of his bow tie. 'Would you believe I'm Jewish?' he said. 'Not one of your Stamford Hill frummers or your Golders Green estate agents. My old man was a horse dealer. The only horse dealer in the City of London. What a character. Christ, I could tell you a story. I should write a book.' He handed a towel to Case. 'When you've fixed the motor,' he said, as Case patted his face dry, 'get yourself suited up and join us at the Casino. They do a lovely buffet.'

'Too busy,' Case said.

'Where are you dossing?'

'A place in the centre. It's cheap.'

'I'll get you a room here.'

'Out of my class.'

'Don't make me laugh. It's a demolition job. Look at those cracks.'

'I don't want to miss Laschen,' Case said.

He began to manoeuvre himself out, but Low detained him.

'Pat,' he said, a smile frozen on his face. 'I like you, but I won't let it get in the way of business. Know what I mean?'

'Yes, chief.'

Low cupped his chin in his hand. He was smiling in a fatherly way. 'Consider yourself on a yellow card. Understand?'

'Yes, chief.'

'Because the next time, it won't be a pop in the face.'

'No, chief.'

'I hope so, my son,' Low said, and ran his finger with the big onyx ring down Case's cheek. 'Act the cunt again,' he murmured, 'and I'll give you a right fucking.'

First, Case went to the Avis office in Gueliz and rented a Peugeot 505 estate with three rows of seats. He said he wanted it for a week and paid the deposit with traveller's cheques. Then he drove to the medina, parked the Peugeot outside his hotel, took a taxi to a back-street hire firm and rented for cash a Renault 4 which he left on a wasteland parking lot after tipping an old watchman ten dirhams to keep an eye on it. He walked back through the Djemaa el-Fna, through the story-tellers and jugglers, but people pestered him for money and he didn't stay long. In the market he found a woman selling poultry and domestic pigeons and on impulse he bought a white dove. In his hotel room he cut the toe-end off a sock, threaded draw tapes around both ends, and put the dove into it. He placed the dove inside his wardrobe and sewed twenty nylon nooses on a cotton harness. It was three by the time he went to bed, but he was up in time to see the light spreading over the roof-tops. At seven he drove the Peugeot to the hotel, and by eight the whole team was on the road.

Low insisted on driving. He was in high spirits. 'You missed a cracker of an evening,' he said. 'Roy did a burster on the roulette. Three hundred quid he walked off with.'

Besant, wearing a baby-blue safari suit, was wedged up against a hungover Fatso, who had outfitted himself in acid-coloured casuals with all the labels displayed on the outside. McGrory fell asleep soon after they left Marrakech and snored in the back seat by himself.

The road ran straight as a piece of string across a yellow-grey plain. The Atlas was a dim presence accompanying them to the south. The sky threatened rain.

'Happy?' Low inquired, beaming at his passengers.

Besant's stomach gurgled.

Low winked at Case as if they shared secrets. 'By the way,' he said airily, 'I've asked Olly to start warming up.'

Besant and Fatso exchanged looks. 'Whose card have you marked?' Fatso asked.

'Just a precaution,' Low said.

'Is that necessary?' Besant asked.

'Can't be too careful, Roy. Can't be too careful.'

That was the third time Case had heard the name. 'Who's Olly?' he asked.

'Olly's wicked,' Fatso said. 'Olly is the *business*.'

'What sort of business?'

Low chuckled at Case's naivety. 'It's like what we was talking about last night,' he explained. 'If a geezer's bent, you call on Olly to straighten him.'

'But to look at – nuffink,' Fatso said. 'Tiny little geezer with glasses. Lives with mum.'

'Remember how he chastised Mad John from Islington?' Low asked. He shuddered. ''Orrible.'

They staged a short silence for Mad John from Islington. McGrory slumbered noisily. Out on the threadbare plain, figures trudged between isolated farms hedged with thorn.

'Did you hear about Olly's bird?' Fatso asked. 'Sylvie her name was, worked part-time for the DHSS, used to perform tricks on her afternoons off. "Caribbean Wild Orchid" the card in the newsagent said. What a dog. Tits like a retread.'

'Don't let Olly catch you rubbishing her,' Low said. 'Olly's a romantic,' he explained to Case. 'Flowers, candlelit dinners, requests on the Jimmy Young show – the works. Old-fashioned, that's Olly. Anyway,' Low said to Fatso, 'what's the story on Sylvie or whatever her name is?'

'Was. She's only gone and topped herself, hasn't she?'

'Get off.'

'My life. She took an overdose and jumped into the Grand Union.'

'Why would she do a thing like that?'

'Love. Olly gave her the elbow for a traffic warden from Walthamstow.'

Low tut-tutted. 'Daft cow.'

'She was religious, too – belonged to one of them fundamental churches in Hackney.'

'A lot of your woollies are, Barry. Frankly, when I see them all flashed up for church, I think: call them what you like, but heathen is definitely one thing they're not.'

'She left a suicide note on her Ansaphone,' Fatso said. 'Signed off with a hymn.'

Low shook his head. 'Ladies, bless 'em. But what can you do? You can't live with them; you can't do without them. Am I right, Pat?'

'I suppose so.'

Low sent him a swift glance. 'You got a girlfriend, Hard Case?'

'Sort of.'

'You rascal. I bet you pull the birds something rotten.'

In the back, McGrory juddered under the strain of snoring and heaved himself into a different position.

'I don't see why you need Olly when we've got a one-man task force on board,' Case said.

For a moment everyone stared, then Low spluttered into laughter. 'Oh dear oh dear,' he said. 'Big Mac's been telling whoppers.'

'He told me he'd seen action in the Falklands,' Case said.

'Maybe the Falkland Arms in Kentish Town at chucking-out time,' Fatso said. 'That's the closest Mac's been to the South Atlantic.'

'You mean he wasn't in the army.'

'For about three days. As a former squaddy yourself,' Low said, 'you will appreciate that it helps if you can tell left from right.'

Case surveyed the sleeping hulk. His copy of the *Puzzler* was rolled in one hand. 'He told me he was a member of Mensa.'

'Mencap, more like,' Fatso said. 'A Ford Fiesta's got more IQ.'

'But he knew all the answers to . . .'

'So he fucking should. He looks them up and learns them by heart.' Fatso tapped his head.

'He got angry when I . . .'

'I should have warned you,' Low said. 'He doesn't like to be contradicted.'

The countryside changed nature, growing hillier, greener. They crested a ridge and Case saw the Atlantic. McGrory woke up. 'I'm hungry,' he said.

'Very tasty,' Low said, wiping his mouth. He cast an approving eye over the quayside. 'Very picture postcard. Reminds me of the Algarve.'

Case had directed them into Essaouira and introduced them to grilled sardines landed that morning and cooked over charcoal on the dock. He watched a bird, black as a bat, flying out to sea. It was an Eleonora's falcon heading back to its nesting site on the Mogador Islands. The falcons bred late in the year, feeding their young on the flow of migrants from Europe. The wind was in the north and cold, Case noted. The flyway should be busy.

'Shall we be going?' Low said, prim as a Women's Institute tour guide.

Case took over the driving, bearing south through dusty green argan forest. He carried the map in his head and counted off the kilometre stones. When he got to thirty, he slowed and peered off to the right. A turning came up, rutted and overgrown, disappearing into the trees. There were no signs. He drove past.

'I think that was it,' Low said, studying the map.

Case drove another mile, keeping an eye on the mirror, then turned and went back, taking the turning fast. A couple of hundred yards down the track he stopped.

'I'm not happy,' Besant said.

Low nodded at Case to proceed with caution. Shrubs in the middle of the track scraped the underside of the car. The forest was open, undifferentiated. Case's eyes were everywhere, but it was a hopeless task. No sooner had he given one thicket the all-clear than his eyes had to dart ahead to another.

'We should be on foot,' he said.

'No one's been down here for weeks,' Besant said. 'It's a fucking jungle.'

Case didn't contradict him. He had spotted an obstruction on the track. The others saw it and craned forward. 'Looks like a dead horse,' Low said.

Case slowed to read the track, dropped into first and put his foot down. He fish-tailed past the carcass, glimpsed eye sockets, a gaping body cavity devoured from the inside, smelt a terrible stench.

'Christ, what did that?' Besant breathed.

'Natural causes,' Low said.

Besant threw himself back from the window. 'Get away,' he screamed.

A dog had hurled itself against the moving car. Half a dozen more raced out of the trees and streamed beside it. They were like no dogs Case had seen – the striped bodies mere appendages of their giant heads, hyenas crossed with terriers.

'Look at the snappers on that one,' Low marvelled. 'Gor, he won't do your Michelins much good.'

Case looked straight into the eyes of the pack leader. He yanked the wheel left, heard a thud, saw the dog rolling in their trail of dust, the others snapping around it.

'On foot, he says,' Fatso jeered.

'Easy, Pat,' Low ordered. 'We're not trying to get home before the lodger.'

Case slowed. The eyes of the dogs were with him still. The mood in the car was fractious.

'Did you see them killer whales on the box?' Fatso demanded. 'I kid you not, the fucking things came right up the beach and snatched off the seals like muggers grabbing old ladies' handbags. Terrifying? Margate will never be the same. Fucking evil they were.'

'Tone it down,' Case said.

'What's the matter with him?'

'He doesn't need your cursing and swearing, that's what.'

'Course he doesn't. He's a Para, and everyone knows Paras are delicate petals.' Fatso leaned on the back of Case's seat. 'I saw some of your mob in a pub in Gib once, well pissed they were, crapping on the tables.'

'I'm going to throw up,' Besant said.

'In the presence of ladies,' Fatso said. 'Fucking animals.'

Low turned, his expression heavy. 'You're spoiling the environment, Barry. I don't want to have to tell you again.'

Fatso sprawled back in a sulk. Case slowed to a crawl.

'Anyone want their fortunes told?' McGrory asked.

They all laughed. 'Go on then,' Low said. 'Do Pat's. What's your birth sign, Hard Case?'

'Libra.'

Haltingly, line by line, McGrory delivered the verdict. 'Socially, this could be a quiet spell, with any partnerships based around work. But a loved one will have your interests at heart and you've little to fret about. Money stars are very powerful – you are hitting a healthy, prosperous phase.'

'Beautifully read,' Low said. He beamed at Case. 'Can't ask for better than that.'

'Do me,' Fatso demanded. 'Virgo.'

'Venus in Scorpio is a wonderful social influence and you should be the life and soul of any party. If you take a few risks, the chances are you'll do well, and earn the glory you always felt you deserve. You should now be giving careful thought to ways of spending your money efficiently.'

Fatso rubbed his hands. 'Got to be something in it.'

A flock of bustards ran off through a glade. Case stopped. 'That's far enough,' he said. 'The sea should be about a mile off.'

'I'm not putting a foot out there,' Besant said.

'I'll go on my own,' Case said. 'See you on the beach in half an hour. Park the car out of sight.'

'Like it,' Low said. 'Alright, boys, under starter's orders. Mac, you stay and keep an eye on the motor.'

Case slung a pair of binoculars around his neck, opened the tail-gate, took out the dove and stowed it inside his jacket.

'What the fuck are you doing with that pigeon?' Low demanded. 'And why is it wearing a fucking corset?'

'Maybe he's going to offer it to the opposition as a peace symbol,' Fatso suggested.

But Case was already out of sight among the trees, moving away from the track. A few hundred yards into the forest, he flushed the bustards again. Nobody was in the vicinity, he decided, making straight for the beach.

Dunes had invaded the edge of the forest, reducing it to a skeletal fringe. Case passed through the dead grey trunks. The beach was blinding white, several hundred yards wide and empty in both directions. At the end of the track, half a mile to the north, was the wreck of a shrine. South, where Fox was supposed to be lodged, the beach curved for miles to the next cape. Through binoculars, Case picked up movement. He smiled in sour acknowledgement. 'X marks the spot,' he said.

Shortening focus, he sighted on a chunky silhouette perched on one of the fossil trees no more than a hundred yards away. 'Hello,' he said in greeting. 'Where are you from?'

Moving slowly, head down so that his face didn't reflect light, he closed the distance. At thirty yards he raised his head and looked into the eyes of a passage peregrine tiercel – a first-year Mediterranean bird, judging by its size. He moved closer and still it didn't move. Its crop was empty. Maybe it had crossed the Straits of Gibraltar that very morning and was gathering its strength for the evening hunting flight.

It let him approach to within twenty yards before taking wing.

Turning his back on it, Case took out the strait-jacketed dove and tossed it into the air. It fluttered lamely to the ground. Over the sea, the peregrine sliced a circuit and came back to take stand.

Leaving cover, Case walked out into the middle of the beach and spread his arms wide.

Three-quarters of the Waltham Forest Fishing Club straggled down to meet him, Besant hanging on to his hair, Fatso kicking bits of flotsam. Fish out of water, Case thought.

They gathered in a morose cluster. 'The map says the villa is down there,' Low said.

'I say we jack it in,' Besant said.

'Do turn it off,' Low said wearily.

Case glanced from one to the other, searching for the object of dissension. Coyly, Low parted his jacket to reveal an automatic pistol. 'Call me old-fashioned,' he said.

'You never said nothing about carrying iron,' Besant complained. 'If the Moroccans nick us, we'll be doing forever. Tell him, Pat.'

'He's right,' Case told Low. 'On the other hand . . .'

He led the way, Besant falling in a long way behind. Low caught up. 'I told you, Pat. Never been the same man since. If he goes on like this, I'm going to have to request his absence.'

'Lovely bit of beach, though,' Fatso observed. 'Beats me why it isn't wall-to-wall deckchairs. Hey, if we come up with Fox, I could set up a resort here.'

'Dream on,' Low said. 'You think the Moroccans don't know about this place.'

'Then why have they left it blank?'

'Killer whales, I expect. Don't go too near the water now.'

'Seriously, Den, this is a prime site.'

Case pointed to an ugly slash of foam fifty yards out. The current couldn't seem to decide on one direction, pulling all ways. 'Take a paddle out there and you won't come ashore until Spain.'

The wind pushed them on, but couldn't disperse the clouds of flies that followed them. The sand hissed at their feet. The whole beach was an unpleasant blur. Flocks of gulls rose and fell, rose and fell. Out to sea a freighter slid over the horizon.

From the water's edge, they were able to survey inland where the house was supposed to stand.

'Remind me to look up that fucking cozzer when we get back to Marrakech,' Low said.

'What's all the activity down there?' Fatso asked, pointing farther south.

'More dogs,' Case said.

'Let's go back,' Besant said.

'What are they doing?' Fatso asked.

'Feeding,' Case said.

Fatso fell into step one side, Low on the other.

'Max would sort that lot,' Fatso said, eyeing the distant pack.

'Do you pit him?' Case asked.

'No chance. Max is show material.'

'But a lot of people down your way fight them.'

'A few, but so many owners got grassed up, it's not worth the aggro. These days it's the West Indian dealers who own the real vicious dogs; they fit their harnesses with pockets to carry their stashes. I mean, a Drugs Squad officer is going to think twice about strip-searching a pit bull. But when it comes to fighting for money, hamsters are the thing.'

'You what?'

'Your hamster is an aggressive little beast. Put two males in a cage and watch the fur fly. All you need is a table in a pub back room. It's very big with the Irish. I've seen hundreds change hands on one fight. There's even this geezer from Bermondsey who'll make you up little harnesses.'

'He's having me on,' Case said to Low.

'Stick with us, my son, and get yourself an education.'

The dogs rose off the sand as they approached. In conformation and general hideousness, they were similar to the brutes they'd encountered earlier. They backed away barking nervously, reluctant to abandon their meal. Their bellies hung like kegs under their hollow ribs. A fight broke out over a bone.

Case halted. The others bunched round him. 'What is it?' Fatso asked.

'Why are you looking like that?' Besant demanded, clinging to his hairstyle.

'I think we've just found Fox,' Low said, staring at Case.

He walked at Case's side. The dogs began to circle round them. One of the dogs loped close, growing in confidence. 'You're the animal expert,' Low said. 'Will they go for us?'

'Not if you shoot one.'

Low fired far too early, the bullet going nowhere, the dog recoiling from the report and then coming closer.

'Go on, give us a go,' Fatso said. He fired three shots, missing. The dogs backed out of range.

Case held out his hand. Fatso cradled the gun to his chest like a kid with a toy. 'Get your own,' he said.

'Give it him,' Low commanded.

Case weighed the gun. A Browning, seven-shot, nine-millimetre – a fair old stopper. Low held up a spare magazine. Case started walking, the pistol hanging at his side, the dogs giving way, falling aside and then regrouping behind. Without stopping, Case shot the nearest in the head, turned thirty degrees and knocked over another as it turned tail. The rest fled over the sand and disappeared into the forest. Case walked back and placed the pistol in Low's hand, having first put it on safety.

Low looked at it as if it was charmed. 'I think we can send Olly back to the sub's bench.'

Case strolled over to the remains of the dogs' feast. It was partially buried, most of the flesh gone. He stirred a bone with his foot and wondered why he didn't feel anything.

'Is it Fox?' Low murmured.

'Forbes Valentine.'

'How can you tell?'

'The hair.'

'Poor Shirley,' Low said. 'And him an accountant.'

Fatso stared bug-eyed. Besant came up. 'Oh my good God!' Clapping his hand to his mouth, he staggered away.

Obsequies over, Low erupted in rage. 'He was my last card,' he cried. 'Someone's going to suffer for this. You hear me?' he shouted to the forest. 'Someone's going to die for this.' Still yelling threats, pointing at the trees, he backed down the beach.

Besant was at the water's edge, thin and old, his hair a mess. 'It's time to fold,' he said, staring out to sea.

Fatso edged a downcast look at Low. 'I think Roy's right, Den, in the circs.'

'Give me a couple more days,' Case said. 'Valentine wouldn't have come to Morocco unless Fox was here, alive.'

'What's the fucking point,' Fatso said. 'Whoever's got him will have ghosted him.'

'Two days,' Case repeated.

Low nodded. 'And then we go back to London and give Rafiq a spin.'

'I'm taking the first flight out,' Besant insisted.

'You don't have to do nothing,' Low assured him. 'Stay at the hotel, put your feet up, work on your tan. Leave Pat to walk on the wild side.'

Case left the argument behind and set off back up the beach. The wind had erased their tracks. The figures behind him grew small and lonely – survivors at the end of the world.

It took him half an hour to get back, and a further ten minutes to locate the pigeon. The peregrine must have killed it within minutes of him throwing it out. It was half-eaten, the tiercel still on it, well and truly snared. As Case made in, it flew in terror but only got ten yards before the line trailing from the pigeon's harness dragged it down. Screaming, it threw itself on its back, wings spread. Four loops of soft nylon held its talons. Gently, Case dropped his jacket over it, seized its legs, jessed and hooded it and then cut it free. He placed it on his forearm where it hissed and snaked its head, striving for the light.

Attracted by the noise, Fatso appeared. 'Hey, you lot,' he shouted, 'come and see what Hard Case has caught.'

Low wandered up. 'I bet that would fetch a few bob down Brick Lane.'

'A thousand or so,' Case said.

'Catch five hundred and we can go home all square,' Fatso said.

'It's taken divots out of your hand,' Low pointed out.

'He's a headcase,' Fatso said. 'Acting like we're on a nature ramble and Valentine a heap of bones.'

'Life goes on,' Case said.

'What are you going to do with it?' Low asked.

For answer, Case cut the jesses, unhooded the falcon and cast it free. Sucking the bites on the back of his hand, he watched it skim the sea-glitter and rise into the wind. Like a soul taking flight, he thought, realizing with a chill heart that Valentine would never see a falcon's flight again and that one day he, too, would be bones in the sand.

18

Iseult woke calm and wide-eyed. The room was lit by a stroke of light angled through a shuttered window overhung with roses. The walls were white, decorated with rugs. Iseult turned her head and saw a fresh vase of flowers by her bedside. She stretched, naked under a single sheet, luxuriating from top to toe.

Like pain, the experience of the last two days had already slipped into the abstract. Her fever must have lasted the first night and all the next day. She could dimly remember her head bursting with crazed dreams, the inside of her skull lined with hot fur. The breaking of the fever had brought not relief but waves of dull sickness, as if her insides were an organ that had rejected her.

Sobered by the memory, she examined her hands. The top layers had been burned off. A white lotion masked the new skin. She remembered a girl applying it, but the recollection might have been a dream.

Slipping back the sheet, she stepped on to cool tiles. The room darkened for a moment and she had to put out a steadying hand. When the dizziness passed, she crossed to the mirror. Her ghost walked towards her.

The swelling had gone down on her face, but the blistering was still apparent and she was glad she was in shadow. On the positive side, she had lost weight. Quite a lot, she decided, turning so that she could see the curve of her stomach. She cupped her breasts and stared at her reflection as if waiting for it to speak.

Warm scents came in through the window. It must be

mid-morning. Still naked, she stole across and peered through the shutters. An old man trailed through an orchard, his hand on a little boy's head. The garden was bounded by a mud wall overgrown with thorn and honeysuckle. On the other side, the hills rose to deckled peaks the colour of parchment.

From directly above came a peculiar clacking sound that started slowly and built up to a rattle like the climax of a flamenco performance. In the breathless silence that succeeded it, Iseult had the uncanny feeling that she had experienced this moment before – stood at this window, looked out on this view, breathed the same scents.

She turned and stared at the door, knowing that in a moment it would open and a girl would enter.

She made a grab for her robe as the handle turned. The girl Iseult was expecting backed in, carrying a tray which she nearly dropped in surprise. Recovering, she dipped her eyes while Iseult slipped into bed. Her face was round and as smooth as soap under a plain white headscarf. There was a small tattoo on her chin. Her clothing was an exercise in the imaginative use of synthetic remnants.

'Rachida,' Iseult said, remembering. 'Thank you for looking after me.'

A smile flitted across the girl's face. 'Iseult,' she said.

Somehow the speaking of her name held the utmost significance, confirming her return to the world of the living. She hugged Rachida and kissed her cheek. Drawing apart, the girl indicated the tray. It held water, white bread, a thin clear soup. Iseult's stomach growled and they both laughed.

The girl watched every mouthful go down, and when Iseult had finished, she sighed with satisfaction, as if she had eaten the meal herself. 'More?' she asked.

'What I'd really like is coffee and a cigarette.'

Rachida's face fell. 'The cook is asleep.'

'He must be a very lazy cook.'

Rachida's smooth face wrinkled. 'But no, it's the afternoon.'

Iseult couldn't believe it. 'Then I've been asleep . . .'

Gravely, Rachida counted off the hours on her fingers, holding up both hands twice, then three more fingers.

Iseult was shocked 'How many days have I been here?'

'Four,' Rachida said. She went out.

The thought of a day lost troubled Iseult, but then she thought, it's a borderline, the start of a better life, and she lay back, wallowing in a placid sea.

Rachida touched her from a doze. The smell of coffee filled the room. The first intake of black tobacco made Iseult see stars and she stubbed out the cigarette. 'Where's my brother?' she asked. He had been an occasional presence in her darkened sickroom.

'In the next room,' Rachida said, and laid her cheek against her hands.

'Is he well?'

Rachida nodded. She pointed to Iseult's sunburnt face, then at a bottle of lotion and made a gentle rubbing motion. Iseult shook her head. She took one of Rachida's hands and unclenched it. The palm bore a henna design that made Iseult think of Celtic runes.

'That's pretty. How do you do it?'

'My mother,' the girl said. She examined Iseult's hand and stroked the palm. 'Would you like?'

'Yes please.'

'I will bring her this evening,' Rachida said, 'before you meet the Count.'

Iseult had forgotten Lemonnier. 'He's here?' she said foolishly.

'In the cellar,' Rachida said. She rose. '*À bientôt.*'

Iseult drank another cup of coffee and pondered what her host might be doing in the cellar. She put aside the temptation of another cigarette, telling herself that breaking the habit was easy. The light had deepened and she was suddenly anxious not to waste what was left of the day.

Her clothes had been put away washed and starched. She dressed in jeans and shirt and went out. There were two rooms on the passage. The house smelt of woodsmoke and

French cooking. Flies buzzed against the sunlit windows. The fittings were plain, made from rough-hewn local wood, but on the landing stood a gilded baroque chest, and formal portraits brooded over her as she made her way down the wide staircase into a lofty entrance hall.

Two full suits of armour flanked the doorway. Above it was a heraldic device comprising a black boar's head surmounting a castle keep. A real boar's head bristled on one wall, along with various other game trophies. A valuable-looking equestrian bronze and a painting of hunting dogs completed the effects.

The garden was deserted, drowsing in silence. Iseult walked through rose beds and went down into the orchard. A white stork glided over the trees and landed on the house, greeting its mate with a courtly dance and the castanet flourish of its beak which she had heard in her room. She reached the boundary and followed it left, halfway round the house, until she reached an artificial pool. A brilliant green snake looped through the thick surface scum, its eyes yellow and unblinking. Not feeling so assured, Iseult gave the pool a wide berth and set off up the hillside.

This part of the garden was reverting to the wild, the boundary wall overrun by banks of briars. Iseult sat down with her back against a tree and watched the sunlight dappling the leaves. She yawned, and then her jaw locked as something energetic pushed through undergrowth behind her. On the edge of panic, she turned in time to see a long, naked tail being sucked into the stockade of thorns. Only a rat, she told herself.

But the garden had lost its charm. She eyed with suspicion an iridescent beetle toiling towards her foot. Small birds in the canopy darted and twittered in a fretful way. Insects made a conspiratorial buzz. The light glancing off the leaves no longer seemed innocent; it was fidgety, mindless, making and dissolving shapes that began to take on the aspect of faces. Iseult decided to go indoors.

She had gone only a few yards when she found her way blocked by a hedge gone wild that enclosed some kind of yard with decaying wooden buildings. As she skirted it, she became aware of a rank smell and heard a rhythmic grunting, a frustrated striving.

Slowly she backed off until she found the right way, then bolted for the house.

Inside, nothing stirred. She tiptoed upstairs, put her ear to Cathal's door and knocked.

'*Entrez.*'

His room was empty, the bed unmade.

'I'm in the bath,' he called.

Smiling, she went in.

The room was steamy and fragrant. Cathal was lolling back, eyes closed, fondling an erection. He murmured something – a name – which Iseult didn't catch.

Disappointment spiralled down inside her. 'It's me,' she said.

His eyes flashed open and his hand pounced to cover himself, but then he thought better of it and sat up, slopping water over the rim. 'Iseult,' he exclaimed, reaching for a glass of wine, 'how wonderful to see you back from the far side.'

'I can see how excited it makes you,' she said, wrapping the words in sarcasm.

'You had us worried. Your temperature went to nearly a hundred and five.'

'Not so worried as all that, apparently.'

'Actually, I was pretty poorly myself,' Cathal said, sounding hurt. His eyes strayed behind her. 'Close the door, will you?'

Iseult turned. 'I'll come back later.'

'Don't run away,' Cathal said. He subsided into the water, eyes glinting. 'Why don't you join me?' He admired himself. 'Seems a shame to waste it.'

'You're gross.'

'I can't help the way you make me feel,' Cathal said. 'Go on, close the door.'

'And disappoint whoever you're expecting?'

'He won't mind.'

235

'Perhaps you'd like us to have a party.'

Cathal brightened. 'Now that's a strikingly enticing idea. I've always entertained a delicious fantasy along those lines.' His eyes went sly. 'I seem to remember you shared it.'

'That's all it was – fantasy.'

'Wait till you see the reality.'

'Better than the waiter in Tangiers?'

'Different class altogether.'

'Better than your flatmate in New York?'

'God, yes. Infinitely.'

'Not to mention Hassan.'

'Rather a non-starter, that one.'

At that precise moment there came a knock on the outer door. Iseult's mouth tightened. She strode out and swung the door wide. A stocky lad with the beginnings of a moustache stood there, smile wasting away. 'Get lost,' she said, slamming the door in his face. She went back into the bathroom and sat on a stool.

'Well?' Cathal inquired, eyes half-closed and watchful.

Iseult felt her face grow haggard. 'He can't be older than fourteen,' she said.

'Quite unspoilt, but impressively mature in other departments.'

'You're . . .' She couldn't find the right word. '. . . evil.'

He began to stroke himself, his eyes dreamy. 'We're on the wilder shores now, Iseult. Don't you feel it? This place is fabulous.' He smiled. 'I could stay forever.'

She took herself over to the window and stared out. 'Does that mean you've given up Fox?'

Cathal's demeanour turned businesslike. 'I've kept in touch with the hotel. There were a couple of messages. Case has apparently tracked down the Israeli, but it didn't sound too hopeful.'

'Anything else?'

Cathal lathered his chest. 'Oh yes, he sends his love.'

Iseult's conscience tugged. The truth was, she hadn't given a thought to Pat. 'What's the Count like?' she asked quickly.

Cathal mulled over the question. 'Mad,' he said at last. 'But as I get older,' he added, 'I find it easier to understand the other fellow's point of view.'

'In what way, "mad"?' Iseult asked, her composure ready to take wing.

Cathal appraised her, gauging how much he should tell her, or what she could tolerate. 'Well, politically he's pretty far out.'

'Pat said something about his father being shot for collaborating with the Nazis.'

'Traditions die hard in that family,' Cathal said. 'Conversation-wise, it can make for a few sticky moments, so best avoid contentious subjects. De Gaulle for one, Algeria of course; Western civilization in general and Americans in particular. Television is definitely out. In fact, best stick to neutral subjects like food and wine – which are *out* of this world. We eat early by the way – seven for seven-thirty. The Count isn't exactly in the pink. Wear your new frock and look beautiful.'

'I can hardly wait.'

'He's dying to meet you. He was most interested to hear you were a painter. I think he wants to give you a commission. A landscape, I think.'

'I don't do landscapes.'

'I rather glossed over your style; I suspect abstract art is another form of decadence that sets the Count off.'

'Does he know why we're here?'

'*Naturellement*, but he won't lift a finger to help. He suspects that Fox has got caught up in something political.'

'Have you told him about Pat?'

Cathal winced at some recollection he wasn't going to pass on. 'Your friend is going to get himself in deep trouble. That was the gist of it.'

'Then why are you looking so pleased with yourself?'

'Several reasons,' Cathal said, and paused as if deciding which ones to select. 'As I guessed, the Count is embarrassed to find himself in possession of a bumper crop of hash that isn't as easy to move as you might imagine. He's a conservative man. He only deals with people he trusts.'

'Solid, dependable types like you.'

'If I can shift dirty money, I can handle dope.'

She eyed him askance, as if viewing a hologram that changes image according to the way light hits it. He seemed to be nursing some private satisfaction. 'There's something else,' she said.

'Nothing concrete. I suppose you could say the Count and I have established a rapport.'

'You mean you've come up with a scheme to rip him off.'

'No I don't fucking mean that,' Cathal shouted, slapping the water in anger. 'Jesus, Iseult, why must you always think the worst.'

'Because that's the way things always turn out.'

Cathal had almost submerged himself in the bath.

'If I'm going to meet this monster, I want fair warning of what's in store.'

'You'll laugh.'

'Somehow I doubt it.'

Cathal mustered his thoughts. 'The Count's old and about to croak. When he snuffs it, that's the end of an ancient line. As you'll discover, he's a great believer in continuity. It's his great regret that there's no one left to carry the flame.'

Despite herself, Iseult laughed. 'And you've deluded him into believing you're the torch-bearer.'

'Nothing wrong in making an old man happy in his declining years – or months, I should say.'

'Lucky old Cathal,' Iseult said. 'Landed on his feet again.'

'I seize my opportunities,' Cathal said modestly.

'Are we free to leave?'

'Free to do anything we want,' Cathal said, and stretched.

'In that case, this is the end of the line for me. Tomorrow, I'm going back to London.'

Rather to her surprise, Cathal didn't try to persuade her to change her mind. 'I shall miss you,' he said.

'You'll find compensations.'

Cathal let her get to the door. 'Darling, you know I'd give you what you want if I only could.'

'You don't know what I want.'

'Normality. Security. A family. A baby.'

Iseult felt like a weary traveller unexpectedly confronted by a mountain. She couldn't bring herself to speak.

'There's more to life than solid bourgeois virtues,' Cathal said.

'Such as?'

'Excitement. Unlicensed fun.'

She looked at him, heart unmoved. 'Fun is what kids have, Cathal. It usually ends in tears before bedtime.'

Abandoning her resolution, Iseult smoked three cigarettes in succession. There was no such thing as a clean slate. Sour of mouth, she fell asleep and dreamt that Cathal and another man were making love to her. The fact that she couldn't remember the other lover's name made her anxious and she woke in a sweat.

It was still daylight and dogs were baying close by. Below the window, a man stood cradling an automatic weapon, eyes cocked skyward as if he was expecting aerial bombardment.

Iseult bathed and showered and began to dress, taking pains, using more make-up than usual. Rachida arrived with her mother – a dark, dumpy woman wearing strings of silver necklaces and a headscarf loaded with coins. They both exclaimed over her transformation and fondled the folds of her dress, shooting shrewd comments about its quality and probable cost.

The mother had brought along a tray with a cloth-coloured bowl on it and a small clay brazier. In the bowl was a mass of what looked like spinach. 'Henna,' Rachida said.

While she brushed Iseult's hair, her mother went to work with the dye, moulding it into patterns which she arranged in Iseult's palms. Her own hands were stained black with henna. Her eyes were like cloves. When the arrangement was to her satisfaction, she closed up Iseult's hands into fists, bound them with cloths and held them over the brazier.

Seeing that it was getting late, Iseult indicated that she still hadn't applied the finishing touches. Rachida painted her lips maroon and her mother brushed her hair. Under their ministering hands, Iseult felt pampered and sexy.

The mother unbound her fists. At such short notice, she warned, the work would be impermanent and of the simplest design. Heat had turned the henna red-black. The mother traced the pattern with her fingers and began speaking in Berber.

'What is she saying?'

'She's reading your fate.'

Fate was not a word that rang comfortably in Iseult's hearing.

'She says two men pursue you – one dark, one light. Two men dance around you. One of them will die of love.' Rachida smiled.

'Which one?'

The finger circling Iseult's palm stopped and tapped.

'Le noir.'

Iseult looked into the older woman's eyes. The dark one. That must be Cathal. But Pat had African blood, didn't he? Which was the dark and which the fair?

Thoughtfully, she put on an antique necklace of silver filigree and green glass. Rachida and her mother sighed with admiration of their handiwork and watched with hands clasped as she went downstairs.

Her host was in the hallway with Cathal. In place of the elongated patrician figure her imagination had concocted, there stood a short, once thickset man with apricot-coloured hair cut *en brosse*, supporting himself on a stick. An elderly spaniel lay at his heels. The only thing that distinguished him from a Midi peasant was his velvet burgundy smoking jacket, worn with a spotted bow tie, workaday cotton slacks, deck shoes and no socks. At first glance, he looked neither ill nor particularly mad. His eyes were alert, his face pink.

Then she came closer and saw that it was all skin-deep. His lips had been glossed in flesh tones, his cheeks rouged, the eyes artificially brightened, the hair coloured from a bottle. Under the powder and paint, his face was a death mask.

The Count bowed and kissed her hand, staring into her eyes. 'Beautiful,' he murmured. Then he frowned and looked from her to Cathal again, as if he was having trouble distinguishing one from the other. 'Forgive me,' he said, 'but are you Jewish?'

'On my mother's side,' Iseult began, before being mowed down by Cathal's emphatic denial.

Choosing not to pursue it, the Count made inquiries about her disposition, starting in French but switching to English, which he spoke with a nasal American intonation.

Cathal was wearing an expression that she hadn't seen him try on before – a judicious blend of airy sophistication and sycophancy. '*Monsieur le comte* was explaining that this armour belonged to an ancestor who fought the Ottomans at Nicopolis.'

'My family took part in four Crusades,' the Count informed Iseult.

'How interesting,' was the best response Iseult could summon.

The Count was frowning at her again, in a way that made her think her own make-up must be crooked. 'I saw you running through the garden. You looked frightened.'

'I heard a noise behind a hedge.'

The Count smiled, showing atrocious teeth. 'That must have been Hubert. He's almost all that's left of my collection.'

'The Count keeps a zoo,' Cathal explained brightly.

'Would you care to see it?' the Count asked politely.

'Well . . .'

'Love to,' Cathal interrupted, eyes signalling wildly.

Outside, he took the Count's arm and they shuffled through the garden, the dog tottering behind and the armed man out on their flank, ever watchful. It was a gorgeous evening –

the house bathed in mellow light, the hills standing out with stunning clarity under a sky of tonic blue.

The Count disengaged himself from Cathal and basked in the view. 'Jacquemart de Hesdin painted skies like that,' he said.

Cathal furrowed his brow. 'De Hesdin,' he repeated, as if he had the name filed somewhere in the back of his mind.

'A medieval painter,' the Count said. 'He illustrated *Les Très Riches Heures du Duc de Berry*.'

'Of course,' Cathal said, with a vexed click of the tongue, dodging Iseult's contemptuous glance.

'Observe how the earth throws its shadow on the sky,' the Count continued, 'dividing it into a terrestrial sphere and a celestial realm.' He raised his chin high, exposing his chicken-wattle neck. 'That is a sky made for angels.'

'Painted in an age of faith,' Cathal murmured, head bent reverently.

'Of miracles,' the Count said. He squinted at Iseult. His eyes, she saw, had already lost their unnatural sparkle. A substance like stale egg yolk had collected in the corners.

'Could you paint a sky like that?'

'With or without angels?'

'Of course you can,' Cathal said to Iseult, contorting his face into a grotesque appeal.

'There's a place I want you to paint. I have all the things you'll need. We'll go tomorrow.'

'I'd like to get back to Tangiers,' Iseult said, ignoring Cathal's rolling eyes.

He intervened at full speed. 'She's far too weak to travel. She should take it easy for a couple of days, shouldn't she?'

'Without doubt,' the Count said, and patted Iseult's arm with a mottled hand.

As they set off again, Iseult kicked Cathal in the ankle. Lemonnier noticed and gave his brown smile. 'Don't you like it here?'

Iseult viewed the surroundings gingerly. 'It's very pretty.'

'My father built it during the pacification. After the war,

I decided to make it my refuge. I haven't been back to France since.'

'Why not?' Iseult demanded, goaded into malice by Cathal's agonized signals.

The Count gave an airy wave. 'Because it's a nest of Jews and socialists. Because it's been colonized by dwarfs.'

They entered the zoo through a rotted gate. The enclosure took the form of a rustic quadrangle surrounded by collapsing timber-framed cabins with steep shingled roofs and carved gables. The architecture was completely at odds with the rest of the property – a gnomish transplant from a colder culture.

Iseult felt the Count's muddy eyes on her, relishing her puzzlement. 'It looks like something out of Hans Christian Andersen,' she said.

A wistful expression came over Lemonnier's face. 'My father was inspired by Romintern, Reichsmarshal Göring's hunting lodge in Prussia, where we were frequent guests. I shot my first stag there in 1937, when I was fifteen. Göring personally invested me with the title of *Jägermeister* – "Master of the Hunt".'

Iseult now saw that the carvings on the gables were variants of the swastika. She sought Cathal out of the corner of her eye, but he had the wisdom to be looking elsewhere. The Count headed across the quadrangle.

'Christ, Cathal,' Iseult said through gritted teeth, 'you really know how to pick them.'

'Just humour the bastard,' Cathal insisted through his smile.

As they caught up with Lemonnier, Iseult smelt a musky emanation and heard the promiscuous grunting that had scared her earlier.

'Hubert,' the Count announced.

Hubert was a wild boar, a tusked porker with huge humped shoulders and a black spinal crest. He trotted over to the Count, genitals bobbing, a line of froth on his jaw and little red sparks in his eye.

'Hubert is showing his cloven hoof,' the Count said. 'It's the beginning of the mating season.' He scratched the boar's flank with a stick. 'Are you familiar with the cult of the boar?' he inquired, as one might ask a sympathetic party if they were conversant with the works of a challenging but worthwhile composer.

'The Count is an expert on the subject,' Cathal declared in a staunch voice. 'He was kind enough to show me a monograph he wrote. Quite fascinating.'

Egged on by his approval, Lemonnier launched into a discourse polished by repetition.

'The word *sanglier* derives from the same root as singular,' he began, 'aptly describing the solitary nature of the beast, who from the age of three leaves his own kind, returning only in the autumn to mate with the sows. The mating is accomplished with extreme vigour, and thus for many medieval writers he exemplified the sin of lust and aroused one of European man's most deep-seated fears – the dread that his lady's shy and tender exterior masks a coarseness of appetite that can only be satisfied by the brutal and lascivious thrusts of a black giant. Your own Chaucer describes fair Criseyde sleeping in the embrace of a huge-tusked boar. Boccaccio had Troilo dreaming that his lady was being pleasured by a boar's mouth.' Here the Count tendered a grotesque smile. 'And of course your own lover's heraldic device is the boar.'

'My lover?' Iseult said, eyes darting to Cathal.

'Tristan. King Mark first becomes aware of his wife's infidelity when a loyal servant has a dream in which a fearsome boar runs out of the forest into the royal court, charges into the royal sleeping chamber and fouls the bed linen with his foam.' The Count shrugged as if elaboration was unnecessary.

'The boar is on your coat of arms, too,' Iseult pointed out.

'He has his virtues; he has his admirers. In pagan times he was revered for his courage, his stamina, his guile. It was only when the heroic age ended that he was associated with evil. I have in my study a fourteenth-century manuscript in which the gates of hell are represented by a boar's mouth. Perhaps you'd care to see it.'

'Er, thank you.'

The tour of the zoo was soon done with. An ape with a white muzzle hunched in the corner of a rusting cage like a long-stay inmate of a lunatic asylum. In an aviary too small for it, an eagle stood on the ground among carrion. Its plumage was dull, its tail wrecked, its bill overgrown into a splintered hook. When the Count prodded the mesh, it lurched off like a muscle-bound turkey.

'*Un aigle royal*, king of birds.'

Iseult contemplated the spectacle with pity.

'He was captured as a baby, and knows no other life.' The Count sighed. 'Just like a real king.'

'You could at least train him to fly free.'

'Impossible.'

'I know someone who could. Pat Case,' Iseult explained, 'the man looking for Digby Fox. He keeps birds of prey. He's a gamekeeper.'

The Count frowned at Cathal. 'You didn't tell me that.'

Cathal laughed in anger. 'It didn't strike me as relevant.'

The Count's expression had settled into something disagreeable. 'I'm a Master of Game,' he said. 'Of course it's relevant.'

Ignoring Cathal's proffered arm, the Count linked elbows with Iseult. They proceeded awkwardly.

'When the doctors told me I had cancer,' he said, 'I decided it would be more dignified to cut myself off from the living. But now that you're here, I realize I was wrong.' He looked up, as if a bird had flown over, and a beatific smile spread across his face. 'After all, what is nature but a cemetery?'

Meekly, Iseult let herself be led through the garden.

The Count began to call out in a commanding voice. '*Joie, Beau, Pitié, Bon, Bride, Pureté, Courage.*'

A chorus of howls turned Iseult's bowels to water.

'No, no,' the Count said, clasping her hand, 'those are not the dogs that attacked you.'

Behind the house was a modern kennel block. The hounds stood as tall as a man's waist. They were loose-skinned, rangy, with blunt muzzles and high-set ears cropped to a point.

'My boar-hounds,' the Count said with winsome pride. 'Seven virtues to counter the deadly sins. I created the breed myself – mastiff for strength, greyhound for speed, pointer for scenting, a dash of native cur for cunning.'

On the hills, other dogs had begun to bay. The sun had slipped below the horizon and the sky had bled of colour. Imagining herself benighted, Iseult shivered.

The Count turned to face the music, his mouth clamped in a disapproving line. 'Five years ago I lost my best bitch. She bred with wild dogs and now the region is overrun.'

'Can't you get rid of them?'

'My huntsman shoots the occasional one, but he's old and they're clever. They're destroying all the game in the area.'

'You could try poison,' Cathal suggested.

'Poison?' the Count said, staring at Cathal with alarm. 'I'm a hunter, not a rat catcher.'

The armed attendant came hurrying through the trees and took the Count aside. Iseult had the feeling that he had news which concerned herself and Cathal.

But when the Count rejoined them, all he said was: 'What an appetite our walk has given me.'

They returned to the house, where the man with the gun was waiting to receive them. He threw open a double door and the Count ushered them in.

Iseult drew a breath and held it, momentarily dazzled. The room was lit by two magnificent crystal chandeliers and beneath it, running the length of the room, stood a black table heaped with more crystalware that excited flashes from every part of the spectrum. And every flash was duplicated, for on the wall hung huge mirrors. It was like standing at the centre of a prism.

The Count sat at one end of the table, Iseult at the other, and Cathal halfway between them. Iseult could see her reflection wherever she looked. It was some time before she became aware of the paintings set between the mirrors. She recognized a Poussin and guessed that the dark and creepy masked ball was the work of Longhi.

Cathal sent her a look irradiated with meaning, as if to say: play your cards right and they can be ours. The Count, too, had noticed her interest. 'All I have left of my inheritance,' he said. 'All I have left of France.'

'Le Comte is forgetting his cellar,' Cathal told Iseult. 'It's mind-boggling. There's a case of pre-Phylloxera claret that men would kill for.'

'An 1866 Haut-Brion,' the Count said. 'I considered serving it this evening, but then I thought: what if it has turned to vinegar? No, the risk of disappointment is too high. It will be a mystery that accompanies me to the grave. You will forgive my caution.'

Iseult's idea of a good wine was Sainsbury's Bulgarian Merlot. 'I'm relieved,' she said, paying no heed to Cathal's wince of pain. 'It would be wasted on us.'

'I took that into account, too,' the Count admitted. 'However,' he added, 'I have tried to choose a few honest wines that might educate and amuse.'

On cue, the all-purpose retainer poured the first selection – a Grand Cru Chablis on which Cathal lavished too much praise.

Surely Lemonnier must see through him, Iseult thought.

Cathal's young friend brought in the first course. As it was served, the Count treated them to a loving description of ingredients and cooking method. It was a *fricassée* of calf's sweetbreads and brains served in a wine-and-cream sauce subtly flavoured with nutmeg and *fines herbes* and garnished with truffles.

'Heavenly,' Cathal declared.

Lemonnier demurred. 'I eat simply,' he said, tucking a napkin into his collar. 'I share the same food as my dogs.'

Iseult responded with an automatic smile. She was an inept cook and an unadventurous eater. 'I've never eaten truffle,' she said, wondering which was brain and which sweetbread.

The Count was shocked and insisted that the boy fetch a truffle from the kitchen. The Count rolled it in his hand, and passed it back to the boy, who held it out to Iseult with his thoughts concealed.

'Smell it,' the Count insisted. 'There. What does it make you think of? No need to be polite.'

'A farmyard,' Iseult muttered, embarrassed.

'Sexual secretions,' the Count said, 'mingled in love and slightly ripened. Why else would men pay a fortune for them? Why else do pigs search for them so enthusiastically?' He snorted and attacked his plate with gusto.

The next course arrived in a smoke-blackened earthenware pot whose lid was sealed by a pastry crust. This, the Count explained, breaking the seal, was *daube de pieds de porc* – pig's feet marinated in cognac and braised overnight in a slow bread oven with aromatics and red wine. With this country dish, a favourite of Lemonnier's from childhood, came a Musigny of ineffable complexity.

'Like a peacock's tail opening in your mouth,' the Count said, as Iseult took her first sip.

Silence settled, save for the chink of cutlery and the chiming of crystal swaying in a draught. The Count ate without pause. Iseult wasn't hungry. She looked down the length of the table into Lemonnier's painted harlequin's face and thought: of course he knows that Cathal is working out how to rip him off. He's encouraging it. He's playing a game.

Sighing, the Count wiped his chin with his napkin. 'Tell me about this soldier of fortune who trains hawks.'

Iseult directed a stare at Cathal, who busied himself with his food.

'He's not only in it for the money,' she said. 'He's doing it out of . . .' She broke off in confusion.

'Ah,' Lemonnier said, his expression softening. 'He is your champion, your Tristan.'

'Is there any chance that Fox is still alive, still in Morocco?'

'*Monsieur Renard* is not easily killed. But even if your friend finds him, then what? Morocco is like a lobster pot – easy to get into, not so easy to get out.'

'You could help.'

'I've already explained that the Count can't get involved,' Cathal swiftly added.

Lemonnier toyed with his glass. 'Perhaps I spoke in haste,' he said. 'After all, what have I got to lose?'

'We wouldn't dream of putting you to any further trouble,' Cathal said, looking daggers at Iseult. 'We've already taken too much advantage of your hospitality.'

'For heaven's sake,' Iseult blurted, stunned by Cathal's uncharacteristic consideration.

'In any case,' the Count said, 'I'm curious to meet the man who trains eagles.'

'I bet he could get rid of those dogs, too,' Iseult said. Seeing Cathal work his jaws, she sent him a smile sweet with malice. And yet she was puzzled. His attitude didn't make sense, unless he had given up Fox as a bad job and decided to concentrate on fleecing the Count.

Finally, the dessert arrived – a moulded almond-milk blancmange of sinister trembly whiteness. To accompany it, the Count presented a dusty bottle of wine aged to the shade of dark honey. The retainer showed the label before pouring: Château-d'Yquem, 1928.

'I chose it especially for you,' the Count told Iseult.

She sipped the oily liquid and found it delicious. 'Like nectar,' she said obligingly.

'Its unique flavour and texture is produced by *la pourriture noble* – the noble rot.' The Count bared his teeth in a malignant smile. 'I, too, have the noble rot.'

Cathal sent an undercover warning that from here on the going was treacherous.

The Count swirled his wine and watched the glycerols slide down the crystal. 'Darwin was right,' he said. 'I'm the living proof. My family is evidence.'

'Evidence of what?' Iseult asked.

'Of the law of natural selection; of the survival of the fittest. For thirty generations my family produced soldiers. Most of them died on the battlefield, and yet the line continued, stronger and more virile than ever, our land manured with their blood. And then what happened?'

Neither Iseult nor Cathal were disposed to hazard a guess.

'Peace. And what has peace brought? I'll tell you. Genetic senility, mental dwarfs. The weak survive with the fit; inferior strains outnumber the healthy. Don't take my word. Consider the Romans, the Greeks, the Mamluks, the Ottomans, the English. History groans with cultures who thrived on blood and adversity and who died feebly of the cancer of peace.'

'History is written by people who didn't have to live through it,' Iseult said curtly. 'Wars make good reading, but I'll choose cancer every time.'

A pall had descended on the table. The Count's face was streaked and exhausted. Outside, the dogs were baying on the mountain. The Count waved tiredly. 'Oh, go away,' he said. 'Can't you see I have guests?'

Next afternoon, after another meal of offal and exquisite wines, the Count took Iseult to view his favourite landscape, leaving a sullen Cathal to kick his heels. The first stage was covered by car, but after a few miles the road stopped. An elderly man – Lemonnier's huntsman – was waiting with two mules on which they rode through thick scrub, the valley closing in, until they reached a wide grassy clearing starred with white flowers and commanded by crags. Iseult looked for a sky with angels.

'Why here?' she asked.

'Because at this spot I won my spurs,' the Count said.

It was certainly a pleasant spot, but it lacked artistic definition. 'It's just a space,' she said. 'It needs figures.'

'You can add them later,' the Count said. He sat on a shooting stick and opened a recipe book – Eduard Nignon's

L'Heptaméron des Gourmets ou les Délices de la Cuisine Française.

Iseult began to sketch in charcoal. She found she was enjoying herself. 'Do you really have no family?'

'I have a Chinese wife somewhere. Nobody that matters.'

'What will happen to the house?'

'It passes to the Moroccans.'

'And your possessions? What about those lovely paintings?'

'Your brother has plans for them.'

The stub of charcoal snapped in Iseult's fingers.

The Count laughed. 'He's ambitious, your brother. That's good. But in more than one respect I have reservations. He's promiscuous, deceitful and greedy – so greedy that I fear one day the head may swallow the tail.'

Iseult could only bite her lip.

'Never mind,' the Count said. 'I was the same at his age.' A senile smile softened his face. 'We'll see,' he murmured.

Iseult looked about from the corner of her eye. 'See what?'

The Count's head jerked. He hadn't been speaking to her at all. He'd forgotten her presence. He shook his fist. 'Go on with the painting,' he urged her. 'Quick, there isn't much time. The light's going.'

19

David Canova's office was in a street given over to commercial services and boutiques off Madrid's Plaza Mayor. Dearborn ran his eye over the polished brass plaques in the lobby and saw that, in addition to the usual clutch of notaries, the building housed the embassy of a tiny African state, an escort agency, a company doctor and several import-export businesses whose titles stressed their global connections. International Procurement was the upfront name Canova had chosen for his arms business.

Dearborn took the stairs. Removal men were active on the first floor and he guessed that a lot of the tenants were short-stay. On the next floor he heard South African accents behind the frosted-glass door of an accountancy firm. So, he thought, this is the kind of place where spies go to turn a buck after their international playing days are over.

Canova's office was next to the photocopier and coffee-vending machine on the third floor. Dearborn peered through a glass panel. The fake mahogany desks were unblemished by paperwork, the hessian-covered walls unmarred by flow charts, calendars or any other sign of ongoing business.

'Can I help you, *Señor*?'

Turning, Dearborn looked upon a flame-haired woman in a suit of ruthless cut with the padded shoulders of a quarterback. He let a smile ease over his face.

'Why, thank you, ma'am,' he said, exaggerating his drawl. 'I was looking for David Canova. I rang a couple of times and left a couple of messages on his machine, but I guess he must be out of town.'

'*Señor* Canova's lease expired two months ago,' the woman said. She had a husky Catalan accent. Her expression told him that he wasn't the first to come looking.

'Do you know where I might be able to reach him?'

'He didn't leave a forwarding address.'

'Maybe his secretary would know,' he ventured, peering through the window as if he might spy such a person under the furniture.

'Dave didn't have a secretary. If he needed a letter typed, I let him borrow my girl.'

Dearborn took note of her familiar use of Canova's name. 'Aw heck, I've flown all the way from Syria to see Dave. We used to work for the same outfit and I was counting on his expertise.' Shaking his head, he turned away. 'It was some darn sweet business, too.'

He had reached the top of the stairs when she swallowed the hook.

'Dave and I stay in touch,' she said. 'If he should call, I'll tell him that *Señor* . . .'

'Doctor John Wesley Dearborn, ma'am.'

'Isabel Vilalta,' she said, taking his outstretched hand. 'How disappointing for you.'

'I mend easily. I guess Dave's the loser. Well, looks like I got myself a day or two off the rein.'

Her smile, which had been strictly in the line of business, reshaped itself. 'Do you know Madrid well?'

'First visit since the old regime. Boy, it's changed. Last time I was here, it was all armoured motorcades and police snipers.'

'Now it is fiesta all the time.' She was still holding on to his hand, appraising him in a way that made him tingly under the collar. 'Are you busy this evening?'

'My plans were all centred on Dave.'

'It would be my pleasure to introduce you to the new Madrid.'

'Why, that would be purely delightful.'

'Come to my office and we'll find out how you like to be entertained.'

There was a directness – almost a coarseness – about the way she looked at him that went straight to the mark. Squeezed into the tiny elevator with her, trapped in her aura of jasmine, he became aware of sensation below the waist for the first time since Magda had left. He coughed and pretended interest in the fluorescent light. Maybe he was on the mend.

Isabel Vilalta's office was an airy suite occupied by a girl pecking away on a word processor.

'What kind of business do you have here – secretarial agency?'

'We provide a complete service for businessmen and women. Can I get you a drink?'

'Too early for me,' Dearborn said. New Woman, he thought. How the world had moved on in his absence.

On the restful wallpaper hung two good reproductions of Goya's Maja portraits – twin canvases of the same young woman in identical poses, one clothed in a dress that moulded itself to the deep contours of her thighs and ripe breasts, the other nude, her gaze fixed contemplatively at about the level of his . . . Dearborn reddened. Under the influence of Isabel's perfume and the provocative stare of the artist's model, he found himself seriously discomposed.

'Some people say she was modelled on the Duchess of Alba,' Isabel murmured at his side. 'Others think she was a fantasy.'

Dearborn gave closer attention to the paintings. The smile on the courtesan clothed was pure allure, anticipation; the way she held her arms crossed behind her head a signal of her defencelessness. But what exactly had transpired after she undressed? Was that smile on the nude expectation or repletion?

Far from allowing Dearborn space to compose himself, Señora Vilalta refused to give quarter, stepping right up until in self-defence he was obliged to back away. His line of retreat was cut off by a low-slung couch into which he gratefully dropped.

'So, John,' Señora Vilalta said, placing a leather-bound album beside him, 'let us see if we can turn your fantasy into flesh and blood.' She seated herself behind an impressive desk and placed both hands before her.

Dearborn grinned like a half-wit at the word processor. 'What kind of service did you say you run here?'

'Total. *Todos*.'

Opening the album, Dearborn found himself studying the prospectus of one Pitusa Bustamente, twenty-three, an economics graduate from Barcelona whose hobbies were horse-riding, literature and . . . Dearborn looked up . . . conversation.

Señora Vilalta countered his astonishment with an executive smile. 'Take your time. If you have specialist interests, try nearer the back. Full details are available on request.'

Dearborn flipped pages. The last one carried the specifications of a muscle-bound black girl with a ring in her nose. He didn't read her hobbies.

'We take all major credit cards,' Isabel Vilalta said.

Climbing out of the couch made considerable inroads into Dearborn's dignity. 'Do I look like I need to pay for my pleasures?'

She smiled at the paintings. 'We all must pay for our pleasures, John. And the best doesn't come cheap.'

At the door, Dearborn checked himself. 'I guess you took care of a lot of Dave's clients.'

'They always expressed satisfaction. Take a card in case you change your mind.'

'Maybe I'll send a friend.'

Feeling all kinds of almighty fool, Dearborn got himself clear. Around the corner he eyed a news-stand bristling with pubic hair and nipples and thought that there certainly had been a great unbuttoning since the Caudillo's exit.

Esther was waiting in the old-fashioned café where he'd left her, sitting under a ceramic mural advertising drinks. She was reading a book and looked about fifteen years old.

He slumped heavily opposite her, ordered a dry sherry and didn't speak until it was secure inside him. 'Canova's gone, closed the store, probably owes rent. Haven't you people done any homework?' He tossed Señora Vilalta's card on the table. 'She runs a deluxe escort agency one floor down. If you want a list of Canova's clients, they're all on computer, right down to which side of the bed they sleep.'

Esther stowed the card. 'That was clever of you.'

The compliment mitigated Dearborn's wrath. It had been a long time since anyone had given him a pat on the head. He took another look at Esther. She had a sallow oval face, an intelligent brow and the most perfectly demarcated mouth imaginable.

'Did anyone tell you you look like an Ottoman princess?'

Esther drew herself up in deterrent fashion. 'My family's from Ethiopia.'

'Even better. Where did you learn to speak such good English?'

'Berkeley.'

'A real exotic.' Dearborn's finger chased his drink mat around the table. 'My plans for this evening fell through. It's years since I saw a movie. There's a Buñuel season showing near my hotel. Would you like to go?' Christ, he thought, it was like taking up circuit training after a ten-year lay-off. 'I'm out of practice,' he confessed.

Esther's astringent expression sweetened. She gathered up her purse. 'I don't socialize when I'm working.'

So Dearborn ate alone again – hake in green sauce served by a shaky ancient who told him about the siege of Madrid. By ten, when the city was starting to roar, he found himself back in his hotel room, toying with the idea of calling Magda. He fell asleep on the notion and woke groping for the phone.

'Doctor John? Dave Canova here. I called as soon as I could. Sorry I forgot to put the gone-fishing sign up.'

He was drunk, trying to sound sober, and nearly getting away with it except for the occasional word that slipped sideways under his tongue.

'Isabel tells me we worked for the same company.'

'Middle East branch.'

'That's great, John. What line are you in now?'

'Oh, same as ever. Analysis, security advisement, forward planning. And that's why I called on you, Dave, because if there's one thing I'm not, it's a hardware broker.'

'Who do I have to thank for the referral?'

'An old pal from Panama City.'

The cagey pause that followed was filled with background hubbub.

'Dave – you still there?'

'Sure. Why don't you outline your requirements?'

'It's a big contract, but definitely not state of the art. Quantity rather than quality. Interested?'

'I just closed a deal not two hours ago. You can probably hear the celebration. Fact is, John, I'm juggling a lot of balls at this moment and I don't want to drop any. Maybe if you gave me a few specifics.'

'Like?'

'Like how big is big?'

'We're thinking around six noughts.'

'There's a lot of interference back here. Did I hear "six"?'

'Maybe nearer seven.'

Canova gave a hungry sigh, almost a sob, converted to a stiff cough. 'I work on fifteen per cent for sourcing the material and arranging shipment. Any other services come extra.'

'Got you. But frankly, Dave, we don't envisage anything out of the ordinary.'

'If you like my quotation, I'll expect a performance bond for seven and a half per cent of the goods' value. Letters of credit are payable on presentation of bills of lading.'

'That's agreeable.'

'You know all this shit, John, but you'd be amazed how many assholes I have to do business with.'

'I can imagine.'

'Okay now, let me see if there's a window in my diary.

Tomorrow, uh-huh. Wednesday is a crazy day for me. Can you do Thursday, seven o'clock, the Sheraton?'

'There's no air in my schedule, Dave. I'm flying to Ankara Wednesday night. Maybe I could come to wherever you are. Whereabouts is that, Dave?'

'Lisbon, but I'm due in Paris for breakfast.'

'Dave, I put you top of my list but I have other names. It's a buyer's market, with a lot of good stuff going begging, as you'll be the first to know.'

For several seconds, the only noise was bar-room surf.

'Let's see if I can rearrange my schedule,' Canova said.

'Hey, no need. I've got a great idea. You like fishing?'

'You mean for fish?'

'I've got a boat up in Marin, near Vigo. How about joining me the day after tomorrow?'

'Tomorrow would be better.'

'Tomorrow's too tight.'

'Well, my margins are tight, too, but if that's the earliest you can manage.'

'There's a mid-morning plane to Vigo, and then it's a half-hour cab ride up the coast. I'll be at the dock. The boat's called *Pyrotechnic II*. Bring a friend. Hell, bring two. Isabel will fix you up. Let me give you a couple of recommendations. Like, there's Nancy – mouth like an oil seal and a . . .'

'Much appreciated, Dave, but I'd sooner leave the partying till after.'

'Commendable attitude, Doctor John. Look forward to getting to know you. Have a nice evening, you hear.'

It was one-fifteen in the morning. Dearborn rang the number Natti and Esther had given him. Waiting for someone to answer, he discovered he was sweating.

Natti answered and told him that Esther was asleep. Dearborn insisted that she be woken.

'I think this approach stinks,' he said, when he had outlined his schedule. 'He's taking tomorrow off to check me out.'

'What did you expect?'

'He's a very unpleasant proposition and I have deep reservations about being alone with him on the high seas.'

'You're frightened,' Esther said softly, as if his want of courage held appeal for her.

'Of course I'm not,' Dearborn intended to say, but in course of delivery he managed to omit the negative.

20

He had always prided himself on being sufficient unto himself, but he found his solitary state dragging like a guest who had long overstayed his welcome. He spent the afternoon doing the Prado – bleeding Christs, stainless virgins, hidalgos arthritic with self-pride – standing for an hour in front of Goya's *Maja*s without getting to the bottom of her enigma. That evening, he gathered his courage to the sticking point and went to a club, took one look at the jostling flesh and reversed step. He ate Chinese, and at eleven, having made inroads on the mini-bar, he called Magda.

'I'm in Madrid. I've been thinking of you all day. Remember that fish restaurant? I ate there yesterday. It's the only joint that hasn't changed.'

'The one where they gave us free champagne?'

'No, that was another place. I'm talking about the restaurant with the oak panelling and the . . . oh, never mind.'

'Sorry, John. I've had an exhausting day.'

'Mother being a trial?'

'She doesn't get any easier, but no, today I started a job.'

'Oh?'

'Secretary in a hospital casualty department. Mornings only.'

'Any other changes you'd like to tell me about?'

'One at a time is all I can handle.'

'So you're not dating anyone?'

'I haven't heard that word since college.'

'Well, whatever you New Women call it these days.'

'Where would I find the time?'

'Magda, remember Goya's courtesan in the Prado? It was her that got me thinking about you.'

'I don't look a bit like her.'

'All women remind me of you.'

'Does that mean you're getting close enough to make comparisons?'

'Quit fooling, Magda.'

'I'm sorry, John.'

'It's tearing me up, Magda. Let's call it quits.'

'John, pain is part of the process.'

'Is that what you tell them in Casualty?'

'John, you refuse to listen. You'll never learn.'

'Learn how to stop loving you? If that's part of the process, I'll go on being a damn fool. Listen, Magda, I've changed a lot already. I'm not the man you left.'

'You'd better let me be the judge of that.'

'I intend to. I'm flying over in a couple of weeks.'

'Lauren will be thrilled. She misses you and she's taking it out on me. Call tomorrow, around six.'

'I'll try. Tomorrow I'm going fishing.'

'Doesn't sound like your idea of fun. What kind of fishing?'

'Shark fishing, I expect. And no, it isn't my kind of fun.'

He didn't sleep much. At dawn he went jogging, then ate breakfast while winging north over the *meseta*.

Vigo was a cross between a Nova Scotia hamlet and the Khrushchev school of high-rise, the tops of the apartment blocks obscured by hanging cloud, their bases planted in peasant smallholdings of maize and beans. All the way to Marin, Dearborn kept an eye out for the Israelis. He thought he saw Natti way down the quayside.

Pyrotechnic II was a converted inshore fishing boat. Canova, black-bearded and tanned to the hue of iodine, stood in a well at the back of the boat, coiling a rope. But the reassuringly nautical impression didn't bear close inspection. His once-handsome face was suffused with toxins, his eyes like something cultured in a test-tube. There was a scab on his lip, food scraps in his beard, a glass of liquor to hand, and even allowing for the brisk wave movement, his gait was unsteady. But Canova drunk seemed more than a match for Dearborn sober. He insisted on frisking his guest for concealed weapons or wires, running his hands over him with brisk competence and chatting about the day's prospects. 'I'd say we're in for some weather by nightfall.'

'It looks pretty rough now,' Dearborn remarked, reacting to the swell with a heave of misgiving.

'*Pyrotechnic* is built to cope. You like her?'

'Neat,' Dearborn said. 'Very shipshape.'

He stood in the cabin while Canova steered. Even chugging out of the harbour, waves smacked over the bows. As they met open water, a school of porpoises frisked past.

'You hear about the Englishman who had sex with a dolphin?'

So they were in for a session of jokes.

'True story. It was a wild dolphin that hung around a harbour. This guy used to go down to the quay and, I don't know, jerk it off or something. There are some funny fucking people walking the planet.'

'Right.'

'Sure you don't want a drink? It'll settle your stomach.'

Granite headlands came into sight along the coast. 'Where are we bound?'

'A wreck about three miles out.'

Shore was a murky smudge when Canova throttled back. He moved to the stern with a couple of rods. 'I'm wondering if I'm making a mistake talking to you,' he said.

'Why would you think that?' Dearborn said, his stomach queasing up.

Canova flashed a smile like a decal. 'You might be after my pension rights.'

'Hell, Dave, I cut my ties with the agency. I'm in the private sector, same as you.'

'Kissing ass for a construction company in Morocco.'

'You've been checking up on me,' Dearborn said, striking a balance between coyness and disapproval.

'Covering my ass is an art I cultivate, Doctor.'

'Glad to hear it,' Dearborn said. He kept casting glances at the seat in the stern while Canova busied himself with the fishing gear.

'A guy with your background, all those years in Lebanon and Tehran. I bet every second guy you met was an arms dealer. Why didn't you just try Beirut Yellow Pages?'

Dearborn dragged his gaze from the seat. 'Well, that might be a little too close to home for our purposes. And you know how Arabs do business – here a commission, there a commission, everywhere a second cousin wanting a percentage. And after you've signed on the line, the buyers open up the crates and find they've bought three tons of hair oil.'

Canova baited two lines with stale herrings and dropped them over. 'Who's the pal from Panama?'

Dearborn's mind clogged. Now or never. 'Lova Hazan,' he said, his insides mushy.

Canova did a quarter-turn. He stared and he stared.

'He sends his bests,' Dearborn added.

Canova laughed loud, long and scarily. 'Lova Hazan,' he said, wiping tears from his eyes.

'Glad it makes you happy.'

Canova poured himself another drink. 'Got the shopping list?'

Dearborn handed it across. He didn't like the way Canova skipped over his answers, as if they weren't worth consideration. He had a bad feeling that somewhere he had made a mistake that couldn't easily be undone. 'I wouldn't have thought there'd be any problems with availability,' he said.

Canova perused the list several times. 'No,' he agreed, 'most of this you can buy in your local K-mart. Yeah, I can source every item from stock.'

'In Spain?'

'Portugal.'

'How soon can you give me a firm quotation?'

'End of the week, but if you want a ball-park figure, you're looking at between eleven and thirteen million.'

'I have to say that's more than we had in mind.'

'Never knowingly undersold, John. What do you want on the EUC?'

'Istanbul. An end-user's certificate should be routine.'

'That depends. I mean, this junk isn't for the Turkish military.'

Dearborn tried to project righteous irritation. 'After the goods are paid for, I figure what we do with them is neither here nor there and not something you need to know. Now let's move on to timing, shall we?'

'Don't know what, John? I mean, that's the fucking problem, isn't it? If I don't know what it is I'm not supposed to know, how do I know if it's worth knowing or not?'

'I follow your logic, Dave, but my principals wouldn't want you burdened with that level of responsibility.'

Canova seemed quietly pleased. 'Responsibility without power,' he said. 'The story of my life. And that's why I'm beachcombing, and guys like you who only saw a combat zone from an embassy compound are on million-dollar contracts. No offence.'

'None taken. Look, Dave, I could feed you any old bullshit.'

'Try me.'

'Okay, the weapons are for an Iraqi-Kurdish group.'

'No shit. In that case, where are the NBC suits?'

'The what?'

'Chemical warfare outfits. Hey, you really are new to the arms market.'

'I've already admitted it, Dave.'

'Tell you what. Call it twelve and I'll throw in a mobile field hospital, still in its box. Cost seventeen million.'

'I don't think so.'

'I guess the Kurds walk away from their wounded.'

Dearborn treated it as a joke. 'By the way,' he said, 'what are we fishing for?'

'Conger. Some brutes down there.'

Dearborn watched the float on his line, imagining the eels in the wreck. He knew he was going to be sick.

'I think we deserve ourselves a celebration,' Canova said.

'You go ahead. I took seasickness pills and booze doesn't agree with them.'

Canova went into the cabin and came out a minute or two later, his pupils furiously dilated.

Dully, Dearborn took note of the shotgun in his hand. 'What's that for? You shoot the eels?'

Canova lurched towards him, the shotgun pointed undeviatingly at his midriff, as if it was mounted on gimbals. 'Show and tell time,' he said.

'This is not the way I like to do business, Dave.'

'You're right, Doctor John. It's not your style at all.'

'You'd better turn this boat round. I'm feeling green as all hell.'

'We're in international waters. I lay down the rules.' Canova put the shotgun close to Dearborn's ear. 'Lova Hazan is all things to all people, you understand, but he's definitely not my buddy.'

'Well, if you don't want to do business, say so and let me off.'

'In fact, the last time we came in contact, the little frig tried to off me.'

'Time's a great healer,' Dearborn said, sweating ice, 'and there's no room for animosity in business.'

Canova stepped back, faking concern. 'You're not looking too peachy, Doctor.'

'I swear to God, Dave, I'm going to be sick.' In one effortless spasm, Dearborn vomited. He hung over the rail, the shotgun barrel cold on his neck.

'The Kurds couldn't buy a BB gun between them, and Lova Hazan was never motivated by anything but bread. You'd better tell me who the principals are, Doctor.'

'Shoot me,' Dearborn mumbled. 'You'd be doing me a favour.'

The cold pressure on his neck lifted as Canova whirled

and fired. Out of a flock of seagulls that had been squawking in their wake, one settled slowly to the water, a wing outstretched, a spot of red on the white.

Dearborn emptied the remaining contents of his stomach. 'Why didn't they tell me you were a crazy?' he groaned.

'Who?' Canova demanded, his eyes fizzing like neurones. He ground the muzzle into Dearborn's left ear. 'Who's "they"?'

Dearborn reckoned he had another second to live. 'The Israelis.'

Canova pumped another shell and fired carelessly. 'What the fuck is this horseshit? You make it up as you go along?' He fired again.

'I swear, Dave.'

Canova backed off, letting the shotgun hang. He sat down as if his legs had gone. 'I want to believe you,' he pleaded. 'I need the contract. This fucking peace and goodwill on earth is killing me.' He raised the gun again. 'But you have to see it my way, Doctor. I've been burned once too often. I carry scar tissue.'

'Please,' Dearborn begged. He half-lifted his arm towards the distant land. 'They're waiting for me.'

Canova laughed to himself. 'Oh, Doctor John,' he crooned, 'you're killing me.'

One of the reels began to click. The line tightened then slackened then tightened again. The float was pulled under.

'Better see what's on the other end,' Canova said.

'Fuck the fishing.'

Canova elbowed Dearborn aside. He took the rod and applied pressure. 'You got something there alright. Oo-hoo, feels damn big.' He couldn't reel in with the shotgun in his hand. 'Stand over there, Doctor John, where I can see you.' He grounded the shotgun against his thigh. 'Conger for sure. The ship was carrying a cargo of horses when she went down. The eels grew big as pigs, take your entire fucking head in their mouths.' He grinned at Dearborn, his face a damaged circuit board.

Dearborn measured the distance to the stern. 'Oh God,' he said, retching, 'here we go again.' He made a rush for the rail, dropped to his knees and hung his head over, his hands dangling down. He felt under the seat, touched cold metal.

'Yes,' Canova was saying, 'let's get this monster topside, and then we'll see what we shall see.'

Dearborn flung himself back and round, rolling over in an inch of sea-water, a Nambu pistol waving at the sky. 'Don't come near me,' he screamed.

'Where in fuck did that come from?' Canova marvelled.

'You hear me? Stay away.'

'Give it to me,' Canova said. Odd pulses spoilt the calm of his face. He bent his knees to recover the shotgun.

The pistol discharged with no volition from Dearborn.

Canova touched his scalp as if checking it was still attached. His expression was stricken by awe. 'You could have killed me.'

'I'm scared enough to do anything,' Dearborn shouted. He poked the pistol at Canova as if it was a pitchfork. 'Let go of the gun. Kick it over here.' He grabbed the shotgun and scrambled to his feet.

'Alright, man, take it easy. That thing's on a hair trigger.'

'So am I,' Dearborn shouted. He whirled the shotgun into the ocean. 'Sit down, put your hands under your butt.'

Canova complied, looking as if he would jump any second. 'You're not going home, Doctor John. No way.'

'See how my hands are shaking,' Dearborn said. 'I'm not in control. Now let's both take a deep breath and start behaving like reasonable adults.' He began to breathe in the manner demanded by the instructor at Magda's antenatal classes.

'Make the most of it, Doctor John.'

'The Israelis are waiting for me, Dave. Give me what truth you can about Lova Hazan and it ends there, with goodwill all round. Refuse, and they'll make sure you stay hassled. That's the choice.'

'Fuck you.'

'There's nothing personal in this, Dave. Lova Hazan is the man we're after.'

Canova stiffened, ready to charge through blood and shit no matter what, then the crazy lights went out behind his eyes. It was a screen gone dead.

'There never was a deal, was there?'

'It wasn't my idea,' Dearborn said. The storm in his brain had passed. He felt ashamed. He took a thousand bucks from his jacket. 'I want to square things with you.'

Canova picked at his fingernails. He looked at the bills.

'Go on,' Dearborn said. 'I know you can use it.'

Canova picked up the money, nodding sadly, as if he recognized that his entire life had been preparation for this moment. He began to flick through the bills, but was distracted by the slow ratcheting of the reel. 'Would you mind . . .'

'If it helps you concentrate.'

Canova took up the rod and pumped it experimentally. He held out a hand. 'Pass the bottle,' he ordered. He took his time with it. When he began speaking, his voice was controlled, his tone measured.

'Lova Hazan drifted into Colombia with a bagful of Uzis, claiming to be an ex-officer of some special forces unit. He was full of shit like that. One day he'd tell you he'd been a racing-car driver, another that he'd been part of the team that freed the hostages at Entebbe.'

'Let me get something straight,' Dearborn said. 'You didn't actually know him at this time.'

'Not until about two years after.'

'Okay, so Lova Hazan arrives in Colombia looking for work.'

'This was the beginning of the cocaine wars and an Israeli bodyguard was considered very chic. Tommy Blanco took him on.'

'Blanco?'

'Aka Jorge Castrillon, Roberto Garcia, Luis Noguero and, to his many enemies, dead and alive, the Nail – because he wasn't a very agreeable person.'

'Tommy Blanco was a big trafficker.'

'Not a member of the Cartel, but definitely a major independent. The Cartel tried to remove him from the population count. That's why he took on Hazan. The two of them decided to transfer business to Panama, but the big boys came after him – paid a guy to do a *trabajito* on him. Hazan earned his keep on that one, because it was the hit guy who had the job done on *him*. So then the Cartel decided they could at least put Blanco out of the game. Four years ago, acting on information received, the DEA picked Tommy up in a Buffalo motel. In his car they found sixteen kilos of coke – ninety-six per cent pure – a million dollars in notes, three Galil assault rifles and an Uzi with a laserscope.'

'Twice, you've mentioned Israeli weaponry. Was that obtained by Hazan?'

'Maybe. He was always claiming he had friends high up in the Israeli defence establishment. I thought it was another of his fantasies until I ran into him in Honduras.' Canova heaved on the rod, took a couple of turns on the reel and heaved again. 'Snagged,' he said.

'Honduras,' Dearborn reminded him.

Canova leaned his full weight against the resistance. The line hummed. Whatever was on the end came free. 'I was up in La Ceiba to take receipt of weapons. This was just after Congress had blocked funds for the Contras, and we were sourcing from Israel, the UK – calling in favours. I went into this bar and Hazan was there with a guy I'd seen on the ship.'

'Did he introduce himself.'

'Yoshi, Moshe – I forget. Big guy, white hair – looked a bit like Arik Sharon. He was a real Nazi.'

'What?'

'Israel must be redeemed, cleansed of the Arabs – all that nice stuff.'

Dearborn recalled with unease his meeting with Zwy Gur. 'If you can remember the name, it might be worth your while.'

'How much?'

'I'll do the best I can.'

'Five thousand. Tell them I know the name of the ship.'

'I'll see what I can do. Okay, let's get back to Buffalo. Blanco is arrested. What about Hazan?'

'Out of the country.'

'Was he the informant?'

'Definitely not.'

'How so sure?'

Canova smiled. 'Because it was me.'

'Oh. In that case, let me run the next bit myself. The DEA introduces Blanco to someone who offers to take care of his legal problems. This person flips him, puts him back on the street on condition he diverts some of the profits from coke to the Contras. Nod if I'm right.'

Canova shrugged.

'What was Lova Hazan's role?'

'Jack of all trades. Sometimes he carried weight, sometimes he couriered the takings to Panama, and sometimes he stayed at home minding the *estancia*.'

'What was he like as a person.'

'Smooth, freaky, an operator. I doubt if even Blanco got to the bottom of him.'

'Where can I find Blanco?'

'Shovelling coke in hell. Some of his *compadres* finally got to him. They taped a pound of HE under his Rolls.'

Dearborn breathed a sigh compounded of disappointment and relief. 'I guess that saves me a trip to Medellín.'

'Medellín, shit. They put his lights out right here. After Irangate, Blanco and Hazan transferred over to Spain and started a new distribution network.'

'That was about the same time *you* came to Spain.'

'Coincidence.'

'You said Lova Hazan tried to kill you.'

'Time's up,' Canova said. Something broke surface under the boat's side. 'A beauty,' he said, 'fifty pounds if it's an ounce. Pass me that hook. Better stand back. These fuckers

270

bite.' Canova leaned over with a gaff and hauled the conger aboard. It slithered into the scuppers and thrashed itself into knots.

Dearborn tried not to be distracted by the eel's spasms. 'Any theories as to why Hazan might want to visit Morocco?'

'They got drugs there, haven't they?' Canova said. He reversed the gaff and brought it down on the eel's head several times.

'You've been a great help,' Dearborn said.

They motored back in silence, Dearborn trying to keep the Nambu trained on Canova as discreetly as he could. At the harbour breakwater, he dropped it over the side. Grey dusk was succeeding the grey day. The wind was shaving the tops off the waves.

'While I'm ashore,' Dearborn said. 'Take a nap. Ease up on the booze. You're killing yourself.'

Canova stood with his hands slack on the wheel. 'Sometimes,' he said, 'I think that I'll fuel up, load a case of Scotch and just turn her towards the horizon.'

Dearborn restrained himself from giving Canova a sympathetic pat. 'Another day,' he said.

With dry land underneath him and Canova safely shipboard, Dearborn had never felt better – intoxicated at being alive. As agreed with Esther, he made his way to a waterfront bar-restaurant and dried himself at the stove. The furniture looked as if it had been made from driftwood soaked in creosote; the other occupants were a few old salts playing dominoes.

After an hour, his host brought him a fisherman's stew – a *zarzuela* of squid, conger, prawns and green-boned garfish. The dessert was figs and the wine came in an unlabelled litre bottle. The entire meal cost less than a Big Mac. Dearborn was dissecting a fig, which set him thinking about sex, when Esther came in, looking very *noir* in a designer trench-coat beaded with raindrops.

He poured her a tumbler of raw wine and pushed the figs in her direction, but she ignored both offerings, standing with her spine very straight, like a young schoolmistress trying to impose her authority over an unruly class.

'Come on,' she said, 'we'll talk as we drive.'

Dearborn was in no hurry and said so.

'We're not staying,' Esther said.

'I've still got business here,' Dearborn said. 'Sit down. And take off that coat will you? You're attracting more attention than Mata Hari.'

Esther glanced around. Everyone was watching. Flushing, she sat, still keeping herself erect, as if trying to create the illusion that Dearborn was nothing to do with her.

'Either your research is non-existent,' he said, 'or this whole exercise is designed to get rid of me with maximum unpleasantness.'

Esther turned her unreserved attention on him for the first time.

'Lova Hazan once tried to kill Canova,' Dearborn said. 'When I brought his name up, he went ape. If you hadn't got things right with the pistol, I'd be feeding the fishes.'

'Have you still got it?' Esther said. She stole another look at the door.

'It's in twenty fathoms,' Dearborn said. He rested his chin on his fist, trying to look unconcerned. 'Esther, I know you want to project a tough professional image, but a little sympathy wouldn't go amiss.'

A fugitive smile crossed her face. The room was filling, fogging up with cigarette smoke and conversation. Under her coat, Esther was wearing a sweater that looked very soft. Dearborn recognized the scent of Chanel No 19. He shut his eyes.

'That was my all-time favourite perfume,' he said, 'until my wife passed a bottle on to her mother. Now my senses are confused.'

Esther swung her hair impatiently. It was black with a slight curl. 'What did you get out of Canova?'

'Not much you don't already know. Nothing you couldn't find out from your local reference library.' Dearborn drank.

'How much of that have you had?'

'Not sure. They bring another bottle as fast as you can empty them.' In fact Dearborn had finished less than half a bottle, but it suited him to let Esther think he was drunk.

'Come on,' she said, 'I want your report while you're still sober.'

'What's the matter? You're like a cat that can't get comfortable.'

By a visible effort of will, Esther relaxed. Dearborn related the details of his fishing trip, saving the best till last. 'Lova Hazan was on drinking terms with a Mossad agent who ran arms to the Contras. Canova has the details and is prepared to share them.'

Esther's small-boned features went still.

'It'll cost you five grand,' he said, 'but it's worth it.'

She made a dismissive gesture. 'We don't owe that animal anything.'

Dearborn was beginning to find Esther a chore. 'In a righteous world, people like Canova would be put down. But this isn't a righteous world, and none of us can bear too much scrutiny – not you, not me and, most of all, not Zwy Gur. I was there with him in the Lebanon and it was not pretty.'

Esther cut him off like an obscene phone call. She slapped a piece of paper on to the table. 'We've got to get back to Madrid,' she said.

There were four names on it: Ahmed Rafidi, Daniel Escobar, Charles Villon, Clayton Smith.

'Canova's clients who were entertained by Isabel Vilalta's girls,' Esther explained, still angry. 'We're checking the first three, but Smith was easy. He works for the DEA in Madrid.'

'Oh, how the wheels go round.'

'Zwy Gur told you it was all linked.'

'Maybe because it was him who put the chain together.'

'Natti's arranged a meeting with Smith tomorrow evening. He can bring Hazan's career up to date. Now let's go.'

'What's the big rush? Frightened Canova will fall through the door? Don't worry; he's out of it.'

Esther forced her mouth into the semblance of a smile. Her slim hands drummed on the table.

'Talking to a burn-out like Canova is one thing,' Dearborn said. 'Pressuring a narcotics official is another.'

'Smith will talk. When Canova came to Spain, he tried to set himself up as a drug smuggler. He thought Smith would be useful.'

'You're saying he's corrupt?'

'Professionally, I don't know, but he has unusual personal propensities which Canova exploited.'

Dearborn laughed. 'Unusual propensities?' He leaned closer. 'Since you obviously studied creative writing at Berkeley, perhaps you'd care to tell me what they taught you to call blackmail.'

'He's a pervert,' Esther said angrily.

'Oh yes,' Dearborn said. 'What's his kink?'

Esther's gaze flickered. 'He likes to be humiliated by women.'

Dearborn clicked his tongue. 'Him, too, huh? For years I thought I was the only one.' He leaned even closer. 'Esther, that's not deviation. That's part of the deal.'

Disdain filled her eyes. She passed over a sheet without comment. It was a matter-of-fact summary of the services offered by thirty-six-year-old Mercedes Martinez, a single parent of young twins domiciled in Madrid.

Dearborn read and was aghast. 'She doesn't take prisoners, does she? Her turnover in clients must be fantastic; one visit and you're maimed for life. And what in hell is "golden rain"? No, on second thoughts I'd rather not know.' Dearborn pushed the sheet back. 'Well,' he said, 'we plumb the lower depths.'

'You'll see him?' Esther said uncertainly.

Dearborn puffed out his cheeks. 'After Canova, even an evening with Smith will seem like a trip to Disneyland.'

Puzzlement turned Esther's face on its side.

'But I need to know how long the chain is,' Dearborn said. 'I have to be in America in two weeks.'

'Two weeks is all we need you for.'

'You make me sound dispensable.' Dearborn checked his watch. 'Have you come to a decision about Canova?'

'I'll send someone tomorrow.'

'You're crazy. His head's chemical soup. By morning he'll have gone through half a dozen personality changes. Before I jumped ship, he was talking about arranging himself a Viking funeral.'

'I'll have to phone Natti in Madrid.'

'But he's right here. I saw him.'

'You were mistaken.'

'Well call him. Get a move on.'

Esther was torn, looking away, looking back. Finally, she said: 'We know about Lova's Israeli contact. The boat was the *Elsevier*, Danish, registered in Panama. It docked at La Ceiba in October, 1985. We have a list of the ship's company. We know the identity of the man who Canova saw with Lova Hazan.'

Dearborn palped his face, his scalp, the back of his neck. 'You're telling me I risked my life for intelligence you've already got.'

'Zwy Gur explained what you're doing,' Esther said impatiently. 'You're backtracking, looking for something we missed.'

Dearborn gripped the edge of the table. 'No disrespect, ma'am, but the difference is that Zwy Gur says it with conviction.'

Esther tipped her face scornfully. 'No wonder your wife left you.'

'What the heck has she got to do with it?'

'I don't like to be patronized.'

'I'm not patronizing you; I'm telling you that your methodology is a disgrace. You fucked up over Canova's place of work; you fucked up about his relationship with Lova Hazan, and now you're about to fuck up the one solid piece of intelligence to come out of this fuck-up.' Dearborn recovered his breath. 'Excuse my strong language.'

She actually and unreservedly smiled.

'You did a very good job in the circumstances.'

'I did?' Dearborn said, caught flat-footed.

'Let's drive back to Vigo together. I'm sure there's a Buñuel movie showing somewhere.'

Dearborn narrowed his eyes and looked at her from various angles. 'You're too subtle for me.'

Her smile had gone demure. She lowered her eyes. 'I've been wondering what an Ottoman princess looks like.'

'You had your chance. Now you'll never know.'

She ran her tongue round the wall of her mouth, definitely vamping. The come-on left Dearborn slightly chilled.

'For your information,' he said, 'they were sly and devious. They spent most of the time lying around in the seraglio having affairs with each other or the occasional passing eunuch, dreaming up ways of getting their own son on the throne.' He stood up. 'Wait here or go back to town,' he said. 'I'm going to call on Canova.'

He left her sitting among the domino players and went out into black night. Rain gusted in his face.

Without surprise, he heard quick footsteps behind him.

'Leave Canova alone,' she said to his back.

'I have two theories I want to try out on you,' he said.

She caught up with him. Her collar was up, her face waiflike and anxious.

'Lova Hazan traded dope for guns in Central America,' Dearborn said, striding at his own pace. 'Perhaps he was trying the same combo in Morocco.'

Esther stumbled in her efforts to keep up. 'France and America supply the Moroccans with all the weapons they need.'

'Like Iran?' Dearborn said. 'I've had a lot of experience of our Middle East allies, and the funny thing is we used to have a lot more than we have now.'

'It's pointless to speculate,' Esther said – although Dearborn hadn't got to the point of speculating.

They had left the inhabited quarter and they were passing warehouses. The wind tugged them off balance. A navigation bell clanged anxiously out by the harbour entrance.

'You said two theories.'

'More fact than theory,' Dearborn said. He stopped. Over Esther's shoulder, the water was a matrix of black and orange. 'Zwy Gur is using me as a bird dog to flush out the baddies. The missing link is the person who gets to me.'

Esther didn't speak for a moment, then she touched his hand. 'I think this is foolhardy. Canova's too unstable.'

'It's a bit late to be telling me that.'

Esther hung back as he approached the boat.

Pyrotechnic II looked deserted, groaning to itself on choppy waters. The wind sawed through its mast. No lights were showing.

'He must be sleeping it off,' Dearborn said.

Esther had eased up to him. 'Let him sleep.' She looked behind her at the unlovely bulk of a fish processing plant, shivered and moved closer. 'I'm cold and wet.' She walked her fingers up his sleeve. 'Let's find somewhere warm.'

He looked down into her sweet face. Rain streaked her cheeks. He bent and felt the cold of her lips, the feathering of her long lashes. She still had her eyes closed and her mouth slightly parted when he stepped back.

'After I've asked him a couple of questions.'

She almost stamped her foot. 'You've already asked them all.'

Without a word, he left her standing there.

'I'm your case officer,' she said in a different voice. 'I'm ordering you.'

He heard her cock a pistol – a chunky masculine sound – and all the bones in his spine fused. Over his shoulder he could just make out the glint of ordnance. He resumed walking as if his back was in traction.

'Please,' she said, her voice faint with distance or despair.

He jumped aboard. The cockpit was empty, lit by green dials. Boards creaked underfoot. He smelt Chanel No 19 and turned to see Esther in a partial crouch, her gun extended in textbook fashion, her face witchy in the gloom. 'He's not here,' she murmured.

'Dave Canova would never walk out on five grand. He's probably down below, passed out.'

She detained him as he reached the stairhead. 'John, I can't hand out taxpayers' money without approval from Zwy Gur. Even if I had the approval, I don't have the cash.'

He touched her cheek. 'Let us see what we shall see.'

'John, don't go in there. John!'

The cabin door was open. The inside was hot, stinking of booze and vomit. A radio played Latin rhythms. A reading light shone down on Canova, who was sprawled face down on his bunk. 'Dave?' Dearborn said, quite loudly.

'Drunk,' Esther said, with feminine disgust.

'Dead to the world.'

Esther's face was screwed up in revulsion. 'Come on. He's in no state to tell us anything.'

Dearborn felt for Canova's pulse. He let the arm drop. Gingerly he lifted Canova's head. His face was frightful, black and congested, eyes bolting.

'Let's get off this fucking boat, right now,' Esther shouted, close to hysteria.

But in the presence of death, Dearborn's locomotor mechanism had packed up. He found himself sitting on the bunk opposite the corpse. There was a photograph of Canova with his shirt open to the waist, a gold chain around his neck, looking like a gigolo, a pretty Hispanic girl clinging to his waist. Dearborn put his hands over his face. 'Why?' he mumbled through his fingers.

'If you don't leave right now,' Esther said in a warning tone. 'I'll . . .'

'What?' Dearborn looked at Esther through parted fingers. 'Humiliate me.'

Esther moved briskly to the foot of the steps, the professional once more. 'He died of asphyxia,' she said.

'He's been juicing and tooting since he left the service,' Dearborn shouted. 'He didn't overdose by accident on this night of all nights.'

'You said yourself he talked of suicide.'

Anger gave Dearborn his legs back. 'Clayton Smith doesn't sound too stable either. I guess my visit will be a death sentence for him, too.'

'Ssh . . .' Esther said, her eyes magnified by alarm.

'Tell Zwy Gur it's finished.'

'Shut your stupid mouth,' she hissed, swinging the gun with real intent.

He caught his breath, waiting for the flash. Her hand was to her lips.

'There's someone on deck,' she whispered.

Above the creaking and groaning of waves and timbers, Dearborn heard a sound like a hand slapping wet wood. On the instant he was scared witless.

Still keeping her finger on her lips, Esther began to climb the steps, keeping to the wall. Dearborn followed, admiring her courage. The cockpit was as they had left it.

'Sounds like it's coming from the stern,' Dearborn whispered.

Esther squirmed over to the door in the approved manner. At the door she swung up on her haunches, gun cocked at her breast, as if tensed for prayer. Even in the depths of fear, Dearborn found time to think that no matter how real, civilians bearing guns indoors looked like bad television. Inch by slow inch, she craned round the doorway. At least a minute went by before she ducked back. 'There's someone there,' she said.

She strained into the dark again, and this time when she

showed her face to Dearborn, it was waxy with horror. 'Oh God,' she said. 'I think it's another body.'

The slapping sound was repeated many times before Dearborn let his breath go. He stood up and and walked to the stern. 'It's not Natti,' he said. 'It's only a conger eel that doesn't know it's dead.'

21

The clouds broke the day after Case found Valentine's body, swamping Marrakech under half its winter rainfall. When it stopped it was dark and Case climbed to the roof terrace with a beer. Four storeys below, kids frisked in the flood and ladies splashed homewards screaming with laughter, their robes hiked above their knees.

Another day, another blank. Low was ready to pack it in, and worse, Laschen had disappeared – probably gone back to his village. In a country where freedom of information only extended to the sports pages, Moroccans were masters of reading between the lines. Laschen didn't need bold type to recognize that Fox was bad news.

Case decided to give it one more day, and then go and trap hawks.

Across the street, a woman drew flimsy curtains and disrobed, bending fluently from the waist. Watching her, Case realized he had spent a lot of time spying on people through windows – domestic havens glimpsed on urban ring-roads where he'd been dropped in the all-shut-up hours; farmhouse kitchens viewed in the spectral light of an image intensifier.

His peripheral vision registered a taxi crossing the intersection, carving a bow wave. Three men in suits and sunglasses got out. After mustering on high ground, they headed for the hotel entrance. Out of reflex, Case checked the roof, although he knew there was no way off it except the stairs.

He continued watching the silhouette of the woman behind the blinds; already he was a little in love with her.

The lights on the terrace went out moments before the three men in sunglasses arrived on the roof. In the semi-darkness they looked for a table that wasn't soaked. Having found one, they did a little *pas de trois* to make sure they were seated according to rank. First to settle was a tall slim man in a double-breasted suit with soft highlights – the governor. The person who made sure he was seated comfortably was the copper from the building site. The other one looked like makeweight, brought along for bulk in case the meeting should turn ugly.

A waiter came hurrying out, rattling a cup of coffee which he put down as if the saucer was scalding his fingers. He fled without looking to see who he was serving.

Police, Case thought, but not municipal.

The copper crooked his finger, indicating that they desired him to approach. He did so, legs fluttering, and pulled up a chair.

The governor didn't like the table setting and was rearranging it, placing his handbag to one side, a pack of Rothmans on the other, the coffee dead centre. He had a casual arrogance bred in. When everything was to his satisfaction, he began unwrapping a sugar lump with long, sensitive hands.

Case's own hands were shaking. He stuffed them under his thighs. 'Why come to me?' he asked.

'Because you have visited Morocco before,' the governor said in American-accented English, 'and know that there are many snakes in our country.'

'And wild dogs.'

The governor acknowledged the truth of it with a slim smile.

'Did you find your friend?' the copper asked in his basic but confident English.

'What was left of him,' Case said. 'I'd go to the police, except . . .' he spread his arms '. . . here you are.'

The governor dropped the sugar lump into his coffee and started on another. His sunglasses were as opaque as a blacked-out limo. Case resisted the urge to snatch them off.

'Why did you murder Forbes Valentine?'

Frowns gathered on the foreheads of all three.

'Valentine?' the copper said. 'This is not the name of the man you asked about.'

The governor was on his fourth sugar lump.

'You murdered Valentine because he knows where you're holding Digby Fox.'

A faint caution disturbed the governor's poise – only for a moment. He stirred his coffee syrup, sipped it, put a Rothmans into a tortoiseshell holder, lit it and exhaled with a sigh of pleasure long-awaited.

'That makes two you've killed.'

'M'sieur Fox? *Mais non*. I made a mistake. He left Morocco two weeks ago. Believe me, you're wasting your time.'

'I'm not talking about Fox. I'm talking about his Israeli friend.'

That froze all three to their chairs. The copper muttered something behind his hand. The governor rose and the others were on their feet a moment later. 'Your flights to London have been confirmed for Sunday. Be at the airport two hours before departure.'

'And if we miss the plane?'

The governor made a tiny feathering motion with his hands, indicating that he did not wish to stray into unpleasantness. He began to lead his underlings away.

'Why the performance?' Case called after them. 'If you want us out, all you have do is sign a deportation order.'

The three men came to a halt.

'Whoever you are, you're the wrong side of the law. Maybe I *will* go to the police.'

The makeweight swung and made a move in his direction. The governor restrained him. He walked back to where Case was standing.

'Why do you want this man?' he asked soothingly.

'He owes money.'

The governor winced at such frankness. 'Your friend is a smuggler of drugs. Our laws concerning smugglers of drugs and their accomplices are very severe. Do you understand?'

As a matter of fact, Case did. He had met a young American who had done time in a Moroccan jail for trying to export a few pounds of hash. As a result of scurvy, all his teeth had fallen out, for built into the Moroccan penal system was the assumption that the feeding of prisoners was the responsibility of relatives.

'I think you do *not* understand, m'sieur. There are criminals in our jails who have not seen the sun for twenty years. They live in night.' The governor inclined his fine head a couple of times to drive home the truth of his statement. 'Do you understand now?'

Case nodded.

'*Bon*. We will not speak again.'

He led his men away, leaving Case to wonder whether the governor meant that Fox was banged up in some black hole, or that solitary confinement without lights was what awaited Case if he failed to heed the warning. He went downstairs to the lobby. The manager had his nose buried in paperwork.

'Those men who just left,' Case said. 'Any idea who they were?'

The manager looked up, his face as blank as an egg, and handed him his bill.

Little more than forty-eight hours to do anything effective. He called Low. After a brief discussion, it was decided that enough was enough; the Waltham Forest Fishing Club would pick up Case en route for the airport. They would leave together, for safety and to preserve some aspect of dignity.

Case called the hotel in Casa and asked for Iseult O'Dwyer or her brother, but the answer was the same: they still hadn't arrived, although every night Monsieur O'Dwyer telephoned. Yes, the messages were passed on, the receptionist said tetchily.

'In that case, tell Iseult . . .'

'Yes, m'sieur?'

'Tell her I'm going home.'

Too dispirited to eat, Case went to bed early.

At three-thirty someone rapped on his door. 'M'sieur, there is a phone call.'

'Who is it?'

'A lady. English.'

He went down to the lobby, where three porters lay strewn in sleep. 'Iseult.'

'Hello, Pat. Who's Iseult?'

'Catty,' he managed to say. 'How on earth did you find me?'

'I remembered the name of the hotel.'

'It's late. Is everything alright?'

'Oh, the little monster's starting to kick up a fuss,' Catty said. Her tone was fond. In his mind's eye Case could see her looking down, running her hand over her belly.

'How are the hawks and dogs?'

'I might have known,' Catty said. She laughed good-naturedly, ever willing to indulge his obsession. 'They're fine. Alastair's thrilled to bits with the gos.' She paused. 'The reason I'm ringing, Pat . . . Dad says he'll buy Auchronie for us.'

'For us?'

'For us to live in.'

'On condition I marry you.'

'You'll keep the house, you'll still have the hawks. I know you're going to like the baby.'

'I can have the house without taking on something I never asked for.'

'No you can't, Pat.'

'What's that supposed to mean?'

'You won't be able to come back here.'

'I'll go where I want. It's a free country.'

Catty sighed, lovingly. 'You always chase after what you can't have.'

'But it's alright for you to take what you fancy.'

'Every baby has a right to his father. You should know that better than anyone.'

'I got by pretty well, didn't I?'

'Did you?'

Case couldn't work up conviction a second time.

'Pat, Archie Thain has asked me to marry him.'

Cruelty seemed to offer the only escape. 'Well don't let me stop you.'

'I told him it's you I love.'

Case grimaced. 'I'm sorry, Catty. I'm not in a position to do anything about it.'

Silence spanned the distance.

'So that's that, I suppose,' Catty said, her voice high and bright, still tinged with hope.

Case steeled himself. 'That's that,' he said, and stood waiting, his breath screwed up inside him, until she gently broke the connection.

He found himself on the roof terrace. The air was still and dense. Fat drops fell from the parapet, shivering the pools below. The city was tarnished under the burgeoning moon and pulsing stars. To the south, the first snows of winter were a soft gleam suspended from the sky. The window where the unknown woman had stood was dark and empty, and Case knew that he had reached another point of no return. For other people, the past was part of the present; it was parents, photographs, childhood books, schoolfriends. But for him it was truly past – a series of sealed compartments, closed doors.

Catty's voice went round on a loop. 'You always want what you can't have. You always . . .'

When he was a nipper, about eight or nine, he'd entered a competition on a biscuit wrapper. If you answered the questions right, you won two minutes plundering the toyshop of your choice. The questions were dead simple. He couldn't remember them now, but they were things like: 'what is the tallest mountain in England; what is the fastest land mammal?' Really, he should have sussed that the questions weren't going to cause too many problems for all the other kids who would enter, but it never occurred to him. And of course there was no parent to put him wise. He was dead certain he was going to win.

During the month before the result was due, he prepared for the big day, visiting the big toyshop in Percy Street, planning how to get the best out of his two minutes.

The month passed and no news arrived. He lived in dwindling hope. When two months were gone, he wrote to the biscuit company and a week later a parcel arrived containing a pack of samples.

He still thought of it as the biggest betrayal of his life. Years later, on the night he did a runner from the Home, he put a brick through the toyshop window.

Nah, the only way to get owt out of life was to grab it. Ask Fox, ask Valentine, ask Cathal O'Dwyer, ask Low. Ask anyone.

Feet whispered on concrete and he spun.

'Rest tranquil, gentle. This is me.'

'Hello, Laschen. Where have you been?'

'I know where this man is,' Laschen said, laying out Fox's snap on the parapet.

'Yeah?' Case said, having no difficulty curbing his excitement.

'He is in a rich house in the Ourika Valley,' Laschen said, pointing south by south-east.

'Whose house?'

'The man who has seen him says it belongs to a rich man from Rabat.'

'So you haven't been there yourself.'

'It is him,' Laschen insisted, prodding Fox's face.

Case smiled at the sleeping ranges. 'Remember the time we tramped through the Atlas for a week after an eagle that turned out to be a buzzard?'

Laschen lifted his chin, taking offence.

Case studied him. It was strange the way different cultures had different blindspots. Mountain Berbers like Laschen saw birds of prey every day. Sometimes eagles killed their lambs, and in return they shot them, they poisoned them, they robbed their nests and made soup out of their young. And yet they couldn't distinguish one species from another, having only three names for the dozen and more kinds that inhabited their lands. Small mousing hawks they called *mnina*; medium-sized raptors, such as peregrines and booted eagles, were classified as *sef*; and large eagles and vultures were lumped together as *n'da*. But their ignorance didn't stop there, for on many occasions Case had found that the identity of a hawk was determined solely by the observer's viewpoint. A *sef* viewed close up was a *n'da*, and a *n'da* spotted half a mile off was a *mnina*. Showing Laschen diagrams and close-up photos didn't help; he couldn't translate abstractions into reality – like those New Guinea tribesmen who couldn't recognize their own images in photos or film.

'It is him,' Laschen repeated doggedly.

Case had to struggle against the twin handicaps of scepticism and fear, but in the end that old killer curiosity won. 'What the shit,' he said. '*Yalla.*'

Marrakech never sleeps, except during the dog days of summer and in the small hours before each Ramadan fasting. Workers were already filing like apparitions through the darkened streets, exchanging soft blessings with watchmen.

Case and Laschen came to the city gates and passed through them on to waste ground, where taxi drivers slept in old American autos with grilles like chromed jaws.

They settled down to wait. Roosters chorused. The sun rose and for a while the Atlas was visible, glazed by mist. Case could see cols that he had crossed, but soon the cloud thickened and it was hard to believe that there were mountains there at all. Out on the plain, the reflective guidance beacons of the airport approaches winked.

Imperceptibly, the day began to fill up with noise. Buses started arriving, the faces behind the windows groggy with sleep after driving all night from oasis towns on the far side of the Atlas. A string of horse-drawn *calèches* clopped past, bound for the international hotels. The first country taxi pulled in and disgorged twelve passengers from space designed for five.

To the west, the sky rumbled as a Royal Air Maroc Boeing spewing jet exhaust climbed steeply from Menara and turned north.

Half a dozen more taxis arrived. By the city gate, vendors were building mountains of oranges. Laschen nudged Case to his feet and led the way to a turquoise Buick trimmed with Dacron bearskin and magazine pictures of fat chanteuses. The driver, a jowly entrepreneur in overalls, was trying to extract the fare from an old Berber who seemed to be entering the cash economy for the first time. Laschen hung back, then presented himself and showed the driver Fox's photo. Busy totting up the takings from the early morning run, the driver managed a cursory nod.

'*Oui, c'est lui.*'

'Where, exactly?' Case said.

The driver gave him an amused glance and held out his hand.

Case repeated the question, accompanying it with fifty dirhams. The price of the information proved to be double this, plus the taxi fare should such transport be required. When Case declared that it wasn't, further haggling ensued. It was half an hour before the deal was struck and Case was able to return to the town to pick up the Renault. He lost another twenty minutes converting all his traveller's cheques, and because he drove north before deciding he had no tail, it was mid-morning by the time he and Laschen were on their way towards the mountains.

The road ran straight as a bullet between eucalyptus trees.

'This is not the road to Ourika,' Laschen said.

'We're taking the long way round,' Case said.

Laschen was carrying Fox's snapshot on his lap. He kept touching it, as if it was a talisman.

Case wondered if he was to be trusted. 'You don't have to come,' he said. 'This could be dangerous for you – for both of us.'

'I will show you where the Englishman is and you will give me a thousand sterlings.'

Money was likely to prove a problem in the short term. 'You could go to prison,' Case said.

Laschen watched the square of light at the end of the avenue as if his life's resolution was framed there. 'If it is written . . .' he said.

Case detoured off the road to avoid being mashed by an oncoming Berliet. At a fork up ahead, a police motorcyclist was checking the papers of a busload of travellers. Case took the left, feeling conspicuous, trying to project the carefree image of a tourist bound for scenic parts. In the rearview he watched the policeman for signs of interest, his breath held almost to bursting.

'What will you do with the money?' he said when they were clear.

'I shall buy a passport and go to Amsterdam.'

'A thousand pounds won't take you far in Amsterdam. Why don't you use it to build a new house?'

'I will not build a new house.'

After considerable thought, Case settled for basic inquiry. 'What's this about a curse?'

He expected no reply and didn't get one until they reached the first serious curve since leaving the city. Laschen, as if freed from the monotony of straightforward motion, began to speak.

'One winter I was hunting moufflon on the plateau above my village and I saw a plane fall from the sky – *boom*! – like that gas stove which exploded in the refuge at Iferd. When I reached the plane, everyone was dead, lying in the snow, and all their things were lying there – watches, bags, clothes.'

Case manipulated the column shift to cope with a gradient.

'I hid the things,' Laschen said, 'and went back to the village. When I saw the people, I knew it would be a big problem for me if I told them what I'd done. Next day the army came in helicopters and found the plane. The police came and took the bodies. They searched them and found things missing, so they went to my village and arrested all the men. "Where are the things you stole from the plane?" they asked. "We stole nothing; we didn't know about the plane until the soldiers told us." And they were speaking the truth. I was the only man who saw the plane crash.

'But the police didn't believe them. "You stole these things," they said to Hussein. "And here is your accomplice." They took ten men to Marrakech and put them in the jail. The police were clever; they took the sons of the chief and his family. The families of the dead people were rich and said they mustn't be let go.'

A sign to the left indicated a backroad to the *Vallée de l'Ourika*. Case took it.

'Then the people came to my house. "You were on the plateau when the plane crashed. It was you who stole from the passengers. You must go to the *caid* and tell him, then you will go to prison and our sons will come home." But I didn't want to go to prison. I said I don't know about the plane.

'Then our *imam* said you must go to the tomb of the *sidi* and swear. I was frightened. I went to the head of my family and asked him to swear for me. "Not unless you give me some of the things you stole." I did what he asked. I gave *cadeaux* to all my relatives and they swore, but one man who I had given a gold watch said Laschen is lying.'

Case was having to concentrate on his driving. The road was buckled and potholed.

'Did you go to jail?'

'In the night the man who refused to swear died. The next day, the chief's sons came back.'

'So it all ended okay.'

'Next year, snow in May killed all my walnut trees.'

'It killed a lot of other people's trees,' Case pointed out. That spring had been the occasion of his first visit.

'In the summer, *djinns* took away my son's legs.'

'I told you: it was polio.'

Laschen began to sob.

Case brought the car to a halt. The ground was perfectly

291

level in all directions. He felt stupid and wished he had not raised the matter. 'Amsterdam's not for you,' he said. 'Go back to your village, make a donation to the mosque and ask the people for forgiveness.'

Laschen smiled across the cultural gulf. 'No, gentle. Only God can forgive.'

If you were a Moroccan who wanted to incarcerate an Englishman with maximum discretion, the Ourika Valley was as good a place as any. It was a green and pleasant dead-end running into the Toubkal massif – a favourite one-day excursion for foreign tourists as well as picnicking Marrakechis, and a popular hill resort for holiday-home owners who valued privacy. Case seemed to recall that Mick Jagger had rented a villa here.

For all Case knew, the villa may have been in the place where Fox or his lookalike had been seen. The properties were mini estates, sited for maximum seclusion, scattered over the thickly wooded base of a mountain. Driving slowly, tucked behind an air-conditioned coach, Case noted surveillance cameras at the entrance to a driveway.

Laschen turned in his seat as they passed a turning leading to the river. 'The house is down there.'

'I know,' Case said.

The resort had no centre. Beyond it the road was a strip hemmed in by spired ridges. Case drove on for a couple of kilometres before pulling in to a track bulldozed by the department of *les Eaux et Forêts*.

'Will you recognize the house?' he asked.

'Blue with a red gate and a stork's nest on the chimney.'

'See if there's a place where we can watch it. Keep an eye out for cameras. Don't get caught, and don't talk to anyone.'

While Case waited, he checked his kit. It contained food, a green maggot sleeping-bag, poncho, cam-cream – all liberated from HM government.

Laschen was away for more than an hour, and when he returned, his expression spoke for him.

'Problems?' Case said.

'It's difficult.'

'Any way in?'

'The gate is locked.'

'I'm not planning to walk through the gate.'

'There is a high wall all around the house, and on the wall there is sharp wire.'

'Cameras?'

'No.'

'See anyone? Any dogs, gardeners?'

'A watchman. It's difficult.'

'Phhh,' Case said through his teeth. He squinted up at the craggy hillside facing the resort. On the ridge trees stood out like Indian ink soaking into blotting pper. 'We'll take a bird's eye look.'

The slope was very steep and thick with rain-soaked brush. On the way up, a black snake whiplashed off a boulder and went undulating over their heads.

Noon had passed before they had made enough height, but there were so many trees around the blue house that Case's view was restricted to a bit of roof, a couple of windows and a patch of lawn.

'If we don't see owt,' he said, focusing his binoculars, 'I'll go over the wall tonight.'

He and Laschen had shared many vigils on mountains. They talked, dozed by turns, ate a can of sardines. A fox came by without seeing them. Once, a falcon swept past like a fast ghost, hugging the contours; in the valley bottom a flock of pigeons sprayed in alarm.

Laschen jabbed an elbow into his ribs. Across the patch of lawn, a man was walking, closely tagged by another. By the time Case brought the glasses to bear, the space was empty. He tried to interpret what he'd glimpsed.

'You see,' Laschen said.

'See what?' Case scoffed.

He checked his watch – a couple of minutes past three, suggesting an after-lunch turn round the garden. He clamped his eyes to the binoculars. Beside him, Laschen gnawed his fingernails.

A few minutes before four the figures reappeared, making for the house. Even with the images magnified by eight, the distance was too great for positive identification, but just as Case could recognize a distant hawk from its wing-beat, so he could infer from the leading man's gait that he was European, and that the man behind him was not a companion but an attendant. It was possible that the object in the attendant's hands was a gun.

'Magic,' Case murmured. In his glee he punched Laschen. 'Fucking magic.'

The Berber muttered.

Case's euphoria was of brief duration. In Armagh, his surveillance operations had sometimes lasted weeks before any decision about action was taken, but he had no more than hours in which to make his move – assuming that he had commit. He weighed up the stack of objections and decided there was no stopping now. He had half a mind to call on Low for back-up, but the other half told him that back-up Waltham Forest style might be effective in an urban context, but would be downright suicidal in the present circs.

Some kind of outline plan came to him as they descended to the car. He worked on it as he drove Laschen back to the trans-Atlas highway. The problem was that it required Laschen's continuing co-operation, and he couldn't even pay him the first instalment.

He dropped the Berber at a filling station close to the fork where the police motorcyclist had set up a checkpoint. It was nearly dark. He scribbled the address and telephone number of a back-street restaurant on a scrap of paper.

'Let's get it straight,' he said. 'You send this note to Mr Low at his hotel. You don't give it to him yourself; you don't visit anyone you know. Tomorrow morning, early, you take a bus back here and wait for me. If I'm not here by seven, go to Mr Low and tell him everything.'

Laschen had walked away.

'Did you get that?' Case demanded

'I have already done what you asked. Now give me the thousand sterlings.'

'I'm not going to argue, Laschen. I don't have the money.' Case was overcome with weariness, anticipating the hours ahead. 'That isn't all,' he said. 'We'll need a place to hide. They'll never look for us in your village.'

Laschen punched the ground. 'This is not what you promised.'

'I'm sorry.'

Laschen turned, his expression venomous. 'I shall go to your rich friend Mr Low. I shall tell him where Mr Fox is and he will give me the money you promised.'

Case closed the distance with ominous silence. 'He's not my friend and he's not yours. He won't trust you. But I trust you, and you trust me. That's why you call me gentle. Gentle means kind, doesn't it.'

'You are not always gentle.'

'No, that's true. I'm not. Remember it. Remember also that Fox is a rich man – richer than Mr Low, richer than you can imagine. We'll charge him two thousand pounds for your help.'

'You speak always of tomorrow. Tomorrow you may be in prison.'

'Tomorrow I'll be waiting for you here,' Case said. He stuck out his hand.

After a while, Laschen touched it and walked away into the night.

Case was so alarmed by his attitude that he risked calling Low from the garage. It was Fatso who came to the phone.

'We was worried,' Fatso said, sounding it. 'We thought you'd been nicked. We was thinking about going to the authorities.'

'I'm touched,' Case said, meaning it. 'This is going to be quick because there may be something dodgy about the phone.'

'Gotcha.'

'I'm sending you a note with an address and phone number. Wait there all tomorrow. If another local turns up offering a bird in the bush, remember a bird in the hand and all that. Stick around.'

He was almost back in his car before he remembered Iseult. He wobbled. For five days, while he had been putting himself on the line, they had been swanning around God knows where, barely acknowledging his calls. He had never put himself out for a woman before, and the thought that this particular woman had used him, was in love with another, was shameful.

On the crest of his anger he jumped into the Renault. A hundred metres up the road he stopped, threw the car into reverse and drove back.

The same voice answered, its customary politeness strained. Case asked if another message could be relayed to his friends. The voice hesitated and said that though it was a cause for regret, the hotel was not in the business of providing an answering service for guests who failed to honour their bookings.

'This is the last time,' Case said. He composed himself. 'Tell Iseult I've found him. I'll be at the *Gazelle d'Argent* tomorrow night, *insh'allah*. It's a limited offer, one night only. That's all.'

'You have forgotten something, m'sieur.'

'Have I?'

'Always, you give the lady your love.'

'Yeah, well,' Case said. 'It's run out.'

The tongue at the other end clicked in Gallic deprecation of such flippancy over matters of the heart. 'Love has endless patience,' the voice said. '*Courage*. I hope she comes. *Bonne nuit, m'sieur. Bonne chance.*'

Fatigue played tricks with Case's eyes on the return journey to Ourika. Disposing of the car for the night was one more problem, but weariness dulled caution and he left it on the same forestry track, hoping that anyone who saw it would think it belonged to campers. Amateur night, he thought, setting off up the hill. He found his way to a place of safety by the light of the half moon and three stars. The sky was fast clouding over, and because there was no ground wind, it looked as though the moon and stars were moving and the cloud remained still. Minutes after Case took up position, the sky blacked out. The darkness didn't bother him. Him and night were old friends.

Wrapped in his poncho against the dew, he tried to see beyond the immediate, wondering where cause and effect would lead him in the days to come. But every move he plotted was so interwoven with 'ifs and buts' and 'what thens?' that he couldn't assign himself to any course with a clear-cut outcome.

He would have to jump and pray for a soft landing. It was Russian roulette, the legendary dread of all parachutists – when you dropped directly above another parachutist and his parachute captured your air, making your own chute collapse so that you plummeted below him, where the positions would be reversed and your chute would re-inflate while his folded up, causing him to drop past you in turn.

And so it would go on, turn and turn about, until one of you piled into the ground.

22

Total darkness and someone moving in it. Iseult tracked the sound, her eyes stiff in their sockets.

Her scream came out as a muffled gasp as the intruder superimposed himself on the blackness above her bed.

'Hush there now. It's only me.'

'Bloody hell, Cathal! What do you think you're playing at?'

'Couldn't sleep,' he muttered, his voice blurred by booze. 'Shift over.'

'No! Get out.'

He slid under the cover and stretched the length of her. 'Ah, but this is cosy.'

'Please, Cathal. It's not fair.'

'Tonight I'm as chaste as a stone. It's five minutes' warmth and comfort I crave after, the soothing touch of a fellow mortal.'

'I'm warning you, Cathal.'

'Not a finger will I lay on you – promise.'

'You'd better not,' she growled.

He fitted his back to the curve of her body. 'There,' he said. 'Babes in the wood.'

Her arm was in an awkward position, avoiding contact. She let it rest lightly on his hip. He took her hand and looped it over him. She tensed, but he made no further move. Gradually her muscles slackened.

'You're getting a belly, brother.'

'That's the lamb's *frivolités* admiring the stuffed pig's ears. What a diet, eh? The Count must be fattening us up.'

'What exactly are *frivolités*?'

Cathal conducted her hand a little lower. She pulled back as if burnt.

'How revolting.'

'You had two helpings.'

'Only to please the Count. For a mortally ill man, he can certainly put away his food.'

'Well, he's eating for two. Death's a hungry guest.'

'That's sick.'

'How's the painting coming along?'

'Nearly finished, so far as it goes.'

'I wish you'd let me see it.'

'When it's finished.'

'When's that?'

'Today, I thought, but now he wants me to add a Moorish pavilion and some figures. It's going to be a Moroccan *déjeuner sur l'herbe*.'

'Careful, Iseult. You're sounding happy.'

'I always feel better when I'm working.'

'You see? Aren't you glad I brought you?'

'In some ways, yes. Yes I am.' She kissed the nape of his neck. 'Sweet dreams.'

Cathal yawned and changed position. 'Night, night. I'll be gone in the morning.'

But she could tell he was awake. She couldn't sleep herself. She was breathing in more often than she was breathing out. The room seemed to have grown hot, charged with static. Secretly she touched her labia. Swollen. Between was moist. She turned over and bit her finger, turned again.

'Cathal, this is not a very good idea.'

'Mmmm.'

'Cathal, do you make love to other women?'

'Sometimes.'

'Who?'

'Iseult, I've a busy day ahead of me. I've no time for a compare and contrast session.'

'I feel frivolous,' she murmured, walking her fingers down his belly. He was limp.

'I told you, I'm here under a vow of celibacy.'

She kneaded him, angry and frustrated, and when he didn't respond, she pulled her hand away and rolled on her back, heart pounding, hating herself. 'What's the matter – shagged out from another session with the servants?' She buried her face in her pillow.

'It's Pat Case,' he said quietly.

She squirmed deeper into the pillow. 'Don't, Cathal. I feel bad enough without having to think about him.'

He touched her on the shoulder. 'Save it for a worthier cause.'

She turned, her neck at an awkward angle. 'Don't start that again. He's gone. We'll never see him again.'

Cathal unburdened a sigh. Slowly, Iseult moved apart from him.

'Has something happened? Tell me, Cathal. You're frightening me.'

'That officer who was injured with Case in Armagh.'

'Ridley,' Iseult said. 'I don't like to think about it.'

'I was curious to find out what really happened.'

'Leave it alone, Cathal.'

'Quite a case, it turns out. For you see, it didn't end with Ridley's shooting. A month later, two of the men who did it were murdered. Shot in their beds in their uncle's house twenty miles south of the border. One of them was only nineteen.'

'Don't expect me to grieve for them.'

'It was a revenge killing.'

'Surprise, surprise.'

'But not an official operation. The Brits said it was an internal feud, and yet within days of the murders, the army patrols had a new chant: "Paras Two, Provos One".'

'You're saying that Pat . . .? I don't believe it.'

'He knew the identity of the men. He'd been keeping them under observation for days. A week after the murders, he was discharged from the army. It was him alright, but the Brits hushed it up like they always do.'

'Where did you get this from?'

'A friend in Paris.'

'And you've been saving it up for this particular moment.'

'I wasn't going to tell you at all.'

'How considerate. What's the point, Cathal? Why tell me now? Am I supposed to feel guilty or something? Because if so, you've succeeded wonderfully.'

Cathal was still, his breathing regular.

'Iseult, the bastard's found Fox.'

Iseult sat up. 'That's not possible. Yesterday you said he was flying home.' She punched Cathal. 'It's not true,' she cried.

'Don't ask me how. He phoned this evening, telling us to get there right away.'

'What are we going to do?' she breathed.

'Let him sort it out himself.'

Iseult began to laugh.

'Ssh, you'll wake the house up.' Cathal put his arm around his sister's shoulders. 'Look, we've got one foot in paradise. You're painting again. I'm learning the ropes of the dope trade. Why spoil it?'

'A week ago you were in terror for your life.'

'No, listen Iseult, I've taken care of that.'

'Taken care of the Provos?'

'They're not going to chase after me in Morocco. In a few weeks I'll have put a deal together with the Count. The IRA will have their money back with interest.'

Iseult was out of bed. She pulled back the shutters. The moon shed its glimmer.

'What are you doing?' Cathal demanded.

'What does it look like? I'm getting dressed.'

'Stay out of it, Iseult.'

'You dragged me here, kicking and screaming every step, and now you tell me none of it was necessary.'

'Circumstances change, Iseult.'

'No they don't. You do.'

'We've got it made right here. I can't leave the Count now. He's relying on me. He could pop off any time.'

'Where is Pat?'

'No, Iseult. I'm not going to let you.'

'Give me the car keys.'

'You'll never get there in time. He's somewhere on the edge of the desert, four hundred miles from here.'

'The keys, Cathal.'

'No.'

'I'll go to the Count.'

'Do that and I'll kill you,' Cathal said, rising up out of bed. Iseult ran to the door.

'Alright,' Cathal shouted. 'Alright.' He flung back the cover, swung his feet to the floor, then stalled, staring at his toes. 'I'll go. You stay here and keep the fucking Count alive.'

Iseult threw his dressing-gown at him. 'We're both going.'

23

Although Dearborn made an effort to avoid pre-judging Clayton Smith, the image he carried to the rendezvous was of a weak-sighted wimp with a small moustache and sad city suit – the kind of man who would wipe his hands and look at them before offering you one to shake.

Clayton Smith, it turned out, was a hunky six-footer with a country-club face, corn-coloured hair and a wedge-shaped chin manfully cleft. It was Dearborn's impression that he was in the presence of muscular Christianity. Clayton Smith, it seemed to him, might very well be the mainstay tenor in a church choir, or the motivating force behind an outreach team for wayward metropolitan youth.

The only conspicuously bizarre aspect of the meeting was the venue and timing. On Smith's instructions, Dearborn had motored seventy kilometres south of Madrid, arriving at a modern roadhouse shortly before 2 a.m. Fairground music was playing inside. He found Clayton Smith ensconced in a backroom cluttered with three steam organs, one of which was playing the habanera 'L'amour est un oiseau rebelle' from Bizet's *Carmen*. The proprietor and custodian, a small vole-faced party in a mothy waistcoat, placed a tray of *tapas* before them and back-pedalled out.

'But, if I love you – beware of me!' Clayton Smith sang along to the dying chords. He selected a slice of *chorizo* from the platter. 'I'm sorry to drag you out into the boonies, but it's kind of a Friday night ritual for me. Also, I'm an insomniac.'

'I'm a bit of a night bird myself,' Dearborn said. He found he had a special gruff voice for dealing with the likes of Smith.

'It beats watching game shows.'

There was a short period of awkwardness on both sides. A clock carved from black oak chimed the hour. A matador emerged from one side of the dial, performed a slow *paron* at a toy bull, and pirouetted into another door.

'You know, John,' Smith said, when the timepiece had stopped whirring, 'I had a long talk with my conscience before I came down here.' He smiled, serenely.

'You made the right choice,' Dearborn said. He couldn't get comfortable on his seat, and he smiled unceasingly – a grimace as if he had bitten into something distasteful.

Smith watched him for every nuance. 'I know that my tendencies must seem repellent to you.'

Dearborn writhed. 'How you seek gratification . . . What you do in the privacy of . . . Look, Smith, your personal life doesn't matter a dime to me. You do a damn fine job and there's no reason why your off-duty activities should be part of the record.'

'Your colleague gave a different impression.'

'She overstepped herself there. I'll have a word with her.'

'Him,' Smith said. 'It was a young man. He threatened to tell my wife if I didn't co-operate.' Once more, Smith gave an unnerving smile. 'There are photographs.'

'Your wife?' Dearborn blurted, a lump the size of a golf-ball in his throat.

'Yes, John, my wife and three lovely daughters.'

Dearborn had the unpleasant suspicion that a part of Smith was taking pleasure in the ignominy of interrogation. 'Put it out of your head,' he said. 'This is a straightforward question and answer session on issues that are in the public domain. You play ball with us, and . . . well, I'm not conducting a witch hunt.'

'Speak,' Smith said, and spread his hands. 'I'm at your mercy.'

'Question one,' Dearborn said, slipping on his half-rims. 'Tommy Blanco. You're familiar with his narcotics activities in Europe.'

304

'Nothing much to tell. He organized a few minor runs and was caught by the Spanish.'

'Bad luck or poor judgement?'

Smith dipped into the platter. 'Blanco had no finesse. You're familiar with the Cartel's motto, *plomo o plata* – "the lead or the silver", the bullet or the bribe. Blanco preferred the bullet every time. In a zoo like Colombia, operating close to the point of supply and with the cops in his pocket, his methods served him well, but drugs in Europe is a more sophisticated enterprise. The competition did not approve of Tommy and his methods.'

'Someone informed on him?'

'I'm not at liberty to divulge.'

'I'm not going to press you,' Dearborn said. 'But since I'm new to this theatre I'd appreciate it if you summed up the competition.'

Smith threw back his head. 'Diddly-dee,' he said – apparently a form of expletive. 'Where to start? Well, clockwise, from the north, you have the Germans, the Dutch and the British on Ibiza. On the Costa del Sol you have the gold Rolex crowd who have diversified into narcotics from other forms of crime. Further south, the Syrians. And of course, the Colombians and the Spanish in the big cities.'

Dearborn decided to let it go for the time being. 'He had a right-hand man – Lova Hazan. Was he caught, too?'

'A non-stick character, John. I always wondered why he pinned his star to that particular mast.' Smith shrugged. 'Still, he knew when to jump ship when the moment came.'

Dearborn divined that the inquiry was about to veer in a new direction. By an effort, he doused his excitement. 'You nailed Blanco. Did he come to trial?'

Exasperation swept Smith's face. 'It wasn't us who nailed him; it was a Spanish effort. As far as we were concerned, Blanco was off limits. He had, as you know, been inveigled into covert activities on our behalf and that conferred immunity on him.'

'Embarrassing,' Dearborn said.

'Very. When he was caught, Blanco threatened to blow the lid off his activities in Central America. The Spanish were determined to put him in court. It took a considerable diplomatic effort to arrange a compromise.'

'Which took what form?'

'He had rendered us service once. Why not again? we suggested to the Spanish.'

'For a man who excites such loathing, the law enforcement agencies have spent one helluva time snuggling up to him.'

'In a war,' Smith said in his precise way, 'you sometimes have to make a pact with the devil. Winston Churchill said that.'

So had a lot of Dearborn's associates. He may even have expressed such a view himself. The thought made his eyelids heavy.

'Who was the target?' he asked.

'Digby Fox,' Smith said, and paused as if the name should mean something.

Dearborn rolled his shoulders.

'A living legend,' Smith said, 'an icon to a generation of pot-heads.'

'I'm new to the scene,' Dearborn reminded him.

Smith filled his lungs and exhaled at length, looking for a starting point. 'Fox is bad seed from good English stock. His father was a bishop, his sister's a merchant banker, his brother's a big fish in some kind of political think-tank. A blue-chip family, well-connected and cerebral. Fox was educated at Harrow where he took all the honours, then he went to Oxford – Oriel College.'

'I know Oriel.'

'This was the sixties and a lot of young men from good backgrounds jumped tracks. Fox dabbled in the politics of the counter-culture. He founded an anarchist club called the After-Eight society, wrote a practical handbook on *coups d'état*. He was the darling of a few lefty professors.'

Dearborn selected an appetiser from the items on offer.

'But in 1968,' Smith continued, 'Fox went to Paris and got

concussed by a cobblestone. The experience persuaded him that he wasn't a street-fighting man. He was already a recreational cannabis user and he had the notion – fairly widespread at the time – that, rather than storm the barricades head on, he'd subvert the system from within, using drugs. He started dealing on campus and got caught.'

'Sounds like you know his file by heart.'

'Digby Fox represents a personal challenge to me.'

'Take me back to the beginning of his career.'

'It's part of folklore. After he was thrown out – "sent down" they call it – he wandered around Morocco for a few months.'

Dearborn coughed on his olive.

'He made friends with an English family who were touring the country. He borrowed their car, removed the spare wheel and stuffed the tyre with hash. Back in England, he called on the family, substituted the wheel and . . .' Smith shrugged. 'That's been his hallmark ever since – simple, effective and risk-free so far as he's concerned. Only the scale and sources have changed. In the seventies it was Afghanistan; in the early eighties Pakistan and Nigeria; and now – who knows?'

'Morocco again?'

'Possibly. He likes to ring the changes. It's one of the reasons why he's still at liberty.'

'You've said nothing about hard drugs.'

'We have no evidence that he's a multi-commodity dealer.'

'Then why pick on him over all the others?'

'A question of pride, John. For twenty years that hippy has made idiots of the drug enforcement agencies of three countries.'

'Yes, but what could a marijuana specialist have in common with a crazy such as Tommy Blanco?'

'A good point,' Smith said. 'A critical point as it turns out.' Smith sighed. 'Fox hasn't dealt in heroin or cocaine so far as we know, but a year ago his fortunes took a knock. Two of his cargoes went down in quick succession. One, from Karachi, literally sank en route to Rotterdam; the other, from Nigeria, was seized in a random search at Valencia. There was no proveable link with Fox, but it was his dope alright and the losses hurt. He always buys big, you see – one or two huge deals a year – and pays up front.'

'With two decades of drugs profits stashed, surely he couldn't have been hurting too badly.'

'Bear in mind that marijuana is not a growth market. To today's youth – today's consumer – it's considered old-fashioned, messy and, for all I know, ecologically unsound.'

Like me, Dearborn thought.

Smith continued, nose stuck to the groove. 'It was felt in some quarters that Fox might be receptive to a quick and dirty deal.'

'You set up a sting, using Blanco.'

'I was against it on several counts. First, Fox would never have dealings with slime like Blanco. Second, by temperament if not morality, he's wary of coke or heroin. The profits are higher, but so are the stakes and penalties, and the risk of violence grows exponentially. Third, the legal ramifications of entrapment are a nightmare, as we know from recent cases Stateside. And fourth – do you know anything about fox hunting?'

'The unspeakable in pursuit of the uneatable. It was coons we hunted where I grew up. My daddy raised very fine blue-ticks. Personally, I could never see the point.'

'The hunted fox pulls all kinds of fancy ruses – like leading the hounds on to a railroad as the express train is going past.'

'Blanco wasn't killed by an express train. He was blown up in his Rolls-Royce. That doesn't sound like Fox's style.'

'It isn't, but don't make the mistake of thinking that Fox would have qualms.'

'A lot of people would have liked to see Blanco dead,' Dearborn said thoughtfully. He snapped his fingers. 'Dave Canova.'

Smith clamped his lips together and splayed the fingers of both hands, as if he were playing a parlour guessing game.

'Hold it,' Dearborn cried, 'we've lost sight of Lova Hazan.'

Smith let out his breath approvingly. 'Precisely. *Precisamente*. It's my belief that Hazan was impressed by Fox, had already concluded that Blanco was a three-time loser, and changed allegiance.'

'You have proof?'

'Since Blanco's death, they've been seen in Gibraltar, where Fox keeps substantial cash assets.'

'How long ago?'

'Three, four months. Soon after his last run.'

'From?'

'Not sure. Lebanon, possibly. If so, it was a small operation – a trial run.'

Dearborn paused to take stock. He felt that he had reached a crossroads and that all directions lay open. 'In his youth, Fox had left-wing sympathies. Is he still political? I mean, what with Hazan's involvement, a Lebanese connection, could there be more to Fox than drugs?'

'The interface between politics and narcotics becomes increasingly blurred.' Smith shrugged. 'Only Fox could give you the answer.'

'That's not a bad idea. Where do I find him?'

'Majorca, but he's not at home; he shut up house a few weeks ago. Although there's no record of him leaving the mainland, a marine engineer answering his description took a flight to South Africa on twenty-eighth September.'

After the initial disappointment, Dearborn thrilled to the news. That was only two days before Lova Hazan arrived in Morocco.

'Any idea where Fox is now?'

'He's not an easy man to keep tabs on. He has a passport for each day of the year.'

'Who else is close to him?'

'Very few. Paranoia is the stock in trade of the successful trafficker.'

'An operation as big as his must need an organization to match.'

'He goes against the trend. While the other big dealers surround themselves with the trappings of a multinational – airlines, shipping companies, banks – Fox still runs his business on cottage-industry lines. He organizes supply and shipment and that's about it. Distribution is left to his wholesale customers; it's a cash-and-carry business.'

'Someone has to handle the financial side – launder the money, invest the proceeds.'

'Yes, he has a money man. Forbes Valentine.'

Forbes Valentine, Dearborn wrote.

'An Oxford contemporary,' Smith explained.

'They started out down the yellow-brick road together?'

'No, Valentine took his degree and became an accountant. Maybe it was part of a long-term strategy, but his early years were spent with a prestigious London firm. He struck out on his own after a couple of years and made a big killing during the oil crisis, advising oil sheikhs what to do with their petro-dollars. He had an entrée because of an interest in falconry, which is still big with Arabs.'

'Any particular kind of Arabs?' Dearborn said, trying to keep the quaver of excitement from his voice.

'Gulf State *nouveaux riches*, a few Saudi princelings. Almost certainly, some of their money financed Fox's activities, but it's unlikely that any of them were involved knowingly.'

'Do you have an address for him?'

'Several. He has a farm in Wiltshire, England, where he's a lord of the manor; a town residence in London's Holland Park; an apartment in Manhattan; a time-share in Bermuda. He also owns several businesses, including a property company in Spain.'

'You make it sound significant.'

'It was in bad financial trouble last year. You may not know, but the Spanish rewrote the laws on foreign ownership of coastal property, causing a big slump in the market. The downturn came soon after the loss of Fox's two cargoes and it coincided with the retirement of some of Fox's main customers-stroke-distributors.'

'Forcible retirement?'

'They got to be middle-aged, that's all, with wives and kids and comfortable homes. It was a blow, because they'd been with Fox from the start. They were irreplaceable.'

'So all in all this was a bad trading year.'

'For Valentine in particular. Fox lives like a bum, but Valentine has half a dozen establishments to maintain. In fact, we asked the British to keep an eye on him because we suspected he'd do something rash in order to recoup.'

'Rash like how?'

'As I said, Fox usually pays up front and leaves it to the distributors to handle the dope once it reaches these shores. But this summer our Spanish counterparts heard that an Englishman sounding like Valentine was inviting some of the expatriate community in Marbella to buy stakes in a major deal at preferential rates.'

'What kind of expats?'

'Marbella is a thieves' kitchen.'

Dearborn began to have difficulty digesting the information. 'Where can I connect with Valentine?'

'At this time of year, Scotland's your best bet. He rents a hunting lodge where he entertains his more respectable clients. Our British friends swept it last year – clean.'

'Can you give me some idea of where the money is spread?'

'Diddly-dee,' Smith said once again. 'You name it – Panama, the Caymans, Gibraltar, Liechtenstein. Valentine formed so many shell companies, offshore trust funds, fly-by-night banks, that it would take ten men a lifetime to uncover them all.'

'You talked about liaison with London. Do me a favour. Give someone a call. Tell them you're following up a new lead and want everything they have on Fox, Valentine, the syndicate he put together – every little thing.'

'I can't do that.'

'Mr Smith, I don't want to intrude between you and your conscience, but the people I'm working with lack my scruples.'

'Who are your people, John? I can't work it out.'

'Don't even try. I've been through this with one curious individual, and well . . . he isn't remotely curious any more.'

Smith's face shadowed, but by and by the equable smile came back. 'Paul Betts,' he said. 'I'll see what he's got.'

'Drugs Squad?'

'Customs and Excise Investigation Division. He's on Fox's case. He says it's like nailing a blancmange to the wall.'

Dearborn gave Smith his number. 'Call me the moment you have anything.' He stood up and held out his hand.

'Is that all?'

'You see, it wasn't such a chore.'

'I expect there'll be others treading in your footsteps.'

Dearborn hesitated. 'If you've got leave due,' he said, 'now might be a good time to take it.'

Smith nodded without absorbing the warning. 'Would you mind staying awhile, John. I feel I can talk to you.'

'I wish I could,' Dearborn said. He looked at the clock. Unnoticed, the matador had made another pass at the bull. 'It's late,' he said, then looked at his hands, not knowing which one to extend. 'Nice talking to you, er . . . Clayton.'

As Dearborn reached his car, the merry-go-round music started again – a military march. Dearborn pounded the steering-wheel exultantly. On the way back to the capital he sang Bizet's 'March of the Toreadors'. He was in full cry now.

Natti and Esther were waiting in the lobby of his hotel.

'You changed your mind,' Natti said, stepping into his path.

'I said I quit working for Zwy Gur and his death squad,' Dearborn said, avoiding Esther's eye. 'I'll do it my way.'

Esther made a move to join them in the elevator, but Natti gently excluded her. All the way up, Dearborn couldn't rid himself of the Israeli's soft dark stare. He found himself liking Natti a little less each passing moment.

When the door hissed open, Natti blocked the entrance. 'You work with us, Doctor Dearborn. Or you work against us. There's no other way.'

Smith's call woke him from sound sleep. It was after eleven. Drawn curtains muted the din of Madrid's traffic.

'I'm at the office,' Smith said. 'I've just had a long talk with Betts in London.'

'Wait until I find a pen,' Dearborn said, fumbling around on his bedside table. He muffled a yawn. 'Okay, go ahead.'

'Nothing new on Fox, and Valentine flew to Paris a week ago. A deal is going down – that's the consensus. But it's the old story. No one knows where from or where to.'

Disappointment chased out the last cobwebs of sleep. 'Anything on the syndicate he was putting together?'

'I'm pretty pissed about that as a matter of fact. The Brits have a name which they forgot to pass on to us. Actually, it's a name we happen to have on file, courtesy of the Spanish. Denis Low. I have his file on screen as we speak. You know, John, you may have started something.'

'Yeah,' Dearborn said. 'Who's Denis Low?'

'Low is the cream of the crud on the Costa del Sol. If Valentine was laying bets off on him, he really must be desperate.'

'Is Low in Spain now?'

'London.'

'Would he talk to me?'

Smith laughed. 'You might find the conversation one-sided. Low is tough; Low is chewy. Among the fraternity he's known as the Humane Killer. It isn't as nice as it sounds. His family sold horse meat. He did eleven years for armed robbery in the seventies. The cops reckon his stake money came from a holdup in which a security guard got wasted.'

'Alright, where does he hang out?'

Smith dictated home and business addresses. 'There's a

club, too – the Low Spot, a place where money and flesh mingle. Low drops in most nights.' Smith hesitated. 'You're getting a long way from politics.'

Dearborn, too, wondered if he had detoured up a blind alley. 'Like you say, it's a blurry line.'

24

With two hours of dark remaining, Case left his place of hiding. The night was pitch black, forcing him to use a torch on the descent, but down on the road he had to feel his way, for there was every chance of meeting peasants stealing a march on the day.

He reached the turn-off to the blue house and withdrew to cover, trying to reconstruct the lie of the land. But his view from above had been partial and Laschen's directions were open to confusion. The river was his best clue. He could hear its rapid progress to his right. The garden of the blue house backed on to it, perhaps two hundred metres down the lane.

Time passed unseen. Case waved a hand in front of his face, unable to believe that a Moroccan night could be so comprehensive. He ducked under his poncho and flashed light on his watch. Only an hour until dawn, even allowing for the cloud. It had begun to rain and that, too, was bad, for Fox – if it was Fox – was unlikely to go outside in such weather. Case swore gently. He would have to lie up all day and effect an entry into the house that night. He swallowed, trying to ease a soreness in his throat. He had a cold coming on.

Rusty squeaking pushed discomfort from his mind. Down the lane a light was wavering towards him. The light went past and wobbled on to the road, accompanied by an unseen presence singing under its breath. Case noticed a lighted window on the hill, where none had been a minute before. If he was going for commit, he had better get shifted.

He considered the bold approach – a two-minute amble

under full beam, a quick shin up the wall and into place with darkness to spare. But if he bumped into anyone, he didn't have the language to answer a greeting or a challenge. No, caution was the way. He would hear anyone before they heard him.

Going into the lane was like entering a tunnel. He shuffled left, hand feeling for the edge of the lane, and slipped knee deep into a ditch. Mouthing obscenities, he pulled himself out and went on, groping hand across hand along a wall matted with creepers. There were at least two other properties to pass.

Without warning, the wall ended. Blindly Case reached for the next hold, touched metal with one hand, and realized he was gripping the wrought-iron entrance to the blue house. His lungs clutched. Only feet beyond the gate a crack of orange showed. He had blundered past the watchman dozing at his master's gate.

Once past the danger point the lane made a bend. Voices were coming; a buttery glow swung into his path. There was only one course. He lay belly down in the ditch, swaddled in his poncho. The voices passed him but he lay still for a count of fifty. The water was as cold as any he'd lain in, and his thoughts turned to the hot shower and dry clothes back at barracks before he remembered that there were no barracks to go home to.

Bugger it, he decided. At this rate, he'd be crawling around at midday. He moved to the middle of the lane. The night was losing its grip. Now there was a sense in which he could see the trees arched over the lane, though it was not exactly a visual thing. The river was loud, muffling his squelching feet.

A sensation as of stepping into unseen danger made him halt. He was in the open. Below him, the river rapids were a faint agitation – like scratches on blank movie film.

His plan was to work his way round to the far side of the house, which was a blind spot so far as he'd been able to tell. To reach it, he had to traverse the river bank under the rear wall of the garden. The bank was steep and rocky, and Case took it steady, measuring his progress against the remaining night. He wanted to go over the wall when there was sufficient light to see what he was jumping into.

A rooster heralded false dawn as he came to the far corner. There was no lane on this side, and no adjoining garden. Beyond the boundary of the blue house was wasteland overrun by brambles. He tried to force a passage along the wall but couldn't make an inroad. Refusing to hurry, he backed out and scrambled downriver, intending to outflank the thicket. Five minutes later, viciously pierced about the hands and legs, he had to give it best.

The rooster crowed again, impelling him back upstream. He'd have to go over the rear wall, and it was a lousy spot – wide open to anyone on the other side of the river.

He was trying to come to a decision. So far as he could estimate, the wall was eight-feet high, made higher by the way the river bank dropped away from its base. He balanced himself, stood on tiptoes and strained. Miles out of reach, with no point of purchase and no space to launch a running jump. The wall was of rubble, and subsidence due to flood action had made it bow out. He made several pathetic attempts to scale it in orthodox fashion.

Panic took over. He began jumping up like a rat trapped in a box.

Somewhere down the valley a mosque official switched on a call to prayer – the dawn observance. For religious purposes, Muslims reckoned sunrise was when a white thread could be distinguished against the dark – or was it sunset? In any case, the night had got beyond that point. Trees bulked on the opposite bank, and the rooster population was carolling.

Back towards the lane, a slabby shape inclined itself at an angle, its top a little higher than the base of the wall and three or four feet out. It was a section of reinforced concrete – part of someone's house displaced by a flood. Rusty steel rods stuck out from the top. So far, Case thought, hardly a thing had gone to plan; he was having to improvise all the way.

Bending, he hauled back on one of the steel ties. Slowly it gave until it was pointing up, giving him another few inches of height. It was quite easy to balance on it with one foot, but impossible to launch himself off with any force. The wall was capped with smooth clay and fenced with four strands of barbed wire.

Stepping down, he retreated to the bottom of the ramp, swung his arms and made a dummy run to see if it was feasible. One thing was for sure: he wasn't going anywhere with a pack on his back. No change of clothes on the other side; no book to while away the hours. He took out what he thought he might need, cached the pack under the slab and made another couple of test runs, getting the feel of it.

Behind him the night was thinning out and the peaks were beginning to make a distinct impression.

His actual attempt was made without thought – three steps, foot on the prong, feeling it give, a slight hesitation to recover balance without losing all momentum, and then off and up.

His landing was a knee-bruising collision, but he had a hold, and then a better one. He hung for a few seconds, getting his wind back, before walking himself up the wall. His feet lost traction. He would have to rely on the wire. It held and he was up, over the wire and ready to drop. A doddle, he thought, and then it occurred to him that just conceivably he had the wrong house.

Dense shrubbery concealed the landing zone below. Beyond that was what looked like a modest orchard, a lawn, a terrace, and finally the house – the upper floor burning electricity and a single light downstairs, behind a pair of French windows that gave access to the terrace.

There was too much undergrowth to make a neat landing at this point. He would be better off to the left. He snatched a quick glance to confirm his antics hadn't attracted an audience and spotted movement on the far bank – a woman coming down to the river with a basket or pot on her head.

He crouched, hung, felt his grip go and went with it, crashing through branches and tipping over into a bush. He lay on his back, every pore straining for sounds of alarm. A couple of garden birds protested with a bar or two of song.

Disentangling himself, he crawled towards the angle of the garden where it met the lane. Here the wall was colonized by some kind of vine with bell-shaped flowers and a network of fibrous branches. An ideal spot for getting out, especially for a middle-aged non-combatant like Fox.

A bank of roses at the end of the orchard obscured the house. To bring it back into his sights, he had to burrow only a couple of feet to the right. He measured the angles, but it was obvious at a glance that this small corner was the only piece of garden that wasn't exposed to casual view.

A wind shook rain from the cherry trees. A garden table and two chairs had been set up under one of them, and after checking his bearings by sighting on the hillside where he'd spent yesterday, he concluded that this was where Fox had digested his lunch. There was a small object on the table – an ashtray. Frowning, he felt for Fox's photo. Yes, there on Fox's right-hand side was a well-used ashtray.

Day had dawned, but without much conviction or cheer; the house lamps continued to burn, effectively blinding anyone looking out. On a snap decision, Case loped over to the table. Crouched down, he began to scribble, hardly looking at his writing, one eye on the house.

He slid the snap under the ashtray. All its corners remained exposed. He tore a little off each. In his haste he smeared the paper with camouflage cream, but still it didn't fit, so he tore some more off and realized he'd sacrificed some of his instructions. Sweat burst out. Every second counted now. He shoved the tatty, hardly legible four-by-three back under, winced at the presentation, told himself that it was meant to attract notice and back-tracked to the shrubbery.

By standing tall and craning, he could just see the house. A little to the right, his view of the house would be entire – and vice versa. Deciding to stay where he was, he sank down to regroup. Seconds later he was on his feet again trying to see if he could see the postcard. He could. So could anyone else.

319

It had stopped raining. His blood cooled and he felt wretched – wet through, hollow in the stomach and raw of throat. He squatted down and forced himself to swallow some Dexedrine tabs and a bar of chocolate. As he chewed, he had an image of himself – face blacked out and scratched, pale eyes blinking slowly and bloodshot for want of sleep, the rest shrouded in rubber like a battlefield corpse. That was good, he thought. Anyone who discovered him would jump out of his skin first and shoot afterwards.

And in between, what would be his response?

Think about it when the moment came.

Something was nagging him. He looked about, not sure which of his senses had been activated. Weak sunlight hung the trees with silver. Steam began to rise. He yawned, checked his watch and moments later yawned again. Like watching grass grow, he thought, eyeing the stems straightening where his feet had crushed them.

He started up, wide awake.

His tracks in the wet grass were dark in the flat light, leading from the table right to his hiding place. It would be hours before they were erased. He couldn't believe he'd been so stupid.

Birds jumped among the branches. In the lane a man went by, berating somebody or just passing the time of day. Berbers were another world, he thought, reflecting on Laschen. Other voices came to him at intervals over the rush of the river.

He woke to his own teeth chattering and the squeak of a door. He stretched himself upright. The French windows were open and a moustached man was ushering someone on to the terrace. In the shade of the room behind was another figure.

Case shrank down, losing sight of the trio. When they came into the orchard there were only two and they had reversed position. The balding, bearded European man in front was carrying a tray with breakfast things, walking with a short, prissy gait as if he wasn't too confident of his balance. He looked more like a vicar than an international drug trafficker.

But if it wasn't Fox, why was the guard walking a cautious two paces behind carrying a fucking sub-machine-gun?

The third man didn't appear. Case couldn't adjust his position because the guard was facing him head on.

Fox sat down, his back to Case, the ashtray to his right. His guard remained standing, eyes roaming. Case never took his gaze from them. His tracks were plain to see and the guard looked conscientious.

Fox said something and the guard's watchfulness wavered. Case took the opportunity to alter his position. He found he was grasping a hefty rock.

Somewhere a radio played Arab music. A voice called and the guard answered.

Fox was reading, absent-mindedly sipping coffee and eating a croissant.

The guard began to mooch, bored or perhaps alerted by some sixth sense. Case made himself ignore him and concentrated on Fox, willing him to use his eyes.

Idly, Fox pulled out a pack of Gauloises, looked up and held out the pack to the guard, who came over feeling in his pocket. Case's stomach performed a revolution. The guard accepted a cigarette, produced a box of matches, struck one, held it out and then lit his own fag. He dropped the spent match into the ashtray as he turned away.

Now!

A telephone had been trilling in the house. Someone shouted and Fox's guard turned. The third man came half running, half walking into the garden. The guard stood up and went to meet him.

Fox was watching them, cigarette forgotten, trying to work out what they were saying. Oh, the blindness of people, Case fumed.

Fox seemed to shrug and took a deep drag, tipped off the accumulated ash into the tray and – went still.

Don't gawp, Case screamed silently. Pick it up.

He glanced wildly at the guards. They were holding on to each other's arms as if for comfort – the Arab prelude to disengagement.

Pick it up, you moron, Case mouthed in fury.

He blinked. By some sleight of hand, the snap had gone. Fox was reading his book for all he was worth.

You little darling!

The guard came back with a purposeful step. Fox looked up with what Case imagined was owlish innocence. The guard ordered him to his feet. Fox murmured mild protest. The guard's attitude hardened. Fox closed his book and stood, yawning. He was scared.

To Case's outrage, he went like a lamb – not even a backward glance. Careless in his anger, Case stood to full height. The terrace was deserted. He could see a shape in a window, back turned. He moaned with disappointment. He had ridden his luck to the limits, and for what?

Fox stopped, said something, turned and pointed right at Case. He was smiling and Case's stomach turned to slush. But the guard made a cutting gesture with his hand, obviously not interested or refusing permission, and continued up the garden. Fox spoke again and turned. His face was pale, his eyes bolting.

Ignoring the guard's shout, he walked back through the orchard and stopped within feet of Case's hiding place. He reached out a hand as if expecting it to be bitten, plucked a blossom and smelt it.

'Stay absolutely still,' Case whispered.

The guard was already running over, face livid. He snatched Fox's arm and yanked, making a half turn at the same time. Fox dug in his heels and the guard went off balance. In the last moment he realized that something was dubious and his gun hand shifted its grip.

Case erupted out of the shrubbery, punching the rock into the side of the guard's head. The guard went down like a collapsed doll, and Case was on him, binding his mouth. He glanced up. Fox's face was clenched in a rictus of shock, his canines bared.

'Watch the house,' Case hissed. He grabbed Fox by the shoulders and swung him round, then bent over the guard. His face was a very bad colour and there was an indentation on his temple. Blood was trickling from his nose.

'Watch the fucking house!'

Fox's head snapped round again.

'What's happening inside with the other one?' Case demanded, securing the guard's ankles with electrician's plastic ties.

'He's on the telephone.'

'Armed?'

'Yes.'

'Any more of them?' Case asked, binding the guard's wrists.

'Only the cook.'

'What about the watchman?'

'He's the cook as well. He left for town an hour ago. He'll be back in a couple of hours.'

Case took the guard under the shoulders and dragged him into the bushes, then retrieved the compact machine-gun. It was a Heckler and Koch, a type he was familiar with. He touched Fox's arm. 'You are Fox?'

A stunned nod.

'That's a relief. You okay?'

'Within tolerable limits.'

'That's my boy,' Case said. He pushed the rock into Fox's hands. 'If this bloke moves, knock him on the head.'

'Look . . .'

Case levelled a stare at him. 'Valentine's dead. So's your Israeli mate.'

Leaving Fox to get on terms with the news, Case ran to the house, taking no precautions. He felt light of foot and immortal – a dangerous state for all sides.

He took the steps to the terrace in a stride and only slowed when he was at the door. Inside, a voice spoke softly, pausing often.

Case waited for the call to end. As soon as the receiver was replaced, the guard began to call 'Mohamed, Mohamed.' Urgent footsteps clicked on tiles.

Case sideswiped his face as he came through the door, threw him off the wall, kicked his legs apart and ordered him to drop with his hands on his head. Case pulled up his jacket and relieved him of his automatic.

When guard number two was immobilized, he waited, listening. Moroccan music galloped up and down the scale. The house had been cleared. He backed out.

Fox looked relieved to see him. He dropped the stone immediately and wiped his hands.

'I think you've killed him,' he said.

'You should see what they did to Valentine. Here, get up there.'

Fox had absolutely no physical talent; his attempt to scale the wall was a cartoon. Case manhandled him up.

'There are people about,' Fox said, ducking.

Case swarmed up the vines. On the other bank, half a dozen women were pounding clothes in the river. Case still had the machine-gun. It was a tempting trophy, but a bit eye-catching. 'Pity,' he said, pulling out the magazine and chucking the rest of the works into the bushes. He retained the pistol.

Fox got snagged on the wire and began to thrash like a rabbit caught in a bush. 'They've seen us,' he panted.

All the women were watching. Case waved cheerily and they ducked their heads as if he'd exposed himself. He got Fox free and lowered him down the other side. He was hooked on the wire himself. He pulled, lost balance, grabbed for another strand, felt it come away and jumped, trying to straighten in the air. But the ground was a rockery and his left ankle buckled right over as he hit. He was up straightaway but the first step told him his plans were undone.

Shaking tears of pain from his eyes, he hobbled over to the slab, unearthed his gear and hobbled back. 'What a dumb thing to do,' he said.

'Is it broken?' Fox said helpfully.

'Give us your arm. If I conk out, get the car and pick me up.'

With Fox for support, he managed to hop up the lane. They met no one and the entrance to the blue house was empty. In the road, a van went by and slowed.

'What are you staring at?' Case shouted at the amazed driver.

'It's your face,' Fox said, as if he didn't like to mention it.

Case realized he was still blacked up for night action. The Renault was where he'd left it. He flung himself the last step and clung to the roof. He felt dreadfully sick, on the point of passing out. He fumbled for the keys and slid them across. He felt Fox take his weight and help him into the car.

'Any particular direction?' Fox inquired.

'Up the valley. No, wait – someone's watching. Down the valley a few hundred yards, then do a U-turn and come back. We cut over to the P501 in a few kilometres. I'll tell you when.'

Case slid open the awkward side-window and had the automatic ready as they went past the lane to the blue house. Once clear of the resort, he put his head out. 'Keep going,' he said, 'I'm going to puke.'

'Righto,' Fox said in a sprightly tone.

Case laughed, and then was sick. He lay back, pale and sweating.

Fox drove like a pensioner, crouched over the wheel, co-ordination between hand and eye at a minimum. 'And you are . . .?' he inquired.

'Pat Case.'

'No, don't tell me. On the tip of my tongue.' Fox clicked his fingers. 'Falconer. Gamekeeper. Friend of Forbes.' His smile was replete with self-satisfaction.

'This isn't one of his initiatives,' Case said. 'I represent Denis Low and the O'Dwyers.' He rolled his head and attempted a grin. 'Debts collected with discretion.'

It eclipsed Fox's smile, but only for a moment. 'Clever

of you to find me, though.' He farted without excuse or comment. 'Forbes . . .' he said.

Case shook his head. 'You don't want to know, mate.'

'Silly old Forbes. I told him to leave well alone.'

'Leave what alone? The last we heard, you were driving down from the Rif to meet the Israeli. No one even knows his name.'

Fox studied Case to the exclusion of the road ahead. 'Are you sure you're not an agent of the law?'

'Would you prefer to go back to the villa?'

Fox sighed. 'I'm taking an awful lot on trust.'

'The Israeli,' Case insisted. 'And while you're about it, would you mind watching where you're going?'

'Lova Hazan,' Fox said, and went into a long silence until dug out by a nudge from Case. 'He was born in Marrakech and thought it would be terrific fun to see the parental home again.'

'Terrific fun,' Case repeated in a wooden voice.

'Dead, you say.'

'A neighbour recognized him, accused him of being an Israeli spy, and someone stuck a knife in him. It didn't make the papers. I don't know how true it is. Stick your foot down, will you?'

'Can't help you there, I'm afraid. Two men abducted me outside my hotel as I was going to meet him. They were in a complete tizz. The one who questioned me about Hazan kept going out of the room. I think he was reporting back to a superior, getting instructions. They went on and on about an American called Dearborn. I've never heard of anyone called Dearborn.' Fox directed a prim look at Case. 'Have you?'

'I think it's someone they picked up by the Israeli's body,' Case said. He began cleaning off his face-paint, using mineral water and harsh Moroccan lavatory paper. 'Keep talking,' he said. 'Who were they? Was one of them a tall guy – very much the governor?'

'I should have said: I was kept blindfolded until they brought me to the house a week ago. I don't think they were police.'

'Oh yes?'

'Mmm. They sounded like army officers.'

In his mind's eye, Case clothed the governor in military uniform. 'It fits,' he murmured.

'I wonder why they didn't kill me,' Fox said. 'Actually, I don't wonder. My bet is that Lova *was* killed by accident, so knocking me off as well would have been a flippety-floppity. I suppose they murdered old Forbes because he came looking. They made me call him, you see, and tell him I'd be delayed for six weeks.'

'What's so magic about six weeks?'

'Oh, they didn't tell me that.'

Case opened his door and lobbed the magazine from the machine-gun into a roadside ditch. 'Right here,' he said, as the turning came up. He had the heater on full and the car stank of wet rubber. He struggled out of his poncho.

'Can I ask where we're going?' Fox said.

'To meet a friend.'

'And is there a plan?'

'There was,' Case said. Gingerly he removed his boot. His ankle was puffed and bruised. 'But that's put the mockers on it.' He flexed his ankle. It hurt like hell but was still attached to his leg. He closed his eyes and tried to revise his thinking. 'Got a passport?'

'No, but I can probably pick one up in Casa.'

'Money?'

'The same.'

'That's awkward,' Case said. He looked at Fox. The bloke might be two left feet, but his gormless manner was a sham. He had the beady eyes of one of the smarter passerines. 'Any bright ideas?'

Fox put his mind to work. 'Casa is our best bet. I have a friend in the cargo trade.'

Case didn't dismiss it out of hand. 'Nah,' he said at last. 'I'm no good in cities, and I doubt if we'd get there before the alarm goes off. Any other suggestions?'

Fox studied him again, coming to a decision. 'In that case, we could try the Count, but he's even further away.'

Case did a quarter-turn. 'Surely the Moroccans know about him.'

'Only if they got it out of Forbes,' Fox said. He took account of Case's disbelief. 'Forbes had to know because he arranges payment, but no one else.'

'Not even the Israeli?'

'About the deal, yes; in fact he was going to buy into it. But as for the supplier . . .' Fox smiled faintly. 'Lova Hazan was not a man of stainless virtue. Fidelity was not his strong point.' Fox raised a hand to deter interruption. 'Do you mind if I free associate?'

'So long as you keep your eyes open and your foot down.'

'Lova had business of his own in Fez. It's a fair assumption that it involved the people who were holding me. They, however, had no idea who I was – not who I *really* was. They found out eventually, of course, but not from me.' He fingered an unhealed sore on the soft part of his jaw. It looked like a cigarette burn. 'I wonder how they found out.'

Case chewed over the possibilities. 'Rafiq Saad?' he said.

Fox wafted out of his reverie. 'Very possibly.' He frowned. 'Where did you cross paths with him?'

'In Scotland, with Valentine. I assumed he was one of your customers.'

'Quite the reverse,' Fox said. He arched himself, trying to extricate something from his back pocket. 'Years ago, Lova Hazan did business with him in Lebanon. Last year, when I was going through a bad patch, Lova fixed up a deal with him to keep the wheels turning.' Fox shuddered. 'Not one of my better decisions.' He was still footling about in his pocket.

'There's a truck coming,' Case pointed out, and fell dumb as the Ford bore down on a collision course, airhorns braying and lights ablaze.

Fox corrected his line with feet to spare and waved casually in response to the truck driver's shaking fist. For the moment, he had stopped trying to reach into his pocket; he seemed to have tied himself into immobility.

Case unclamped his whitened fingers from the tinny dash. 'You're a menace,' he said.

'Exceptionally,' Fox said, 'I paid Rafiq through Lova, which makes me think there was some kind of settlement in kind – arms, I suppose. It doesn't take much effort to believe he moonlighted for the Israelis. Before I met him, he kept some very strange company.'

Case watched the road for the next peril. 'What – like terrorists?'

'Wouldn't be surprised. By the way, Rafiq's a Christian.'

'Yeah?' Case said. 'Well, he told me he was on the Moroccan royal family's Christmas card list.'

Fox took it serenely. 'Putting all the odds and ends together, it makes you wonder what's supposed to come off in six weeks.'

'Only four weeks now,' Case pointed out. 'I don't intend to stick around.'

They reached the trans-Atlas highway and headed in the direction of Marrakech. A rainbow curved down to a hilltop village.

'Turned out rather nice, hasn't it?' Fox said.

Case's mind had been see-sawing. It came down on the side of common sense. 'I'm going to lose you in the mountains for a few days. A Berber called Laschen will take care of you. I'll join you when my ankle's working again and we'll decide whether to risk the Count.'

Fox forgot about driving. 'Aren't you coming too?'

'It's a long walk,' Case said, using one hand to steer the Renault to the correct side of the road. 'Pay attention. In half an hour we'll be with Laschen. I'll drive the two of you as close to Marrakech as I can, and then it's up to you. Take a taxi to the Fez road; better still, take two. Jump on the first bus going east. Laschen knows where to get off. A truck will take you another forty kilometres, and then it's three days on foot.'

Fox had finally rooted out the object of his search – his crumpled Gauloises packet. Sadly, he shook out tobacco crumbs. 'I don't suppose you possess some snout.'

'I don't smoke,' Case snapped.

'I would kill for a cigarette and a proper cup of tea,' Fox said. His eyes widened. 'I've just thought of a joke. Why do anarchists drink mint tea?'

'For crying out loud,' Case said.

'Because proper tea is theft.' Fox snuffled with amusement. 'Rather good, I think.'

'Did you hear a word I said?'

Fox repeated them exactly.

'Do you think you'll be able to hack it?'

Fox looked down. He had on a grubby blue shirt, a pair of corduroys and sandals. 'I'll need a woollie and a pair of stout shoes.'

'Sure you don't want a hottie and a teddy bear,' Case said. Wearily he indicated his pack. 'Take whatever fits.'

'Decent of you.'

Case sneezed.

'Bless you.'

They were approaching the roadhouse where Case had phoned Iseult. It was only ten-fifteen. 'Pull in here,' he ordered. Stiffly he manoeuvred himself out.

'Who are you calling?' Fox asked, helping Case across the forecourt.

'Denis Low,' Case said, then yelped with pain as Fox missed a step. 'Oh yes,' he said, glad to be able to inflict some suffering on his own account, 'you've got quite a following.'

It took several minutes to link up with the number he'd given Low. Fox pottered off to buy some 'snout'. We've got a right one here, Case thought, keeping watch on the road. He had the Dexie fidgets. Every passing car made him jump. He was about to quit when Low came on. He gave him no chance to speak. 'If our Moroccan friends know where you are, this is goodbye.'

'We're sweet. George arrived in the motorhome. We spent

last night sleeping five-up on a bleeding campsite. It was horrible, but the filth has no idea where we're located. What about you?'

'I found him.'

'You little tinker. You fucking prince. Where?'

'Doesn't matter. He's not there now. I got him out.' Case swivelled. 'He's standing right beside me. He's a nutter.'

'And you're a jewel. Stay right where you are, my son. We're on our way.'

'No hurry. By the time you reach me, he'll be somewhere else. I'm sending him into the country for a few days.'

'Are you out of your fucking crust?' Low demanded. He dropped his voice. 'Listen, I've been on to a friend who owns a cabin cruiser. Know what I mean? We can have Fox back in Spain inside forty-eight hours. Get him into my possession and we're coasting.'

Case covered the mouthpiece. 'Denis wants to know if you fancy a trip to Spain on a friend's yacht.'

'Lovely,' Fox whispered.

Case uncovered the mouthpiece. 'He says he'd rather not.'

'You're at it again,' Low shouted.

'Do you want him or not?'

'Does the fucking Pope have bullet wounds?' Low bellowed.

'First, you give me the thirty thou.'

'COD,' Low yelled. 'CO-fucking-D is what we agreed. I can't pay you until I get the body.'

'What's all the fuss?' Fox whispered.

Once again, Case muffled the phone. 'Denis wants to know if he can have his money back.'

'Could be a trifle tricky,' Fox whispered.

Case restored contact with Low. 'He says you're entitled to a full refund. Statutory rights not affected.'

Low breathed on this for a while. 'If you're trying to shaft me, you're meat. You both are.'

'Before you blow a valve,' Case suggested, 'here's what

you do. Try not to attract attention. If you're followed, we are in bad trouble. Tonight I'll be on the other side of the Atlas. Take the Taroudannt road as far as Ijoukak and stop the night at the hotel. I'll call you at ten and let you know where to come. Don't bust a gut trying to reach me. Fox will be out of my hands within the hour.'

Low breathed down the phone. 'There'd better be extenuating circumstances, Pat, because I am well . . .'

Case cut off the threat and smiled at Fox. 'He's thrilled to bits.'

Fox was muted as he helped Case back to the car. 'The offer of a sea passage seems reasonable to me.'

'He hasn't told you the fare.' Grunting, Case lowered himself into the driver's seat. 'Low has gone to a lot of trouble; he thinks that turning you over is a lot easier than robbing banks.' Case cocked a bemused eye. 'Personally, I'm not so sure.'

Fox smiled faintly, cigarette dangling from his mouth. He stared south, where flashes of snow showed between rolls of cloud. 'It's not the most enticing prospect,' he murmured.

'Given a toss-up between the mountains and a watery grave,' Case said, 'I know which I'd choose.'

Fox wrung his hands. 'Oh, I do hope I'm doing the right thing.'

25

Army roadblocks at close intervals were the first sign that not all was calm in Tangiers. At the second check Cathal asked a dewy-faced lieutenant what the matter was, but he only smiled into Iseult's eyes and wished them a nice trip.

Driving downtown, Iseult kept casting rabbity glances at all sides. The atmosphere was eerily familiar – like a note stretched too thin for normal hearing. Sullen groups of young men had corralled themselves on building lots, under the uneasy surveillance of soldiers in olive drab. Sirens complained in the distance. Mute faces peeped from windows. A mother ran across the road towing her child, her distraught expression familiar from a thousand photojournalistic images.

The square where Iseult had intended to cash traveller's cheques was the main trouble spot, now cleared of protest and cordoned off by military with dangling gas-masks and bulging ammo pouches. She saw two burnt-out buses. The ground was littered with stones and glass and crushed placards.

An officer ran towards them semaphoring 'stop'. Iseult coughed on tear gas. The air reeked of wet ash and spent diesel. Upon finding their passports in order, the officer insisted they go back to their hotel.

On the road to Casa, Iseult had to pull over to let a long convoy hum past. A truckload of soldiers cradling rifles gave her the thumbs up and automatically she smiled back.

'Bastards,' Cathal said. He fiddled with the car radio, but every channel fed a diet of music. At least it wasn't martial music. In a filling station the attendant told them that a labour march had been crushed and there were casualties. The situation in Casa was best avoided, he said, and Fez should be given a wide berth.

Taking his advice, Iseult turned south at Rabat. On the map the journey looked a reasonable day's drive, but away from the coast the distances were continental – grassless plains with pyramids of phosphate spoil, stony barrens and vast fields watered by pipelines. They drove in three-hour shifts and reached Marrakech after dark, just too late to catch the bank before tackling the High Atlas. It was Iseult's turn at the wheel and she was glad of that, for snow warning signs had been planted on the climb, and the Tizi-n-Test was rutted with frozen slush. They passed two accidents, one of which looked nasty.

Cathal slept. He hadn't spoken much all day. Iseult was too exhausted to wonder what was gnawing him. She drove on the brake, her forehead almost pressed to the windscreen, hallucinating pitfalls and black spots on the empty road. The music on the radio was strenuous. When the road straightened in its descent she switched it off. For the first time in her life, a desert night stretched before her.

It was nearly midnight when they reached the hotel. Palms hung limp around it. There was a light at the entrance, but all the windows were dark. Iseult's balance was unsteady. Every time she blinked she saw headlights converging on a collision course.

The door was open. It gave on to a hall which led to a dining-room. In the gloom it looked like a sultan's palace, with intricately fretted cornices, hanging rugs and fine candelabra.

Cathal called for service but received no answer. 'What happens if he's not here?'

Iseult stepped out through French windows. The guests' quarters were small pavilions arranged around a garden with an illuminated swimming-pool at its centre. From out of one of the changing cubicles emerged a tiny man in pyjamas. As soon as he saw them he dived back, to appear again a couple of minutes later, dressed in a dinner jacket, settling a set of false teeth in place. His effusive greeting was in English. He was Monsieur Khader, and though dinner was not available, the cook having gone home to his village, no other demand would be refused.

'We arranged to meet two English friends,' Cathal said.

'Only my good friend Mister Pat is here.'

He conducted them into the dining-room and turned on the lights. The switch hung off the wall by its flex; water stains spread over the sagging ceiling; the table-cloths hadn't been changed. With a modest flourish, Monsieur Khader threw another switch, piping music into the room. Iseult recognized *Eine Kleine Nachtmusik*, the Serenade in G major, orchestrated for synthesizer and drums. Parts of the tape had been erased, and the tempo was erratic, sometimes threatening to come to a stop.

'Whisky?' Monsieur Khader said, briskly dealing with crumbs.

'Yes please. A large one.'

But apparently he was asking if they had brought any. Cathal had. Monsieur Khader removed the bottle to the bar, went into a huddle over it and returned with two full glasses. He settled himself at their table and watched Iseult closely as she sipped. The whisky had been switched; it left an aftertaste of boiled sweets. She took out her cigarettes and, after a moment's doubt, offered them. Monsieur Khader accepted one and sucked hard on it, staring at his guests with simple pleasure.

'I like the English,' he said. 'They are philosophers.' He crossed his legs and waved his cigarette. 'Arthur Scargill,' he said. 'Maggie Thatcher, the Iron Lady.'

'We're Irish,' Cathal said. He was not enjoying himself.

The Irish and their philosophers were dismissed with a puff of smoke. 'Do I speak good English?'

'Excellent,' Iseult said.

'Because my teacher is Winston Churchill,' Monsieur

Khader said. He explained how as a boy he had waited on the great man during his vacations in Marrakech.

His reminiscences dried up. Iseult's breath snatched. Her hands contracted into weak fists.

Pale and mean, Case stood in the doorway. His face had been cut. He walked across with the aid of a stick and shook hands. His eyes were like pincers. He sat down with a wince and glanced at their glasses.

'Bring them proper whisky,' he ordered. 'And turn that din off.'

Monsieur Khader complied with a simper. Pyjama bottoms showed between his trouser cuffs and bedroom slippers. He shifted to a neighbouring table and rested his chin on his bridged hands.

'Nice holiday?' Case inquired nastily.

'Very agreeable,' Cathal answered.

'Yeah?'

Cathal wouldn't look at him.

'They are looking for a friend,' Monsieur Khader volunteered.

'He's gone trekking for a few days. We'll sort it out later.'

Cathal stiffened, then lolled back. 'You've been in the wars,' he said.

'Nah, it was a stroll,' Case said. He looked away. 'I'll need a sub – as much as you can afford.'

'We couldn't change our cheques,' Iseult explained. 'There was a riot in Tangiers and by the time . . .' She faltered.

But Case only nodded, a faraway look in his eyes, as if the excuse was reasonable and his mind had already turned to other matters. 'Things have changed,' he said, addressing himself to Cathal. 'I want ten per cent commission.'

Iseult glanced at Cathal. 'But you said you'd do it for . . .'

'I know I did,' Case said, 'but so far it's been all one-sided.'

Cathal fingered the rim of his glass. 'You *do* have him?' he said.

'Oh yes – alive and kicking.'

Cathal found a smile from somewhere. 'Well,' he said, 'that's a huge relief.'

'Ten per cent,' Case reminded him.

'Sure, but only on production of the goods.' Cathal got to his feet. 'I'm ripped,' he said. 'Speak to you in the morning.'

Case watched him go, his expression sour. 'Overcome with gratitude.'

'Don't take it to heart,' Iseult said. 'He's exhausted.'

Case fabricated a smile. 'From his long holiday.' He gazed at Cathal's retreating back. 'I don't like your brother,' he said. He shrugged.

Iseult had to look away. 'We'd given you up,' she said, a quaver in her voice.

'For dead?' Case seemed to enjoy the phrase. 'I was thinking the same. Where have you been this last week?'

'Oh, wandering around, killing time.' Lying was easy, Iseult thought – much easier than admitting the truth. She smiled brightly, hating herself. 'You look so different.'

Case ran his fingers over his skull. 'Moroccan barbers put your head in a pencil sharpener.'

'No, it's your . . . manner.'

'I've got a stinking cold and I'm coming down from Dexies.' He held out his hand to show he had the shakes. He stood. 'Come for a walk.'

Outside, he felt for her hand and she had no choice but to let him hold it. The sky was eternal, layer upon layer of starry mesh. Through the trees was a great sheet of still water, and on the other side, at some remote part of the darkness, a fire was burning, tugging this way and that in a wind unfelt where they stood. The far-off yipping of a jackal only accentuated the silence.

'I've never been in the desert before,' Iseult said.

'This is only the edge. Imagine how quiet it is in the centre.' Case tilted his face to the stars. 'I thought about you a lot.'

Iseult stood in discomfort, wondering if he'd be offended if she freed her hand. 'I'd better get some sleep. We started at four this morning.'

'We have to talk.'

'I'm filthy; I need a bath.' She realized that what she'd said was open to misinterpretation.

'Baths is off,' Case told her. 'Use my shower. It's probably the only one that works.'

'I'll wait until morning,' she said. She couldn't interpret his mood, but she suspected he was close to an act of violence. She sneaked a step in the direction of the hotel.

Case stood still. 'There's this bloke called Orpheus,' he said. 'One day he sees these women riding along beside a river, all carrying falcons. Among them is their queen, who he really fancies. But when he tries to speak to her, she can't hear him. There's a kind of invisible barrier between them. They're in different worlds, you see, and though they're, like, in love, they can't reach each other.' Case went silent.

Iseult fiddled with her watch strap. 'Alright,' she said.

She showered in a dribble of tepid water. As she was drying herself, Case knocked on the door and pushed through a parcel. 'I got this for you in Marrakech,' he said.

Unwrapping the cheap paper, Iseult found a white *djellaba* embroidered in royal blue. She grimaced. Everything about it was wrong – material, colour, style, concept. 'I'll wear it in the morning,' she called out, her eyes tight-shut.

'Try it on now, may as well. Exchange it if it doesn't fit.'

It didn't. Seams gave as she crammed herself into it. The ghastly material wrinkled over her hips and formed a slick curve over her stomach, making her think of a car panel. Where it wasn't an interference fit, it clung by static attraction. And yet confronted with her humiliation in the mirror, Iseult found it suited her very well. This gross and clumsy bag was the real her.

Case's eyes were cast down. He raised them cautiously, and his dismay was almost comical. 'It's too small,' he said, as if the possibility had never occurred.

'Not very,' Iseult said gaily.

'Take it off.'

'I like it,' Iseult said. She did a twirl. 'I'll have to lose a few pounds.'

Case's face went small. 'I said take the fucking thing off.'

Her smile froze. He looked demented. She teetered back but his hand snaked out, seizing the front of the dress, and wrenched. The collar cut into her neck before the material gave, ripping from bodice to hem. She stood with her hands at her throat, as if caught in a gale. He began to strip off his own clothes.

She backed away but he was between her and the door. Naked, he herded her towards the bed and shoved her back. He knelt above her. She jabbed her hand in his face and he laughed, drew her hand between his teeth and bit the webbing between her fingers.

And as the pain lanced through her, she melted into it, certain it was what she wanted.

She bit the hand that held her own and tasted blood. He convulsed, panting obscenities, but she pulled him back, clutched him close, raking his back with her nails. 'No,' she gasped, 'go on, go on, go on!'

They fought and writhed, fucking and sucking. On each wet thrust he gasped out the awful things he would do to her. She laughed and urged him on, wanting him to hurt, wanting brute ravishment with nothing of thought or tenderness. And that . . . oh God! . . . was . . . oh yes, yes! . . . was what he was . . . giving . . . ramming home as no one had . . . yesyesyesyesyes . . . aaaaah! . . . NOW!

And again.

And again.

And this time he throbbed inside her.

Drenched with sweat, her breath sawing, she untwined her legs from around his back and slid from under him. For a time she lay without touching him, her hair damp and matted, one hand trailing on the cool floor.

She swung back her hair and looked down at him. There were weals on his shoulders. Her own back smarted. Inflamed still, she climbed astride him with a little growl, drew the tent of her hair about them and undulated to a rhythm of her own, her eyes open and then glazing over as another succession of jolts first raised her in an arch and then brought her sagging forward, lower and lower, until with a last small gasp, a thin squeal almost painful in its intensity, she pitched across him, the whole structure flattened and complete.

But even then there were twinges of pleasure to be squeezed out.

Laughter bubbled inside her. She felt an enormous sense of accomplishment, a great liberation that made her kiss him hard. She felt his mouth move under hers in a smile.

'Why me?' she whispered a little later, her head lodged in the crook of his shoulder.

He didn't answer for a long time. 'When I was a nipper,' he said at last, 'I nearly drowned at the seaside. I was paddling at the edge and a wave knocked me down and I couldn't get up. Every time I tried, another one flattened me. I could see the supervisor and all the other kids playing rounders on the beach and I couldn't understand why they couldn't see me. I tried to shout and took a lungful of water. I went under and could hear the sea roaring in my head. Then someone had hold of me. It was a girl – well, I don't know how old she was, but I remember she had a black swimsuit and dark hair, and when she got me to the beach I didn't want her to let go of me. I could feel her breasts.' Case turned his head. 'I must have been five or six.'

'I never saved anyone's life.'

Outside the window a bird piped a melancholy tune.

'Rhapsody,' Iseult heard herself say at a distance.

'That's a bulbul,' Case said, 'the Arabian nightingale.'

She half raised herself. 'Fancy you knowing the story of Orpheus and Eurydice.'

'I don't. A friend sent me the bit about the falcons.'

'It's sad,' she said, and yawned. 'A queen is abducted by the king of the underworld, but when her husband rescues her, she dies because she can't survive in the light.'

340

'The bit I know reminds me of a fairy story – about a prince who escapes from a beautiful witch. When she sees she's lost him, she says: "If I had known you'd betray me, I would have given you two plugs of wood for eyes." I always rememember that – "two plugs of wood for eyes."' Case looked down into her eyes. 'I love you, Iseult.'

Her gaze wouldn't hold to his. She struggled upright and reached for her cigarettes.

'You'd better get your head down,' he said as she smoked. 'We're in trouble. I want you gone first thing – both of you.'

He fell asleep, hot and twitching. After an hour he quietened down.

When at last Iseult shut her eyes, she found herself back in Belfast, walking not through the leafy suburb of Malone but some blighted section of the Falls. It was night-time and sodium lights leached everything of colour. On the greasy road some way ahead, she saw her mother stepping on to the boarding platform of a bus. She remained standing on the platform when it moved off, and Iseult began to run after her, hearing her feet beating on the wet pavement. She ran for miles before she caught up, but when she jumped aboard her mother was no longer there. Turning, Iseult saw with no surprise that her mother had alighted at the previous stop and was briskly walking back the way she had come, past rowhouses with cement windows and doors and nationalist murals on the walls. Not daring to jump, Iseult watched the gap widen until by the time she reached the next stop, her mother was tiny in the deserted street. She set off in pursuit. Hurry, she kept telling herself, but she wore a tight skirt that impeded her. The buildings fell back, leaving a dereliction of flattened factories. Her mother was climbing a footbridge over a motorway. Iseult followed, heart pounding, out of breath, and found that the bridge had no centre, although her mother had somehow crossed to the other side and was walking away as if late for an appointment. Iseult ran back down the steps and found herself in the middle of the motorway, headlights stabbing to each side of her, horns blaring, faces contorted with hatred or scorn. Something was stifling her. She couldn't move. She was smothering.

Her eyes opened. A hand was clamped over her mouth and in terror she thought that Pat was trying to murder her. But it wasn't Case's face hanging in the dark. In the ambient light of the shuttered room, the face acquired features. She mewed.

'Remember me, wee pet?' the Landlord whispered.

He took his finger away and pointed right. Iseult's eyes rolled in their sockets and she recognized the Poet, bent over Case, holding a gun at his head. She could tell Case was awake.

Reaching down, the Landlord switched on the bedside lamp, then whisked off her sheet. Iseult gasped. The Landlord whistled softly.

'It's a focking blessing your grandpa didn't live to see the day.'

The Poet's mouth tightened as if on drawstrings. 'Get your bodies dressed,' she said.

26

In the first crack of day, with the black palms edged by sky the colour of teal feathers, the Landlord and the Poet escorted Case to their Citroën, discreetly moving him along at pistol-point. They swung round, startled by a muffled detonation. Out beyond the oasis, a cloud of waders swarmed up over the trees and formed into long black fingers pointing south.

The Landlord showed Case to his place in the rear. He was burly and proletarian, his face winey and his movements laboured – not the picture of health. He spoke in the phlegmy growl of old Ulster and had the long-suffering manner of a much put-upon family man. He had a way of moving his eyelids slowly down over his eyes that made Case think of a toad.

The Poet reminded Case of the sort of junior bank-teller who never engages your eyes except to tell you you're overdrawn. She had lank hair and a thin washed-out face – like kids he remembered from the Battlefields Estate, where a lot of the inmates of the Home came from, and where even the social workers had to have a police escort. She had thoughtful hands, though, which carried the .357 Ruger aimed at Case's kidneys. Her speech was of the rural south.

They drove in convoy, Iseult leading in Case's Renault, Cathal making up the tail in his Fiat. The sun forged orange buttes from cold purple hills. Ahead, cloud girdled the Atlas, leaving only the ice-caps bare. Case had never known snow come so early. He wiped his runny nose on his sleeve. His hands were cuffed by the same device he'd used on Fox's guard. His cold smouldered in his sinuses.

'Only a dumb Mick would take this road,' he said.

'Don't be going on again,' the Landlord said. 'It's the quickest way, and that'll do us.'

Case sniffed noisily. 'Quickest way to die,' he said, looking around. He could bait his captors with impunity. For now he was precious cargo and by the time they chose to kill him, they would be dead themselves. Of that he was certain.

The Poet said something in Gaelic.

'Ach, pay no mind,' the Landlord told her. 'He's only creating mischief.'

Half an hour into the ascent the Landlord slowed on a hairpin, an impressive drop to the nearside. 'Here's a good place to lose the Renault,' he said, and flashed his lights at Iseult. She stopped.

'Please yourself,' Case said, 'but that shepherd will think it odd to see you ditch a perfectly decent car.'

'I don't see any shepherd.'

'You must be blind, man. Over on the scree there.'

The Landlord showed a trace of exasperation. 'The fockers get everywhere. Have you noticed that, Deirdre? There's one behind every rock.'

'No hurry,' Case said. 'We'll be up in the clouds soon.'

The Landlord breathed a little harder.

The sunlight paled. Plumes of mist wafted across the road. The Landlord switched to headlights. At times the lamps of the Renault disappeared.

Fog swallowed them – a dazzle of white that thickened to clammy grey and cut visibility to yards. The Landlord switched on wipers and rubbed the windscreen as if it was the glass that was the problem. He flashed his lights. 'We've lost her,' he said.

'One down,' Case said. 'Two to go.'

'We'll pick her up soon enough,' the Poet said in clear English. She wiped the rear screen and peered back. 'Wait for the welcher.'

They halted. The atmosphere floated lazily past, condensing into beads on the glass. Lights nosed out of the murk. Behind the screen, Cathal's face looked like a paper mask.

Once again the Poet spoke softly in Irish.

'We'd better take him with us,' the Landlord said. He lumbered forth. 'Out,' he ordered. 'We're dumping your car.'

'But it's rented in my name.'

'Get you out before I beat you bloody.'

Cathal stumbled on to the road, limbs not properly functioning.

'They've lost your sister,' Case informed him.

'Shut your focking gob and put your shoulder to this heap,' the Landlord ordered.

'There could be a village below,' Case pointed out.

'Tough tit.'

The Fiat went over with a satisfying crash. It stuck on a rock then slithered away.

They went on, the road leading ever upward. Sealed in the steel and glass, Case detected a palpable disimprovement of spirits.

The Poet muttered something.

'What are you gurning about now?'

'We could be going head on into disaster.'

'For Christ's sake, I'm not doing above fifteen miles an hour.'

'It's not your driving that's the matter – though I wish to God you'd give the horn a wee toot at some of these corners.' The Poet looked at the cliffs sliding past. 'I'm thinking the Brit could be a problem.' She cocked the Ruger at Case's temple. 'Give us the name of the village.'

'Bou Redine.'

'Ach, he's mixing us about,' the Landlord said.

The Poet altered her aim. 'Would you have me clean out your ears?'

'Leave it,' the Landlord advised. 'We'll ease it out of him somewhere quiet.'

'It won't do you any good. How far do you think a pair of wallies like you would get without me?'

'Wallies,' the Landlord murmured. His glance suggested he

was wearily familiar with Case's brand of bravado. 'Tell him who he's mixing with,' the Landlord ordered Cathal.

Cathal showed no haste to answer, so the Landlord swung an elbow into his face. 'Tell him!'

'Company Commander in the Belfast Brigade.'

'And what do they call me?'

'The Landlord.'

'And why is that?'

Cathal risked an anxious glance. 'Because you used to run a drinking club.'

'The Nail Bomb,' Case said, 'near the Divis. With a soundproof romper room in the back.' He engaged the Landlord's eyes in the mirror. 'I know who you are. You're Joseph Tolan and you're a bad bastard. You were in Long Kesh for murder and extortion.' He leaned close to Cathal. 'You'll be alright with these two.' He reclined again. 'So,' he said, 'what's the going rate for ripping off IRA funds?'

The Landlord smiled over his shoulder. 'These days, it's all rationalized.'

Case prodded Cathal with his bound hands. 'That sounds nice. They're going to rationalize your knee-caps. Or maybe,' he suggested, 'it's a nut job.'

'You Brits are always trying to put the wrong on us,' the Poet said in a surly tone.

'Don't encourage him,' the Landlord said, but then laughed and slapped his hands on the wheel. 'Did I tell you about that geg who traded in his knees?'

'A thousand times,' the Poet answered, sulking.

'When I came out of the Lazy K,' the Landlord said, 'I was put in charge of policing Clonard. Well now, most of the boys up in front of me were glue-sniffers and joy-riders, but there was one fellow – Dosser Pearse, a Derryman – who I had occasion to reprimand over his persistent thieving of his neighbours' smalls.' The Landlord gave a bronchial laugh. 'Some of the wifies hardly had a pair of knickers to cover their arses with. Well now, we finally caught the bugger and he admitted it straight out; he couldn't do anything else. You should have seen the amount of bras and panties we recovered – "and you haven't found the half of them", Dosser boasted. Aye, he was like you, Pat – a real gamester. Even when he was taken to the place of punishment, all he said was: "Would youse mind if it was the left knee, because I'm striker for the local footer team?" I said this isn't a focking self-service; you'll just have to learn how to kick with the other. So bang goes his knee.

'Well now, a few months later I see this one-legged man walking up the Springfield, and it's Dosser, just out of the Royal Victoria with his artificial leg – aye, it had to be amputated. He sees me and smiles and shakes my hand like we're the best of muckers. It was all for the best he says, and he's four thousand pounds better off from the compensation board.' The Landlord shook his head. 'But I tell you: I'd want more than four thousand pounds for any leg that belonged to me.' He smiled contentedly. 'Still, Dosser Pearse plays darts now and is a match for anyone in the Six Counties.'

'That's what I love about you Rum and Cokes – the wonderful community spirit.'

Cathal buried his face in his hands.

Case grinned. 'How did you come to take on this blouse?'

'Through his grandda – a cracking fighter and one of the staunchest patriots Ireland has had.' The Landlord glanced at Cathal and sighed. 'Breeding's a perplexing business.'

Case eyed the Poet. 'Who's your pasty-faced girlfriend?'

'Deirdre Coghlan from Connemara. She's a poet.'

'Like Yeats?' Case said, interested.

'As good as, if not better, but you'd have to speak the Gaelic to get the measure of it. And now, enough of us: let's be hearing about you. Would it be true what they say, Pat – that you're the Lone Ranger?'

'The what?'

'The fellow who shot those two players in Monaghan.'

'Oh them. Yeah, it's all true – every word.'

The Landlord let the driving take care of itself so he could engage Case fully. 'Well now, that puts us on a common footing,' he said. 'We'll have a good crack when we're away from the hurly-burly.'

'I'm looking forward to that. Eh, Cathal?'

Cathal cringed from Case's touch.

'G'wan, cheer up,' the Landlord said. 'It might never happen.'

Slowly Cathal lifted his head. 'We agreed,' he said hoarsely.

The Poet flicked Cathal's ear. 'Hush.'

'Agreed what?' Case asked.

The Poet spoke rapidly in Gaelic.

'Nawh,' the Landlord said in a musing tone. 'I'm thinking a little frankness could clear the way ahead.' He made sure he had Case's eyes. 'You've served in Belfast, so you know what a hard oul' station it is. I've done one whack in the Lazy K, and if I go back it's dead certain there'll be another.' He bestowed a kindly look on Cathal. 'I was thinking we might settle out of court.'

'Take the money and run?' Case said.

The Landlord wasn't perturbed. 'There's more to life than stiffing Brits, and two million is a handsome sum in anybody's language.' Some kind of signal passed between him and the Poet. 'Are you on?'

'Sure,' Case said. He laughed, and the Landlord laughed along with him. Between those two, at least, there was quite an amicable atmosphere.

A roadside hamlet sprang from the pall. Beside a deserted tourist stall offering crystals of amethyst was a grocery kiosk constructed mainly of beaten cans and manned by two beady eyes in a *djellaba*.

'No point hoping to run into a Tesco,' Case said. 'We'd better stock up while we have the chance.'

The Landlord clicked his tongue at Cathal. 'None of this gallivanting about would have been necessary if you'd stuck with him.' He heaved himself out and crossed the road. Half a minute later he was back, shaking his head. 'What a language,' he said. 'The buggers can't find a decent vowel

348

between them. What's Moroccan for sardines? For that's all they've got.'

'Sardines,' Case told him. 'Watch out for the ones with chilli. They're murder.'

The Landlord closed his eyes. 'You go.'

Under the supervision of the Poet, Case bought almost the entire stock – sardines in oil and tomato sauce, scrotal little dried dates, mud-coloured pasta, a metal teapot made in Poland, a block of sugar shaped like an artillery shell, some chocolate that smelt like air freshener, condensed milk, oranges, four extra cartridges for his butane stove. Case piled the provisions into the back and they resumed the climb.

Snow rustled on the roof. The windscreen wipers squeaked. The tyres crackled on ice.

'If we make it to Marrakech,' Case said, 'one of you will have to stop to buy clothing and sleeping things. Even when it's a hundred down in Marrakech, it can be five or six below on the plateau.'

'Look at him,' the Poet said quietly. 'He's plotting sneakiness.'

'Give my head some peace. It's all I can do to see what's in front of my nose. The road's sheet ice and . . . Focking hell, I can't . . . Jesus, Mary and holy Saint Joseph!'

A truck had slewed on the apex of a bend, partly blocking the road. Figures were clustered at the rear wheels. Case leaned forward and felt the pistol jab.

'Not a squeak,' the Poet hissed.

'Good morning, campers,' Case murmured, sinking down.

One of the men came forward, arms spread in apology. It was Fatso, dressed for the beach. He halted and his jaw hit his chest. He ran back.

'We've just been clocked by the Waltham Forest Fishing Club,' Case said.

The Landlord put his foot down and the wheels spun uselessly, the car sliding with the camber towards the unprotected brink. They stopped feet short. Nobody was in sight by the motorhome.

'Have they got weapons?'

Case hesitated. 'Only the one pistol.

'Go on, Joe,' the Poet urged. 'There's plenty of room.'

'We're on a skating rink,' the Landlord said. The back of his neck had flushed brick red.

Through the fog Low's disembodied voice sang out, his words bouncing off the cliffs above and reaching them with all resonance taken out.

'Here we are again, happy as can be. All good friends and jolly good companeee . . .'

'Who's that focking eejit?' the Landlord demanded.

'Give me Fox,' Low shouted.

'Answer him,' the Landlord said, activating the window.

'He's not here,' Case called.

'Who's that mob then?'

'Tell 'em we picked you up hitchhiking.'

'Tourists who gave me a lift.'

Low laughed. He fell silent for a moment. 'Ask them if they'd be so good as to step outside.'

The Poet and the Landlord nodded at each other. 'Youse uns stay tight,' the Landlord murmured, beginning to open his door. As he shifted his bulk Cathal flung open his own door and was out like a rat through a crack. The Poet swung with the chance of a snap-shot but held her fire. Cathal dropped over the edge and, for all anyone in the car could tell, into messy oblivion.

'You done me wrong, Pat,' Low shouted.

'It's not what it seems, chief.'

'Don't call me that, slag. You're off the firm as of this moment.' There was a pause, and when he spoke again his voice was choked. 'Why, Pat? I gave you the best start you ever had. You could have made something of yourself.'

Someone was coming through the fog, arm extended as if feeling the way. It was Roy Besant. The tip of his nose glowed red with cold and the Browning in his hand trembled like a diviner's rod. More spectres were ranged behind him.

'Do like Denis says,' Besant commanded, the Browning jiggling.

The Landlord and the Poet exchanged another nod, in perfect understanding, and cautiously vacated the car, holding out their bare hands with the uncertainty of bystanders. Besant instructed them to step aside.

'Where's Fox?' Low shouted.

'Safe and sound.'

'You'll have to square it,' Besant said.

'I'd like to, Roy, but I'm in no position at present. Put the gun away.'

Besant looked at the gun. 'You know I never wanted to come,' he said. 'I want to go home, Pat, back to my own patch, back to my family, and watch crap on the telly.'

This plea, making up in feeling what it lacked in eloquence, touched Case. 'My hands are tied right now,' he said, 'but let us through and I'll do my best.'

'Understand me on this one,' Low bellowed. 'I want Fox. Come up short and you are shish kebab.'

'That's about the strength of it,' Besant said. He adjusted his hold on the gun and came a step closer. Case opened his mouth in warning as the Poet rolled and fired. Besant reared up on tiptoes as if trying to see where the shot had come from. Then quite slowly he took a couple of halting backward steps and sat down. The Poet fired again and Besant's wig fell off into his lap. He looked at it for a moment, making extraordinary gargling noises, before toppling back.

His colleagues had faded away. The Poet stood up and fired with deliberation, emptying the magazine at ten degree intervals. She picked up Besant's gun and reloaded her own before backing into the car. The fog held the sweet stink of cordite.

The Landlord came back chuckling, agile with action, but he got the car under way carefully enough, easing it through the gap between the motorhome and the mountain. From above a voice called in anguish.

'I know where you live, Hard Case. You'll never walk

alone.' Low paused, reconsidering the force of this particular threat. 'You'll never fucking walk *again*.'

'We've lost the welcher,' the Poet said, staring back as if she was the only one who'd noticed.

'Two down, only me to go,' Case said. He was trembly.

'It's no loss at all,' the Landlord said. 'The man's a bucket of jelly.' He turned in glee. 'Are we not fine innovators?'

'Yeah, but that lot are on our side. Wait till you meet the baddies.'

The Landlord's shoulders bunched. 'Whack him,' he said. 'Knock his bollocks in.'

The Poet looked about for a heavy implement.

'Use the gun, girl. It won't break.'

The Poet reversed her grip and struck out. Case parried the blow easily. The Poet tried again with little better success.

'Don't make such a meal of it,' the Landlord growled, intent on his driving.

'It's like you courting me on the back seat,' the Poet panted. 'And you know how far that got you.' She raised the gun again, lunged and missed by a mile as the Citroën swerved to avoid an oncoming car full of men. 'Mercy, that was close,' she cried, swivelling rearwards.

'Did you see the glimp they gave us?' the Landlord said thoughtfully.

'That's because they're the people who were holding Fox.'

The Landlord increased speed as much as he dared. He began to hum. The Poet kept an anxious lookout to the rear.

'What will we do?' she asked.

'They won't catch us in a hurry. There must have been six big fellows in that car.'

'We still have to get down the other side,' Case said. 'They may have a radio and . . .' His tone grew urgent. 'Listen, they must have passed Iseult without a thought. If we can catch up with her, we can swap cars. Leave the Citroën on the road. It'll throw them for long enough.'

'He's a devil for ideas,' the Landlord acknowledged.

In the car there was hardly any sensation of progress. It was like driving into a thick blanket. Case felt sick.

'What will we do with the O'Dwyer girl?' the Poet asked.

'Take her along.'

'If she comes, I don't,' Case said.

The Landlord chuckled. 'That was a great performance you put up last night. Aye, raving and romping like beasts of the field. Your fancy French tricks stirred my own blood, so they did.' He gave Deirdre a soppy smile.

'No bad talk,' she snapped, blushing. 'Eyes on the road.'

'What pigging road?'

Case watched behind. The angle of the climb lessened. In another minute they were at the pass. A sign said they were at 2,100 metres. To the right was a parking area.

'There she is,' the Poet cried.

Iseult put up some resistance before the Landlord bundled her into the passenger seat. She was weeping.

'What's she so upset about?' Case jeered. He had an ache which was partly in his chest and partly in his throat.

At the sound of his voice, Iseult hunched forward, as if nose to nose with an adversary.

Case leaned as close as he could. He could smell her, the ammoniac residues of their love-making. 'Two wooden plugs for eyes,' he whispered.

Iseult flinched. 'I'm not talking to you.'

Case laughed and laughed until the Poet, taking advantage of his distraction, gave him a good smack in the gob with her pistol.

Case spat a tooth into his palm and inspected it. It was the one Low had loosened.

'That's still a few dozen more than I've got,' the Landlord told him. 'Where I grew up, teeth were considered such a lot of bother, you had them all taken out for a twenty-first birthday present.'

'Here they come,' the Poet murmured.

Lamps starred the fog then receded to fuzzy points.

'Give us your duty-free,' the Landlord ordered, extending one arm towards the Poet.

'I'm not watching you get stotious,' she snapped.

'Just a drop to get the brain cells up and dancing.'

Reluctantly, Deirdre handed over a litre of sweet red Martini.

'It's the right one, the bright one – it's Martini,' the Landlord sang. He drank from the bottle, one eye on the mirror. 'What's he up to?' he asked after a while.

'Nothing yet. Can't you go any faster?'

'Not in this candyfloss.'

'He's dropped back. No, here he is again, on sidelights only. I think he means to push us over at his leisure. Shall I take a shot?'

'If those boys are peelers, there'll be holy murder.'

'I'm not so sure of that,' Case said.

The Landlord weighed up the situation. 'I'm reluctant,' he said, 'us being guests of a foreign country. What do you say, Pat? Can you contrive something more cute than shooting?'

'I don't know,' Case said, thinking on several tracks at once.

'You'd better come to a decision quick,' the Poet said. 'We'll not outrun them in this tub, and once we're out of the cloud, he has us any way he wants.'

The Landlord took another swallow and put the Martini aside. 'It's a misfortune,' he said, 'but I'd say it looks like a beaten docket.'

By this Case understood that the Poet was free to fire at will. 'Not yet,' he cried.

The Landlord looked at him with an expression of polite inquiry.

'He can see even less of the road than us,' Case explained. 'He's reacting to our brake lights. Before the next right-hander, accelerate, then switch off the ignition and take the turn as fast as you can. The brake lights won't come on and they'll just keep going.'

'You'll lock the steering, you eejit.'

'Renault Fours don't run to a lock.'

The Landlord turned the key and gave the wheel an experimental turn. 'He's a quality thinker, you know, but there's one small error: I can't see where the next focking corner is hiding. Whoops, there it is!' he cried, spinning the wheel and just avoiding the mountain.

'There'll be another one along soon,' Case said. 'Keep an eye out for a crash wall to the left. Leave your braking until the last moment.'

They all strained forward.

Whitewashed stones flickered past. The engine note hardened as the Landlord reached for the key.

'Too late, abort,' Case said, seeing the stones curve into the bend. The Renault heeled over. He squeezed his eyeballs.

'Where are they?' the Landlord asked.

'God in heaven knows. No, there they are, kiting along as cool as you please.'

'If I brake hard with that lot up our arse, it'll be us that gets shunted into space.'

'Take your timing from me,' Case said. His eyes flicked from the road ahead to the dim eyes behind and back again. 'Okay,' he said, 'give it the lot.'

'I'm blind.'

'Now! Flat out.'

The Landlord obeyed. He began to hum again. His neck sweated what looked like thin oil.

'Oh glory,' the Poet murmured.

'Have we lost them?' Case demanded, his gaze fixed in front.

'Not quite, but they're dropping back.'

'Don't slow,' Case cried, sensing the Landlord backing off as the curve tightened. 'Switch off . . . Now!'

In silence the Renault free-wheeled into the hairpin. Under braking it ploughed straight on, and as the road ran out and only cloud remained, Case grabbed for the door with the skimpy hope of flinging himself clear. He was slammed against it, pinned there by gravity and the Poet's weight as the car abruptly changed direction, almost putting its rear out over the drop. Case and the Poet piled against the opposite door as the Renault spun and stopped almost in its own length.

'Did it do the trick?' the Landlord said, fumbling for the ignition.

'I had my eyes shut,' the Poet said. 'For all I know they're sitting on the roof.' She rubbed strained neck muscles, then pushed Case away and brushed herself down as if he had taken some naughty advantage during their contact.

'They've gone,' Case assured them.

The Landlord managed to start the car, which was now facing uphill, and drove to the edge. Down in the gorge the clouds were tinted reddish.

'Three good cars used up,' the Landlord marvelled, 'and it's not yet breakfast time.' He reached for the bottle, took a deep draught, then laid his forehead on the steering-wheel. 'What now?'

'Now you've got me to think about,' Case told him.

27

Jetting up to London, Dearborn found a paragraph about the Moroccan riots in the *International Herald Tribune*. He asked the steward for every English and French newspaper on board, and supplemented them at Heathrow with half a dozen others which he scoured on the crawl into Mayfair. The consensus was seven dead in Tangiers and an unknown number of fatalities in Fez, where – according to one of the more clued-up French correspondents – the protests had been orchestrated by a local Sufi brotherhood whose membership, it was rumoured, included elements of the Moroccan officer corps.

As Dearborn chewed it over in his hotel room, his perplexity thickened into anger. What the hell had Cody been playing at, pretending that the Moroccan situation was serene? He buzzed the operator and asked to place a call to the United States embassy, Rabat.

International lines were busy, and while he waited for them to clear, he began to vacillate. Cody was a veteran of civil strife; of course he had been anticipating trouble. If he hadn't taken Dearborn into his confidence – well, why should he?

The phone bleeped. 'I have that number you requested, sir.'

'My apologies,' Dearborn said. 'I'd like to cancel.'

'You're welcome.'

With the afternoon going begging, he took a stroll through Piccadilly. London was gridlocked, the fine autumn light misted by traffic fumes. Dearborn had never seen so many attractive women. Returning up Bond Street, Dearborn watched one walking his way, and something about her – her bold, life-affirming stride – made him feel good. He caught her eye, smiling.

Her reaction was more irritable than angry – a quick toss of the head, as if he was the tenth undesirable to have given her the eye that day. Dearborn found his reflection in a store window, and his smile withered in his mouth. He saw a middle-aged man with the beginnings of a stoop, the face unexciting, the clothes uninventive. His self-image was woefully out of date.

The store was a fancy men's boutique. In a fit of madness, he went in and blew fifteen hundred bucks on an Italian leather blouson.

At eight, dressed in his new outfit, he took a cab to the Low Spot. The club was in a refurbished reach of London Docklands. Expecting a funky drinking den with muscle on the door, he was startled to find a deconsecrated church with a lobby as cool and tasteful as a plastic surgeon's waiting-room. The pretty receptionist beamed at him.

'Good evening, sir. Are you a member, sir?'

'Forbes Valentine recommended I drop by any old time.'

'Forbes Valentine,' she mused, examining the register. She looked up with regret. 'I'm afraid Mr Valentine doesn't appear to be with us tonight.'

'I believe he intends to call in later,' Dearborn said, starting towards the inner door, 'so if I . . .'

'I'm terribly sorry, sir. Guests must be accompanied by a member.'

'I'd be happy to join up right now.'

'I'd love to oblige you, sir, but . . .' She slid across an application on heavy paper. 'There's an eighteen-month waiting list and you'll require two sponsors.'

While Dearborn was trying to think up something imaginative, a smartly turned out young lady entered, swinging a briefcase with executive assurance. 'Evening, June,' she called. 'God, what a ghastly day. Is the poison dwarf in?'

'I'm afraid so.'

'Pissed?'

'No more than usual.'

'Fuck.'

'Excuse me, ma'am,' Dearborn said. 'I was expecting to meet a friend here, but he's been delayed. I wonder if I could ask you to sign me in.'

The woman rolled her eyes at June.

'I'd be happy to show my appreciation by buying you a bottle of champagne.'

'Get lost,' the woman said, blending indignation with lofty indifference.

Sweating from the put-down, Dearborn forgot restraint. He slapped a twenty-pound note in front of June. 'How about we ignore the rules?'

The suggestion quite took the shine off June's smile. 'I'm sorry, sir.'

'Look, it's Denis Low I want to see. Give him a call, will you? Tell him one of Forbes Valentine's buddies is in town.'

'Mr Low is away on holiday.'

'Where?' Dearborn demanded, losing control.

June must have activated an alarm. A pudgy, sharply dressed young man came out, a co-operative but not entirely convincing smile to the fore. Behind him trod a powerfully built man wearing a tieless black shirt buttoned to the neck. 'Good evening, sir,' the managerial one said. 'How may we help you, sir?'

'Derek, the gentleman doesn't understand the rules of admission.'

'Quite simple, sir,' Derek said. 'Members only.'

'That's what I told him,' June said. 'It doesn't seem to get through.'

'In that case, let me put it another way,' Derek said, sliding a hand under Dearborn's arm. 'You're in or you're out.'

'He says he's a friend of Forbes Valentine,' June said. 'And,' she added darkly, 'he was asking for Denis.'

'Is that right?' Derek said. He studied Dearborn's face as

if he was going to be tested on it later. 'How is my old mate Forbsie? I hear he's not been too well.'

'He was looking pretty good when I saw him in New York.'

'Great city,' Derek said. 'Business or . . .' His eyes took Dearborn's measure. '. . . personal?'

'I run a video company. Forbes was advising me on markets in the Gulf.'

'Nice work,' Derek said approvingly. He jerked a finger at the bouncer. 'Alright, Nicky, I think we can make an exception for . . .?'

'John Wesley Dearborn.'

'Derek Jargon,' his host said, shaking hands as if a deal had been clinched. 'Welcome to the Low Spot, John.'

Dearborn fumbled for his wallet.

'Put it away,' Jargon told him. 'It's a trial offer.' He smiled brightly. 'You might not find it to your taste.' He moved off. 'I'll catch up with you inside and you can give me the latest on Shirl . . . Forbsie.'

Inside it was crowded and smoky and animated, the laughter rising in waves, as if cued. The sexes were represented about equally and there was a lot of unreserved hugging between the women, which put Dearborn in mind of Middle East despots.

A world-weary barman with a stud in his nose served Dearborn a white wine. On the walls hung photographs of showbiz types dedicated with fond expressions to Denis.

Someone jogged his arm, spilling wine down his jacket. 'Hey,' Dearborn called after a small, tightly wound man who was making for the protective custody of the woman he had propositioned in the foyer. She flashed him a triumphant grin. Despondently, he ordered another drink. The wine left a sour film on his teeth.

'Denis in?' he asked the bartender without enthusiasm.

'Abroad, heart. On his hols.'

'Seen Forbes Valentine lately?'

The barman pouted. 'Not for *ages*.'

'You disappoint me, John,' Jargon said behind him. 'You practically elbow your way in and then sit around like a spare dick at a wedding.' He pulled himself on to a stool and smoothed down his jacket. 'Same again for John, and make mine an Aqua Libra.' His eyes cruised the room, monitoring the interplay of relationships.

'Pretty crowded,' Dearborn said.

'The usual ratpack,' Jargon said. 'Monday's our meet-the-press evening.' To judge from his air of distraction, it appeared that not everything was to his satisfaction. Frowning, he caught the attention of a middle-aged woman with mean eyes sharpened by expensive optics. She hurried over.

'Rita,' Jargon said with a crimped smile, 'have a word with Calypso, there's a good girl.'

'I already have,' Rita said, her tone vicious.

'Well have another fucking one, and make sure it's the last.'

From the direction in which they were looking, it seemed as if their concern centred on a slim black girl in a leather micro-skirt who was being pressed indecently close by a grey-haired gentleman.

'Actresses,' Jargon said, shaking his head in irritation. 'One five-minute spot on *Blankety-Blank* and they think they're Greta Garbo. "I vanna be alone,"' he mimicked. He shrugged. 'So update me on Forbsie.'

'It's been a few weeks,' Dearborn said, watching Rita work her way through the crush. Something about the set of her shoulders made him want to call out a warning to Calypso.

'Videos, eh? Very tasty.'

'Educational videos,' Dearborn said, 'mainly in the field of health.'

Jargon winked. 'Health and beauty, doctors and nursies, right?'

Dearborn obliged with a laugh.

'Hey, maybe I can help with your casting requirements,' Jargon said, magicking a card from his jacket. *Oxygen*, it said in gilt. *Image Enhancement*. 'Most of my clients are actresses, models.' Jargon's hands described extravagant curves. 'Only we're not talking Royal Shakespeare Company, right?'

Rita was having the definitive word with Calypso. The grey-haired man sent them a furtive smile. His eyes made Dearborn think of oysters.

'A patron of the arts,' Jargon said, and flashed a Polaroid of black limbs folded around white anatomy. 'Whaddya say, John? Any shape, any size, any colour. I practically factory-farm them.'

'I think not,' Dearborn said. His eyes crossed. He had just unscrambled the photo and realized it was an informal shot of a black woman sitting on a man's face.

Jargon tapped the side of his nose. 'Diversify or die,' he said. He looked at the photo, sighed, and put it away. His expression drifted. 'What did you want with Denis?'

'Forbes made him sound like an interesting man to meet.'

Jargon chuckled roguishly. 'Old Forbsie's a riot.'

It seemed to Dearborn that his host's interest had strayed to a booth occupied by Nicky the bouncer and two other men with night-time faces. Nicky was eating and his colleagues were watching him as if at any moment he might spring a request for salt or ketchup on them.

Dearborn realized just how much at the mercy of events he had placed himself. He checked his watch. 'Doesn't look like Forbes is going to show.' He stood, yawning.

Jargon evinced alarm. 'Hey, no hurry.'

'Tired,' Dearborn said, stretching. 'Long day.'

'C'mon, John, lemme organize a connection.'

'What is this,' Dearborn said, trying to laugh his way out, 'a lonely hearts club?'

'On the house, John. Lemme see, you're the thinking type, right?' Jargon scanned the throng and snapped his fingers. 'Got it, the perfect mix-and-match, all the attributes.' He slid off his stool. 'Turn round. No peeping. Big surprise.'

Dearborn did in fact face away, and he may even have closed his eyes. His thoughts wandered to home. He was not cut out for the bachelor life. His playing days were over. He yearned to hold his little girl again.

'Hello,' a small voice said behind him, 'I'm Chelsea.'

Moving with cautious imprecision, Dearborn turned to confront a vision of golden hair, a soft swell of breast over a turquoise bodice, wide blue eyes – a walking, living Barbie doll. Angry and incredulous he searched for Jargon and found him delivering a big thumbs-up from the other side of the room.

'Chelsea Tudor,' the girl said, and dipped her lashes like a maiden up for auction at a slave market.

'John Wesley Dearborn, ma'am,' he said, remembering his manners. 'Can I offer you something to drink?'

'Mineral water, please,' she said, taking a seat. She gave a pleasant, if slightly artificial, laugh. 'I don't think anyone called me ma'am before.' She mouthed the word again.

Dearborn couldn't think of a thing to say. He watched the bartender pouring her drink. 'The price they charge,' he said, 'it would be cheaper drinking gasoline.'

Frowning, Chelsea thought about it. 'But it wouldn't taste so nice.'

'No,' Dearborn said, astonishing himself. 'You're right.'

They watched the bubbles rising up the glass. They both opened their mouths at the same time, though Dearborn hadn't a clue as to what might issue. 'Please,' he said, 'go ahead.'

'Derek says you're in films,' she said. 'In New York.' She made her eyes full.

'That's putting it a mite strong. I make learning packs for Third World countries.'

'Oh, that sounds interesting.' She looked at her hands, then she examined the selection of bottles.

With every passing second, Dearborn was revising her age downwards. She couldn't be more than nineteen – less than half his age. The thought filled him with complicated feelings. 'I guess you must be an actress,' he ventured.

'Well, sort of.'

'Are you famous?'

'Well, not really.'

'You should be,' Dearborn said, finding his stride. 'You look like Marilyn Monroe.'

That was untrue. She didn't resemble Monroe in the slightest – except at the superficial level of tits and hair. Plus the vapid voice and blue eyes. And for all Dearborn knew, those items were false.

'I was in an episode of *'Allo 'Allo* last spring,' she said, and paused to see if it meant anything. 'I was offered a chance to try for *Emmerdale Farm*, but Derek said "no".' She wrinkled her nose. 'He says I should wait for the right vehicle to come along.'

The grey-haired man was leaving, propelling Calypso in front of him. His face was inflamed and he had one hand inserted in the cleft of her ass.

Dearborn coughed. 'I think you should do whatever you think is right.'

'Do you really?'

'Sure I do,' Dearborn declared in a bluff voice. She made him feel protective. Shedding his useless prejudice, he saw what a nice, straightforward girl she was – a healthy English rose unspiked by cynicism, her skin withered neither by age nor excess, her eyes wide with candour. Candid interest. Interest in him.

To his consternation, he felt his belly warm. He envisaged Chelsea's breasts unrestrained, his head on . . . Squirming, he half turned as if searching for a familiar face. 'I was hoping to run into a friend – Forbes Valentine.'

'Oh, do you know Forbes? I met him at a house-party in Scotland only last month.'

Dearborn's base thoughts were swept aside. 'That must have been fun.'

'Not really,' Chelsea said. 'It poured most of the time and I had a bust-up with my ex.'

'I can't imagine you being anyone's ex.'

Chelsea's laugh was coarser this time. 'You don't know Rafiq.'

'From where I'm sitting,' Dearborn began, before the delayed-action charge went off in his chest. 'Rafiq?' he said, his face furrowing in concentration. 'I believe I heard Forbes mention someone of that name.'

'Rafiq Saad,' Chelsea said. 'They're in business together.'

'Oh, right,' Dearborn said. He frowned intensely. 'Banking, isn't it?'

'Something like that. Rafiq never discussed his work. All I know is that him and Forbes were on the phone morning and night. I hardly saw him.'

Dearborn had the feeling that he was lit up like a beacon, the object of all eyes, but when he stole a look he saw that Jargon had his back turned, pressing flesh.

'Is that what you rowed about?' he asked Chelsea.

She gave him a friendly prod in the chest. 'You're ever so nosy.'

Dearborn assumed gravitas, the demeanour of a man wounded by events. His heart was racing. 'Personal relations mean a lot to me. My wife and I split up. Well, truth be told, she walked out on me. I'm trying to learn from my mistakes.'

'Why?'

'So I won't make them again.'

'No, why did she leave you?'

In the midst of his excitement, an insight dawned on Dearborn. 'I bored her, I guess.'

They both laughed as if the admission wasn't to be taken too seriously.

'You don't want to hear about that,' Dearborn told her. 'You were explaining how you and Rafiq . . .' He left a delicate silence.

'He was a real crosspatch all week. One night at dinner an Irish girl – Isobel I think her name was, ever so striking, tall with lovely hair . . . well, anyway, she had an argument with Forbes about some money she said he owed her brother. Rafiq was there and he was *furious*. So was Denis.'

'Mr Low was there, too?'

'Not then. He turned up the next day, and him and Forbes had a long talk. Afterwards Forbes looked like death warmed up. If you ask me, he lost some of Denis's money, because when we'd all relaxed, Denis said, "Chel!" – that's what he calls me – "Chel," he said, "do you know how to make a million with Forbes?" Chance would be a fine thing, I said. "Start with two million," he said.'

Dearborn joined in her laughter. 'Shame he's not around.'

'He's abroad.'

'Yes, I know. Spain, isn't it?' Dearborn had a boyhood picture of himself tickling steelheads in the brook that ran through his daddy's wood lot.

'Tunisia. June had a week there last Christmas and said it was ever so nice, although I think it must be funny eating turkey and mince pies in the desert.' Chelsea frowned. 'Did I say Tunisia? I meant that other place.'

Dearborn's heart was threatening to wrench itself off its mountings. 'Morocco?'

'That's it,' Chelsea said admiringly.

Careful, Dearborn told himself, putting his shaky hands out of sight. 'Did Rafiq go with him?'

Chelsea pouted. 'I don't know and I don't care. Good riddance.'

Dearborn put his hand over his mouth and coughed. 'Maybe you'd like to go on somewhere. I'd be honoured to take you to dinner.'

Chelsea patted her trim stomach. 'I only eat lunch.'

Dearborn tried to think of alternative entertainments. 'Dancing?' he said, letting his doubt show.

'I prefer talking,' Chelsea said. She looked straight at him and fluttered her lashes. 'Honestly.'

A roar of laughter from a gaggle of media types gave Dearborn his opportunity. 'Kind of noisy for meaningful conversation,' he shouted.

Chelsea lowered her eyes. 'We could go somewhere quiet.'

'I'm afraid I don't know London too well.'

Chelsea thought about it. She smiled mischievously. 'I know,' she said, 'I'll take you to an all-night sitting.'

Dearborn's palms moistened as he followed her out, but no one interfered with them and they were lucky enough to catch a taxi almost at the door. Chelsea ordered the driver to take them to the Houses of Parliament.

The security men knew Chelsea by name and greeted her with affectionate badinage. She led the way confidently to the Visitor's Gallery. Half a dozen members were debating in the Chamber. 'Look at them,' Chelsea said. 'Aren't they awful?'

For half an hour they listened to the opposition trying to talk out a bill on agricultural subsidies, and then they walked along the river. It was a beautiful night. Chelsea talked politics. She was a Green. Listening to her, Dearborn felt a smile cross his face. Under Waterloo Bridge he kissed her.

'Rafiq must be mad,' he breathed.

'He's not losing any sleep, believe me. To him, women are possessions.' She sniffed. 'That's the Arab male mentality for you.'

'Saudi?' Dearborn murmured.

'Lebanese, but he's a Christian. His grandmother was French. He knows a lot of Arab leaders. When we were in Scotland I heard him boasting that he was friends with the king of Morocco.'

Alleluiah, Dearborn thought, clutching Chelsea in gratitude.

She pushed him away. 'I got my own back,' she said in a new, sharp voice. 'A girlfriend told me what to do. I'd still got a key to his flat in Duke Street, so I bought fifty packets of mustard and cress seed, poured water on his Persian carpets, turned the central heating up full and left the lights on. When he comes back his bloody sitting-room will be a field.'

'Neat trick,' Dearborn said, taken aback. He looked across the river. 'Duke Street? That's a very exclusive address.'

'Oh, he's got pots of money. The flat is only where he entertains his . . . I mean, it's his town apartment. His proper house is in Hampstead.' She looked at him, her finger to her lip, and giggled. 'Shall I tell you what else I did?'

'Please do.'

'You know them porno chat-lines, where women talk dirty . . .'

'Hypothetically,' Dearborn said.

'I called one in Los Angeles and left the phone off the hook. I worked out it's costing Rafiq ten thousand a week.'

Dearborn couldn't think of a suitable response. 'Serves him right.'

She swung his hand gaily. 'Don't let's talk about him.'

Hand in hand they strolled across the bridge. 'I'm not really called Chelsea,' she said. 'I expect you guessed that. My real name's Lynn Stapler. Chelsea was Derek's idea. He wanted to call me Thyme, like the herb – Thyme Preston, but my mum put a stop to that.' Chelsea looked over the bridge. 'I don't know why I'm telling you this. I must be feeling sad. I don't think Derek's interested in me being an actress.' She wrinkled her nose again. '"Fulfil my potential," that's what he calls it.'

'Chelsea's how I think of you.'

They walked on.

'A lot of men ask me out for dinner,' Chelsea said, 'but I nearly always refuse.'

'Wise,' Dearborn said, imagining with some indignation the kind of characters Chelsea must encounter.

'I tell them to save their money,' she said. She stopped. 'Well, not exactly save it.' She faced him. 'I can't see the difference between accepting a meal from a man I like and, well, just taking the money.'

Put like that, Dearborn couldn't muster any overriding objections.

'I expect you think I ain't got no self-respect,' Chelsea said, her accent slipping drastically, 'but straight up, John, I get a lot more respect from my boyfriends than they give their wives.' She fixed him with stern eyes. 'I make sure of that.'

'Yes,' Dearborn said humbly.

'You're sweet,' she said, and touched him on the tip of his nose. She moved close. Her breath warmed his cheek. 'Let's pretend you just bought me a six-course meal at Chez Nico.' Her tongue feathered his ear. 'With liqueurs for afters.'

Chelsea lived in a cosmopolitan terrace off Queensway. As she fitted her key into her lock, she smiled over her shoulder at him and he smiled back. Everything's going to be alright, he exulted. Better than alright.

She took one step into the room and stopped. 'Oi!' she said.

Nicky and one of the other leg-breakers from the Low Spot had convened in her sitting-room. The other one had an athletic build and receding blond hair shaped close to his skull. He was chewing gum and reading a paperback.

'What the hell . . .' Dearborn said.

'Here's a good bit,' the blond one said, not looking up: '"Fiercely, Dominic took her in his muscular arms. With every fibre of her being she strained against his great . . ."'

'Bleeding cheek,' Chelsea said, taking a run at him. He threw the book at her, caught her by the elbow and pushed her into a bedroom, slamming the door after her.

Dearborn still had his finger pointed accusingly. 'You're from the club,' he said.

'Quick off the mark, ain't he?' the blond one said.

Nicky stood up.

'I'm warning you,' Dearborn said, taking a step backwards.

Nicky advanced until they were chest to chest, a manoeuvre that involved him standing on tiptoe. He lifted his chin, inviting Dearborn to hit it.

'Derek says you like a bit of rough.' There was a foreign component in his accent – Greek or Cypriot.

'I don't know what you mean,' Dearborn said, leaning away from Nicky's spicy breath.

'Yes you do,' Nicky said, toppling him on to the couch.

'Empty his bins,' the blond one said. 'You never know: he might be the Mafia's number one button man.'

The contents of Dearborn's pockets were scattered on to a glass coffee-table. It so happened that he had equipped himself with a large sum of cash to meet contingencies.

'If it's money you're after,' he said, 'take it and get out.'

Nicky picked up a book of matches from the Westbury and tossed it to the blond one, who dialled the hotel and asked in a civil voice to speak to Mr Dearborn. Politely he offered his thanks and replaced the phone.

'He's from out of town, alright,' he said.

The bedroom door opened and Derek Jargon walked out, wearing an unbuttoned overcoat over his suit. He appeared to have a lot on his mind. Chelsea followed, dressed in jeans and sweater, carrying a large plastic carrier bag.

'Chel's popping down to the laundrette,' Jargon said.

She scowled at Dearborn. 'What about my fee?' she demanded.

'There's his poke,' Jargon said, gesturing at Dearborn's money. 'Help yourself.'

Chelsea took him at his word. 'We agreed four hundred, okay?' she said, glowering at Dearborn, challenging him to contradict her.

The blond one laughed and poked him in the chest. 'You dirty old man.'

When Chelsea had gone, Jargon sat down opposite Dearborn, stretched out his legs and examined his socks. 'He's been nosing around after that scumbag Rafiq.'

'Oh dear,' the blond one said, his expression suggesting that Dearborn had consigned himself to an infinitely worse category than he had imagined.

Jargon raised his eyes, his expression sad. 'You're the law,' he said.

'I can assure you I'm not.'

'Hear that?' the blond one said. 'He talks like a fucking brief.'

Jargon pointed an accusing finger. 'FBI, drug enforcement – which is it, John?'

'Neither. I told you how I earn my living.'

Jargon swept his possessions to the floor. 'A video producer going out on the town without his cards. That's like Florence Nightingale clocking on without her thermometer.' He shook his head affably. 'Besides, John, you don't have the personality.'

Dearborn tried to keep his eye on Nicky, who had worked his way behind him. The tart taste of fear filled his mouth. 'Valentine gave me Rafiq's name. He said he had a lot of useful contacts in the Gulf.'

Jargon laughed without humour. 'Better raise your game, John.'

'I swear.'

'He swears,' Nicky said soberly, wrapping a hank of Dearborn's hair around his hand and forcing his head down. The book the blond one had thrown at Chelsea lay face-down on the floor. *Tender is the Tyrant*, Dearborn read – A Regency Romance.

'You ain't seen nothing yet,' the blond one said.

Dearborn's head was wrenched back so he was looking into Nicky's face. Viewed upside down, it was a savage sight – the nostrils sprouting hair, the jowls stubbled with what looked like iron filings.

'You're making a colossal mistake,' Dearborn groaned.

'There's no reasoning with him,' the blond one said.

Jargon detached a piece of lint from his jacket and stood. He buttoned up his overcoat. 'I think we'd better adjourn this interview to the piggery. The porkers John's been telling, he'll feel well at home.'

Dearborn was hoisted up by the hair. At the door he braced himself. 'Okay,' he said, 'okay, I'll tell you.'

'Amazing,' Jargon said.

'I've never met Valentine. I never heard of Rafiq Saad until tonight.'

The blond one blew a bubble. 'And Denis Low is the fucking tooth fairy.'

Dearborn looked at each of them in turn. 'I'm a security advisor to the American State Department.'

'He's got a fucking wild imagination,' the blond one said.

'I work in an advisory capacity with the Moroccan government.'

Three pairs of eyes made contact. 'Let the gentleman go,' Jargon said with a sigh. He unbuttoned his coat and wearily patted the couch. 'Sit down, John.'

But Dearborn remained standing. Confidence trickled back. Jargon was a hustler left to mind the store while the boss was away, and the other two were not of an independent cast of mind. The truth would undo any violent designs they had.

'I'm investigating the murder of an Israeli in Marrakech. My inquiries have established a link with an English drug-trafficker called Digby Fox, whose partner, Forbes Valentine, has business dealings with Rafiq Saad. Some of this you know.'

The blond one popped gum. 'It's the way he tells them,' he said.

''Ere,' Nicky complained, 'I thought you said you wasn't the law.'

Jargon waved his colleagues down. He observed Dearborn without expression. 'I don't hear Denis Low's name.'

'Low's of minor interest. It's the collateral aspects that concern me.'

The blond one frowned. 'This is England, tosh. We talk English here.'

'Politics,' Dearborn said, letting the word expand to fill the room. 'It's my belief that there is a political dimension to the activities of Rafiq Saad.'

Jargon rose out of his seat and paced. 'It's like Denis said,' he murmured.

'I know who you are,' the blond one said. 'You're fucking CIA, man.'

372

'Why don't I hit him?' Nicky suggested.

'Belt up,' Jargon snapped. 'You want the kind of heavy pressure Denis is under?'

'Pressure?' Dearborn inquired.

Jargon laughed softly. 'Where is he, John? What have you done with him?'

'Morocco. I have no idea. I didn't even know he was abroad. If I'd known, I wouldn't have gone looking for him at the club.' Dearborn discerned that a critical moment had been reached. 'I'll trade,' he said hastily. 'Help me trace Rafiq Saad and I'll give you information of vital significance to Denis Low.'

Jargon nodded with caution. 'It had better be.'

'Derek,' the blond one said uneasily, 'I think you should consult Mr Low before mouthing off.'

Jargon smiled at him with barely controlled impatience. 'How can I fucking consult with him when he's off the map? Go on,' he said to Dearborn.

'If I were you, I'd tell Denis to scoot back behind the bar as quick as possible. The Spanish police and the DEA know he's lining up a drug deal. They'll be waiting.'

Jargon laughed bitterly. 'This is what comes of branching out.'

'Rafiq Saad,' Dearborn reminded him.

'Try Lost and Found. He's done a runner. His gaff's been empty for the last month.' Jargon shrugged. 'All square, John.'

'Valentine?' Dearborn said. 'Maybe he can put me in touch.'

Jargon smiled oddly. 'Don't waste your time chasing Shirley. He's off the park.' He moved towards the door. 'You're on a caution, John. Show your face in the club again, and Nicky will cave it in. Are we clear?'

'As crystal.'

'Hey, you're not letting it go,' Nicky complained.

'You heard what he said,' Jargon said in disgust, heading for the door. 'Fucking politics.'

When he was sure they had gone, Dearborn curled up on

the couch, his eyes open, fear lodged like a sickness. Cody was right, he thought: he had no capacity for violence – neither meting it out nor receiving it. He pushed himself to his feet. Of all courses now open to him, only one carried acceptable risk.

He found that he had wandered into Chelsea's bedroom, a shrine to femininity, smelling like a beauty parlour. He touched things, picked up a nightdress and let it slither through his hands, then cast it away from him. Feeling despoiled, a despoiler, he went back into the sitting-room and stared out of the window. The street was still busy. He watched the people go by – the innocent, the hopeful, the casualties, the accidents looking to happen. He took his place among them.

28

All morning and early afternoon, Dearborn skulked in his hotel room. Several times he reached for the telephone, then drew back his hand, checked by an intangible fear. He looked at the bedside clock. Three fifty-three. He would do it on the hour, he vowed. At one minute to, he placed his hand on the instrument. The hairs on his arm were standing up. He took a breath as if he was preparing to pump iron and lifted the phone.

'I'd like to make a person-to-person call to Jerry Cody, United States embassy, Rabat, Morocco.'

'Are you sure?'

'Why shouldn't I be?' Dearborn blurted.

'Last time you cancelled, sir.'

Dearborn swallowed. 'This time I'm sure.'

As he waited, he felt the skin tighten on his skull. The operator's voice made him flinch.

'I'm sorry, sir, the party you request is not available.'

He couldn't accept it. It was like opening a door to find a hole where he had expected solid floor. 'What do you mean?' he demanded.

There was a slight pause, and then the operator said: 'The party you request is not available.'

Jolted into action, Dearborn rang Rabat himself. Cody's office said he was out of the country, but refused to say where, or when he was expected back.

'Don't you know who I am?' Dearborn shouted. 'Don't you remember me?'

He began to feel he didn't exist. For hours he sat without

moving. Dusk fell, but he didn't switch the lights on. In the gathering dark he smiled at the phone. 'Well, Cody, old buddy,' he whispered, 'I tried.'

He dialled the London embassy. 'Give me Byron Field,' he demanded without preliminaries.

'Who may I say is calling?'

'John Wesley Dearborn.'

He waited in a thin sweat.

'Hi, John,' Byron said, his voice issuing from a world of light and order. 'Am I in Okinawa?'

Dearborn laughed weakly. It was he who had told Byron the tale of the Jewish *émigré* who, having kept one knock-on-the-door ahead of the pogroms in Russia, the brownshirts in Hamburg and the SS in Amsterdam, had diligently set to to find the safest place on God's earth, finally settling after months of painstaking research on a flyspeck in the Pacific – an island called Okinawa. After the débâcles in Tehran and Beirut, anywhere where Dearborn was was Okinawa.

'I'm in transit,' he said. 'How about getting together for a drink?'

'Tomorrow,' Field said without hesitation. 'Six-thirty, the Ritz.'

'Great,' Dearborn said. He shut his eyes and tried to cross his toes inside his shoes. 'I wonder if you can help me out with a name. Rafiq Saad, a Christian Lebanese.'

'I didn't get that, John.'

Dearborn remembered that Byron's eardrums had been perforated by the Beirut suicide bomb.

'Rafiq Saad, a Christian Lebanese from Baalbek, domiciled in Britain about fifteen years. He has an apartment in Duke Street, just down the road from you, and a main residence in the Bishop's Avenue, Hampstead. At the moment he's abroad, whereabouts unknown.'

When Field didn't speak, Dearborn began over again.

'I heard,' Field said impatiently. 'I can't oblige. This isn't an information service.'

'There could be a quid pro quo.'

'If you have something we should know, John, take it through the proper channels.'

'You are the proper channel. What do you want me to do – put it in writing?'

'Good thinking.'

'Please, Byron, at this stage I prefer to keep it informal. All I'm asking is for you to punch a few keys on the memory bank. If nothing shows – fine, we'll have that drink anyway.'

'Goodbye, John,' Field said, and cut him off.

Later, when Dearborn's rage had abated and he had finished off the vodka in the mini-bar, he was able to convince himself that no CIA man would ignore such a tempting lead.

At six next day he took up position in the Ritz Bar. Six-thirty came and went. The room filled and latecomers cast covetous eyes at Dearborn guarding an empty table. Sick with disappointment, he prepared to relinquish his place.

Just before seven, Byron Field came tripping lightly up the steps, his head down, like a television compère making an entrance. But when he looked up, his face had the impatient air of a man keeping pace with a hectic schedule. Sighting Dearborn, he lowered his head again and wove a course between the tables. In passing, he touched the arm of the head waiter, who smiled after him as if he'd been blessed.

Dearborn half-rose to attract service.

'I fixed it,' Field said, dropping into his seat.

Dearborn indicated the opulent décor. 'Your friendly neighbourhood bar.'

Field frowned at the blue and gilt. 'After a day at the office, this shit is balm to my soul.' He lifted the cuff of his expensive suit and glanced at his watch. 'I have a dinner date at eight – Italian magazine columnist.' He pursed his mouth in a kiss. 'Cute.'

Dearborn was envious. Field was always romancing someone. It was sickening. 'I'm a free man myself now,' he said. 'Magda and I parted company.'

Field looked right at him. He had cool blue eyes and straight black hair. 'I'm surprised it lasted so long. I guess it was the attraction of opposites.'

Dearborn was stung. It occurred to him that perhaps he had overestimated the depth of his friendship with Byron.

The waiter brought Field a champagne cocktail. Field watched the sugar lump fizzing in the bottom of the glass. 'I hear they terminated your Moroccan contract.'

It was only natural, Dearborn reasoned, that Field would have refreshed himself on his curriculum vitae. 'I didn't feel comfortable in it,' he said,

'Is that the end of the bad luck, or only the beginning?'

'The start of something new.'

'You got another job lined up?'

'I decided to finish the book.'

Field laughed in amiable derision. '*A Short History of the Middle East*.' He sprayed imaginary machine-gun fire at the other guests. He stopped smiling. 'Does Rafiq Saad rate a footnote?'

'I'm damned if I know,' Dearborn said.

Carefully, Field put down his glass. 'Why didn't you take your request to your old trail-boss?'

'I tried to. I can't reach him.'

'From what I hear, you two aren't on speaking terms. You know, John, I always thought that was an unhealthy relationship.'

'Cody and I had a personal difference. He thinks my soul is in jeopardy.'

'It's your ass he should be looking out for,' Field said. He leaned back, his eyes watchful. 'He must be worried that the Moroccan problem could spoil his retirement party.'

'Yes,' Dearborn agreed. 'He wants to go out on a high note.'

The response irritated Field. 'All we want is for him to maintain the status quo.'

'That's what I meant,' Dearborn said, his spirits lowering fast.

In silence, Field finished his drink. 'I scrolled that name, John.'

'I'm immensely grateful, Byron.'

Field stirred the remains of the sugar lump with his finger. 'Care to tell me where you came up against it?'

'A hooker gave it to me.'

Field looked pained. 'John, a mid-life crisis isn't a plea in mitigation.'

'I thought I'd broaden my horizons.'

Field eyed him with displeasure. 'Don't get clever, John. If the flat-earthers are right, you'll drop off the edge.'

'Am I to interpret that as a warning about Rafiq Saad?'

Thoughtfully, Field sucked the syrup off his finger. 'He's a deluxe currency shark with a list of Arab clients who want a secure nest-egg in case the pot boils over at home. His philosophy is that money, like refugees, deserves a safe haven.'

'Is that all?' Dearborn said, his jaw slack with disappointment.

'We targeted him as a potential asset a few years ago, but we never followed it up.' Field shrugged, checked the time and rose. 'Thanks for the drink,' he said. He paused. 'Speaking of names, I wonder if you recall Adnan al-Jalil. Now there's material worthy of a book.'

Dearborn frowned. 'He's head of *Sa'eqa* – or was. I helped compile his file.'

Field's face was blank, as if the explanation hadn't registered.

'"Bolt of Lightning",' Dearborn translated, 'the Syrian-sponsored wing of the PLO. He has his headquarters in . . .' Dearborn's mouth fell ajar '. . . the Bekaa Valley.'

Field stared down with a grim smile. 'You really have no idea, do you?'

'Byron, that's why I'm speaking to you.'

'I was up half the fucking night accessing every contact Rafiq Saad ever had.'

'And?'

A bemused expression crossed Field's face. 'God knows how we missed it.'

'Missed what?'

Field passed a hand over his eyes. 'Rafiq Saad is Adnan al-Jalil's half-brother.'

'Let me get you another drink,' Dearborn said when the world had resumed its motion. He tried to snap his fingers, but the joints had turned to putty.

Field leaned over, his hands on the table. 'John, if this involves Morocco, I want to know, and know fucking fast.'

'Byron, I have to talk to Cody first. I owe it to him.'

Briskly, Field straightened to full height. 'We won't let it go, John. If necessary, we'll sweat it out of you.'

'Give me a week.'

Field turned away. 'Twenty-four hours.'

29

Eyes pressed into the crook of her arm, Iseult lay face up on a butcher's slab in the centre of a deserted village market-square. Small flies pestered her. A loose piece of tin roofing banged in a wind that blew hot and cold by turns. She turned her head, apathetic, and saw the Landlord and the Poet stretched out on their own slabs, looking bloated and fly-blown in the duvet jackets which they had picked up in Marrakech.

Grit scraped past and spiralled viciously as the wind rounded on itself. A fly found its way into Iseult's throat and she struck out, gasping under the indignation.

Hate it, she thought, squinting into the dirty white light of the plaza. The wind blew her hair over her face and she clawed it back. It was a mess, dull and tangled; she had lost her grooming kit and nothing would induce her to borrow a comb or slide from that Deirdre bitch.

Hate them, she mouthed, projecting venom on to her captors. She looked across the square at Case. Hate him, she thought dully.

Before she could stop herself she was groping for another cigarette, although there were only three left and she knew that smoking wouldn't give pleasure. She lit one anyway, and dumped it after a single puff.

Case propped himself on his makeshift crutch and hopped over. As he passed, Iseult sent him a beseeching look. If only he would let her explain, but not a word or a glance had he given her in the last twenty-four hours.

'Is that our transport?' the Landlord murmured. 'Or is the

fellow with the black hat rode into town?' He stirred his bulk. Skin was sloughing from his boiled face.

Case didn't answer until they could all hear the whine of straight-cut gears under load, and then he said: 'I'll give you a break. It'll be hard going on the plateau and even harder getting off. The best thing you can do is leave me here and take the truck back down tomorrow morning.'

'Ach, you're a decent spud,' the Landlord said, 'but you're stuck with us.'

Case just nodded.

A yellow truck entered in a swirl of dust, briefly brightening up the outlook. But only the driver and one other man alighted, leaving their human cargo penned in the back. The square slumped back into lethargy.

Soon after midday the driver swaggered forth, wiping his mouth and conveying the impression of important work ahead. Case led the little band over. Curious, unblinking eyes stared straight down at them. Case said something to the driver and he gestured for Iseult to get into the cab.

'Thank you,' she said to Case in a formal voice.

'So long as you're out of my sight.'

Iseult held her hands stiff at her side. 'You don't have to be so spiteful,' she called to his back.

Four other passengers squeezed up to make room. Everything non-functional had been stripped from the cab; the gauges were either dead or missing. Local music cantered from a cassette-player taped to the dash.

Between the village and the plateau lay limestone steppe, with the strata exposed at angles, so that the truck strained forward axle by axle, lurching like an overladen camel. The land danced in shimmers. The driver kept up a heated monologue, clinching his arguments with back-handed slaps to his assistant, who was in charge of gear-shifting – a two-handed operation. The veiled woman next to Iseult fanned her face and appeared to be hyperventilating. Someone handed round pistachios.

Head aching from the glitter and scratchy music, Iseult

dozed until a drumming on the roof brought the truck to a jerky stop. A young man in army fatigues alighted, picked up his suitcase and strode into the barrens. At other intervals that were impossible to predict, there being no trace of habitation en route, more passengers got off. Some of them remained sitting by the roadside like dumped baggage.

Gradually the geology changed. Highlands loomed and the driver shut his window against cold gusts. They breasted a ridge capped by an abandoned French telegraph station. A hammering on the cab roof brought the truck to another squealing halt.

Case's face appeared at the window and one of the passengers obligingly opened the door for Iseult. Caught unprepared, she saw the road looping down before straggling east under a cinder-grey tableland streaked by snow. With no destination in sight, she grew agitated.

'I'm not budging,' she said.

To laughter from the other passengers, Case yanked her out and pushed her towards the Landlord and the Poet, who were huddled together like refugees cast on an alien shore.

The truck moaned away and a keening wind closed the space it had left. Iseult's eyes scavenged over raw hills prickling with dry shrubs. She had never seen so much fresh air; it sucked the strength out of her.

Having turned in a full circle and failed to spot a point to aim for, the Landlord faced Case with a rueful smile.

'Up there,' Case said, nodding at an extension of the mountain wall. 'Once we're on the plateau, we'll follow the rim east. That way we're less likely to meet anyone.'

'It would be a quair kind of fellow that made his home on top of that.'

'Nomads from the Sahara,' Case said. 'They'll be heading back to the desert for winter.' He slung on his pack. 'Sure you want to face it?'

'If you can stot along on one leg, I'll do well enough on two.'

Case showed a smile lacking one incisor. 'That's not what I meant.'

The Landlord managed a sort of laugh. 'We'll see.' He turned to the Poet. 'Are you fit, Deirdre?'

'Sure,' she said in stagey Irish. 'Was I not born in the Connemara bogs, and the nearest shop eight miles distant by hard wet road?'

Iseult heard these exchanges with rising anger. A speck of yellow, their last contact with the known world, was slinking away under the range. 'Well I bloody well don't,' she shouted.

'Awh, it's nothing for a great strapping young girl like yourself,' the Landlord said.

Iseult sat down and crossed her arms, making herself heavy. 'You can't make me.'

'Can't I just?' Deirdre said.

But then Case took a step away and they stopped bickering and looked at him, holding their breath for sudden movement. He had his hands up as if the sky was blinding him, and the slant of the unseen sun struck a bleak Asiatic light from his eyes.

'What is it?' the Landlord asked, a twinge of unease in his voice.

'Eagle,' Case murmured.

They all looked into the empty sky. The Landlord broke the tension. 'Awh, go on, pet,' he pleaded, placing a small rucksack by Iseult's side. It was a kid's model with a picture of Yogi Bear on the flap.

She pushed it away. 'Carry it yourself. I've got weak ankles.'

'I've had enough of her blather,' the Poet cried, running forward with upraised hand.

Iseult ducked her head and gripped her knees, but the blow never fell. Instead, Case's feet planted themselves in front of her. Slowly she looked up into his impassive face. Her eyes shifted in confusion. 'Oh, alright,' she said. She stood up and the wind pulled her hair. 'I need to borrow a comb,' she muttered.

The Poet laughed, short and sour, but dug into her pack. She laughed again. 'I've got a better idea,' she said, and held up a pair of scissors. 'This'll take the weight off her ankles.'

Eyes stuck wide-open with shock, Iseult backed into the arms of the Landlord.

'Now, Deirdre,' he said. 'That's not a very republican thing to do.'

'Get away Joe Tolan,' she screamed, her face scalded with fury. 'I've seen you lusting after her, you dirty old ram.' She brandished the scissors at Iseult. 'This is what you've got coming for, for, for . . . going with the likes of that.'

Enfolded in the Landlord's sturdy arms, Iseult kicked and screamed while Deirdre Coghlan chopped off her mane lock by lock. The wind blew it away and hung it on thorns. When the Poet had finished, Iseult saw through a blaze of tears Case standing with his lips parted in what she assumed was a snarl of triumph.

She woke stone cold to see solid earth above and the clouds below, giving her a topsy-turvy feeling that made her sit up and put her hand to her head. Her *hair*! Under the weight of the monstrous violation she began to pant, clenching and unclenching handfuls of stones.

Lying back, weak and murderous, she heard a sound and whirled to see Case huddled against a rock like the survivor of a shipwreck, wrapped in a Berber blanket. His mouth was outlined with blue and his cheeks were waxy. From his bound hands a length of climbing rope led into a flimsy tent where the Landlord and the Poet were asleep.

'Pat?' she said, her grief forgotten. 'Pat?' She scrambled over and pulled hard on the rope. 'Quick,' she cried. 'Pat's freezing to death.'

The Poet's dreepy nose poked through the tent-flap. A moment later the Landlord's bleary face stuck out.

'It's no wonder,' he said, scratching his eyelids. 'I'm near perished of cold myself.'

The Poet crawled out and walked around Case as if she

was circling a sick calf that might have to be put down. 'Not so jaunty today.'

Case voiced no complaint.

After a sardine breakfast, they climbed the last stage to the plateau, to be met by a level wind and miles of sun-scorched pasture on which boulders a stone's throw away proved to be giant outcroppings half an hour's walk distant. In the lee of the ridges, dunes of snow had formed, scalloped and delicate, bursting into powder under their feet. Iseult's lips blistered in the dryness and her jeans chafed the insides of her thighs. Despite Case's claim about nomads, she saw no one or any other living thing.

It was a bizarre caravan they made – like a package tour gone badly astray. The Landlord led, a jolly blue giant in his down mountain jacket, fifteen yards of gaily coloured sheathed nylon linking him to Case, who was pegging along as best he could, closely watched by the Poet in a Rifian leather Stetson from a souvenir stall and cheap sunglasses with pink-framed, heart-shaped lenses. Shorn like a penitent, Iseult stumbled behind, tears drying to salt in the corners of her mouth.

It was like a sea crossing, the wake of the pierced horizon falling back on each side. The punishing wind stayed constant. At sunset they had reached a part of the plateau indistinguishable from what had gone before.

While Deirdre tried to concoct something hot and nourishing, the Landlord sneaked to Iseult's side. 'Bogging sardines,' he complained. 'I'd walk another thousand miles for a good fry-up.' He half extended his hand towards her hair. 'Ach, it's a shame,' he muttered.

Shame was the word. Her attention darted to Case, but he was hunkered down in his blanket, his eyes narrowed to shards.

'Deirdre's just jealous,' the Landlord said. 'We're supposed to be married in the spring, but I don't know.' He gave his intended a furtive glance. 'They're funny about sex in her parish. Two of her sisters are nuns, and her ma made her wear a shift in the bath so she didn't see her own body until she was full grown.' He put all his weight into a sigh. 'I'm still waiting for a glimpse of it myself.'

Iseult removed herself to a distance. Her ankles were stiff and swollen with fluid, elephantine. With not a shred of self-esteem left, she smoked her second-last fag and watched the light passing to the west. When it was completely gone, she returned to camp.

By nine they were wrapped up for the night. The air had grown still and hard frost had fallen. The sky was in a ferment, milky whorls spinning through space. A few yards away, Case shivered as if rough hands were shaking him.

'Are you alright?' Iseult whispered.

'Top of the world.'

Iseult's heart surged at the sound of his voice. She began to speak, her voice tripping over itself. 'They've given me your sleeping-bag. Do you want it back? Shall I come over?'

He didn't answer. Hearing him suppress another spasm, she glanced at the candle-lit tent, then crawled over to Case and pressed herself the length of his back, trying to infuse him with her warmth. He didn't react. His blanket was harsh and smelt peppery.

Grunts and whispers came from the tent. The light had been extinguished. Soon the commotion stopped and the Landlord swore – whether through desire frustrated or prematurely fulfilled was not clear.

'I'm going to kill that bitch,' Iseult said, her anger rearing out of nowhere.

'You got what you deserve.'

Her anger fizzled out. 'I didn't know about those two.'

Case gave a monosyllabic laugh.

'I knew that the money belonged to the IRA, but I never imagined Cathal would bring them to Morocco. When I saw them at the hotel, I . . .' Nightmare recollection struck her cold. In a different voice, she said: 'Pat, I know that what I did was wrong, but if I'd told you, you wouldn't have helped, and they would have killed him.' She waited. 'Don't you understand? It was the only way I had of saving his life.'

'I hope you think the trade-off is worth it.'

'I was too mixed up to see where it might lead.'

Case's voice was coiled flat. 'Oh, wonderful, terrific. Forget your lies. Forget Roy Besant. You were in a funny emotional state.'

'Yes,' Iseult said, 'I was.'

'The sooner your brother's put down, the better. He cheats his clients; he robs the fucking IRA; and then he betrays the bloke who tries to dig him out.' Case swallowed audibly. 'You must be as sick as he is.'

'Yes,' Iseult said, 'I must be.' She began to speak fast, spilling out her confession. 'It's not the first time. In the past, I've forged signatures for him, perjured myself to the police, even stolen.'

'Why? What kind of hold does he have on you?'

She opened her mouth but at first no words came. 'You know what it's like when you share a secret with someone – a bad secret that you'd never dare admit to anyone. It binds you. Well, that's how Cathal and I are. Bound by a secret.'

'Secret?'

Her silence was more eloquent than words. She could sense him skirting around the unacceptable truth, sniffing at it like a dog. Slowly, he sat up.

'My God, it's *him*,' he whispered.

'Yes,' Iseult said – a flat assertion. She waited for the feedback of guilt, and when it didn't come she felt cheated. 'Aren't you going to tell me how revolting I am?' she demanded, flinging herself the other way.

'You mean you let him screw you?' he asked incredulously.

Iseult tried to reframe the question, without success. 'Yes,' she said weakly. 'That's what I mean.'

'But he's a poof!'

She wanted to laugh and cry. Poor Pat, she thought. 'Incest isn't that uncommon,' she said, as if this was a topic they could debate with reason and restraint.

He lay very slack, his face to the stars. 'What a fucking fool I am,' he breathed.

'It wasn't all sham,' she whispered, clutching him. 'I truly liked you. Part of me even hoped that we . . .' She didn't bother to go on.

'The other night,' Case said, tensing up for more revelations, 'was that Cathal's idea to soften me up? Was he watching at the window, too?'

Iseult soothed his clenched hands. 'No, I wanted to,' she said. She prised apart his fingers and linked them with her own. 'It's the first time I've had an orgasm with another man. It was lovely, the best ever.'

'Christ!' Case shouted, unstifling his rage.

'Would youse uns let me get some sleep?' the Landlord cried.

Extricating herself from the morass of wounded sexuality, Iseult arched over Case and began to speak in a rapid whisper. 'We went to the *Sanglier Blessé* and met the Count. He says he'll help get Fox out of the country.' She hesitated. The next part was much harder. 'Cathal will try to find his way back there.'

Case laughed. 'I hope so. I really do.'

Iseult's heart thudded. 'You said you loved me.'

Case laughed again, but this time it sounded more like crying. 'Love? Don't make me laugh.'

'If you really love me, you must promise not to hurt him.'

Case punched the ground. 'Even now he's all you care about.'

'I'm begging you, Pat.'

When he spoke it was with a drawn-out finality. 'No,' he said. 'This time he pays.'

She experienced a cleansing gust of anger. 'What gives you the right? I'm not the only one who's hiding the truth. You lied about those IRA men in Armagh.'

Case's sigh sounded like a yawn. 'Not you as well.'

'It's true, though.'

'Technically, I suppose I'm an accessory. I know who killed them; it was me who told them when and where. I'd have done it myself if I could.'

'Oh, Pat.'

'If you think I feel guilty, forget it. They were in a war.'

'They were asleep in their beds.'

'Like the odd couple over there,' Case said, staring at the darkened tent. 'You lot claim to be soldiers, but as soon as anyone takes you on, you start whining about us murdering innocent civilians. I despise you Irish. If I had my way, I'd let the whole murdering lot of you get on with it.'

You lot, Iseult repeated to herself. Micks, Paddies, Taigs. She looked at Case's starved features and her barely articulated hope that perhaps they might have had a future seemed preposterous. There was no common ground; their roots were in different soils. Once passion cooled and the newness wore off, she knew she would come to despise his tabloid certainties, his half-digested scraps of knowledge. Already their love-making shamed her, a gorging of gross appetites, a wanton blow-out.

'What about those two?' she asked in a wooden voice.

'They're in the bag,' Case said, shrugging.

'Me, too?' she said after a time.

He looked into her face. Lifting his tied hands, he rubbed her hair – rubbed it, not caressed it.

'Don't,' Iseult said, catching his wrists.

He continued staring at her.

'Is it awful?' she asked in a monotone. 'I haven't dared look.'

'It's only hair,' he said, lying back. 'It'll grow again.' Some connected thought remained unvoiced.

Iseult, too, had nothing else to say. Her heart dilated, closing round a vision of Cathal lost and afraid. For a time she stared blank-eyed into the plateau, then with a sigh she rested her forehead against Case's back. 'Good night,' she whispered.

In the morning he was gone, a speckling of snow over the spot where he had lain.

Stupefied, the Landlord examined the untied end of the

rope. The Poet's shiny nose twitched. Her eyes lighted on Iseult and she pointed the Ruger.

'It wasn't me,' Iseult cried, shrinking back.

'He's left his pack,' the Landlord said. He raised his head, sluggish with cold. 'There's his tracks leading to the edge.'

Part elated, part frightened, Iseult followed them as they worked along the trail. An air frost veiled the plateau, threatening to crystallize into snow. Out of this shining haze Case emerged like a figure from legend, swathed in his homespun blanket, holding prey in his hands.

'Where the fock have you been?' the Landlord demanded, aiming the other pistol.

'I'm sick of sardines,' Case said, raising two striped creatures on wire snares.

Closing up on him, the Landlord peered suspiciously. 'What kind of cratur's that?'

'Ground squirrel.'

'Can you eat it?'

'Sure.'

The Landlord stepped back smartly, as if all this was fogging the important issue. 'Why didn't you flit?' he demanded.

'We've got a bargain,' Case said, holding out his hands.

For a second the Landlord was nonplussed then, catching on, he tried to smile. 'Sure we have.' He pulled the knots tight on Case's wrists as if sealing a pact. 'Sure we have, Pat.'

All morning the air frost hovered – a delicate glaze that would have been dispersed by the lightest breath of wind. Iseult's thoughts, such as they were, wandered along beside her.

Why couldn't she love two men? Why couldn't she love who she liked, how she liked? Where was the sin in that?

Two men pursue you. One of them will die of love.

The caravan had stopped. On a rise ahead, the Poet was standing entranced, one bare hand held out, speaking softly in Gaelic.

'A poem just came to her,' the Landlord explained.

'On a lonely corner of a distant mountain, a single snowflake fluttered from a clear sky, falling as dew into the warmth of my waiting hand.'

'It's better in Irish,' the Landlord added quickly, cringing under Deirdre's eye.

'It's a piss-poor poem in anyone's language,' Case scoffed.

'It's a kind of Irish haiku,' Iseult said, glad of the diversion. 'That's a Japanese poem,' she explained for the benefit of Case and the Landlord. 'Listen, why don't we all try one. It should contain three lines of five, seven and five syllables respectively, and it should convey a sense of time, place and mood.'

Undaunted by their want of enthusiasm, Iseult applied herself to the exercise. The Atlas, she thought. On the shoulders of Atlas. That would do for line two. Four travellers walk / on the shoulders of Atlas. That took care of place, but not season. Alright:

> Four travellers walk
> On the shoulders of Atlas,
> Winter at their heels.

But it was the Landlord who got in first. 'I'll give you a focking haiku,' he said, and spread his hands like a god.

> 'Fock all to look at
> Feet near destroyed by walking.
> Not a pub for miles.'

'No sense of place,' the Poet snapped. 'It could be the Wicklow hills on a wet Sunday.'

'And no colloquialisms,' Iseult added.

'Aye,' the Landlord said, scowling at the emptiness, 'not even one of them buggers.'

They finished that stage at a shepherd's summer encampment, with the sun still over their heads.

'You said we'd see the village tonight,' the Poet complained.

'Over there,' Case said, pointing at a stony hillock blocking the view south. 'I'll show you when we've set up camp.' He gestured at the crude hamlet of stone corrals and huts. 'This is one of their *azibs*.' He threw the ground squirrels down. 'Give me a knife and I'll get supper started.'

While he skinned and jointed, the Poet and the Landlord searched for the makings of a fire and Iseult went to collect water from a nearby spring. She lingered by the cold trickle, soothing her feet in a poultice of wet moss.

Evening was settling in when Case led them up the hill. At first, Iseult's gaze squandered itself on nothing, then she took another few steps and a solid map sprang into view – ranges and mesas diminishing into a plain lit by floating columns of sunlight. But all this was across a gulf of air, a giddy split of rock.

Serenely balanced at the edge, Case levered a boulder over. Long seconds later it burst to smithereens that went clattering down like broken shackles. 'Nearly three thousand feet,' he said.

The Landlord snorted and shied.

Shuffling forward, a hundredth of her normal weight, Iseult looked down. When her horizons tilted back to level she saw a crawl of river, forest matted like fleece, a random pattern of fields and, miles to the west, the curving white slash of a dam.

'Where's Fox?' the Landlord asked, keeping the whole length of the rope between himself and Case.

Lazily, Case's hand targeted the head of the valley. After making the necessary adjustment of scale, Iseult picked out a village – a haze of smoke under a cathedral of rock.

The Landlord swept the valley floor with Case's binoculars. A short silence ensued, and then the Poet spoke for everyone. 'How are we supposed to get down?'

'There's a goat path.'

'You're codding us,' the Landlord said, his mouth stretched in a reflex smile of fear.

'The devil he is, too,' the Poet blurted.

'He told you it was difficult,' Iseult cried.

'You can climb down the back way,' Case said, 'but it adds two more days. We can't come up the valley because there's an army post at the dam.'

Blood flowed into the Landlord's face. 'If I thought for a moment you could make eejits of us, it would end right here and now. For a moment, you hear?'

'Joe,' the Poet said quietly, her face pallid. 'I think there may not be another moment.'

Case displayed a crumpled Gauloises packet. 'Fox's,' he said. 'He passed this way with Laschen.'

The Landlord fingered the packet as if it was an object of veneration. He looked up. 'Nawh,' he said pathetically. 'A bargain's a bargain. Right, Pat?'

'Right, Joe.'

Determination hardened the Landlord's face. He stood taller. 'Well now, I hope there's no climbing involved, because I'm not built for leaping about mountains.'

'Neither is Fox.'

'If it's that easy,' the Poet said, 'what do we need the Brit for?'

'It's not much of a path,' Case told her. 'You won't get to the bottom on your own.'

They went into conclave. Iseult moved towards Case, her intuition crying foul. 'I don't understand,' she said. 'You could have got away this morning.'

He smiled, the sun masking his face in gold.

'Why *did* you come back?' she asked.

'When I dump them, I want them to stay dumped.' His stare challenged her. 'Don't imagine I came back for you.'

'No,' she lied. She fiddled with a box of matches.

Below them the calm airs were thickening into dusk. Small clouds had marshalled in the north. The sky glowed to a deeper blue and the colours of the formations intensified, from yellow to red, lavender to purple and then one by one, into a luxurious black. Under hard blue lights, the dam was exquisite, a jewel sepulchred in darkness.

'Everybody has a dark side,' Iseult said, as if picking up a conversation broken off only moments before. 'I bet you have. I bet everyone has. In the street I'd look at people and think: what nasty little secret are you hiding?'

'I've got nothing to hide.'

'Then you're the exception.'

'Do you still love him?'

Confusion and anger seethed in Iseult. Without thinking, she lit her last cigarette. 'Love isn't something you can pick up or drop at your convenience.'

'Yes or no?'

Iseult watched the tip of her cigarette glow hot. 'Oh God, what does it matter? Yes.'

Case nodded.

'You know why Cathal loathes you so much,' Iseult blurted. 'Because you're so fucking straight, so fucking natural. You're the hawk who can't cheat.'

Case blinked. 'I cheat all the time,' he said. He glanced at the Poet and the Landlord. 'Tomorrow, when I give the word, don't think. Just do it.'

'Do what?'

'Whatever's necessary.'

'I'm not going to help you kill them.'

'Whatever.'

A gulf of vapours confronted them. Behind their backs the huge sun was floating free of the horizon, throwing their shadows on to the clouds smoking out of the canyon. Two soft thuds fluttered Iseult's chest.

'Blasting at the dam,' Case said.

'Now you're sure you know the way?' the Landlord asked, simulating jollity.

'Vaguely.'

'Well mind how you go.' The Landlord tugged on the rope. 'Remember, if I fall, you fall too.'

'And if I go,' Case said, 'everyone's a loser.'

They descended into a blinding whiteness that soon grew

dark and drenchingly cold. The clouds coiled and parted and coiled again, giving Iseult intermittent glimpses of a mossy black subterranean world, an orgy frozen in stone – thick shafts rearing up from matted growth, dank triangles.

The clouds drew shut and absorbed them. Slippery planes of rock floated past. Local sounds were magnified – the creaking of jeans, the sawing of breath. Stones rattled underfoot and went bouncing downward.

Goat droppings and the occasional scar of an iron nail pointed the way, but as Case had warned, it wasn't much of a track, and over long stretches there didn't appear to be a path at all. With many false turns, hesitations and back-trackings, they went teetering down. An hour passed. Tempers stretched, feet jarred, concentration faltered. If Case hadn't been roped, he could have escaped at any moment of his choosing.

At a kink in the path, Iseult blundered into Deirdre, shunting her against the Landlord. All three jostled like nervous sheep. Case was a few yards ahead, pondering.

'What's the hold-up?' the Landlord demanded.

'We've lost the track.'

They all scanned about as if the path was a small discrete object that had been casually mislaid. The Landlord clawed at his face as if he had walked into cobwebs. 'Well where the fock is it?'

'Down there,' Case said, leaning out. 'I think.'

Closing the gap, the Landlord risked a cagey inspection. He flinched, his legs trembling. 'It's a sheer drop.'

'That's an exaggeration,' Case said.

'I'm not focking risking my neck on that.'

'I'll check,' Case said, sauntering forward.

'Stay still,' the Landlord yelled, yanking him back. He glared wildly about. 'Nobody move. I want to reason this out.' Laying his Browning at his feet, he sat down to consider the situation.

No one stirred. They waited in sniffling irritability. The rain had thickened to sleet. Iseult sweated in the cold. Wherever she looked, her gaze stubbed itself on rock. It was a hideous place, implacable and utterly hostile to life.

'Let's get back to the top,' the Poet said, her voice slurred.

As one, they turned. The cloud seemed to be pressing down from above. Iseult's heart sank into her boots.

She watched the Landlord gnawing his fingers, working out the permutations. It was like the teaser about the man who wanted to ferry the fox, the goose and the sack of grain across a river in a boat that would take only one passenger at a time. Given a chance, the fox would eat the goose, or the goose would gobble the grain.

An icy trickle slid down Iseult's neck. 'Look,' she said, startling herself, 'you'd better make your mind up. Deirdre's not well.'

The Poet's face was blanched and her eyes held a wild light. Hypothermia was setting in.

Hauling himself up, the Landlord advanced to the edge. 'You sure about that focking path?'

'Well, it's not up here.'

'If it is the path,' the Landlord said, pleading for reassurance, 'how much further?'

'Maybe an hour,' Case said. He shrugged. 'Maybe two.'

'Fock it,' the Landlord said. He hitched up his trousers. 'I'll go first. Pat comes next, then Iseult. Deirdre, you'll have to come down on your own.' He frowned. 'Deirdre?'

Anger and fear swarmed over the Poet's face. A rush of Gaelic burst from her. Holding the Ruger in both hands, she pointed it at Case's head.

With an oath the Landlord lunged and knocked the gun up in the instant it fired. The bullet rang off rock. Grimacing at Case, he wrestled the gun from her grasp.

'Every step was contrived,' the Poet said in a dull voice. Her gaze was lifeless. 'Kill him before he kills us.'

'For Christ's sake,' the Landlord shouted. 'We need him.' Lightly he slapped her face.

She sat down as if her legs were wet cardboard and began to

cry. Face burning, the Landlord stroked her hand. He kissed her cheek. He wiped her eyes. When she had been restored to some semblance of reason, he gave her back her Ruger, strode to the edge and stood straight, as if he was poised on the scaffold.

Case thrust out his tied hands. 'You'll be a lot safer if I can hold you with two hands.'

The Landlord laughed on phlegm. 'Ah well, easy glum, easy glow.' He set Case free. 'You sure you've got me safe?'

'As a row of houses.'

Eyes shallow with fear, the Landlord backed over the edge. His tortured breathing grew faint. Case paid out rope. At last a hollow shout signalled that the Landlord had touched bottom.

'What does it look like?' Case called.

'Focking awful. You'd better get yourself down.'

Case descended without strain. Then it was Iseult's turn. Shutting her mind to the silent disc-like faces upturned below, she set off, turning inwards as the drop steepened. About a third of the way down her feet stirred around without finding a hold. She glanced down and the world turned topsy-turvy. She froze with her face to the cliff, everything shrinking down to the few square inches of wet rock in front of her nose. She had the illusion of weightlessness – of holding fast to a floor in zero gravity. If she relaxed her grip, she would simply float free. Her fingers clutched convulsively.

'Hold on,' Case's voice cried. 'I'm coming up.'

Eyes shut, she clung tight. The fog caressed her like a chill breath, numbing her body and her senses. Case's hand touched her ankle, cupped her foot. Trusting blindly in his strength, she let him lift her down.

The Landlord handed her the Martini bottle. 'Any time, any place, anywhere,' he sang.

She drank and coughed and looked for the promised path, but the ledge fell into nothing – a slow exhalation of vapours nosing hungrily at her feet.

Deirdre's pinched face craned over. She started down with

assurance, but balked at the same spot where Iseult had frozen. She laughed.

'What's so funny?' the Landlord asked.

'I'm stuck.'

'Don't be stupid,' the Landlord said. 'It's easy.'

'Easy for you. You had a rope.'

'Shall I give her a hand?' Case asked.

'Pat's coming up,' the Landlord called, and took another immoderate swig.

'No,' Deirdre cried, her voice shrill with fright. 'He'll get my gun.'

'Toss it down then.'

'And what happens when he reaches me? He'll throw me off, that's what.'

The Landlord closed his eyes. 'Well, you'll just have to come down on your bogging own, won't you?'

Deirdre lowered one foot as if she was testing hot water. She drew it back as if she had scalded herself. 'It's no good. I can't move.'

'Climb back up,' the Landlord ordered carelessly, up-ending the bottle as if he had disavowed all responsibility.

Deirdre groped with one hand and snatched it back. She pressed her face into her arm and said something they didn't catch.

'Stop footering about,' the Landlord shouted in sudden rage. 'We can't stand around on this pigging mountain all day.' He lobbed the empty bottle over his shoulder. It shattered with a puny crash.

'Joe,' Deirdre called in a much sharper tone, 'get up here and rescue me.'

The Landlord huffed in frustration. 'I can't leave these uns on their own.'

'Tie them up,' Deirdre ordered. She began to wail. 'I warned you he was messing us about.'

'Mary, mother, what a focking performance,' the Landlord said. Cursing weakly, he lashed Case and Iseult back to back, shoved his pistol into his waistband, and set off up the cliff.

Iseult watched him go. 'Is this part of the plan?' she asked.

'Shift over where they can't see us,' Case said. 'Get down on your knees.'

'Putting your trust in prayer?' Iseult said. She was in a strange state of mind, almost dreamy.

'I've got a knife.'

As he levered himself down, she braced herself upright.

'What are you playing at? We only have a minute.'

'Pat, swear you won't harm my brother.'

'For Christ's sake.'

'Swear!'

She resisted his savage jerk. She felt him go slack.

'I swear.'

Iseult fell to her knees. She felt him working at their bonds.

The Landlord's voice floated down. 'Are you there, Pat?'

'Where else would I be?' Case said, cutting away.

Iseult felt the rope spring.

'Joe?' Case called, strolling into view. In his hand he held a blade as fine as a scalpel.

The Landlord compressed his mouth and shook his head. 'No mistake, Pat, you're a sleekit bastard.'

'Chuck your guns down and then we'll think what to do.'

'Nawh, we'll find our own way, thanks.'

'No,' Case said, 'you won't.' He turned away.

'Maybe, see you,' the Landlord said. He smiled grimly into the fog. 'If we're spared.'

'No,' Case said. 'You won't be.'

Iseult soon understood the finality of his leave-taking. Without a guide there was no way down. It was late afternoon before they emerged from the cloud, still some height above the village. Soon they met a boy guarding a flock of goats. He stared in puzzlement at the mountain they had walked off. The valley was sealed in. Cold rain fell.

'We can't abandon them,' Iseult said.

'It won't make world headlines.'

'*Bon-bon,*' the goatherd begged. '*Donnez-moi un stylo.*' His scalp was scarred with ringworm.

'Pat,' she cried, tugging his sleeve. 'I think I can hear them calling.'

He glanced back, pitiless, shrugged, and said:

> 'Hearing a man's cry,
> the shepherd looks up and frowns.
> Just the mountain wind.'

30

All next day the valley lay cocooned in cloud, but the morning after dawned clear and Case, under duress, went back up the mountain. From the moment he left the track and started climbing, he knew he was in serious error. His body was stiff and unresponsive, balking at straightforward moves. He told himself he was exhausted, all his reserves used up, but in his heart he knew it was fear. The fear and the sense of futility at what he was doing made him terribly angry. He knew that the Poet and the Landlord were dead, frozen in each other's arms or spread like jam on the rocks below.

Stepping clumsily between ice-glazed shadows and dizzy sunlight, he gasped and slithered towards oblivion. For a minute he remained with his legs dangling over a blue drop, too frightened to move, and when at last he dragged himself to safety he stayed there, calling out to the silence every so often, until the sun had burnt down to the level of his eyes and he had almost persuaded himself that he had done as much to find them as anyone reasonably could.

When he staggered into the village Iseult was waiting, her face a flash of white in the shaded guest-room.

'They probably went back over the plateau,' he lied.

Concern hushed her voice. Her hands wouldn't stay still. 'We should ask Laschen to organize a proper search party.'

'And have the whole village know what happened?'

As she opened her mouth to protest, an image pushed its way into his recall – Roy Besant's hands twisting anxiously on his toupee as he lay dying in the slush on the pass. Something snapped. 'They're dead,' he cried, his voice rising out of control. 'And if you want to make something of it, you know where to start.'

For the first time since he'd known her, colour flooded her cheeks. Her eyes filled. She moved back jerkily, one step at a time, as if the flat of a cruel hand was pushing her, and then she turned and fled.

Blindly, Case pushed his way out of the house. He found himself down by the river, a place of gentle contemplation in happier times. The fields here were walled plots no bigger than gardens, and in the spring they were invaded by poppies, so that from the plateau the eye was startled by a mosaic of red and green.

This had always been his special valley, a place where his imagination returned when winter winds groaned, but now he knew that it had become one more place he would never see again. The atmosphere had been defiled. Wherever he looked, he saw only the Landlord's veined face and the Poet's famished eyes.

A voice hailed him in Berber. It was Fox, who had made substantial progress in the dialect, regardless of the fact that it didn't travel – was, in fact, as incomprehensible as Japanese to a Rif Berber. He stood at a distance, a twittish expression on his face, one hand raised like a child awaiting permission to speak.

'Not now,' Case muttered.

With the exaggeratedly hushed tread of a parishioner taking his place late for church, Fox joined him. He flicked up a cigarette and removed it with his lips. He had acquired a large stock of the local brand – 'moderately acceptable snout', he called it.

'Do you know Omar Khayyam?' he said through smoke, watching the sun retreat up the cliffs.

'Film star, in't he?'

'Ignorant peasant,' Fox said in mild reproof. 'He was a poet. You know – *A flask of wine, a loaf of bread and thou beside me were paradise enow*, etcetera.' He rounded on Case. 'I do think you're being unfair on Iseult.'

'Did she tell you about her and her brother?'

'Poured out her heart, the poor poppet. What does it matter? She loves you; you love her.'

'No she doesn't; no I don't.'

'Take it from Foxy.'

'You're an expert, are you?'

'On women? Never risen to the challenge; but I'm a keen student of humans and their funny little natures.'

Case was in no mood for Fox's drolleries. His attention strayed to an adjoining field, where a peasant had prostrated himself for the evening prayer, bowing and scraping with moans and groans.

'Laschen's found religion,' Fox said. 'He's been labouring on the new mosque.' Fox frowned. 'Watching these chaps stick their bums up in the air six times a day – it makes you wonder.'

A minute passed. 'Wonder what?' Case said.

'How they reconcile their piety with their frightful cupidity.'

'They have to live.'

'I suppose,' Fox said, 'that since they believe all material blessings come from Allah, it's an act of faith to milk every last drop of his munificence – especially if the goodies are routed through infidels such as ourselves.'

'What are you wirelessing on about?'

'I believe Laschen is unsound,' Fox said. He detached a twig of tobacco from his teeth. 'He talks to himself in a most unsettling way.'

Case turned a dyspeptic smile on him. 'So do you.'

'He talks about money. He feels we've short-changed him.'

'He's not far wrong.'

'The question is: what does he intend to do about it?' Fox pointed his cigarette challengingly. 'I imagine he'd earn a handsome reward for turning us in.'

'We're his guests. Berbers take hospitality seriously.'

'And all Africans have a wonderful sense of rhythm, and the

Scots are mean, and the Chinese are inscrutable little blighters.' Fox blew a large smoke circle and then puffed another five or six rings through it. 'In the days when smoking was deregulated,' he said, 'a tobacco company offered a lifetime supply of snout to anyone who could blow ten smoke rings through one of those. I trained assiduously, sixty a day for a month, but come the moment, I could only manage eight. My *embouchure* failed me.' Fox shrugged. 'Stage fright.'

'Laschen's okay,' Case said.

'He's throwing a feast for us tonight.'

'What's the big occasion?'

'What indeed?' Fox said, and articulated his eyebrows. He stood up, always a touch-and-go procedure. 'I vote we skedaddle while the going, as they say, is good.'

'Look, Laschen and me have been mates for years. If it hadn't been for him, you'd still be banged up.'

Fox placed a finger to his lips. 'Trust old Foxy. Foxy knows best.' He went away with his lopsided gait.

His warning squirmed into Case's assurance. There had been incidents in the past – a sum of money stolen from a tent, one or two items of kit that had gone missing. He had dismissed these petty rip-offs as part of a cultural pattern which he didn't understand.

Back at the village he found Laschen dragging a goat from a pen.

'I hear you're giving a party,' Case said ungraciously.

'For the m'sieur,' Laschen panted, throwing the goat on to its side. 'With music.'

Case watched him lash the goat's front legs. 'I'm afraid it's a good-bye party.'

'Excuse me?'

'We're leaving tomorrow.'

Laschen drew a curved knife. 'What you wish,' he said with no change of tone.

'Are you going to come with us?'

Laschen kept his eyes on the terrified goat. 'I am going to work on the new mosque.'

Case tried to interpret what was going on behind those tea-coloured eyes. He had a vision of bodies strewn like dolls on the snow-covered plateau, Laschen panting as he stripped them of their artefacts.

'I thought you were set on Amsterdam.'

'No Amsterdam,' Laschen said, and slit the goat's neck with one stroke. Shocking arterial blood spouted. 'No money.'

Case smiled tightly. 'I told you: we'll send the money.'

Unblinking, Laschen regarded the goat's death spasms. 'I think you do not have the luck.'

Case did not enjoy the party.

Iseult showed up white and defiant in a borrowed *djellaba* and jewellery. Fox, too, had opted for ethnic dress. Laschen brought around a salver of water and towels. The meal itself was seven courses spread over four and a half hours, with lengthy interludes and even naps between courses. First came a range of soft drinks in primary colours, followed soon after by coffee and dates and bread and butter and honey. By the time mint tea had been disposed of, Case felt that his teeth were dissolving in sugar.

Next came kebabs of mutton and the precious fat from around the kidneys, then a woman waddled forth with a huge dish of couscous.

Probing the communal platter, Case and Iseult addressed each other with hideous politeness.

'The way the grease squirts between your back teeth is interesting,' Fox observed.

A *tagine* of mutton came next. The final dish was a *mechoui* of goat.

More tea was served on the roof-top, where the musicians had gathered – half a dozen men and about ten women, swathed in brilliant fabrics and hung with antique metalwork.

Their performance started at the same leisurely tempo as the banquet. One man laid down a slurred, introspective rhythm on soft membranes; another plucked an instrument like a lute; a male singer began a melancholy solo.

'A shepherd bemoans his lost love,' Fox explained. 'Gender unspecified. Fill in the rest for yourself.'

It went on much longer than Case had bargained for, and he was caught out when, with only a half-beat pause, the singer burst into an impassioned tremolo, accompanied by the full orchestra, each player complicating the beat with counter-rhythms.

The music made the women restless. They smoothed down their robes and shifted their feet.

Over the edge of the mountain the moon drifted. A thrilling ululation rose from the women. Seeing Iseult clapping, one of the girls dragged her into the swaying line. Her face shone. She's forgotten already, Case thought with disgust.

He looked for Laschen and spotted him talking to the *imam*. It was the first time Case had seen him socializing. Something had changed.

But eventually even he surrendered to the hypnotic rhythms. The music was a drug, altering perception, for looking up he saw the moon was drawing closer.

He must have nodded off, because when he next looked Laschen was gone. The roof-top was packed. He shouldered his way through the crowd, asking if anyone knew where Laschen was, but no one could or would say. Case looked down the length of the valley to the phantom light above the dam. All his doubts congealed in a hard block.

Fox was wafting about as if draped in yards of chiffon. Case touched him on the shoulder. 'We're leaving.'

'Good. I could use some exercise.'

Iseult was in a trance and he had to shake her roughly. 'Get changed,' he shouted. 'We're going.'

'When the music stops,' she said, not hearing him properly.

He pulled her out of the line. 'If we're here when the music stops, we're dead.'

Their unscheduled departure imposed a mood of stealth on them. They crept up behind the village and passed through a wooded ravine, following a stream frozen in silver. Apes crashed away through the trees. The cliffs radiated a ghostly light. It was like leaving by the back door of the world.

The music was still playing. It stole after them, floating and fading, emanating from all directions. Case drove them on, hounded by the fear that pursuit would begin the moment the music stopped.

It ended with a staccato rattle of drums. The silence ached.

Walking with a strong wind at their backs, they reached the Atlas watershed at noon the next day. They climbed a crooked defile and ate in a blustery gap beneath boulder fields and crags. Fleeces of cumulus slanted overhead, approaching slowly and scudding past with their edges curling, almost close enough to touch.

The wind made Case skittish. All morning an acute sensation of vulnerability had been lodged between his shoulderblades. Fox was jumpy, too. Immediately they had finished, he was on his feet.

'I'll stop a minute,' Case told him.

He watched them grow tiny, casting the occasional glance behind, into a sage and pink basin dotted with scrub like puffs of smoke. Only the wind moved, but when he stood to leave, the premonition of danger held him to the spot. Twice more he turned to go, and twice more he couldn't break the compulsion to stay. Bloody neurotic, he told himself, like getting up in the middle of the night to check that a door was locked.

Finally he overrode his apprehension, but when he had descended a little way, the feeling crawled through him again, bringing him to another stop. This is ridiculous, he raged to himself, yet the more he studied the gap in the skyline, the more his intuition hardened into certainty that on the other side a threat was drawing close.

Moving cautiously, he approached the top. His mouth tightened in self-derision. The plateau was empty except for an eagle quartering the ridge, methodically working the contours. He stayed to watch it, and by the time it had covered the entire slope and set course for a new hunting ground, Fox and Iseult had passed from view. Case made no haste to follow. He would catch them up before dark.

With a last throwaway look, he turned away. He froze in a crouch, his chest tight. Dropping to a squat, he focused on a far-off speck, a dark pulse in the puddled light. Stretched flat, he observed it draw nearer. It was a man on a white mule, and Case knew from the rider's red bobble hat and the rifle carried vertically on his back that it was Laschen.

He's changed his mind about coming with us, Case told himself, but even when he repeated the hope aloud, it rang just as false.

Soon Laschen would disappear into the defile. Quickly Case examined his situation. Above him fields of shale and tumbled boulders rose three or four hundred feet to the summit. Provided he took pains not to leave a trail, he had an infinity of hiding places to choose from. He would lie up until Laschen passed and then follow at a distance, waiting for nightfall, when he would decide what was to be done. At the prospect of outwitting the Berber, an intense excitement shook him.

Laschen had stopped and was surveying the ridge, his head raised like a hound questing for scent. Light winked on binoculars. Case was impatient for him to move on, but the minutes passed and Laschen went on scouting. A primitive chill settled on Case. With binoculars, a watchful eye might have spotted movement on the ridge.

Impatient to change his position, he fretted while Laschen completed his inspection. Before heeling the mule forward, he turned in the saddle, looking back the way he had come. Case had no time to ponder the significance of that backward look. As soon as Laschen was out of sight, he began climbing, making slow progress on the splintered surface. Giving up his plan to reach the top, he took cover behind a sun-rotted column and waited for the sound of the mule picking its way over rock.

Again, the expected didn't materialize. Instead, three more

blips wavered out of the light. Cursing his bravado, Case edged forward to get a better look.

A crack like a violent electrical discharge stunned him; something stung his face. Flat to the ground, he saw that the bullet had impacted only a foot from his head, gouging splinters. The bridge of his nose had been cut. Calculating the angle of fire, he guessed that Laschen was not far below, hidden behind a line of rocks like knobbly vertebrae. Shocked into flight, he sprinted away, his only thought to reach the top first. A silhouette sprang up a hundred yards to his left. From the corner of his eye he saw Laschen stop and snatch the gun to his shoulder, but he made himself hold his course another half-second before swerving and ducking aside. The bullet ricocheted to the right.

Falling upwards, he scrambled on hands and knees through cushions of thorn. Gulping for breath, he blundered over another ledge, tripped, and landed with his outspread hands inches from a tight coil of dirty brown and black. His eyes stood out on sticks. It was the biggest rock adder he'd ever seen, and he had nearly thrown himself on it. He forced himself into stillness. The snake didn't move. Perhaps it was dead, but he couldn't be sure because he couldn't locate its fucking head. Blood and sweat dripped from his nose. The pressure in his chest was unbearable. He began to let his breath ease from his lungs and caught it again as the coil slackened. The head probed forth, mean eyes gleaming and tongue darting. Case flung himself aside without waiting to see which way it was aimed.

Laschen was gone from sight. Alerted by the shots, the three riders had stopped on the low ground.

Case found himself conducting a furious dialogue with himself. The high ground was the only place to be, but Laschen might already be waiting for him. If he descended, he would be forced out into the open. He shook with indecision. He didn't know which way to turn.

At the edge of his vision, the snake was straightening out. The brute was at least four feet long, its fangs packed with enough venom to kill a horse, but it was cold and torpid, moving with painful slowness – not a threat.

Something else snagged his bolting eye – a dark blotch buried in a cave beneath an overhang on a south-facing crag out of sight of anyone on the summit. White splashes and streaks beneath it confirmed it was the nest of a raptor – perhaps the nest of the eagle he'd seen hunting.

Even as he identified it, he dismissed it from consideration. It was too obvious. Once Laschen spotted it, he would smile and shake his head and make straight for it.

Nowhere was safe.

Stampeded by fear, he ran and stopped, glanced back, looking for the snake. It was gone. No, it was flowing between two boulders. His gaze switched back to the nest.

Laschen hated snakes. It was not a sensible respect or even the conventional atavistic fear of all things scaly and legless; it was a full-blown nursery horror responsive neither to reason nor experience. Two memories stuck in Case's mind. Once, he had gone swimming in a mountain lake and two grass snakes had converged on him. On the other occasion, he had casually shone a torch from his tent to discover that they had pitched it on a nest of vipers. On both occasions Laschen had become unstrung.

Scrambling down, Case whipped the viper out by the tip of its tail. He fumbled open his pack and tipped his tent from its nylon carrying bag. He looked in vain for something with which to handle the snake. There was no time for caution. His hand hovered over the snake, pounced and pinned it behind the head. It came alive in his grasp, writhing and thrashing. He couldn't get it into the fucking bag. Oh please, he prayed, as its tail threw a loop around his arm. He half-spilled, half-crammed it in and pulled the drawstring tight.

Gathering his breath, he searched for Laschen, scared that he had wasted too much time. No, he was pretty safe where he was, but to reach the nest he had to cross an open fan of scree, and if Laschen was in position, he could empty a magazine into him before he made cover.

Time and time again he assessed the risks and always they seemed stacked against him, but with each moment he dithered, the odds against lengthened.

Dumping his pack, he made his dash, tensed for the gunshot, although he knew the bullet would slam into his back before he heard it. He reached safety and toiled up a fall of boulders. Distance was deceptive. The closer he got, the bigger the nest grew. It must have been occupied on and off for generations, growing with each season's use until now it bulked to the height of a grown man. Not a golden eagle's nest, he decided, but a lammergeier's – a rare vulture for which, ironically, he had spent many weeks searching with Laschen.

It was incredibly easy of access, but Case hesitated. His feet had left a clear path in the shale. Once he was inside, all other options would be closed. He would be blind and trapped. The nest offered only one advantage. Even if the presence of the snake didn't convince Laschen that the site was empty, he would have to come in to check, and once inside he would have small room for manoeuvre and precious little time to react.

Decision made, Case pulled himself up on to a shallow, compacted dish with hanks of wool and scraps of cloth woven into the structure. Crawling deeper, Case grazed his back on the sloping roof, where strange succulents like babies' clenched hands hung. The cave was as dry as a tomb. Dust clogged his throat. He thought with disgust of the mites and blood-suckers infesting the debris.

In the semi-darkness, he toppled into a crevice at the back. Thrashing around, he made enough space to curl almost flat, invisible to anyone crouched at the entrance. He had a moment's triumph; he thought he had made a smart move.

From the heel of his boot he took his leather-cutter's blade.

His hands were inflamed and for a bad moment he was convinced that the snake had bitten him. Raising them to the light, he saw that he had been punctured by hundreds of thorns.

As he tried to pick them out, he found himself running through the hunting strategies used by birds of prey – direct aerial pursuit, the stoop from a commanding height, the glide attack, quartering, ambush, still-hunting . . . Get a grip, he ordered himself.

His position wasn't as spacious as he'd first thought, and several times he had to shift about to restore circulation. He remembered that the bag with the snake had tears in it. It wasn't a comfortable thought.

The first hour passed in tight-wound expectation; the second lapsed into miserable suspense. A bird, one of the dowdy desert species, chirruped close by. Risking a look, Case saw only blue sky. The cave faced south-east and one side of the entrance was lit by the unseen sun. He licked his caked lips and another dread surfaced. He wasn't equipped for a long confinement. Food wasn't a problem, but unforgivably he had abandoned his water with his pack and he had sweated buckets. All Laschen had to do was sit it out on the summit. With the weather set fair and the moon only a few days off full, night wouldn't offer an opportunity to escape.

Trapped in the silence of bones, Case waited. His hands throbbed. The light moved off the cave entrance. In the darkening sky the clouds had slowed.

Rocks chased each other down the cliff. Laschen was above. Silence came back. Case bit the ball of his thumb. His nerves would not tolerate this blind and helpless waiting.

He shut his eyes, all his other senses straining to absorb the signals of Laschen's presence. He pictured him pausing and listening between each step, not a trace of expression on his face. He would be suspicious of ambush, even a little fearful, unable to blot out the image of a hand shooting out to grab or a stone lobbed to make him whirl in the wrong direction. His rifle was an old bolt-action type, Case remembered. At close quarters he would be able to loose off only one shot.

Now Case could sense him very close. He lifted the bag, wincing at the alien rustle it made. The snake was heavy and still.

Scree grated below.

Timing was crucial. Holding the bag at full stretch, Case up-ended it into the centre of the nest. The snake flopped out and lay in an unseemly pile. It's dead, he thought with indignation. What fucking use is a dead snake?

Fingers curled into claws, he reached for the viper, but almost at the moment of contact he stayed his hand. Working feverishly, he pulled a stick from the nest and poked the snake. A loud hiss filled the cave and with sudden, shocking fluency, the viper glided straight at him. Gibbering, he flicked at it with the stick, managed to turn it and then watched in dismay as it slid towards the light. Twice he tugged it back by its tail. 'Stay,' he whispered, as if commanding a dog. Sweat blinded him.

The snake was determined to get out. Throwing aside caution, Case grabbed it, but this time he had it too far back and it whirled and struck. He fell back, not knowing if he'd been bitten, the snake lashing at the full reach of his arm.

A rock thumped into the nest.

'What are you doing, gentle?' a voice asked.

Well may you fucking ask, Case mouthed, still grappling with the viper.

'Come out, please,' Laschen commanded. He laughed. 'You are not *n'da*.'

The weight of the snake was cramping Case's arm.

'You make some big problem for me,' Laschen said in an aggrieved voice.

Knowing what would come next, Case cowered.

A bullet careered on a crazy course around the cave, ending up God knows where. Two or three of those, Case thought, and he was finished. If he surrendered, he reasoned, it was unlikely that Laschen would shoot him out of hand. He tensed to call out, but shrank back as he picked up a vibration through the nest. Laschen was climbing. Case felt the nest give. Shadow blotted out the light. Case heard Laschen's even breathing.

Another crash paralysed him. Too late, he heard the clunk

of the bolt pushing another round home. That, he decided, was his last chance.

He bottled up his breath. Laschen was crawling forward.

The hiss of the snake disturbed the silence. Puzzled, Laschen stopped, shifting his weight as he peered around. The snake hissed again – a throaty sound, similar to the threat of a frightened hawk or cat. Laschen muttered. The tight-packed arrangement of sticks communicated his alarm. He was backing out.

But that was the last thing Case wanted him to do. He had been discovered. Laschen would summon reinforcements, or – Case had been suppressing the horror since hearing the first footfalls – he could torch the nest.

Clumsily he flung the viper towards the light. Laschen yelped as if the breath had been knocked out of him and reared back, cracking his skull on the roof and discharging the rifle. Almost simultaneous with the crash, Case drove forward, lunging for the gun and getting one hand to the muzzle as Laschen snatched it back. They were at opposite ends of it, Case trying to drag himself forward, using the barrel for purchase, Laschen struggling to work the bolt. Case couldn't hold on; his hands were slick with sweat. With all the leverage he could muster, he brought his knife arm up and over, aiming for Laschen's forearm and missing, plunging the blade so deep into the nest that he lost his grip. For a moment neither of them could exert any force, then Laschen's eyes widened and Case, glimpsing the viper pouring over the Berber's legs, bellied forward, gouging and pummeling. Laschen was giving ground, more frightened of the snake than Case. They were at the entrance. Case had hold of Laschen's sleeve. The material wrenched and tore out of his grasp as the edge of the nest gave way and Laschen went with it.

He didn't fall. He hung on by his forearms, one hand paddling like an exhausted swimmer, the other still clutching the rifle. Case wrenched it from his grasp and rose to his knees, fumbling the bolt, swinging the muzzle. Laschen stopped struggling. He looked into the bore of his own rifle, and then looked up at Case with the resigned stare of a prey animal.

All the jubilation and rage went out of Case. Exhausted and confused, he held out a hand and helped Laschen up.

For some time they sat side by side, like fledglings taking stock of the hostile world, then Case lowered himself on to firm ground and traversed back to find his pack. Laschen joined him and looked on despondently. Taking out his water-bottle, Case swallowed half, emptied some on his head, and threw the bottle to Laschen. He wiped his bloody face with the back of his filthy hand and studied the three men waiting below.

'Who are they?' he asked.

'Police. One of them comes to the dam. He makes trouble when someone tries to kill the American.'

Case hadn't given any thought to the American. 'Is he still around?'

'Maybe. His house is not far from the dam.'

Case looked north, wondering if he should risk it, but his situation was bad enough without getting involved with dodgy Americans. Also, he wasn't feeling too good – hot and shivery. He fingered his tender throat with puffy hands.

Consciousness of his plight squeezed another spurt of anger from him. Sighting on the figures, he loosed off one shot for each. The mules danced. Return fire zipped among the rocks.

Whatever weaponry they had, Case knew they wouldn't advance to the col, and at this halfway point on the plateau, they couldn't get back to the valley before he reached the road.

Shadows wrinkled the plateau. The clouds were becalmed, their undersides pink. In an hour it would be dark. 'I'm taking your mule,' Case told Laschen.

When he led it back, Laschen was still there, head downcast. 'I'll leave it with somone when I reach the road,' Case told him. He hesitated, then offered his hand. Without looking up, Laschen brushed it, touched his own hand to his heart and kissed it.

31

Spooked by the fear that Byron Field would grab him off the street for questioning, Dearborn checked out of the Westbury and took a week's rental on a studio in an early modernist apartment block off Highgate Hill. The name of Adnan al-Jalil had shaken him out his blind, complacent stumbling; like a sleepwalker, he found that he had woken up in a position of peril, a seething drop ahead and no idea how to retrace his steps.

His best hope was to stay right where he was and shout for help. He called Rabat again, but the same voice told him that Cody was still out of contact.

After a night of disorderly dreams, he went jogging on Hampstead Heath, hoping that the exercise would kick-start his brain into some kind of independent initiative. The fair weather was holding, although the weather forecaster had warned that air quality was way down. He found his legs carrying him into the billion-dollar Arab quarter north of the Heath – a dreamtime garden suburb of shuttered mansions and empty sidewalks where Rafiq Saad had his London residence. One glance showed that it was as lifeless as the next. But even if he'd been at home, Dearborn asked himself, what did he plan to do? Press the buzzer and demand an explanation?

When he returned, he saw the eye on the Ansaphone winking for attention, but when he pressed the replay button there was only a breathing silence, as if whoever knew where he was hiding wanted him to know that they knew.

That evening he booked dinner at an expensive Italian

restaurant in Hampstead Village. The room was full, and as befitted his solitary status, he was given a table in the corner. He wasn't the only diner eating alone. At the next table sat a woman reading a book while she waited for her order to be taken. The table placement meant that every time the woman looked up from a page, she caught his eye. Her flared cheekbones and air of self-possession reminded him of Magda.

Her proximity made him feel absurdly self-conscious. He couldn't take any pleasure in his meal; it was like eating wet feathers. Gratefully, he turned his attention to a diversion at the door. Apparently, there was a problem of overbooking an angry shuffle of excess guests refusing to leave.

'Excuse me.'

It was his neighbour. She had a low, pleasant voice that might well have been trained for the stage.

'You had the mussels,' she said.

'Yes?' Dearborn said, slightly alarmed.

'And I heard you order the wild duck stuffed with olives and anchovies.'

'Did I make a mistake?'

'I hope not; I ordered it too.' She glanced at the commotion by the door and smiled. 'Since we're eating the same meal,' she said, 'why don't we share it at the same table?'

It was such a simple solution, so neatly accomplished, that Dearborn cursed himself for not thinking of it himself.

She was called Sarah Dupont and she owned an antique business – successfully to judge by the quality of her outfit and grooming. Yes, she had once been a stage actress, but she hadn't made the top grade and she had given up the theatre to help her husband establish his business.

'He died two years ago,' she added. 'Both our children went away to university this year. I'm still finding my feet again.' She shrugged. 'And you? Do you have children?' Dearborn's married status was taken for granted.

'Er, one. I'm divorced.'

When his conscience had assimilated that lie, the evening

418

flowed. Sarah was a delightful companion, informed and witty and interested, able to open up common ground at every turn in the conversation. But as the meal drew to a close, a tension crept in.

The waiter offered them more coffee. Wanting to put off the moment of parting, Dearborn opened his mouth to accept, but Sarah stilled him with a touch. 'Perhaps,' she said, turning her smile on the waiter, 'you could call us a cab.'

Nothing more was said as they walked towards the cab. Nothing more needed to be said. They would go to Sarah's home, talk late and then wordlessly become lovers.

'John!'

Dearborn whirled to behold a young woman in a lipstick-pink jogging suit, her black hair held back in a sweat-band. She looked as pretty and wholesome as a breakfast TV keep-fit artiste.

'Esther! What are you doing here?'

'I always take a run before going to bed.'

'Why are you chasing me?' Dearborn demanded, his senses dislocated by shock.

Esther made a face at Sarah. 'John,' she said in a wronged voice, 'you promised to stay in touch.'

'No I didn't,' Dearborn blurted. 'We're finished. Leave me alone.'

'I thought you must have gone back to your wife.'

Dearborn glanced wildly at Sarah.

'John,' Esther said, 'you know I can't let you walk out of my life.'

Dearborn stood paralysed.

'You're too important to me,' Esther said. 'We're too important to each other.'

Sarah smiled as if she was reflecting on something pleasant in her past. 'Well,' she said, 'obviously you two have a lot to talk about.' She put out her hand decisively. 'Goodbye, John. It was a lovely evening.'

Dearborn groaned with mortification as he watched her

climb into the cab. 'Thanks,' he said bitterly. 'You just ruined the one decent thing to come my way in months.'

Esther slipped her hand under his arm. 'I'll make it up to you.'

Dearborn entered his apartment cautiously, half-expecting to find Zwy Gur and Natti admiring the Max Ernst reproductions. Esther asked him for tea – preferably herbal.

When he came out of the kitchenette, she was lying on the bed, her eyes closed.

'Hey,' he said.

She stretched her arms and arched her neck. 'Don't you find that exercise makes you feel sexy?'

He looked down on her stonily. 'No, it makes me tired.'

'All in the mind,' she murmured. She opened her eyes and appraised him with candour. 'You're fit. You have staying power.'

Dearborn recalled the small-boned, feline feel of her at the harbour shortly before she threatened to blow his head off.

'You're wasting your time,' he told her, 'I'm not susceptible.'

She crossed her hands behind her head. 'You have too many inhibitions. You should learn how to realize yourself. Take a course.'

'Is that how you passed time between classes?'

'We can all use a little therapy.'

'West Coast self-assertion meets Israeli self-conviction. I bet they could hear the primal screams in Seattle.'

'John.'

Dearborn shifted uneasily. 'What?'

Esther pulled off her hot pink top. Underneath she wore a singlet like a second skin. Her flesh was smooth and honeyed.

Dearborn swallowed. 'I thought you wanted to talk.'

'Talking won't save you.'

Dearborn ran his fingers through his hair. 'This isn't a good idea.'

420

'Why not?'

'I'm married,' he said weakly.

She laughed derisively and slipped out of her jogging pants.

'In all modesty,' he confessed, trying to avoid looking. 'I'm practically a virgin.'

'How sweet.' She slid into bed, keeping her eyes on him. 'I suppose the girl in Marrakech doesn't count.'

Dearborn had forgotten the girl in Marrakech. 'An aberration. The exception that proves the rule.'

'What made her so special?' Esther asked, removing her singlet.

'I didn't go out of my way. It just happened.' He couldn't tear his gaze from her breasts. 'For God's sake, Esther, is this relevant?'

She didn't answer. She pulled up the coverlet and masked her face until only her almond eyes showed. 'I like you,' she said.

He shifted uncomfortably. 'Look,' he said, determined to draw the line, 'I admire your straightforwardness, but this kind of approach is woefully out of date.'

'Some things never go out of fashion,' she said. Throwing off the cover, she crawled naked across the bed and reached for him. 'See?'

He had forgotten how resilient young flesh was. She was more active than Magda, but not so pliant, defter but not so assured, less inhibited but more demanding.

'Surprisingly nice,' she murmured, patting his hip. She eyed him at an angle, then nudged him in the ribs. 'The lady would appreciate a kind word too.'

'It was terrific,' Dearborn said. 'Like driving a new car – nice and tight, no squeaks or rattles, suspension firm but nicely damped, impeccable ride quality, still under the good Lord's warranty.'

She punched him without malice. 'You're so cynical.'

'It's my only line of defence.'

The phone rang. Dearborn stared at it, mesmerized, before

picking it up. Again there was only a loaded silence. Slowly he replaced the receiver. Esther was looking at him.

'They did that yesterday,' he muttered.

'They?'

'I thought it was you.'

'It wasn't,' Esther said, 'but if *we* can find you, so can others. Of course,' she added, 'they'd need a reason.'

Dearborn thought of Byron.

Esther settled back, not taking her eyes off him for an instant. 'Perhaps it was your lady friend.'

'Sarah? She doesn't have my number. We only met tonight, over dinner.'

'Do you often pick up strangers in restaurants?'

'Actually,' he said, 'it was the other way around. She was . . .' The implications halted him.

Esther shook her head. 'You're so irresistible,' she said. 'It must be your innocence.' She kissed him on the nose. 'Her name?'

'You're crazy. She's an antiques dealer.'

'Name,' Esther demanded, leaning towards the bedside table.

'Dupont,' Dearborn snapped. He stared furiously away as Esther thumbed through the household directory and the Yellow Pages, but he couldn't prevent unpleasant doubt from weaseling into his mind. The pick-up *had* been too neat. In retrospect, the convenient table placement and the mess-up over the booking had a programmed feel.

'Not listed,' Esther said. She stared at him. 'I think, John, that you'd better bring me up to date. Apart from us, who else wants to stay in touch with you?'

'Give me those,' Dearborn snapped, wrenching the books away. He scanned the columns – Du Pont, Dupont. Suddenly all the names and addresses blurred.

'What am I doing?' he whispered. 'How did I get into this mess?'

'You see,' Esther whispered. 'Without us you can't separate real from imaginary.' She rocked him in her arms.

'Tell me what you've been doing in London. Let me make sense of it.'

Dully, Dearborn relaxed against her. 'Not until I've spoken to Cody.'

She pulled away and sat with her back to him, applying a tissue between her legs. 'Cody isn't interested. That's why you came to us.'

'That was before I had anything to tell him.'

Her shoulder-blades stood out like little hatchets. 'Like what? What have you come up with?'

'I have to speak to Cody first.'

'He's in Liberia all week – a communications seminar.'

'I'll wait.'

'No you won't,' she snapped, swinging round. Her expression sweetened again. She took hold of his hand and ran her finger down it. 'Zwy Gur wanted to pull you in. I begged him. I promised him you would talk to me.' She lowered her lashes.

'Let me give you a tip,' Dearborn said. His fingers circled down her belly. 'Always make sure you have the goods *before* you hand over the candy.'

Her hand trapped his on its descent. 'John,' she said, 'this was fun.' Her fingertips jabbed nerves. 'Next time it won't be.'

Dearborn was taken by a fit of aggression. He caught her wrists and toppled her on to her back. 'I'm an American citizen,' he declared, straddling her. 'You can't fuck with Americans.'

The little Abyssinian cat's face stared up at him.

'You want to trade information for sex,' Dearborn said, pinning her arms back. 'Okay, it's a deal.'

She lay like a rock while he fucked her in the style and tempo of his choosing. Afterwards, sensing the threat of retaliation in her furious stillness, he held her tight, his mouth close to her ear.

'Finished?' she said.

'Lova Hazan was into a big marijuana deal with an English pair called Valentine and Fox.'

'I'm not interested in Lova Hazan's drug connections,' she said. 'Get off me.'

'Fox has a money man called Valentine.'

She grunted.

'Who is active in business with a Lebanese wheeler-dealer by the name of Rafiq Saad.'

She squirmed under him.

'Who has a half-brother called . . .' Dearborn relaxed his hold and raised himself so that he could witness Esther's astonishment.

'Adnan al-Jalil,' she said.

Dearborn opened and closed his mouth for a few seconds. 'Wonderful,' he said when his voice came back. 'Wonderful.' He laughed bitterly.

She frowned. 'Tell me where you got Rafiq Saad's name?'

'From one of his girls.'

'And al-Jalil?' Esther said, her frown intensifying. 'Was that another bedroom confidence?'

Dearborn was beginning to find his position uncomfortable. 'Not exactly. I tapped a friendly source.'

'Friendly?' Esther asked, her shapely mouth beginning to stretch in a snarl.

'Well . . .'

Esther pulled one hand free and chopped him under the nose. The pain was excruciating. 'You went to the Americans,' she hissed.

'Listen,' Dearborn blurted, 'that hurt.'

'You fucking fool,' she said, rolling out from under him.

Through smarting eyes he saw her dialling. She spoke in Ethiopian, keeping one cold black eye on him, then stood and headed for the bathroom. 'Get dressed,' she commanded.

Limply, Dearborn did as he was told. When he was clothed he stood watching her silhouette through the frosted glass of the shower stall. He cleared his throat. 'Suppose you tell me the connection.'

'What?' Esther shouted over the rush of water.

'Between Lova Hazan and the Syrians.'

The shower was turned off. 'If we knew that, I wouldn't be wasting my time with you.' Esther put her head round the curtain. 'Pass me a towel.'

Dearborn held it out. 'So al-Jalil isn't the final link.'

'You're nearly there.'

'Me? This is as close as I get. I'm not putting myself in the way of any more bodily harm.'

'Only one more step.'

'That's what the hangman says.'

'John,' she said, moving up against him, 'I didn't mean it when I said I was wasting my time.' She stroked his bruised upper lip. 'You've been very good – better than anyone could have expected.'

Dearborn stepped back, discomfited as much by the warm damp elasticity of her body as by the thought that she expected him to complete the chain. 'Are we talking sex now, or what?'

'Now it's work, work, work,' she said, towelling herself with vigour.

Dearborn peered at her suspiciously. 'One step in which direction.'

Esther wiped a damp curl from her cheek. 'What does your intuition say?'

'I don't know. Morocco, I suppose.'

Esther nodded slowly and withdrew. 'But this time,' she called, 'we stay close, you and me.'

'Sure,' Dearborn said faintly. 'Sure.' Then, obeying his intuition, he walked back into the living area, gathered up cash and passport and tiptoed out.

He fetched up in a commercial travellers' bed-and-breakfast off the Edgware Road. When he had unpacked, he put in another call to Cody, vowing that if he didn't get through, he would turn himself and his half-formed suppositions over to Byron Field. Cody wasn't available, but Dearborn noted a difference in tone, and this time the voice suggested that if he leave his number, a return call might be forthcoming.

He waited an hour, then called Magda. The warmth of her manner caught him unprepared.

'I was thinking of you this very moment. Lauren was asking when she would see you. Are you still planning to make that trip?'

'In a couple of days – as soon as I finish up my work here.'

'You didn't tell me you'd found a job. I've been wondering what you were doing.'

'Part-time, unpaid research – for that book I told you about.'

'Oh, I'm glad you're going ahead with it.' She hesitated. 'Does your research leave you any time for a social life?'

'You mean women?' Dearborn said. 'Not exactly.'

'Liar,' she said pleasantly, and laughed. 'I know you, John.'

Dearborn swallowed. 'In the circumstance, I'm not sure I have anything to be guilty about.' Suddenly he was fired up with indignation, ready to justify his infidelities, but as he took breath to launch into his defence, he heard a muffled snuffling from the other end. 'Magda?' he said cautiously, 'Why are you crying?'

'It's every woman's right.' She sniffed. 'Sorry, it's all getting on top of me. Nothing turns out as you hope.'

In her voice Dearborn heard the anguish of disappointment, the frustration of someone who thinks they have escaped, only to find that they have run into a different set of bars. And then he knew that his wild accusation on the night of the storm had been right; during their vacation she *had* had an affair with the lawyer whose name he couldn't remember and didn't want to know. She had fled Morocco not just to escape from him, but to pursue an infatuation, and the object of her desires had escaped or proved less enticing close up or impossibly married or . . . The details weren't important at this stage, and it would be wiser not to worry about them later. What was important was that he knew the basic state of her heart just as certainly as she knew about his. They both had each other's number. It was the privilege and the price of marriage.

'Hang in there,' he told her. 'I'll be with you in a couple of days.'

Cody's call came in the dead of the night.

'Thank Christ!' Dearborn exclaimed, fumbling awake.

The connection crackled with Cody's fury. 'I've had that cocksucker Byron Field crawling over my ass because of you. You went against me, John Wesley, sneaked around behind my back, and now I'm telling you our friendship is over.'

'This isn't a social call. This is a crisis.'

'In a pig's ear, cowboy.'

'For God's sake, it's nearly cost me my life. I'm looking into a black hole with something very nasty lurking at the bottom.'

Cody laughed. He sounded unhinged. 'Thus were they defiled with their own works, and went a-whoring with their own inventions.'

Anger squirted through Dearborn. 'Well I know another psalm and it goes like this: "Who is this asshole that darkeneth counsel by words without knowledge?"'

'In your mouth,' Cody roared, 'those words are blasphemy.'

'Blasphemy, shit. Byron has threatened to annex me if I don't turn over what I've found.'

'That fornicator has no authority to piss on my territory.'

'And if he doesn't get me, the Israelis surely will.'

'Traitor! Judas!'

'Are you nuts? Why do you think I've been calling your office all week. What I've got is for your evaluation.'

Cody breathed on this. 'Okay,' he said at last, 'tell me.'

'Not on the phone. Can you come to London?'

'Hell no, I only just got back.'

Dearborn's mouth clenched decisively. 'You'd better set your mind to it, because if you don't come up with something positive by morning, I'm taking a ride to Grosvenor Square.' He slammed down the phone.

Half an hour later Cody rang back. His voice was emotionless. 'You're reserved in the name of Richard Barnes on the afternoon RAM flight to Casa.'

'But the Moroccans have got an exclusion order on me.'

'I fixed it,' Cody said. He hesitated. 'Does anyone know where you are?'

'I'm completely out of sight.'

'Stay there.'

32

'It must be the nomads,' Iseult murmured, squinting at a yellow column of dust over the next horizon.

'Did Pat say if they're tame?' Fox asked.

At the mention of his name, Iseult automatically glanced back towards the white sun.

Fox caught the look. 'He'll show up eventually,' he said, not hiding his impatience. 'Come on, we might make the road tonight.'

'Half an hour,' Iseult pleaded.

'That makes two hours lost,' Fox snapped.

Both of them were on the ragged edge, with no idea of their position, or whether they were going in the right direction. Seeing that Iseult was immovable, Fox lit another cigarette and watched the dust trailing away south. Long before the thirty minutes were up, he flicked his cigarette away and stood. 'Iseult, we're wasting our time.'

'Half an hour's not a lot after what he's done for us.'

'I don't mean that,' Fox said. He laid a hand on her shoulder. 'He's had a whole day to catch us. Either something happened or he's taken another route.' Judging that the alarmist approach was counter-productive, he switched to optimism. 'I bet he's ahead of us, kicking his heels by the road.'

She shrugged off his hand. 'I'll wait.'

'I'm not sure I can afford the gesture,' Fox said with care. He hefted his pack but didn't move. 'I'd much rather we went together.' He gave a high-pitched laugh. 'Who knows what unspeakable things the nomads might do to a lone male? Or,' he added, 'to a female for that matter? I mean, I'm sure you have as much desire to be the sex-slave of a desert vagrant as I have to be a eunuch. Probably much less, if truth be told.'

'You go on,' she said tiredly.

For a moment, indecisive, Fox stood above her. 'Only if you're absolutely sure,' he said. His cheek muscles bunched as he pumped up his resolve. 'Well then, I'll be sloping off. See you this evening – first tent on the right.'

Through half-closed eyes, Iseult watched him leave, almost tiptoeing at first and then breaking into an ungainly stride when he had reached a decent distance. He won't wait, she thought, not caring one way or the other. Faint with hunger and fatigue, she allowed her eyes to close completely, neither awake nor asleep, but suspended in a protective state of semi-consciousness.

It popped like a bubble. The dust was only a faint wisp in the sepia sky and the long empty rises were hardening into their evening shapes. Her predicament engulfed her with a rush. She had left it too late to reach the road, and Fox's childish joke about the nomads had rubbed a nerve. She would have to sleep where she was and go on when daytime revived her courage.

Rooting through her pack, she discovered that Fox had left her only her clothes, sleeping-bag, about a pint of untrustworthy water, some stale scraps of bread and one or two tins.

'Rotten bastard,' she said weakly. A cramp in the pit of her stomach doubled her over and she groaned, knowing that the monthly cycle had come full circle and that she lacked any sanitary provisions.

Sniffing back her tears, she rested her chin on her knees and waited for the sky to darken. Every other minute, without being aware of it and with no expectation of reward, she looked backwards. Cold, she rose and searched for a place to lay out her sleeping-bag.

When she looked again, a rider was approaching out of the blood-red sun. Shielding her eyes, she watched in apprehension, then perplexity, and then tingling recognition.

'Pat?' she said softly, sitting up a little. 'Pat,' she called, scrambling to her feet. Relief flooded her. She broke into a trot, waving and shouting, but he didn't acknowledge her and suddenly she felt foolish gesticulating in the emptiness. She waited silently while he slouched forward and reined in, staring off over her head.

'Where's Fox?' was all he said.

'Gone on,' she muttered, joy quenched. Not wanting him to see her disappointment, she faced south. 'The nomads aren't far ahead,' she said.

'Is Fox dossing down with them?'

'He wants to get to the road.'

'Who doesn't?'

'He's only interested in saving his own skin.'

'Who isn't?' Case said, sliding off the mule.

'I waited,' she said, hungering for the acknowledgement that was due.

He smiled and looked at her properly. 'I told you females were stronger.'

'More biddable – that's what you said. Bitches are more biddable.'

He seemed exhausted. Like a weary combatant conceding an honourable draw, he rested his forehead against hers.

She gasped at the touch. 'You're burning up,' she cried. Drawing back, she was horrified by his appearance. His face was contracted around a core of pain, his eyes narrowed to shards of glass. She put her hand to his hot, damp brow and bit her lip.

'Have you got the first-aid kit?' he mumbled. 'I packed some antibiotics.'

She bit her knuckles. 'Fox took them. What's wrong with you? Where have you been? What happened when we left you? Where did you get the mule?'

'Borrowed it from Laschen.'

'The rifle, too?'

He didn't answer. She seized his hands and his mouth gaped and he buckled forward. He laughed weakly.

His hands were mottled and abscessed; threads of red were creeping up his wrists.

'We have to get you to a doctor,' she whispered.

'That's the general idea.'

They didn't fall in with the nomads that night. In the early hours Case called a rest and insisted she get some sleep, but though she was exhausted she knew that Case wouldn't have stopped if he'd been alone, and when she saw him feel the glands in his armpits and wince, she forced herself up.

'If you can face it, I'm happy to carry on.'

Case lifted his hands to the mule's bridle and let them drop. 'Would you mind steering. My arms are a bit stiff.'

They rode under wheeling constellations, Iseult dozing when the going permitted, and emerged into the light of day to see dust hanging in the sky like the smoke of battle. The way was downhill, through a shallow valley. Ahead they heard a bleating that swelled to a mighty lament, and rounding a corner they found the way blocked by complaining mutton – trickles flowing into streams that broadened into rivers that brimmed into a flood. Iseult saw her first nomad. Mounted on a camel, he seemed to her unreliable eye to be wearing a lounge suit and Ray-Bans.

All morning they continued down the valley. From the entrances of black tents women watched them, their cheekbones smeared with wood-ash against the glare. Small dogs barked at their heels. The valley narrowed and deepened into a gorge harsh with dust and primeval echoes. A camel train heeled past, loaded with chattels and women veiled in black gauze.

With the sun a huge fireball on the escarpment, they funnelled out of the gorge and looked across stony desert to a road straddled by a bellowing oasis – a caravanserai with stockyards and busy trucks ferrying away the nomads' surplus livestock. Iseult and Case dismounted half a mile short.

He removed the bolt from the rifle and buried the parts separately. 'Guns have been in and out of my hands since I arrived in Morocco, but I never have one of the damn things when I need it.' He sat beside her. 'We'll wait until dark. How much cash have we got?'

Turning out their pockets, they counted less than fifty dirhams between them.

'That won't take us far.'

'I've got traveller's cheques,' Iseult said.

'Gold fillings would get you further.'

'Couldn't we sell the mule?'

'Too risky. Besides, I promised Laschen I'd leave it for him to collect.' Case pulled himself up by the mule's reins. 'See if you can scrounge a lift going east.'

Iseult entered the oasis with trepidation, conscious that her sex, race and state of dishevelment were not in her favour.

The acrid smells of dung and grilled meat hung over the encampment. Generators thumped. To one side of the animal mart was a café lit by hissing gas mantles where the drivers were congregated, drinking and playing cards. Their eyes lifted as she entered. To steel herself, she ordered a milkshake made with fresh apples. In the chromed blender she saw her reflection – spiky hair, dust-caked face, red eyes. She went from table to table, but the men looked away, dismissing her with a shake of their hands, as she herself had dismissed beggars in Tangiers. She worked the café without success, and then asked the serving boy for advice. Wiping a glass, he pointed out to the glare around the animal pens.

Fat wholesale meat merchants were hammering out deals with gaunt patriarchs and their formidable wives. Drivers were tendering aggressively for the transport concessions. When the transactions were completed, eager boys drove the sheep towards the trucks.

Carried away by the haggling, the drivers looked right through Iseult. One man pushed her roughly away. Hope flagging, she decided to try the lorry park itself.

She heard footsteps and swung round. Blinded by the light, she saw an arm outstretched to grab. She choked back a cry.

'You want to go to Fez?' a voice said in barely comprehensible French.

Iseult wasn't sure of her bearings. 'Anywhere east,' she said, too eagerly.

The silhouette came forward. Iseult smelt motor-oil and beer; she discerned a ratty face and acquisitive eyes. She stood still while he sidled around her, checking her over with the same avid interest with which the buyers had inspected the livestock. 'I have a friend with me,' she said hurriedly. 'My husband.'

'French?' the driver demanded.

'Irish,' Iseult said gratefully. Several times abroad, she had found that her Celtic connection, with its connotations of cheerful resilience in the face of oppression, had charmed foreigners with no tradition of affection for the English.

The driver poked out his tongue and waggled it obscenely. He said something about French women and their carnal appetites. 'Come,' he said, seizing her elbow. She resisted. 'Come,' he demanded.

Gritting her teeth, Iseult followed him, but instead of heading towards the trucks, he walked into the oasis, into the darkness. The hubbub was left behind, but there were people nearby. Shadows moved between the boles of the palms. She heard female laughter.

She balked. 'This isn't the way.'

He addressed her in impatient Arabic.

'I'm sorry, I don't understand.' Her legs were quaking.

With the back of his hand he stroked her from throat to stomach and growled.

She shied away. 'No, you don't understand. We want to get to Fez. We'll pay you.'

His eyes caught the light. 'One thousand dirhams.'

That was nearly a hundred pounds. 'Too much,' she said.

'One thousand dirhams *each*,' he insisted, thrusting out his hand.

'I can't give it to you now. I have traveller's cheques I can cash in Fez.'

He shouted, stamping the ground, then fell ominously quiet, head pushed forward, arms akimbo. It seemed to Iseult that a furious internal dialogue was raging behind his eyes.

In a gesture inspired by panic she emptied her pack out. Her necklace glinted on the sand. 'There,' she cried, 'that's worth more – ten thousand dirhams at least.' She made her voice wheedling, as if she was trying to entice a fractious child. 'Look, it's beautiful. Your wife will love it.' Tears rolled down her cheeks.

Muttering, he held the necklace to the starlight. 'Not enough,' he said, stuffing it into his pocket. He dropped to his haunches and began rifling her pack. The first item that came to hand was the *djellaba* Case had given her. The driver tossed it aside with a grunt of contempt. Then he found the precious green silk dress and let it ripple through his fingers. Bunching it up, he buried his nose in it. His eyes burned up at her. He stood and looked around. 'Okay,' he said casually. '*Yalla.*'

Thanking God, Iseult stumbled after him, past the stockyards, her eyes hunting for Case, finding him waiting in the gloom beneath the trucks. She signalled that all was well. Suddenly she was proud of herself.

The driver took one look at Case and wiped the air very fast with his hand. '*Malade,*' he said.

'Yes, he's ill,' Iseult agreed.

'*Malade,*' the driver shouted as if she had tried to cheat him. '*Malade.*' He walked off to his truck.

'You promised,' she cried.

The driver glowered, then pushed Case towards the back of his vehicle and pointed up. A restless bleating came from the cargo.

'He can't go in there,' Iseult protested.

'Don't make such a song and dance,' Case said, catching her eye in warning.

He was so feeble he could hardly climb the high sides. Contemptuously, the driver shoved him up and over and then installed himself in the cab, slapping his hands as if to wipe out any contagion or simply in pleasant anticipation of the task ahead. The cab had a sour, feral odour.

With the aplomb of a maestro, the driver got the truck underway, pressing his hand on the horn to scatter stray nomads. On the open highway, he took pride in demonstrating the complete range of channels available on his radio. Despite her misgivings, Iseult couldn't keep from dozing off. Whenever she woke, she found the driver smiling at her. Her jaws ached from the effort of maintaining an agreeable expression.

The next time her eyes snapped open, his hand was on her knee. She pried it off in a way calculated to give the minimum of offence, and he laughed to show that none had been taken and put it back. When she reached for it he snatched it away and shook his finger in mock reprimand. For a mile or two they played this game of catch as catch can before the driver got bored with it and grasped her knee in a grip she couldn't break without escalating her resistance to all-out conflict. Almost too exhausted to care, Iseult allowed it to remain, but when his hand slid up her thigh she tore herself away and pressed herself against her door, out of range. His hand lay palm up, like a dead animal, then it felt behind the seat and drew out her dress. He hung it over the steering-wheel. With his other hand he fumbled open his trousers and began to masturbate.

Disgusted, she looked away to be confronted by his reflection in the window. Every so often he leaned to inhale the perfume from her dress. His breath harshened. The truck weaved as he shuddered to a conclusion. Eyes tight-shut, Iseult prayed that her ordeal was over.

She was thrown forward, banging her head on the windscreen and almost sliding into the footwell. The driver yanked her up by the hair. In his other hand he had a knife. He jabbed the point to her throat and with his other hand switched off the ignition. They were on a straight stretch of desert road, black mountains to one side, the starry sky to the other. Since leaving the oasis, they hadn't encountered a single vehicle.

Holding the blade towards her, the driver rolled down his window and stuck his head out. 'Hey, my friend, you want some tea?' Receiving no answer, he repeated the invitation, loading it with even more geniality. Only the sheep answered him.

Pat must be unconscious, Iseult thought. In a coma. Her heart thudded. Dead.

Smiling good-naturedly, the driver leapt from the cab and peered through the slats. He pounded on them then stepped back, hands on hips. Iseult took the opportunity to undo her own door, but her terror of what would happen if she stayed was outweighed by her fear for Pat and the terror of the consequences of being caught running away.

Losing patience, the driver began to climb hand over hand. Iseult slid across and watched in the wing-mirror, ready to shout a warning. She saw a shape duck from under the truck, heard a yelp and saw the driver falling, landing on his back with a smack. Case was on him, kicking, kicking, kicking.

He wouldn't stop. Iseult tore her eyes away and switched on the radio to full volume and screamed and screamed, her hands over her ears so that her own screams were all she could hear.

The door flew open and Case glared up, his neck corded with anger. 'Turn that bloody racket off.'

In the sudden silence she heard weak groans. 'What have you done to him?' she whispered.

He tossed a leather bag at her. 'Count it.'

Inside were nearly four hundred dirhams in soiled notes.

He made three efforts before he succeeded in climbing into the cab. He rested his head on the steering-wheel. Iseult sagged against her door.

'This is a nightmare,' she said.

They sat in silence at opposite sides of the cab, then Case raised himself up. He looked like a corpse. 'You'll have to drive,' he mumbled.

The gear-shift seemed to have no discernible pattern and the heavy clutch defeated her first attempts, but finally she got the hang of it. They rolled east through moonlit wastes. Her soiled dress lay crumpled at her feet. Lifting it as if her fingers were tongs, she pushed it out of the window. When it was disposed of she felt less awful, but not by much.

'How did you know about him?' she asked.

'I'm beginning to get a feel for the type.'

'He'll go to the police.'

Case gave her a febrile smile.

'You look ghastly,' she said.

He laughed. 'If you don't get a move on, you might have to amputate.'

She was so far gone she couldn't be sure he was joking.

He folded himself up in the corner of the cab, his mouth half open and his eyes half shut. He was breathing very fast, one breath overlapping the next. Dawn was an age away. Iseult blinked determinedly and pressed her foot to the floor, willing the truck onwards. Behind her the sheep bleated their hearts out, sensing that they were consigned for slaughter.

At Case's insistence she pulled off the road to sleep for an hour, but otherwise she drove all night – along the edge of the desert and then up and over the Middle Atlas. Mercifully, they didn't run into any police checks. Because a female trucker would have caused Moroccan eyes to pop, Case took over the wheel before it grew light and drove to the outskirts of Fez. He was still lucid enough to organize the ditching of the truck, overriding Iseult's sentimental plea that they liberate the sheep, but if anything he looked worse by daylight than he had by the glow of the instruments. With some of the stolen cash, they took a taxi into a salubrious downtown quarter, where Iseult cashed most of her cheques. Then they went in search of medical assistance.

Entering the glass and stainless steel environment of a pharmacy was like passing from one world to another. The scents of soaps and perfumes made Iseult reel. The assistant's surgically clean smile of welcome puckered into alarm and she darted into the back.

Warily the pharmacist emerged from his sanctum and inquired if he could be of assistance. Iseult led Case forward and asked if he could give them something for his infected hands.

Frowning, the pharmacist inspected them and then pulled up Case's sleeves. The red lines had spread beyond the elbow. Slowly the pharmacist looked up. 'Your friend has blood poisoning. You must take him to hospital immediately.'

'No fucking hospital,' Case mumbled.

'Can't you prescribe antibiotics?' Iseult begged.

The pharmacist bridled at such a feckless attitude. 'This man is very sick. He must go to hospital.'

'I want a doctor to examine him.'

For a long time he stared at her then he scribbled an address on his pad. She took the opportunity to stock up on items of personal hygiene and beauty care. On top of her other purchases, the pharmacist placed a bottle which she hadn't asked for. Outside she read the label. It was lice lotion. Behind his plate-glass window the pharmacist stood with his arms crossed.

A taxi drove them to the doctor's surgery. Three other women waited, but the receptionist took one look at Case and hurried him in for examination. The doctor, bearded and middle-aged, with eyes magnified behind spectacles like bottle glass, pronounced the same diagnosis as the pharmacist.

'We're flying back to London tomorrow,' Iseult told him. 'He can go to hospital there.'

'He can't fly in his condition. I forbid it.'

'The day after tomorrow. Can't you give him something?' She waved money.

Her desperation made him suspicious. He searched her face, then shrugged.

He called in a nurse who prepared a fearsome-looking syringe. The doctor would not allow Iseult to stay to watch the injection.

In the waiting-room she fell asleep. The doctor came out alone and sat beside her.

'Where is he?'

'He fainted,' the doctor said. He sat down beside her. 'If the infection doesn't respond in twenty-four hours, you must take him to hospital. If you don't, there is a possibility he will die. In my judgement, he *will* die. Do you understand?'

'Yes.'

'*Bien*. Which hotel are you staying in?'

'We've only just arrived in town. We've been in the mountains – trekking.'

He gave her an oblique look. Case leaned in the door, pale as paper, massaging his buttocks.

The doctor stood. 'A hotel would not want to take responsibility for your friend. I have a small apartment which is empty. You are welcome to stay until your friend has recovered.'

He looked at her again, with solicitude, with kindness. It was all too much for Iseult. He made her lie down and gave her a check-up. He said she was anaemic and needed a rest.

Throughout the morning and afternoon, Case's fever stayed at danger level, and in the evening he was delirious. Most of what he said was incoherent babbling, but some of it wasn't. The doctor called on his way home, took Case's pulse and temperature and left looking grave, having told Iseult that if there was no improvement by morning, the patient would have to be removed to intensive care.

Iseult napped on a couch beside him. About three she woke and realized that his breathing was quieter and less rapid. Tiptoeing out for a drink of water, she sensed his eyes following her. She leaned over him and wiped his brow.

'How do you feel?'

'Like I'm having an out-of-body experience. Like I'm dead, basically.'

His temperature had fallen by two degrees. The tracks in his arms had faded and the swollen glands were going down. He had no idea where he was. Before dawn he fell into healthy sleep and by mid-morning, when he was still out to the world, Iseult left him to replenish her wardrobe and rehabilitate what remained of her hair. She returned to find Case standing in jeans before the bathroom mirror, getting reacquainted with himself. His ribs were like wash-boards. He began to dress.

'Where do you think you're going?'

'Collect my bounty.'

The row that followed left Case so groggy that when the good doctor called in on his way to work, he was unable to counter his professional fury and fell back in surrender, insisting in defiance of medical advice that he was hitting the road first thing in the morning. In minutes he was unconscious.

Iseult sat at the window and smoked, her distress about Pat effortlessly transmuted into concern for Cathal.

33

Lights were beginning to sprinkle the coastal strip as the Boeing banked for its descent into Casa. Strapped into his seat, Dearborn jumped when the glossy stewardess offered him a boiled sweet to take the pressure off his ears. 'Everything's going to be fine,' she murmured, mistaking his rigor for dread of air disaster.

Dearborn unlocked his jaw. Sure it was, he told himself. In an hour or two he would have discharged his responsibility and be at peace. He watched the lights sliding under the wing and imagined Cody's reaction – the foul-mouthed growling giving way to grunting respect. Yes, everything was going to be just fine.

A passenger squealed as the plane pitched heavily on to the runway. Dearborn waited until the aircraft was nearly empty before making his way to the door. He breathed tepid air saturated with rain and aviation fuel.

At the bottom of the landing steps a conservatively dressed young Moroccan cut him out of the herd. *'Marhaba,'* he murmured. 'I am Allal. Mr Cody sent me.'

Dearborn eyed the other passengers being shepherded on to a waiting bus. 'I was expecting one of the embassy drivers.'

'Officially, you are not permitted to enter Morocco,' Allal said apologetically. 'Procedures to countermand the ban would have taken several days.' He had to raise his voice to be heard above the rumble of a taxiing 747. 'Colonel Douaz took the appropriate steps.'

'Colonel Douaz knows I'm in Morocco?'

'Naturally.'

'Dammit,' Dearborn fumed. 'That isn't what I arranged.'

Allal looked at him, his face deadpan.

Seething, Dearborn turned away. Out on the tarmac apron the 747 shook under the build-up of thrust. Damn, he swore, swallowing the unpalatable fact. Since he was on Immigration's shit list, Cody would have had no option but to enlist the assistance of Douaz, who obviously would insist on being an active party to the debriefing. As the eloquence of Allal's silence indicated, it was Colonel Douaz's country.

Resigned now to the inevitable, consoling himself with the prospect of opening a few cracks in the colonel's smooth façade, Dearborn faced Allal and cupped his hands to his mouth. 'Well, I'm glad you're taking it seriously,' he shouted.

It was a long walk across the tarmac. Allal made polite conversation about the flight and the weather in London. 'Mr Cody said you contacted the London embassy. Do they know you're in Morocco?'

'No,' Dearborn said. 'No one.'

Bypassing the passenger terminal, Allal led Dearborn through a freight hangar and across a garishly lit compound fenced with razor wire. A soldier opened a barrier in the perimeter and saluted them as they passed into a loading area, where a Peugeot was waiting, the driver leaning on the roof. He sprang to open the rear door.

'Please,' Allal said, showing Dearborn into his seat. He took his place beside the driver. The car cowered on its suspension as the 747 lifted off, lumbering overhead like a flying apartment block. It was the New York flight, and seeing faces at the window, Dearborn thought of Magda. It occurred to him that perhaps he had gained more from the separation than she had, and that he could afford to be magnanimous.

In the car Allal lost interest in him. They turned on to the Rabat road, following the same route that Dearborn had taken on the day Cody had summoned him. He rehearsed his story until fatigue dragged down his eyelids.

When he opened them again, he became aware that the

traffic had thinned. He peered back through the rear screen and rubbed his eyes. 'You missed the turn-off,' he said, and as he said it, he had the disconcerting notion that everything that was happening or was about to happen had happened before.

'We are on the right road,' Allal said.

'Are we meeting Cody at his club?'

'We are going to Fez.'

Dearborn leaned forward on the back of Allal's seat. 'What's Cody doing in Fez?'

'Colonel Douaz lives there.'

Again the level stare deflated Dearborn's unease. He closed his eyes again. It would be a three-hour drive.

The squeak of wipers cut short a fretful dream. In the headlights of oncoming cars fat raindrops spread on the glass like snow crystals. It had gone ten. He felt frowsy, his mouth badly used. He ran his tongue over his teeth. 'Have we passed Meknès?' he asked.

Allal nodded and held up one finger. 'Not far.'

The rain eased off on the approach. Dearborn did not know Fez well, but it seemed to him the most mysterious, the slowest and the least-changed of Morocco's cities – a snail curled in its shell.

Idly he wondered what kind of establishment Douaz maintained. From experience of other high-ranking Moroccan officials, he guessed it would be a ranch-style villa with a Roman pool and a Mercedes in the carport. The colonel would probably also own a villa in Azrou for the skiing, and rent a beach cottage near Mohammedia to escape the heat of summer.

Dearborn was obliged to revise his guess as they left the suburbs behind and entered the massy bulk of the city. A purpose-built apartment then, interior-designed to the nth degree, loaded with domestic gadgetry bought by the colonel's wife on her annual pilgrimage to Paris. She would be beautiful, but undoubtedly the colonel would have a mistress, whom he would tend with consummate *savoir-faire*.

The possibility that the wife might also have a lover exercised Dearborn's imagination for a time.

His musing gave way to dry-mouthed anticipation as they reached the downtown district. They crossed it at a tangent and went on, leaving the neon and the crowds behind. Now they were on a road flanked by stalls of corrugated iron, doing brisk trade after the rain. The shacks petered out at a site flattened for development. Beyond, grim tenements reared. The car banged into a pothole and the driver grunted. He navigated between mounds of rubble.

A faint foreboding sneaked into Dearborn's mind. They were in a slum. The headlights picked out grubby children naked from the waist down baling out puddles with cans. Each street resembled the one that had gone before, except that it was a little narrower, and as the district closed in on him, Dearborn had the sensation that the alleys radiated from a centre, shrinking to some claustrophobic and ancient core. He stiffened and shifted to the edge of his seat.

'I thought we were going to the colonel's home.'

'Soon we will be there.'

Dearborn clamped his tongue for another minute, but when they nosed into an alley barely wide enough to admit the car, his anxiety couldn't be stilled. 'Hey,' he said.

'Soon.'

Sweat had started in Dearborn's armpits. The Peugeot went forward at walking pace. The rain had become a thin mist and there were few people about. Those whom they encountered pressed close to the walls and hid their faces from the light.

The driver stopped. No one moved. Dearborn's stomach cramped up. 'Colonel Douaz doesn't live here.'

'Pardon?'

'You told me you were taking me to his home.'

'But yes. His family has resided in this quarter for six centuries.' Allal opened Dearborn's door and beckoned him out. The driver remained at the wheel.

Dearborn stepped into stench and darkness. The rain must

have flooded the sewers. The houses were turned in on themselves, their outer walls blank and windowless, like the tombs of a necropolis. The night sky seemed to be part of another world. The noise of the city was a faint whisper, like a distant sea.

'Come.'

They squelched down the lane, Allal solicitously showing Dearborn where puddles were to be avoided. Imminent menace seemed to surround him.

'What!' he yelped as Allal touched his arm.

'We are here,' Allal said, and loudly rapped on a studded door set into a wall.

An ancient watchman showed his face. He was dressed from a bygone era, a dagger in his belt and a kerosene lantern held high in his hand. Having satisfied himself as to the callers' identity, he ushered them into a spacious courtyard smelling of wet earth and honeysuckle. Carriage lamps cast soft shadows in a colonnaded arcade that ran round three sides of the patio. A mule stamped in its stall. The building was faced in white stucco, with corbelled windows and balconies with wrought-iron railings in the old Moorish style. Dearborn gave an appreciative sigh. The building was a medieval treasure. Like a Medici prince, Colonel Douaz lived in a palace completely unsuspected from outside.

A grilled gateway gave access to the main door, where the servant waited until Dearborn took off his brogues and put on a pair of *babouches*. The sight of a furled umbrella was oddly reassuring. Allal had removed himself. The retainer escorted Dearborn down a passage, constantly looking back as if he feared his guest would disappear between steps, and halted at double doors painted with a faded motif of interlocking vines in red and gold. Putting his ear close to the door, the servant gave the lightest of knocks, then softly swung it open and ushered Dearborn over the threshold.

He was in a room paved with tiles so old that the ceramic glaze had been partially worn away. Heavy damask curtains opened on to a balcony. Two divans flanked a sandalwood coffee-table , and exquisite Berber rugs decorated the walls, but the rest of the furniture was up-to-the-minute Italian, in impeccable taste. A television and video recorder occupied one corner.

'Mr Cody?' Dearborn said, turning, but the retainer had gone.

Too keyed-up to sit, Dearborn paced the room. Near the door hung some antique photographs of men on white horses, armed for a tribal gathering. One of them carried a hooded falcon on his wrist. They must have been taken early in the French conquest. Examining them, Dearborn recognized a family likeness – the long features and aristocratic eyes. The eyes seemed sad with the knowledge that the future held no place for them. There was one blurry photo that took some interpreting. It appeared to show a cage hanging from a city gate, a crowd under it, the majority gawping up, a few bystanders shiftily returning the unblinking stare of the old box Brownie.

Parting the curtains, Dearborn stepped on to the balcony. He smelt flowers bruised by the downpour, rotted straw and human waste. Two pencil-slim minarets pierced the faintly breathing membrane above the city. Standing there was like looking out from one century to the next.

Somewhere children laughed. Hearing footsteps tripping downstairs, Dearborn hurried inside and sat down. A moment later he jumped up as Douaz entered.

The colonel wore a dove-grey silk *djellaba* over city trousers and a white shirt with a neatly knotted tie. 'Forgive me,' he said. 'The rain woke my children and they couldn't go back to sleep. They are at a mischievous age.' He feigned a gesture of helplessness. 'I am like clay in their hands.'

Dearborn found it hard to believe that even the most delinquent juvenile could resist the colonel's effortless authority. Standing before him, he felt like a catalogue of Western deficiencies. 'How many children do you have?' he asked.

'Three boys, blessings be to Allah.'

'Blessings indeed. I have only one – a little girl.' Dearborn was aware that he had spoken apologetically, hanging a question mark over his virility.

'You will have others,' Douaz said, *'insh'allah.'*

'My wife has decided otherwise,' Dearborn confessed, completing the sketch of a man sadly wanting.

Douaz looked at him with concern. 'You are tired after your journey. You haven't eaten.'

'I'm not hungry. Perhaps some tea.'

'I have already ordered it,' Douaz said, gesturing for Dearborn to be seated.

Dearborn perched at the edge of the divan. 'Where is Cody?' he inquired with as much nonchalance as he could summon.

'He is in Rabat.'

Dearborn was stupefied. 'But I was told he was with you.'

'Surely not,' Douaz said, frowning at the thought that his subordinates might have misrepresented the truth.

'Whatever they said, I insist on seeing him.'

Douaz rode the insolence with gentlemanly ease. 'Doctor Dearborn, if a Russian criminal was murdered in Washington, would you let the KGB investigate his death?'

Dearborn twisted under the force of his dismay. 'I expect we would co-operate with them.'

'That is what we are doing. I am co-operating fully with your American representatives – or, to be more accurate . . .' the colonel left a loaded pause '. . . they are co-operating with me.'

The fossil retainer entered with water, soap and hot towels. The touch of the warm compress was blissful, but reminded Dearborn how much the trials of the last few weeks had taken out of him.

An aged maid brought tea and and a plate of tiny cakes. In silence, Douaz poured two glasses.

'Bismillah.'

'Bismillah,' Dearborn echoed. He sipped the tea without tasting it. 'Nevertheless,' he said, deciding not to give in, 'Cody isn't present and that causes a problem.'

Douaz offered him another sweetmeat. 'Mr Cody is ill. Soon after you called him, he succumbed to an unpleasant gastric disorder which he contracted in Liberia. Unfortunately there was no opportunity to inform you, but tomorrow you will be able to visit him. I have booked you a suite at the Hotel Palais Jamais.'

'Then,' Dearborn said with finality, bracing himself to rise, 'let us postpone our discussion until tomorrow.'

Douaz was unperturbed. 'Mr Cody said the matter couldn't wait. He told me that your life had been threatened. I took considerable trouble organizing your entry.'

'I'm grateful, but since what I have to say involves United States' interests, I'm unable to speak freely in the absence of a witness from Cody's department.'

A damp breeze stirred the drapes at the balcony, wafting ripe odours into the room. Douaz turned to face the smell. 'It is surprising, is it not, that Fez, the city at the heart of Morocco, has no diplomatic community beyond a few trade officials. I myself regret that Fez was not chosen as the capital, but of course the decision was not entirely within Moroccan hands.' Abandoning his reflections, he leaned towards Dearborn. 'You are agitated, Doctor. Perhaps I should leave you for an hour.'

'Colonel, a formal meeting with a senior member of the Moroccan security services is not what I expected. My intention was to speak off-the-record to an old friend.'

'But this conversation *is* informal. You are a guest in my house.' Douaz gave a doleful sigh. 'I see that I must take you into my confidence before you will allow me into yours.' He offered the dish of cakes. 'Please,' he said, 'eat.'

Dearborn declined emphatically.

'As the last few weeks have shown,' Douaz said, popping an almond pastry into his mouth, 'Morocco is not immune to political strife. As a committed supporter of the broader democratization of government, I can say frankly that we have some way to go before we attain the freedoms you enjoy. But I think you will agree that my country occupies a most favoured position, situated at the crossroads of Europe and Africa, its faith founded in the east, its eyes facing west. It is a bridge between the old world and the new.'

'It is a lion among countries,' Dearborn said, deploying a phrase he had picked up from the Minister of Tourism.

'A neutral lion,' Douaz amended.

Dearborn shifted his posture, determined not to sit still for a load of bullshit. 'I wish I'd been allowed to get to know it better.'

Douaz raised his hand as if Dearborn had touched the nub of the matter. 'The reasons for your expulsion will soon be made clear.' He opened a silver case, took out a cigarette and fitted it into a holder. 'It has long been the endeavour of His Majesty to bring about a reconciliation between the Palestinian and Israeli nations.'

'His unceasing efforts in that regard are well-known and warmly appreciated.'

'As you say – unceasing,' Douaz said. He puffed elegantly on his cigarette. 'In three weeks, His Majesty will host an informal meeting of Middle East leaders to discuss the Palestinian issue. There is no agenda, no preconditions. The participants will arrive carrying only goodwill.'

You bastard, Cody, Dearborn thought, half admiringly. 'I wish the initiative the success it deserves.'

'And yet you look sceptical.'

'It isn't the first time that such talks have been held under His Majesty's auspices.'

'The difference, this time, is that all interested parties will be represented.'

'All?' Dearborn said. The shockwave hit him. 'Including the Israelis?' He put down his glass. 'You're saying that the Israelis are meeting the Palestinians in Morocco.'

Douaz shrugged modestly. 'You cannot expect me to confirm that. All I will say is that the omens are propitious.'

'Wow,' Dearborn said, groggy with the news, 'that is one hell of a coup.' He reached over and shook Douaz's hand. 'My congratulations.'

The colonel accepted them gracefully. 'Now to return to your own position. An Israeli is murdered in Marrakech and a former CIA officer with a long career in the Middle East is apprehended by the victim. Yes, yes,' Douaz said as Dearborn opened his mouth, 'evil luck, you say, and I can attest to the truth of that, but you have lived in Islamic society long enough to know that bad fortune in our culture is not regarded as a matter of chance. The incident, if it had been broadcast, could have clouded the atmosphere of the talks and may even have made some of the parties question the wisdom of attending. I speak, of course, as the officer in charge of the security arrangements.' He settled back on his seat. 'I think now you understand why we thought it desirable that you leave Morocco.'

'I understand very well, and in your position I would probably have done the same. I only wish that Cody could have taken me into his confidence.'

'Doctor Dearborn, it was not his secret to give away.'

Dearborn hesitated. 'I feel the same way about what I have learned.'

Douaz frowned and placed his fingertips to his chest. 'But *your* secrets concern Morocco, yes?'

'I believe so,' Dearborn said. 'Yes.'

'Therefore they rightfully belong to me.'

Dearborn was in half a dozen minds. 'Look,' he blurted, 'I haven't uncovered conclusive evidence. All I have is a chain of names and events with a lot of links missing, but what I've got is damned sinister.' His voice trailed away.

'Tell me. Let us see if, together, we can piece together this chain.'

And Dearborn, succumbing to the colonel's soothing voice, to his own desperate need to confide, began. Unburdening himself was like having an abscess lanced, and yet when he had finished he felt flat. The pay-off just wasn't there. He began to gloss, justifying some of his suppositions and adding others. Diplomatic constraints obliged him to slide over Zwy Gur's role.

Douaz waved him into silence. 'Do you intend to continue your investigation?'

Dearborn laughed vigorously. 'I know my limitations, colonel, and I've already overstepped them.' He gave another gusty laugh.

Douaz nodded distractedly. He held up one finger on each hand and steered them about as if he was imagining the protagonists and trying to assign them to their rightful positions. 'Among the links that are absent are the ones connecting Lova Hazan, Rafiq Saad and Adnan al-Jalil.'

'As to the first two individuals, the circumstantial evidence is overwhelming. In respect of Saad and al-Jalil, they are bound by ties of blood.'

'But not by country or religion or ideology. There can be no crime without motivation, and that crucial element is missing. What you have found is disturbing, but it does not constitute proof of any political activity aimed against Morocco.'

'The proof is there, I'm certain, but that's for you to establish.'

Douaz made a steeple of his fingers and slowly nodded at Dearborn over them. 'There *is* a common factor – drugs. When the Syrians occupied the Bekaa valley, they took over the hashish fields. The President's own brother has been implicated in trafficking, and it would be entirely logical for Adnan to take advantage of his relation's connections in Europe to organize the distribution and sale of the hashish crop under his control. The thief Lova Hazan probably bought drugs from that source when he was stationed in Lebanon.'

'Don't overlook his meeting with the Mossad agent in Latin America.'

'A runner of guns, a mercenary, a Zionist rogue. What else but money would make allies of such people?' Douaz's voice sharpened. 'I'm sorry, you are not listening.'

'No, wait.' Dearborn was quaking with excitement. 'In three weeks the PLO, the Israelis, and . . .' Dearborn looked to Douaz '. . . the Syrians I presume, will be meeting here to discuss a resolution of the Palestinian crisis.'

'Yes, Doctor,' Douaz said icily, 'you presume.'

'Lova Hazan,' Dearborn said, counting him off on his thumb, 'an Israeli known to have contacts with Israeli intelligence. Adnan al-Jalil, a Syrian PLO commander whose antipathy towards the state of Israel is well-documented.'

Douaz appeared to be having difficulty tracking the line of thought.

In triumph, Dearborn counted off another finger. 'Rafiq Saad, a cut-price Khashoggi with contacts among the Arabic leadership, including your own royal family.'

The colonel's face paled in anger.

'I'm only bouncing ideas around,' Dearborn said. 'Me and Cody used to do it all the time.'

Douaz seemed fascinated as well as angry. 'Go on,' he insisted. 'Bounce some more of these ideas.'

'Suppose,' Dearborn began cautiously, 'that someone – not necessarily Rafiq Saad,' he added quickly, 'knew of the forthcoming conference in Morocco. Suppose he passed on this information to Adnan al-Jalil or another hardline opponent of Israel.' Inspiration blinded Dearborn. 'Or suppose that the recipient of the information was in fact an Israeli right-winger equally determined to thwart any rapprochement between Israel and the Palestinians.'

'Lova Hazan?' Douaz said sarcastically.

'The Mossad agent he met in Honduras. Lova Hazan could have been the go-between.'

Douaz rocked back in relief. 'Conjecture, all conjecture.' He wagged his finger playfully. 'Be careful, you will give me bad dreams.'

His derision brought Dearborn to earth. 'It would help if we could trace Fox or Valentine,' he muttered.

'More smugglers of drugs,' the colonel said gaily.

'Lova Hazan was in partnership with Fox. Presumably he bought his way in. Find out where the money came from and the final link might be established.'

Douaz looked dubious. 'We have followed every step the Israeli made during the three days he was in Morocco.

He never met either of these Englishmen. And why is that?' Douaz opened his hands. 'Because they are not in Morocco.'

'However,' Dearborn said, 'I have firm evidence that the man Low entered Morocco three weeks ago.'

'A common criminal; I do not concern myself with common criminals.'

'But he obviously knows something about Lova Hazan's death. Why else would he come here?'

Douaz passed his hand over his eyes and brooded, then coming to a decision, he smiled at Dearborn, placed his hands on his knees and sprang to his feet. 'We will continue in the morning. There is a lot to be checked, much to organize.'

Reluctantly, Dearborn stood. Ideas were still leap-frogging through his mind. Douaz stood at the door, waiting. Dearborn took a last look at the room. 'Your house is beautiful,' he said. 'It's a privilege to have seen it.'

Douaz bowed.

'When I was young,' Dearborn said, 'I imagined living in such a house.'

'When I was young, I dreamed of living on a Wild West ranch.' Douaz smiled at the ludicrous ambitions of youth. 'I wanted to be a cowboy.'

Dearborn lingered in front of the pictures. 'Your family,' he said.

Douaz nodded. Observing Dearborn's interest in the photo of the cage suspended from the city gate, he said: 'That is my great-grandfather, a contender in the struggle to unite the kingdom.' Douaz stared at it for a time, then shrugged. 'We are cruel to those who fail to win power.' He stuck out his hand, Western fashion. 'Goodbye, Doctor, you are a brave man, but . . .' he gave Dearborn's chest a playful prod '. . . too imaginative, I think.'

He showed Dearborn out to the waiting car and waved him off. Busy trying to formulate a coherent structure from what Douaz had told him, Dearborn barely noticed that his escort had been increased to three. The new arrival was sitting beside the driver, while Allal had taken a seat in the back.

The King of Morocco was trying to broker a Middle East peace agreement. There would be many on all sides who would want to blow it out of the water. An alliance between them was a possibility, but the colonel had dismissed that hypothesis with contempt. Well, the colonel didn't know everything and he would obviously be protective of his ruler's brainchild, but that still left the question of ways and means. Lova Hazan had been killed in Morocco, suggesting local involvement. In Dearborn's mind the recent unrest took on a more sinister aspect. Provoke enough trouble at home, and grand diplomatic ventures might have to be postponed or even abandoned.

The rickety edifice he was piling up broke under its own weight. He yawned. Better wait and see what Cody had to say.

It dawned on him that they had been driving for some time. A *bidonville* sprawled to one side, but the city was falling away to the right. He glanced at Allal.

The driver took a left. The *bidonville* was behind them and now open country lay ahead.

'What kind of crazy route is this?'

'A short-cut.'

A moped had come up behind. '*Attention*,' Allal murmured.

The passenger in front turned and grunted. The light from the motorbike slid across his face. A moment later it was eclipsed, but the countenance had imprinted itself on Dearborn's memory. A slow chill spread over his neck. 'I know you,' he said, his tongue large and dry in his mouth.

'*Oui?*' the man grunted.

Dearborn licked his lips. 'You're the man in the alley.'

The man didn't answer.

Behind veils of fearful incomprehension, Dearborn discerned the threads of an inexorable and awful logic. Douaz had been in Marrakech the day the Israeli was murdered;

his underling had been standing at the very spot where Lova Hazan had died. But why? Why?

Wildly he glanced at Allal, who slid a hand under his jacket and brought out a pistol. *'Douce,'* he murmured.

Dearborn sat still, but inside he was sick with terror. 'Where are you taking me?'

Finding a gap, the motorbike overtook, the pillion passenger raising a contemptuous finger in passing.

Allal tensed and touched the driver on the shoulder. The car swung right. They were off the tarmac now, proceeding very slowly. Ahead was the ragged outline of a low hill. Still idling forward, the driver switched off the lights.

Dearborn lunged for the door, but Allal was alert to the move and held him. The stranger ran round the car and dragged him out. The stink of wet burning garbage pinched his nostrils. Somewhere a cur was yapping.

They grin like dogs and run about the city, Dearborn thought.

Allal pushed him towards the hill. Disabled by fear, he had no control over his legs, but stumbled on in brutish obedience to the Moroccan's prods. The hill loomed. It was a garbage dump. Mist rose from the piles like a miasma. Fires were burning within the mass, and he could smell singeing wool and rubber. 'No,' he pleaded.

A final push impelled him into the dump. Too shocked to comprehend what was happening, he shuffled forward, more concerned by what he was treading in than anything else. A mound of rubbish blocked his way. He tripped and cut his hand on jagged metal. I'm going to need a tetanus shot, he thought.

The pile in front of him was suddenly illuminated. From among the layers of rags and cans protruded a doorless white fridge, a rat standing on its hind legs inside, its eyes gleaming back at the light. Turning, Dearborn saw the headlights of the Peugeot flash lazily. Allal and the stranger were frozen in a guilty attitude.

Another biblical quotation fleeted across Dearborn's mind.

'Let them perish through their own imaginations.' A gust of incredulous anger for Cody shook him, and then, with the icy jolt of revelation came the knowledge that they were going to kill him – that no appeal to justice, no manoeuvres, no exercise of willpower could save him.

'Better check,' he heard Allal say softly. The stranger argued. Still peering towards the place where they had left the car and driver, Allal gave him a nervous push.

Cats squawled over carrion. Imagining what he would look like by dawn, Dearborn groaned. Angrily Allal shook him into silence.

They waited. Dearborn thought of bodies seen at dawn in Beirut – the night crop.

Allal tensed and pulled him closer. 'Abdselam?' he said softly, seeking reassurance. He held Dearborn very tight and shifted from foot to foot.

Footsteps were running their way. 'Abdselam?' Allal said, a little more sharply. He raised his gun.

The footsteps slowed. Dearborn heard panting, and then an out-of-breath voice said: 'The colonel wants him brought back.'

Dearborn swayed in Allal's grasp. Oh dear God, thank you, he prayed.

Dragging Dearborn down with him, Allal squatted so that their outlines were lost against the dump. The Moroccan turned his face slightly away from the approaching footfalls so that he could hear better. His eyes were distended in concentration.

'Allal?' a voice whispered. 'What are you doing? Where's the American?'

Allal muttered an imprecation. Dearborn thought he saw a shape coagulating in the darkness.

'Stop!' Allal shouted.

Light burst in Dearborn's face, and at almost the same instant Allal's gun went off next to his ear, deafening him to a shouted command. Allal wrenched him. 'Get down!' someone shouted.

Dearborn was already on his side. Allal was shooting over his head. The banging ceased and Allal was scrabbling away up the heap of garbage and Dearborn became conscious of another noise – a subdued, almost apologetic *brrrp*. After a few seconds all commotion stopped. The light had gone off.

Dearborn became aware that figures stood above him. He recognized Esther and he tried to smile at her, but she went straight past without looking. Natti knelt and peered into his face, then slipped back into the dark. Another shape materialized.

'If we shot you, Doctor, you have only yourself to blame.'

'My hand's gashed.'

Zwy Gur hauled him up and began propelling him to the car. He stopped and swung him round like a sack. 'Did Lova Hazan sound like that?'

Sprawled on the garbage, Allal was whispering fierce encouragement to himself.

Only a part of Dearborn's mind attended to the question. 'Yes.'

'Tell me again what he said.'

'I've forgotten.'

'Nine! He said nine!'

'Yes.'

Zwy Gur shook him. 'And then something else.'

Dearborn's mouth opened and shut, but no words came.

Zwy Gur slapped him on the back. 'Something else!'

'Call him,' Dearborn gasped.

'Again!'

'Call him.'

'Again!'

Dearborn's mouth flooded with saliva. 'Thassall.'

Zwy Gur rattled the teeth in his head. 'Lova Hazan was dying,' he shouted, 'choking on his own blood. Say it again.'

'Carrim,' Dearborn said.

'Again! Look at him this time. Imagine it's Lova Hazan. Imagine you're back in the alley.'

All Dearborn could see of Allal was the restless whites of

his eyes. 'Carrim,' he groaned, his throat filled with mint tea and almond cake. He pitched forward and retched. 'Oh God, please,' he moaned, suspended in Zwy Gur's grasp. He looked up, whipped. 'Can we go, please? I want to go now.'

Zwy Gur nodded at Esther who, stepping forward, held the pistol in both hands and shot Allal through the head. The way the Moroccan relaxed gave the impression that he welcomed the release.

He had told the Israelis everything he knew, suspected or imagined, but his mind couldn't find rest. It was like a partly run-down clockwork mechanism; the slightest nudge set it whirring again.

In front, Zwy Gur was conversing softly with Natti. Beside Dearborn, Esther kept a check on the road behind. They had switched cars once. The radio was on, tuned to the police frequency.

'Carrim,' Dearborn said, watching the darkness rushing by. 'Lova Hazan was trying to say sicarrim.'

Nobody paid any attention.

'Greater Israel freaks,' Dearborn said, 'false prophets who claim that the Messianic age is just around the corner. If a lunatic like Meir Kahane can win election to the Knesset, imagine the kind of places where sicarrim supporters turn up. They're probably in every ministry, every branch of security.'

'Get some rest,' Esther said tiredly.

'The Mossad man Lova Hazan met in Honduras was sicarrim.'

'Let it go,' Esther snapped.

'It's alright,' Zwy Gur told her. 'He's only talking in his sleep.'

'He sent Lova Hazan to meet Douaz. Afterwards, in that Marrakech alley – well, Lova Hazan couldn't believe anyone could have recognized him after all those years. He thought sicarrim had decided to dispose of him.'

Zwy Gur chuckled. 'Notice how his mind works by leaps and

bounds.' He half-turned. 'But why Douaz? He's not a disciple of the Palestinian cause; he's no friend of Israel. What's in it for him?'

Dearborn leaned his head back on his seat and shut his eyes. He saw a cage suspended above a mob. 'Douaz is heir to a noble Fez family who were in contention for the leadership until the French arrived. As far as Douaz is concerned, the king is a desert upstart.'

Zwy Gur nodded approvingly. 'It's rumoured that a Fez-based religious fraternity is behind the unrest. Well, I can confirm those rumours. Among its adherents are a group of middle-class army officers who want democracy extended in Morocco. We suspect that Douaz is a member.'

Dearborn's flesh thrilled. 'A coup?'

Zwy Gur applauded softly.

Suddenly, Dearborn was appalled by where his speculations had led. 'A handful of high-minded military aren't going to overthrow the whole apparatus of government.'

'A coup is like a judo throw, John, where the weight of the government is turned against it; one calculated heave while the opponent is off balance, and down he topples.' Zwy Gur's face was half-outlined by the glow from the instrument display. 'Douaz is in charge of the security arrangements for the conference. He knows every detail of the programme. Very well, let us imagine the worst. Let us imagine that Douaz has passed on this precise information to people who arrange to have the king assassinated as he sits across a table from representatives of the PLO and Israel. Better still, kill the Israelis as well. But it doesn't matter if the attempt succeeds. The outrage and sense of betrayal felt by the Moroccans would express itself in the most violent civil disorder. The army would be compelled to step in, as they have been tempted to do in the past.'

'But the Americans wouldn't allow it.'

'That's what you said about Iraq, Greece and half a dozen other countries.' Zwy Gur sighed. 'A coup isn't a revolution, John; it's a seizure of power from within the existing system.

I expect you'd find it possible to accommodate the change of leadership.' Zwy Gur stretched. 'I speak hypothetically, you understand. There will be no assassination because there will be no conference.'

An unpleasant conjecture wormed into Dearborn's mind. Zwy Gur might not be on the extreme fringe of the Israeli right, but his politics were firmly planted in that direction. He would shed no tears over the nonfulfilment of the king's dream. Dearborn opened his mouth to voice the suspicion, but then thought better of it. 'What will happen to the colonel?' he asked.

'I expect he'll fall on his sword,' Zwy Gur said. He yawned. 'Shut up now, Doctor.'

For a moment Dearborn felt a twinge of pity. 'Fuck him,' he said. 'All I want to know is why Cody dumped me.'

Zwy Gur heaved himself round in his seat. 'Why don't you ask him?'

34

A falcon leaned on a thermal above the Wounded Boar, pivoted and fell at a stroke, disappearing into the scenery. The afternoon sky was two-tone indigo, the woods splashed with autumn tints.

Iseult stood at Case's side, a small but conclusive distance between them. They were like two travellers who, having fallen into intimacy on a long journey, adjust their dress and grow awkward as their destination nears and they prepare to resume their separate ways.

In no hurry to get it over with, Case took another look at the Wounded Boar. His fever had knocked the stuffing out of him, leaving him with the feeling that his moment of opportunity had passed and that the initiative lay in other hands. He tried to recover impetus. 'Let's get it done.'

Iseult reined him in with the lightest of touches. 'I'm holding you to your word, Pat.'

'I don't know what word you mean,' Case muttered.

She parried his gaze. 'Cathal.'

The name hung between them.

'We don't know if he's there.'

'But if he is . . .?'

Out of the welter of emotions, vengefulness gained the upper hand. 'Then he gets what's due to him.'

'You owe me your life,' Iseult said. 'Yours for Cathal's. It cancels out.'

'I'd have managed somehow,' Case mumbled. Gratitude, being beholden, was not easy to cope with.

'If you won't do it for me,' Iseult said, 'then for the sake of the woman who saved you from drowning.'

Puzzled, he studied her. He was getting used to the changed shape of her face without its dark frame. Despite the days under fierce sun, her complexion remained weirdly pale, the whiteness glowing beneath the skin.

'What will you do afterwards?' he asked.

She sunk her head into her shoulders and shivered. 'Go home and shut the door.'

A strange sensation welled up from his chest, a sensation so physical it felt like drowning. He loved her. The thought of losing her was insupportable. He had to look away. 'I was hoping you'd come up to Scotland with me.'

'Pat, I'd go mad.'

He kicked a stone. Over the mountain, the falcon had risen again, accompanied by her mate, cutting lazy circles. 'Did you know that falcons mate for life?' he said. 'I mean, it's because they're so aggressive and everything, but basically, once a pair get it together, that's it.'

Iseult frowned at him, her head on one side. She gave a nervous laugh. 'Is that supposed to be a proposal?'

Case didn't know what it was. He felt as flat-footed as he had the day he met her. Until this moment, the prospect of marriage had never occurred to him. 'Why not? Yeah, sure.' Suddenly, perfectly, he was certain. He caught hold of her. 'Absolutely.'

She smiled at something far removed. 'Would we have children?'

Case was sobered. 'In time.'

She leaned and brushed his lips. Her eyes were miles away.

'But?'

Iseult's mouth, not her most generous feature, contracted. 'But apart from anything else, Catty may have something to say about it.'

His eyes rolled skyward. 'Women,' he said bitterly. 'They don't miss a thing.'

'You talked about her when you were delirious. She's expecting your child.'

463

'I'm not going along with it.'

'Oh,' Iseult said. 'I see.' She was eyeing him with frank curiosity.

'We get on okay, but there's something missing.' He gathered breath. 'Basically, I don't love her.' He hesitated, trying to organize his feelings into words. 'With Catty everything's so painless. She makes it too easy.' He was floundering. 'There's no risk involved.'

Iseult made her eyes wide, mocking him. 'Marry her as quick as you can. You've got the woman of every man's dreams.'

'You're the one I love,' he said.

She was still smiling, though in a way that didn't suggest she was flattered. 'Because I'm a challenge. Because I'm an exciting risk.' She rounded on him. 'Because I'm worthy prey.'

Case knew that he had completely buggered things up again. 'The other way round. You can twist me round your little finger. You *have* twisted me round your finger. Look, I don't mind. Whenever two people are in love, the feeling's never completely equal, and that means the one who loves less has power.'

'Not in my case,' Iseult said. 'When I love someone it has to be on an equal footing.'

Her self-deception made Case vindictive. 'Yeah? Who can make you lie and cheat for him? Who trolls round with anyone he fancies and then, when he wants something out of you, just has to smile and snap his fingers?'

She shut her eyes and straightened her back.

'I won't touch him,' Case said, 'but I'll tell you something: if it isn't me, it'll be someone else. Sooner rather than later.'

The Count – broken-framed, heavily made-up and with tranquillized eyes – threw up his hands in horror at the loss of Iseult's quattrocento ringlets. 'Your hair! You left here a beautiful young woman; you come back – a *punk*.' He fixed his dopey eyes on Case. 'The gamekeeper.'

'That's me,' Case said, surly with nerves. The motorhome

he had seen at the pass was parked outside the house and people were gathered in the hallway, but he couldn't make them out because two armed attendants were frisking him for weapons.

'Is my brother here?' Iseult blurted.

'But of course,' the Count said. 'Everyone is here. You will meet them at dinner. First . . .' He put his blotchy hand on Case's arm. '. . . I want to show you something of interest.'

'His zoo,' Iseult said over her shoulder.

Case made a face. 'I thought that was inside.'

First, the Count showed off his pack of boar-hounds. Case praised them for what they were worth. When the Count complained that they were too thin of coat to tackle the thick cover where wild boars lay up, Case suggested that he introduce some blood from wire-haired German pointers.

'If I wasn't about to die,' the Count told him, 'I would ask you to join my service as huntsman.'

'Thanks, but this kind of country is too enclosed for me. Too enclosed for decent hawking.'

'Yes, yes, I'd forgotten. Come with me.'

Ignoring the ape and the wild boar, Lemonnier led Case to a cage holding a golden eagle – the most miserable specimen of raptor Case had set eyes on.

'*Alors*,' the Count said with pride. 'What do you think?'

'I don't know where to begin.'

'Can you train him?'

'Her. Big eagles – especially females – are one bird of prey I wouldn't touch. They can fast for days, their flight isn't suited to falconry, and if they don't kill, there's a good chance they'll have a go at the first person they see.'

Whatever medication the Count was on, it made him hear selectively. 'But how long does it take to train one?'

'Two to three months for a healthy bird.'

'Two months,' the Count said, doing mental arithmetic. 'Can you teach my huntsman?'

'Look, this eagle will never kill anything again. I could repair its plumage and even put its beak back into shape, but there's nothing that can be done about its feet.'

The toes were calcified, the balls grossly swollen.

'Bumblefoot,' Case said.

'Bumblefoot?' the Count repeated to his attendant. 'Bumblefoot?'

'Too far gone to be cured,' Case told him. 'I'm surprised the thing has lived this long.'

The Count's face slackened with disappointment. 'But what can I do?'

Case held his counsel.

The Count's mouth made a decisive line. He jerked his chin at the attendant. On his way back to the house, Case heard a shot, closely followed by another.

Clean but not rested, he went downstairs at eight, arriving outside the dining-room to find both armed retainers on guard at the door, and London voices within. He stood there, his legs weak, afraid in a way he couldn't define – afraid not of Low, but of Cathal.

'Lovely drop of vino,' he heard Low say, 'but I'm not so sure about your amuse girls.'

'*Amuse-gueules*,' Fox said.

'Foxy, don't go all verbal on me. Just list the ingredients by weight.'

'Strips of pig's ear in a marinade of white wine, capers and olives.'

There was the sound of a plate being lowered.

'Something wrong?' the Count's voice inquired.

'Pork doesn't agree with me.'

'You are Jewish?'

'Not kosher, squire.'

'Why does he keep calling me "squire"?' the Count asked in bafflement.

'Mark of respect, guv,' Fatso said.

Case discerned a rattled tone; the lads were not feeling at home. He breathed in and out quickly and entered. A million facets of crystal struck him. When his vision cleared, he saw Low in his tux with a ruffled pink shirt that set off his carotene tan alarmingly. Fatso and Big Mac were present, and there was a stranger – a fleshy, fair-haired man out of the same stable as Low. Case's gaze bonded itself to Cathal's. Iseult took her brother's hand.

The Count was already seated, his expression serene. '*Le garde-chasse,*' he announced.

'Jolly glad you could make it,' Fox said, putting a glass of champagne into Case's hand. He was dressed in a chef's apron and his face was steamed red. 'I'm cooking a grand reunion supper. The Count and I have been ferreting about in the cellar all morning.'

'Well, well,' Low said. 'Well, well, fucking well.' He turned in what looked like triumph to the stranger. 'George, this is him – this is the serpent's tooth.'

'Who's been a naughty boy then?' George said.

'Trust Pat to turn up in injury time,' Fatso said. He seemed nervous.

'The game's over; now it's pay-day.'

'Would you care to redraft that?' Low said in his gentlest voice.

'I've explained everything,' Cathal said quickly. 'Almost everything.'

'You!' Low shouted, shooting out a finger. 'You're not in this conversation.' He strolled over to Case. 'Now, where were we?'

'You wanted Fox. Here he is.'

George chuckled. 'More fucking front than Dick Tracy.'

Low circled Case and stopped behind him. 'But I wanted him *then*, not now. And you know when *then* was, don't you? *Then* was before Roy got his insides shot to mush.'

'I'm sorry about Roy,' Case said.

'Ah, he's sorry,' Low informed his companions. His face swelled. 'Roy's missus will be *gutted*,' he shouted, 'and when I've finished shelling out compensation, I will be *pauperized*.' He worked round to Case's front and his voice fell away. 'But even if Roy was in the pink, I would have to disassociate you. Because, Hard Case, when I signed you up, it was for exclusive services, and I do believe a penalty clause was attached.'

'I work for myself.'

Low stepped back, squinting. 'Why me? Why not the Irish nonce?'

'I'll make sure you get the money,' Cathal said.

Case didn't know what came over him. 'My agreement was with Iseult,' he said, 'and money never came into it.'

'Bless him,' Low said, cradling Case's chin in his palm. 'Bless his bleeding romantic little heart.' He pushed Case's head back.

'If you don't let go,' Case said, so that only Low could hear, 'I'm going to drop you in your socks.'

'Denis,' Fatso said in warning.

The two gunmen were framed in the doorway.

'*À table, Messieurs, Mademoiselle,*' Fox cried, clapping his hands.

Low let his hand fall. 'Appropriate time and place,' he murmured. 'You and both those fucking Micks.'

Cards had been set before each place. Case read:

« « » »
Terrine de Lapereau Saint-Hubert
Château-d'Yquem 1928
« « » »
Perdreaux Rouges Belles Toulousaine
Château Malartic-Lagravière 1975
« « » »
Salade Verte
« « » »
Fromages
Château Haut-Brion 1866
« « » »
Pain des Houris

'You'd better talk us through it,' Low said, eyeing the card with suspicion.

'A game theme,' Fox said. 'First, a terrine of rabbit and *ceps* named after the patron saint of hunters and served, rather daringly, with a Sauternes aged to dryness – a wine that Iseult is particularly fond of.'

'Something for the ladies, eh?' George said.

'For the entrée, roast partridges stuffed with chicken livers, *foie gras* and truffles. *Exquis*. And to accompany it – a relatively little-known, but nevertheless ravishing, Graves, still somewhat jealous of its youthful attainments, but beginning to open out into voluptuous maturity.'

'Foxy, you'd make someone a lovely wife.'

'*Après*, a green salad to refresh the palate before the cheeses which, being local and therefore undistinguished, are presented solely as a foil to *la pièce de résistance* – a bottle of Haut-Brion 1866. This, my friends, is a unique experience, but one which makes me tremble to contemplate. For despite the considerable pains *le comte* has taken to maintain his cellar, and although it is not unknown for such a great growth to reach its century with equanimity, there is every possibility that after such a span of time, the wine has turned.'

'If it hadn't before,' Low muttered, 'it will have now.'

'And finally,' Fox said, 'an almond and pistachio soufflé, served tepid – heavy but comforting. *Bon appétit*.'

A young servant brought in the terrine and Fox poured the Sauternes.

'To Roy,' Low said, raising his glass, his smouldering eye fixed on Case, 'doing forever in a better place. God bless him.'

'Roy,' his comrades intoned.

Brooding silence descended. Everyone was trying to watch everyone else.

'Well,' Fatso said, breaking the ice in down-to-earth fashion. 'Monday, we'll be back eating Lean Cuisine in front of the box.'

'How do we get out of here?' Case asked.

Again, he felt a frisson of tension.

'We embark for Spain on Sunday night,' Fox said. 'I

assume you want a lift. Safe passage guaranteed,' he added, intercepting Case's glance at Low. 'Mr Low and associates have made alternative travel arrangements.'

'I'll be waiting the other end,' Low said.

'I've lost track of the date,' Case said.

'Tomorrow's the first of November.'

'All Saints' Day,' the Count muttered to himself.

'You know what that means,' Low said. 'We're only going to miss Spurs at home to Chelsea in the Rumbelows. Football derby,' he explained to the Count. '*Le football* as I believe you Fro . . . French call it.'

The Count had been sinking in his chair, but now he pulled himself more or less upright. 'Perhaps I can offer you gentlemen sport of a different kind.'

'Oh yes?' Low said. He eyed his team over the rim of his glass.

'In my family All Saints' Day is traditionally the opening of the boar-hunting season.' He showed rotted teeth. 'From All Saints' to the feast of Purification of the Virgin Mary.'

Cautiously, Low pushed himself back from the table with his fingertips. 'You mean hunting as in shooting?'

'If that is your preference. In the days when I ran *Le Sanglier Blessé* as a sporting estate, my guests sometimes shot as many as thirty on a single drive.'

'Wild boar,' Fatso said. 'I could go for that.'

'You said preference,' Low said, keeping the Count under narrow scrutiny. 'Preference to what?'

'I myself have always despised the *battue*,' the Count said. His eyes settled on Cathal. 'My own passion is for the hunt *par force des bras*.'

'By strength of arms,' Fox explained.

'I'm not stupid,' Low said, still staring at the Count as if he expected him to change form before his eyes. 'Tell me squire, how does one, like, kill a boar with one's bare hands?'

The Count spoke to his servant. The young man went out, and a few seconds later the old huntsman entered, carrying a spear about seven feet long, with a crosspiece lashed above the oval blade.

'You can't be serious,' George said.

The Count fondled the wooden shaft. 'As a young man, I achieved the feat myself, with this very spear.'

'It's a bit medieval, isn't it?' Fatso said. 'Try that on in Angleterre and the Cruelty would be down on you like Tower Hamlets.'

'I saw some of that jousting at Hatfield House,' George said, keeping up his conversational end. 'A lot of fairies poncing about in suits of armour – civil servants, most of them.'

'Is it dangerous?' Fatso asked.

Low laughed indulgently. 'The pillock wants to know if it's dangerous.' He frowned at the Count. 'Well, is it?'

Spots of natural red showed through the Count's face-paint. 'Gaston Phoebus considered the wild boar to be the most dangerous quarry in the world. More than once he saw one strike a man and split him from knee to chest so that he fell dead without a word. But even when the boar doesn't kill outright, it will remain worrying the hunter with the hounds hanging off it.'

'Doesn't sound like it'll go to penalties,' George said, pulling a face. 'So who fancies a spot of pig-sticking?'

'Don't look at me,' Fatso said. 'I like my bacon in rashers with a couple of bangers and a grilled tomato.' He eyed his crowded plate. 'Prefer it any day.'

'Mac, you're about a wild pig's weight. Go on, give us a laugh.'

'Leave off,' McGrory said through a mouthful of stuffed partridge.

'Anyone else?' Low said.

The Count's eyes darted from person to person, coming to rest on Cathal. The light faded from his eyes. 'No one?' he said mournfully.

'Ah well,' Low said, 'looks like it'll have to be shooters.'

The meal proceeded in silence. The table was cleared and the servant bore in a single cobwebbed bottle of Haut-Brion.

'Shouldn't it be decanted?' Low asked.

Like a priest, his eyes on the observance not the observers, Fox drew the cork, cleaned the neck and poured out a liquor like red lymph. Shutting his eyes, the Count inserted his nose into the glass, swirled the wine, sucked noisily through his teeth and gargled. 'Ahh,' he sighed. His eyes flicked open and his gaze was borne heavenward. A great hush had fallen.

'Well?' Cathal demanded anxiously.

The Count's eyes came drifting back. There were tears in them. 'For a moment it was there, the exquisite structure holding together by gossamer, and then – gone, like a corpse collapsing into dust.'

Taking the Count's glass, Low tested the claim. 'Vinegar,' he said.

'Pleasure deferred is pleasure lost,' the Count said, the tear breaking in his eye.

Low's head went up and down with feeling. 'You only get one lap of life's short circuit.'

Cathal cleared his throat. 'What will you do with the other bottles?'

Holding him with a malign eye, the Count beckoned to the servant and handed him the bottle. 'Go down into the cellar and pour away the rest. Bring us two bottles of the 1923 cognac.' He aimed a dim smile at his guests. 'Laid down in the year of my birth, drunk in the year of my death. A consoling symmetry.'

The dessert was dealt with; the brandy was brought. Case refused it. He'd hardly drunk a drop, but he felt dazed. Dimly he was aware that the conversation had turned back to hunting.

'Hey, Pat.'

Case opened his eyes to see Low's grin clamped around a cigar.

'Take on a wild boar single-handed and I'll think about letting bygones be bygones.'

'Handsome offer,' George said.

'Stuff it,' Case said, his wits recovered. 'I'm only interested in the money.'

'What are they saying?' the Count bleated. 'What are they saying?'

'I believe that Mr Low is offering terms to Pat in exchange for fighting a boar,' Fox whispered excitedly. 'Mr Low is offering an amnesty but Pat, quite rightly, is holding out for cash.'

Lemonnier was bemused. 'But one takes the field for honour.'

'Honour's no use to me,' Case told him.

Fox leant towards the Count. 'Wasn't one of your ancestors a professional champion during the Hundred Years War? Made quite a decent living out of it, I recall.'

The Count eyed Case. 'You are serious about putting your courage to trial?'

'Depends what you're prepared to pay.'

The Count sighed. 'Very well. One thousand pounds for taking the field, ten if you kill the boar, thirty to your next of kin should it kill you.'

'Can't lose,' Low said.

Looking into the grinning faces, Case had the urge to sweep the crystal from the table, to reach up and bring the chandeliers crashing down. 'I'll give it a go,' he said.

'What a lark,' Fox said.

'You're despicable, the lot of you,' Iseult shouted. 'Can't you see he's ill?'

'Get down off your hind legs,' Low growled. 'No one's forcing him.'

'I'd rather do it myself than let Pat risk his life.'

'Hey, Den,' Fatso called, 'remember them mud-wrestlers we saw at Barking Town Hall.'

'No, no,' the Count cried in horror, reaching out to Iseult. 'I want you to *paint* the spectacle.'

Amid the confusion, Cathal rose, and one by one the voices were stilled. He bowed to Lemonnier. 'I can't avoid the conclusion that it's me whose prowess *le comte* wants to see put to the test.'

'No!' Iseult screamed.

Turning, Cathal raised his glass to Case. 'I'll take your place on the same terms.'

'Bog off,' Case said. 'I fight my own battles.'

'No, no,' the Count cried. 'I'll pay the gamekeeper, but not you.' He held up his hands and drew Cathal's face down, kissed it on both cheeks. 'For you there'll be a greater reward.'

'Looks like we've got a two-bout card,' George said.

'How's the wild boar situation?' Low asked the Count. 'Got enough to go round?'

The Count summoned his huntsman and conferred. The huntsman shook his head and held up one finger to the assembly.

'There are plenty of sows,' the Count explained, 'but my huntsman has found the bed of only one boar – a five-year-old beast in its prime.'

'So who's going to top the bill?' Fatso asked.

An argument broke out, the majority wanting Case to take the challenge, others favouring Cathal.

Fox rapped on a glass. 'The Count has decided,' he announced. 'Since both men are inexperienced, they will face the boar together.'

Under the weight of shock, Iseult had sat down. She pushed herself up, resting her fists on the table, and stared first at Cathal, then at Case. 'One of you is going to get killed,' she said. She hung her head over the table. 'I know.' Her eyes swept over every man in the room. 'I *know*.' She walked out.

Low laughed awkwardly. 'Women take everything so fucking personal.' He rubbed his hands. 'Right your lordship, run through the programme again.'

The Count ordered Fatso to stand and play the part of the boar, so that the huntsman could demonstrate the correct way to hold the spear – in the middle, at a slight angle to the boar's line of attack. He demonstrated the proper stance, side on, with the leading leg slightly bent to damp the initial shock, the trailing leg braced. The Waltham Forest Fishing Club sniggered. Shifting his grip, he transferred the butt of the spear to his armpit and jabbed and twisted the point in the direction of Fatso, who backed off, grinning sheepishly. Low stood, rolling his shoulders, moving in a fighter's shuffle. 'Get in there, Barry my son. Duck and dive. Punish him.'

Case declined the spear. Cathal took it nervously. The huntsman scolded him. The Count was beside himself. Spittle flecked his chin. 'You're standing too square,' he cried.

Low nodded sagely. 'Stands to reason. Bigger target.'

'A softer one. The boar knows a man's weak points. Give him an opening and he will charge through your legs, cutting with his tusks.'

Low sucked air through his teeth. 'Nasty.'

'Come through in one piece,' George called to Case, 'and I'll bung another big one on top of the Count's prize money. Can't ask for fairer than that.'

Low shook his head. 'You always were a big softy, George.'

'My money's safe. The girl's right; he couldn't hold a knife and fork.'

'Don't be fooled by appearances,' Low warned him. 'It's cost me dear.'

'You want to win some back?'

'A bet? Alright, a pony says that Pat comes through without a scratch.'

'Twenty-five nicker? C'mon, Den. We're talking life and death. A ton at least.'

'Cash is tight, George. Keeping this firm on the road has destituted me, and that's before I settle up with you.' Low frowned. 'By the way, what's the running total?'

'Door to door, you're looking at the thick end of twenty thou, Den.'

'Twenty thousand!'

'Hire of motorhome, passports, my day rate – it all costs.'

'Fucking hell,' Low said, slumping in his chair. He brooded, then opened one eye. 'Tell you what: the Merc against my bill.'

'Bleeding hell, that's upping the stakes.'

'Life and death, George. Life and fucking death.'

George inspected Case again and gave a breathy laugh. 'The Merc, you said?'

'Minus the personal plates. Even then it's got to be worth forty.'

'You're on.'

Low winked at Case. 'See the trouble you keep getting me in?'

Leaving them to it, Case walked out into the garden. The moon leapt from behind clouds. He heard footsteps in the grass and tensed, not wanting it to be Iseult, praying it was her.

'If we were doing it properly,' Cathal said behind him, 'we would spend the night confessing, hearing mass and making our communion.' He thrust a bottle at Case. 'Make the most of it; back home this would set you back two or three hundred pounds.'

In the house, someone had put on a record – a female singer.

'The Count's in seventh heaven, playing his old Edith Piafs and looking forward to the hunt.' Cathal hummed a few bars. *'Je ne regrette rien.'*

'Why did you do it?'

With a long sigh, Cathal settled himself beside Case. 'You must have heard the fable about the scorpion that begs a buffalo for a lift across the river. Knowing the scorpion's reputation, the buffalo refuses, but the scorpion points out that it will drown if it harms the buffalo. So the good-hearted buffalo agrees, and halfway across the river the scorpion stings it. "Why?" the buffalo cries.' Cathal drank deep. 'Because it's my nature.'

Clouds drew over the moon. 'Because you have a death wish,' Case said.

He sensed Cathal smile in the dark. 'Did Iseult tell you about our parents?'

'She said they were killed in a road accident in France.' Case realized that he was talking to the man whom he believed he loathed and feared more than anyone he had known, but in his heart there was no fear and no loathing.

'Near Carcassonne,' Cathal said. 'We were on our way to Lourdes, as it happens.' He laughed. 'It was August and we'd been driving all night to avoid the rush. My father fell asleep and drove off the road into a ravine. He was killed instantly; my mother wasn't. I wasn't badly hurt, but I was trapped in the back seat. I couldn't move. I couldn't get out. My mother was lying half out of the door, the car on her legs. She was moaning – an awful sound. I tried to comfort her, then I begged her to stop. I'd keep thinking she had, and then she'd start again. On and on. I screamed at her to get it over with and die.' Cathal swallowed. 'Well, eventually she did.' He drank savagely. 'But even then she wasn't quiet. Did you know that dead people make noises – trickles and gurgles like drains.'

Case watched the moon sail through a gap in the clouds.

'It was a lovely summer day,' Cathal said, 'very hot and bright. There were flowers around the car and the place was buzzing with insects. Butterflies kept landing on the blood, opening and closing their wings in that ecstatic way they have. The whole time, I could hear traffic rushing past, cars full of families like us, heading for the resorts, looking forward to their first sight of the Med. It was evening before I was found. By then my parents had begun to smell.'

On the mountain dogs began to howl.

'It put me off nature for life,' Cathal said. 'I was the boy who pulled wings off flies.'

'Is that why you hate me so much?'

'Nurture against nature?' Cathal mused. 'Yes, quite plausible.' He stood, adjusting his footing. 'What do you say, Pat? Is to know all to forgive all?'

'It makes a difference.'

Cathal laughed. 'You're right to be cautious. I was an evil brat long before I lost my parents.'

Case wasn't interested. 'What did the Count mean about rewarding you?'

'I'm taking over here, going into partnership with Fox.'

'He's not fussy is he?'

'It makes you wonder what formative nursery influences he suffered at the hands of his father, the bishop.' Cathal raised the bottle. 'Denis Low's our first client. He's bought the entire harvest at a knock-down price. He's organizing shipment himself – some friend with a boat. They'll be sailing the day after tomorrow. You can go with him if you like. He won't hurt you. He's got a soft spot for you.'

'No thanks,' Case said. 'I'll go my own way.' He stood and dusted his hands. 'So everyone comes out a winner.' He laughed.

Cathal was quiet for a moment, staring at the lights of the house. 'Iseult . . .' he began.

'Shut it.'

'She's in bed,' Cathal murmured. 'Waiting.'

Case writhed inside. 'Don't let me keep you.'

'For us,' Cathal said. He smiled radiantly. 'Both of us.' Tentatively, he laid a hand on Case's arm. 'Since this is our last night together, and since we've got a grisly day ahead of us, I thought . . . well, Pat, what I was thinking was that you and I and Iseult could pass a few hours in pleasant abandon – you know, snatch a morsel of comfort from the jaws of death.'

Case stared at him. 'Is that what Iseult wants?'

'Intuitively. Subconsciously.'

'Intuitively? Fucking hell, Cathal, you're out of control.'

'Shush,' Cathal said, raising a finger to the sky, as if a heavenly presence was listening in. 'If it brings peace, then that's what Iseult wants. It's what I want. Peace between you and me, between all three of us.'

And after the shock of indignation was out of the way, Case couldn't muster any overriding objections. Rules were for normal life, and he didn't have much experience of that.

It was time he started making up his own. The word 'peace' stung his eyes. He looked away.

'She loves both of us,' Cathal said, stepping close, 'and we love her. Why not accept that? Come on, let's close the triangle.'

Case smiled at the eagerness on Cathal's face. 'Two minutes plundering the toyshop of your dreams.'

'What?'

Case turned, the spell broken. 'Not tonight, mate. I'm knackered.'

Cathal's grasp tightened in desperation. 'Tonight might be our last chance.'

Gently, Case loosened his hold. 'Tonight, tomorrow, any time – you'll not find peace this side of the grave.'

Cathal seemed to shrink. 'If Iseult's right,' he murmured, 'that might not be so far away.'

'In that case, winner takes all.'

35

Arc lights flooded the dam under blue glare, isolating it among the darkened architecture of the mountains. At the bunker guarding the approach to the walkway, Dearborn chatted to two conscripts in oversize fatigues and undersize berets. He had an irresistible urge to engage with strangers; every encounter added to the conclusive evidence that he was alive.

They raised the barrier and saluted him through. In the frosty air his feet rang on the concrete and he felt suspended above the night. The harrowing light gave him two shadows, one striding ahead and the other behind. He stopped and shielded his eyes.

Cody was leaning on the parapet above the very centre of the slipway, gazing up the valley.

Dearborn's fists balled up. Inside he was quaking with anger, and yet there was fear there, too. It was a feeling he associated with childhood – the confusion of emotions aroused by parental wrongdoing. He walked on, slowing as he approached.

Cody turned and peered at him, apparently not trusting the evidence of his eyes.

'It's me alright,' Dearborn told him. 'Surprised?'

'Colonel Douaz said he'd put you on the flight out.'

'The colonel's prone to wishful thinking.'

Cody frowned. 'Are you on the run?' he demanded, 'because I can't turn a blind eye to you being loose inside Morocco.'

'You don't need to worry about that.'

Cody shot another suspicious glance along the walkway. 'You alone?'

'Just me.'

'Well, you picked a damn funny place to meet,' Cody said. He stamped his feet and beat his hands together. 'Christ, you forget how cold it gets in these mountains.'

Dearborn looked around. 'I chose this place because it has a nice symmetry.'

Cody appeared to relax. He grinned, his breath misting about his face. 'Yeah, ain't it just the prettiest sight? They've caught up with their schedule too.'

Dearborn went to the other parapet and looked down on the silent earth-moving machines – toys abandoned at bedtime. 'I guess,' he said, 'that if you're looking for a venue to hold talks on the Palestinian issue, a brand new dam has a certain symbolic rightness.'

Cody's bomber-pilot's eyes took aim on him. 'You'd better tell me on whose authority you came by that knowledge.'

Dearborn glanced back at the soldiers shadowed against the lights. His gaze travelled up the valley walls. 'I bet they were going to do it here,' he murmured.

'Do what?' Cody demanded.

Dearborn turned to face him. 'Kill the king.'

Cody groped for a cigar. 'My God,' he whispered, 'I hope you can substantiate that.'

Dearborn shrugged. 'I don't have to. It's academic now.'

For a moment longer Cody stared at him, then he detonated. 'You blackmail me into organizing illegal entry, you drag me down here, toss out some half-assed allegations about an attempt on the king's life, and then you tell me it's *academic!*'

'Sorry to piss on the parade,' Dearborn told him, 'but the king has changed his itinerary. The conference is off.' His mouth held a tight smile. 'It seems that the security of his guests cannot be guaranteed.'

Cody fumbled his cigar alight. 'This is what fucking happens when you leave the office for a week.' He stabbed his cigar at

Dearborn. 'Who says?' he shouted. '*You*? You're nothing. I've been making inquiries about you and I know that you have no official status – not with us, the Moroccans, or anyone else that matters.'

Dearborn wanted it over with. 'Remember the man I found dying in the alley – the petty thief who was taking a trip down memory lane?'

Cody stood with legs and arms akimbo, like a bear.

'He was playing go-between for the Syrian PLO, some far-out members of Israeli intelligence and an anti-royalist faction in the Moroccan army.'

Cody smiled cunningly. 'I know your game, cowboy. Zwy Gur put you up to it. This is another lame manoeuvre by the Israelis to sabotage the talks.' Cody swung round in a fury. 'What the fucking hell is Douaz playing at – giving you the liberty to go round stirring up trouble?'

'The colonel believed me, Cody.'

Cody jammed his cigar into his mouth as if to bottle up his anger.

'He believed me so much, he tried to murder me.' Dearborn's own anger burst. 'He tried to murder me because he was the leader of the coup, the man who was going to make it happen – right here, Cody, in front of you and all the other dignitaries.'

Cody stared at him.

Dearborn swallowed. 'I want to know why you connived at my death.'

'I swear to God.'

'Why weren't you there with Douaz? It was you I called, you I agreed to meet.'

'I've been ill,' Cody pleaded. 'I needed Colonel Douaz's help to clear your way into the country. He said he'd debrief you himself and then call me if you had anything worth discussing. He phoned just before midnight, said you'd concocted some wild scenario about a palace coup that was being organized with the backing of the Israelis, and that he was putting you on a plane before you could cause any more embarrassment.

Cody took a step towards Dearborn. 'What was I supposed to do? I trusted him.'

'More than you trusted me?'

Cody was silent.

'Would you have gone on trusting him if you'd heard that I was dead?'

Cody flinched. 'I pray I'd have done the right thing.'

'You're pathetic,' Dearborn roared. 'You're a pathetic lying old hypocrite who can't face the consequences of his own actions. You'd better start praying alright, because it's judgement day, and when they find out what you've done, you're going to hang.'

For several seconds Cody remained staring at him, then he made an off-balance turn and caught hold of the parapet edge. 'The night me and Colonel Douaz came up here,' he said softly, 'I had a premonition that you were the agent of the Almighty's wrath come to find me out.'

'Leave God out of it,' Dearborn snapped. 'Find what out? That you were part of the plot?'

'No,' Cody said. He shook his head, stupefied. 'No.'

'Then what?' Dearborn demanded, stepping close.

Cody moved to the middle of the walkway and looked down at his shadow. 'Like I said, you stand in the sun, only one step from the dark.' He shuddered. 'I'll tell you, John Wesley – no one else.' But he didn't speak for a while – just stood there examining the tip of his cigar. Then suddenly he said: 'Have you ever loved someone?'

Tensed for just about anything, Dearborn laughed in astonishment.

Cody looked at him sadly. 'It's a straight question.'

Dearborn sobered. 'Of course I have. I love Magda. I love Lauren.'

Cody shook his head as if Dearborn had missed the point. 'Deep down in love – body and soul? Crazy in love?'

It was embarrassing to hear Cody talk like this. 'Sex has made a fool of me more than once, if that's what you mean, but I never let it get in the way of national security.'

'Then you don't know the power of earthly love, the mortal temptation that it presents.'

Dearborn squinted at him, not liking the direction the conversation was taking.

Cody sighed. 'I hired a boy to tend the garden – a Berber boy from near Imilchil. He had a crippled foot but he was a very fine boy in every other respect. One time he took me up to his village to meet his folks and they said, in that dignified way the mountain people have: "Monsieur Cody, his father is dead; you must promise to look after him like a son."' He drew hard on his cigar.

Dearborn had no wish to hear his hardening suspicion put into words. 'You know Cody, you should try smoking two at a time.'

'I tried to do what they asked. I grew fond of that boy, and then more than fond, but not in the way a father feels for a son.'

Dearborn squirmed his toes. 'Christ,' he muttered, and threw back his head as if he was short of air.

'I succumbed to temptation. I entered into a homosexual relationship with that boy.'

Dearborn couldn't hold back the shock – and the disgust. If it had been anyone else, he wouldn't have given a damn. But Cody – Jerry Cody, champion of the moral majority, advocate of fire and brimstone for any and all who deviated from the one true path. 'Cody,' he said, shakily, 'try and keep things in proportion. You're not the first American intelligence officer to find out he was gay.'

'Don't use that word,' Cody shouted. For a moment it looked as if he would hit Dearborn, but then his face softened in an expression of sublime remembrance. 'Our relationship was many things,' he said. 'It was beautiful and it was . . .'

Dearborn closed his eyes. 'I'd really rather not hear the details.'

Cody shook himself from his reverie. 'No,' he agreed, 'that's between me and my Maker.'

'God doesn't give a shit about your sex life.'

'Yes he does,' Cody roared. 'Yes sir. Haven't you read your goddam scriptures?'

Dearborn wrenched his mind back to temporal matters. He let his breath go in stages. 'Colonel Douaz blackmailed you.'

Cody pondered a while. 'He never referred to it straight out, but yes, he knew, and he took advantage of it to enhance his understanding of US policy.'

'Like what?'

Cody shrugged. 'What was our assessment of Moroccan intentions on the disputed Sahara region? Any thoughts on how the crown prince was shaping up? What was our strategy in the event of a coup?'

'A coup? He actually raised the possibility?'

'Given the number of previous attempts, he'd have been fucking irresponsible not to. Look, it was all very conversational. He never applied any overt pressure. Our dealings were always courteous and discreet.'

'Until Lova Hazan was killed.'

Cody worried his lip. 'The colonel wanted it played down. He was concerned that if it became widely known it might jeopardize the success of the conference. And I didn't need any persuading that he was correct.'

'And when those two tried to kill me up the valley. Did he convince you that tourist bookings would take a plunge if it got out?'

'In my judgement – both our judgements – that was the work of locals opposed to the dam. The colonel insisted that he lead the investigation himself, and what was wrong with that? I don't tell the Moroccans how to conduct police procedure in their own country.'

'You seem to have absolved yourself of all responsibility.'

Cody looked haggard and old. 'No, John Wesley, I haven't.' He straightened his back. 'I'd better get going. They'll be wanting to talk to me in Rabat.'

Dearborn hesitated. 'That depends on the Israelis,' he said. 'I haven't spoken to anyone else.' He avoided Cody's eye.

'I'm sorry,' Cody said again, and began walking away.

Dearborn made himself stare into an arc light until the fiery core had branded itself on his retina and he couldn't see anything else. He turned in the direction Cody had taken. 'Wait,' he called. Panting, he caught up. 'No one knows I'm here except the Israelis. There's no need to tell anyone about your . . . indiscretion.'

'My lover. Why are you scared of that word?'

'The Israelis were after Douaz, and the colonel's finished – dead or fled to Libya. In a few months you'll be retired. At worst they'll accuse you of negligence and bring your leaving party forward a few months. You'll be home for Christmas.'

Cody smiled as if he was contemplating that prospect. 'No John, I'm not planning on going home.' He looked over the parapet. '"He shall return no more to his house,"' he murmured, '"neither shall his place know him any more."' He flicked his cigar stub away and watched the spark fall. 'I've chosen my place, John, and it's dark.'

Dearborn stood cold and still.

Cody turned, his manner suddenly animated. 'What about you, cowboy? Do you have a home to go to?'

Dearborn nodded miserably. 'Magda wants a reconciliation.'

'That's great. You be sure to give that little girl of yours a big kiss from Uncle Cody.' He hesitated, his face grave with an unspoken plea. 'Listen, cowboy, I need a few hours to straighten out a couple of things.'

'Don't try and run,' Dearborn warned him. 'Running would be the worst thing to do.'

'*Run*? Hell, where would I go?' Cody took his arm and briskly began to lead him away. 'No John, I've got a stack of leave I can't carry over, and I guess I'll use some of it up on that hunting trip I promised myself.' He grinned at Dearborn. 'Did I ever tell you I saw a leopard up in these mountains last fall?'

'I don't believe you did,' Dearborn said, his throat tight.

'A wonderful sight, John Wesley.'

'I bet it was, Cody. I bet it was too.'

36

Case and the Count's two armed attendants went early to the appointed place – a theatre in the round, with a thick curtain of forest in front and a backdrop of wooded crags scrolled in mist. The sun was a black pearl. It was going to be a beautiful day.

While Case inspected the arena, the servants began to erect a tent on a grassy knoll. It was only a white canvas shelter of the kind used to house Moroccan road gangs, but in that setting it made a brave showing.

Hunger made Case queasy. The Count had advised him against taking the field on a full stomach. A stream ran down through the meadow. He washed his face and hands, rinsed his mouth and rested by the water.

The sun burned through the mist and a cheerful breeze tugged at the pavilion. Birds trilled in the woods. About nine-thirty the guests arrived, gorgeously attired in chain-store casuals, with bottles winking in their hands.

Lemonnier and Fox escorted Cathal to his place. He had on dark glasses and white shirt and conveyed an impression of morning-after fragility. The Count had dolled himself up in a green huntsman's uniform and a leather hat with feathers; on his chest he wore a medal which he claimed had been pinned there by Hermann Göring for shooting a twelve-pointer in Prussia.

'A fair field of folk,' Fox said. 'Badly hungover but looking forward to an enthralling contest. As am I.' He peered at the two contenders. 'A touch of the collywobbles?' he inquired.

Far away, the hounds had started to give tongue. The Count initiated a respectful silence.

'They will bring the boar to bay in there,' he said, indicating the covert. 'If they can't drive him out, you'll have to crawl in to finish him off.'

Privately, Case decided he would do no such thing. 'How fast does a wild boar charge?' he asked.

'Over this distance, as fast as a galloping horse.'

'Now then,' Fox fussed, 'what about favours?'

'For starters,' Case told him, 'why don't you fuck off?'

'I mean favours from your lady.'

Case glanced towards the pavilion. Iseult had set up an easel to one side. He looked away.

'A last word of advice if I may,' Fox said. 'Apparently the trick is to watch out for the boar's eyes. When you see them roll, that's the time to stiffen up the sinews.' He raised his hand and began to back away. '*Courage, mes braves*.'

Case and Cathal stood in uncomfortable proximity. The sound of the pack had settled down to a steady baying; they were hot on the scent. Case paced out the distance to the edge of the forest – about forty yards. He walked back to Cathal, calculating how much time they would have between the start of the onrush and the moment of impact. 'About two seconds,' he said.

Cathal returned his wan smile. 'It doesn't sound like much.'

One elephant, two elephant, Case recited to himself, like he used to before pulling the rip-cord. Put like that, it didn't seem so bad.

The clamour of the dogs was drawing closer. Case tried to conjure up an image of the boar, but it was just a dark rushing shape – nemesis.

He yawned so hard he nearly unhinged his jaw. He always felt sleepy and sick when he took his life in his hands. Sometimes, before a jump, he'd feel so nauseous he'd think he really was ill, but when he hit the ground and smelt the grass and felt the earth between his fingers, he'd feel fucking marvellous, like he'd been washed clean – like the whole world was new.

'Scared?' Cathal asked timidly.

'A bit,' Case said. He studied Cathal with curiosity. His bearing had deteriorated badly. 'What about you?'

'Cold feet,' Cathal admitted. 'Not at all enthusiastic.'

The crying of the hounds rose in pitch; they must have sighted their quarry.

'I wish I'd gone to the lavatory,' Cathal said.

'Plenty of time,' Case told him.

'I'm not sure if I can move,' Cathal said. He sniggered. 'I don't dare try to find out.'

The music of the hounds was breaking down in ragged discord.

'They've lost the scent,' Case said.

'If it gets away,' Cathal said anxiously, 'we won't have to go through it again, will we? I mean, the Count said there was only the one boar.'

'That's right.'

Cathal shut his eyes and Case could tell he was saying a prayer for the boar's deliverance.

Suddenly the hounds spoke in unison; their tumult made Case's hair stand up. He tightened his grip on his spear.

'You know the phrase: "his bowels turned to water"?' Cathal said.

'Quiet!'

Holding his breath, Case listened. The birds had left off singing. The leaves reflected the light and in the breeze their agitation made every bush look inhabited. He flinched at the snapping of a twig. Something was in there. A shrub shook and parted, and Case gave a convulsive jerk and then a blustery laugh. It was only a porcupine. An ironic cheer went up from the Waltham Forest Fishing Club as it scuttled busily across the clearing.

Over the next couple of minutes more creatures fled the scene – hares, birds, a genet. A hound came panting out of the thicket, its tongue lolling and its tail waving like a flag. It glanced at the two men without seeing them, all its senses concentrated in its nose, then it turned and loped back into the wood.

Once again Case let his pent-up breath go and grounded his spear.

'It's really true,' Cathal said miserably.

'What is?' Case said, his eyes fixed on the forest edge. Inside, the hounds were baying in frustration, unable to force their way through to the boar. He imagined it couched in ambush, and then he pictured himself tunnelling towards it on hands and knees.

'About bowels turning to water,' Cathal said.

'Before a jump,' Case said, 'the boss used to offer a hundred quid to anyone who could get a hard-on.'

'Did he ever have to pay up?'

'Are you kidding?'

'I'm serious, Pat. I'm shitting myself.'

Case's eyes flickered. Cathal's face was grey and sweaty, his eyes unfocused. He'd seen that look many times on Paras who couldn't take the last step. The boss dealt with them by pushing them out – but at least *they* had parachutes.

Case faced the covert. 'Chuck it in,' he said, making his mind up. 'Bugger off while you can.'

'And lose my inheritance.'

'You have to be alive to collect it.'

Case could smell Cathal's disgrace and wondered if it would attract the boar's attention.

'The last time this happened,' Cathal said through chattering teeth, 'was on my first day at primary school. I was so ashamed.'

Case eyed the guests. They looked as if they were painted against the scenery. 'They're scum,' he said. 'Who gives a toss what they think?'

'I can't back down in front of Iseult.'

Case threw him a scornful glance. 'She doesn't care if you make a complete tit of yourself, so long as you're in one piece.'

'Digby told me about a woman whose champion was killed in a tournament. She wore his blood-stained shirt until it rotted away. I wonder if Iseult would do that for me.'

His fear was infecting Case. 'Frigging shut it,' he snarled.

From close by came an anguished yelp and a fearful howling.

'Bloody hell,' Case breathed.

The hound bayed its agony with unvarying intensity.

'Why doesn't it stop?' Cathal muttered. 'God, why don't you stop?'

The injured dog's cries died to a painful whimper and then stopped altogether. Now there were surreptitious movements throughout the covert. Case thought he saw a dark shape massed in a thicket. Branches trembled. He hefted his spear.

'Is that it?' Cathal whispered. 'Oh my God.'

Excitement shook Case. 'Stay where you are,' he murmured. 'It's mine.'

The boar broke cover without a sound. Razor-backed and massive, it stole forth like an assassin. It stopped and turned, listening for pursuit and Case saw its distended wet snout sampling the air and caught the glint of its tusks.

It began to trot away down the edge of the forest.

'Oi!' Fatso shouted in disappointment.

Cathal was forgotten. The guests didn't exist. Everything had gone deathly still.

'Over here, you bastard!'

The boar spun at incredible speed – a blur like a storm cloud vanishing into a black whirlpool. For just an instant Case saw its hot little eyes, then it lowered its head, gouged the earth, and pounded towards him.

Foam flew from its jaws. Case adjusted his stance, digging in with the side of his right foot. The boar filled his vision and he braced to receive it, but it was charging wider than he'd calculated, making him shift his position and pulling him off balance so that his spear-thrust was a weak lunge. The point caught high on its shoulder and the shaft broke, splintering with a shock that shivered Case's arm numb. Whirling, he saw Cathal in mid-step, running away.

'Cathal!'

He halted, glimpsed the boar and tried to turn. The boar seemed to brake and then it shot forward as if propelled from a catapult, taking Cathal in full gallop and collapsing him like a sack of paper. It wheeled in its own length and charged again, buckling Cathal's body up under its thrusts.

Case was no longer master of time. Cathal's spear lay where he had dropped it, but ages passed before he could reach it. The boar was still mauling Cathal, and Case had an image of something lifeless and insensate – a car in a breaker's yard being shunted by a bulldozer. He couldn't be sure if the grunts he heard were made by the boar or came from Cathal as it drove the breath from his body.

Over the turmoil Case heard voices shouting at him to stand aside. The guards were hopping from foot to foot trying to get a clear shot. Case plunged the spear into the boar's side.

A hound flew past and sank its teeth into the boar's hindquarters. Another threw itself over its shoulders. Case had the boar pinned and it was backing away, hounds hanging off it. Its hindquarters collapsed and it sat down on its haunches like a performing pig, head swaying as it tried to gore its tormentors, its red mouth open down to its throat. With a grunt it settled on to its belly. The entire pack swarmed over it and all Case could see were its front legs, trotters twitching as if it was having a bad dream.

He realized he was still pressing the boar down with his spear. He unlocked his grip and ran to Cathal. Shock brought him up short.

Cathal lay flat on his back, one knee drawn up, his intestines coiled across his shirt and blood everywhere. Case recalled a spaniel he'd owned which had tackled a wounded deer and been gored open. He'd shoved its insides back where they belonged, stitched up the tear on the spot and carried it home. And it had lived.

'You'll be alright,' he said.

Cathal's eyes were rigid, as if he was staring at something fearful. He wasn't feeling pain. Case felt for his pulse, but before he could find it Iseult knocked him aside. She was screaming and pulling at her hair. She stopped screaming when she saw Cathal's injuries. She looked up at Case. Somehow blood had got all over her clothes. 'This is your fault,' she shouted, and then her eyes narrowed, honing all the hatred and contempt that she harboured for him to glittering slivers. 'I hope you're happy,' she said, as if delivering a curse. 'I hope you're fucking happy.' Slowly she knelt over her brother.

Case found himself on his feet, walking towards the audience. Fatso was clapping. Low raised a bottle in one hand and a glass in the other. 'Nice one, Hard Case.'

Case turned away, weaving like a drunkard, walking until there was nothing to be seen and nothing to be heard.

37

Magda and Lauren were at O'Hare Airport to meet Dearborn off the Casa flight. He took his sleepy daughter out of her mother's arms and enveloped her in his own. Magda looked on fondly, tears sparkling in her eyes. She kissed him on the mouth. 'Hello, John.'

For days he had been looking forward to this moment, but now that it was here, the anticipated joy was nowhere to be found. He looked at his wife and could summon nothing. A flame had gone out in his heart.

'You're tired,' she said. 'It must be four o'clock in the morning where you are.' She put her arm around his waist and began to lead him away.

'You've lost weight,' she said.

'I've been keeping busy.'

She edged a look at him. 'I'm sorry about Jerry Cody.'

'So am I,' Dearborn said, looking straight at the sign that said EXIT.

'How did it happen?'

'Damn fool hunting accident,' Dearborn said. He planted a kiss on his daughter's forehead.

'Poor thing,' Magda said. 'She insisted on coming. She was so excited.' Magda hesitated. 'So am I.'

'How are you?' he asked across the gulf.

'Clear in my mind. Clear about wanting us to stay a family.'

'I still don't understand why you left me.'

'You don't understand women, do you?'

Dearborn laughed. 'I don't understand men either, but with women the shocks are cushioned.'

'John, I wanted a change, that's all.'

Dearborn halted. 'And did you get it? Have you had it?'

Magda smiled, a little wistfully. 'Sometimes everything must change for things to stay as they are.'

Anger lit a spark. That's your version, he thought. It's not the only one.

Magda stroked their sleeping daughter's brow. 'There,' she murmured. She linked Dearborn's arm in hers and gave it a fierce squeeze. 'Let's get you home. It's way past this child's bedtime.'

38

Drifting through the Camden afternoon crowds in a Donegal tweed overcoat that had belonged to Cathal, Iseult became conscious of the attention her appearance attracted – her height, her cropped hair, her dark, wounded beauty. The strollers suspected a trend, a cult.

A man was following her. He had been loitering outside the newsagents where she had gone to stock up on cigarettes and current affairs. She had been back from Morocco three days and this was her first excursion from her flat.

She paused to view the window display of an art-deco gallery – nymphs crafted into ashtrays, aeroplanes disguised as lamp holders.

'Did anyone ever tell you that you look like Rosa Ponselle?'

She moved away. He trailed after. 'She was a diva of the twenties – better than Maria Callas in my opinion.'

'Get lost.'

She walked back towards the tube station. Today was the fifth of November and Irish tinker kids as raggedy as any of the urchins she'd seen in Morocco were demanding money from the passers-by, using Guy Fawkes's attempt on Parliament as a pretext. The man was still after her. She turned into a bookshop and browsed in the Women's Fiction section. A book was thrust in front of her face and she flinched from a photograph of a statuesque woman with stern brows and a small mouth, her arms folded across a Valkyrian chest, black hair trailing to her waist, yards of white gown.

'That's her,' he said, 'playing Bellini's *Norma*, high priest of a Druid temple.' Melodiously he hummed part of an aria.

Iseult took herself to another section.

'Don't you think she's wonderful?'

'I think she looks like a ship.'

'A yacht,' he said. 'One of those ocean-going America's Cup types.'

Dismayed to feel her lips twitch in a smile, Iseult plucked a paperback at random and marched to the pay-desk.

'Do you like music?' he asked behind her.

'Not opera.'

'Shame.'

Handing the book to the assistant, Iseult saw that she had grabbed a thriller with a title like the name of a guided missile system and a jacket illustrated with a lurid composition of weaponry and female flesh.

'Why?' she said, startled out of her defences.

'I'm a composer,' he said. 'I write operas.'

'What kind?'

'Minimalist. No fat ladies. Like John Adams without the tunes.'

She looked down on him but resisted the cheap jibe. He was a head shorter than her, with an easy-going smile and bisexual eyes. She guessed he was some years younger than her and a lot smarter.

'Actually,' he said, 'my first opera débuts at the North London Polytechnic next Friday. It's based on the disappearance of Mallory and Irvine on Mount Everest. Have a ticket. Have two. Swell the numbers.'

She narrowed her eyes at him. 'If I take it, will you leave me alone?'

He wrote his number on the back of the ticket. He was called Rupert.

She knew she wouldn't call him or see his opera, but meaningless as the encounter was, it restored to her a small sense of unity with the living. She hadn't stopped mourning Cathal; there would be grievous moments in the weeks and months to come; but she had progressed into the very smallest beginnings of acceptance.

When she got home, she saw what a tip her flat was – the dishes stacked in the sink, her suitcase lying half-unpacked on the carpet. She upturned it, and there on the floor lay the unfinished painting, the canvas torn from side to side. Holding it to the light, she gave a professional frown. In Morocco the colours had seemed true, but here under a sky like washing-up water, they resembled the ingenuous blues and greens of childhood daubs.

A sky made for angels, she thought, a tear squeezing from her eye.

Sniffing, she turned away and saw the ruined *djellaba* Case had given her. She could have sworn she'd got rid of it. She picked it up and the feel of it made her shudder. It was the kind of gown mad women with crooked lipstick and a secret gin supply used to wear at cheese fondue dinners in Dublin's posher suburbs.

Absent-mindedly she had raised it to her face. It smelt of Morocco – dust and spice and black tobacco. For a moment she thought she would keep it as a souvenir of foreign parts – a piece of tourist trash to keep alive memories of sun, sex and sand.

But it was ripped beyond repair. Remembering how the damage had been sustained, she felt a tingling in her extremities. She took a deep breath. Bloody Case, she thought.

Dumping the *djellaba* on top of the painting, she carried them down into the patch of garden. Dusk had fallen and an occasional rocket curved up over the roof-tops. This would be her bonfire night, she thought, holding a match to the torn canvas. When it was well alight she dropped the dress on to it. It didn't burn; it melted, giving off smoke like a burning well-head and attracting neighbours to their windows. In seconds it had shrunk to a bubbling drop of tar.

Bloody Case, she thought, miserably hunching her shoulders against the cold.

On her way back upstairs she remembered that he had given her something else. She began to search for it, at first half-heartedly, and then with increasing determination and frustration, pulling out drawers and reducing the room to chaos. Where the hell had she put it? Her eyes fell on the laundry basket, untouched since her visit to Scotland. God, what a slut she was. She plunged her hand in and withdrew a shirt. Feeling in the pocket, her hand closed around a small spherical object. She took it out, held it to her ear and shook it. A cheerful discordance filled the room. She unclenched her hand. In her palm rested a hawk's bell.

Bloody Case, she thought, standing at the window.

Automatically, she had lit up a cigarette. She looked at it with mild irritation. She really ought to give up smoking, but the time never seemed quite right.

39

Case woke with his thoughts scattered in darkness. The truck was thundering through a tunnel of conifers and at first he could make no sense of where he was, although the very featurelessness of the place was familiar. Clues gathered. They had overshot the turn-off to Auchronie by twenty miles.

'There's a garage coming up on the left,' he told the driver. 'That'll do.'

With a hiss of hydraulics the rig stopped. Stiffly Case climbed down on to a forecourt puddled with ice. A sign advertising videos blurred in a bitter wind blowing all the way from Norway. The first tatters of sky were showing out to sea and a light was on in the office. Case walked towards it, past the pump that still clocked up sales in pounds, shillings and pence. The blistered sign over the door said *Thain's Garage. High Class Tuning Our Speciality*. Deer skulls were nailed above the workshop entrance.

Thain was sitting at a cluttered desk. Betraying no surprise, he reached under and pulled out a bottle of Bell's and two glasses.

'You look like you could use a livener.'

The sting of neat liquor pulled Case's face out of shape.

'That's a nice tan you've picked up. Morocco was it?'

'Morocco,' Case agreed. The booze warmed him with an instant glow.

'And have you come back rich?' Thain asked, peering around the words.

'About evens.'

Thain relaxed visibly. 'So you'll not be buying that ruin like you said?'

'Looks that way.'

Thain shook his head sympathetically. 'It's a hard fight.'

'Anything happen while I was away?'

Thain exerted his memory. 'The Tullos bobby died, skidded on black ice – and him on four-wheel drive. Her down at the hotel has got herself one of those bloody so-called toy-boys.' Thain poked out his cheek with his tongue and poured himself another drink. 'Aye, and Archie's to marry Catriona Bell the first Saturday in December.'

The whisky turned sweet and oily in Case's mouth.

'A quiet wee ceremony,' Thain said. 'You'll understand if you don't receive an invite.'

'Yes,' Case said. He gulped back his drink. 'I'll be away by then in any case.'

Thain stood. 'Aye well,' he said. 'I knew you weren't the settling kind.'

They shook hands and parted. A mile up the road Case cadged a lift with Bill the postie to Alastair's place. The Dancer had died – inflammation of the crop, according to the vet's post mortem. The Barbary was fine. He took her up, but said he would come back for the dogs the next day, when he had settled in. Alastair offered to drive him home.

Not a word of their conversation stuck. He asked to be dropped at the foot of the track.

He couldn't open the door of the house and had to effect entry by smashing a window. The furniture was embedded in two inches of ice. Pipes had frozen and burst and frozen again. Case mooched about, still not sure what to do, made listless by the thought of winter and having to start all over again from scratch.

He made some coffee and ate cold beans out of a can, then slept for an hour, with the hooded Barbary perched at the foot of his bed. Waking, he studied her. *Falco peregrinus*, he thought – the wanderer.

Decision made, he packed a bag with the bare essentials,

then took a last look round. His guns were at the police station; there was nothing else he needed to take. The dogs tugged at his conscience, but Alastair had always coveted the hound and there were plenty of falconers who would be happy to take on the pointers. No, he decided, there really was nothing to keep him.

Leaving his bag by the track, he walked up the hill with the Barbary on his gloved hand. Half a mile from the house the trees ended and the moors began, stretching from sea to sea. He climbed to a rise topped by a cairn where a wild peregrine had killed; the winged keel of her prey quivered in the wind like a fetish. He felt the Barbary's breast. She was fat but not flabby, with enough reserves on her to keep her going even if she didn't kill for several days. She was a haggard; she knew how to survive in the wild.

He stripped her of hood and jesses but left a bell on one leg in the hope that its sound might deter hunters. He held her into the wind but she was reluctant to fly, and when at last she relaxed her hold, she fluttered only as far as the cairn. She combed her flight feathers with her beak, bobbed her head at the sky, then stared at him with acute, expectant eyes.

'You're on your own now,' he said.

He sat down beneath the cairn, and when he heard her fly he did not look. For a moment he regretted the loss. He would never have another like her. But that's what he always said, and another one always came along, special in its own special way.

As he made his way back he heard the tinkling of her single bell. She was waiting on in expectation of being served with prey. All the way down the track she held her position, and he told himself that if she was still in her place when he reached the house, it would be a sign that he should stay.

But when he reached the trees she began to rake away, each circle taking her further south. She turned to beat back upwind, stalled and swung in the air, wavering like the point of a compass needle – and then the wind flung her round and she flowed with it. Case stared after her long after she was quenched by distance.

He picked up his bag without looking at the house, returned to the road and walked south until the light went. At the bottom of a brae he passed a driveway curving between rhododendrons. He walked past, hesitated, and then went in. Rounding the corner, he looked across a lawn at a modern bungalow with a sitting-room lit up behind a picture window. Even from a distance the meticulous order of the interior set his teeth on edge. After a few minutes he was rewarded by the sight of Catty processing stiffly past the window, a tray balanced on her belly. Her mother stood up to take it. The family was settling down to a TV dinner. Her father came in, walked to the window, stood looking blindly out at Case, then firmly swept the curtains shut.

Case crossed to the door. He knew that if he rang the bell and stood there, a smile on his face, she would throw herself into his arms. He liked her; she was fun, and sexy, and her dad would buy them Auchronie and he didn't mind the thought of being a father. Kids were just like dogs and hawks, probably. His hand reached out.

Nah, he told himself, pulling back, despising his momentary weakness.

Thumb cocked, he continued south. Traffic was light, but he hadn't gone far when a rig carrying fish from Kinlochbervie passed, buffeting him with its wash. Brake lights came on. He began to run.

The cab was immaculate – a wheeled sitting-room with all the comforts of home.

'Where are you headed?' the driver asked.

'South,' Case said. 'London.'

'I can take you as far as Perth,' the driver said, giving himself a let-out should Case prove an uncongenial companion.

'That's fine,' Case said. He looked out of the window and imagined the Barbary on her long passage, skirting the wilderness of cities, the darkness flowing back like an estuary, gaining on the sun with each beat of her heart.

The driver glanced at him. 'Looking for a start?'

Case fixed his eyes on the road where the headlights intercepted the dark. 'Yeah,' he said, grudging the admission, 'looking for a start.'